A SPICY SLOW BURN M/M PARANORMAL ROMANCE

AK NEVERMORE

Cover design by BookMojo

Paperback ISBN: 978-1-964466-30-9

Digital ISBN: 978-1-964466-23-1

Dedication

To my dear friend JJ.
Thank you for all you do.

CONTENTS

This book explores themes which some readers may find uncomfortable and/or offensive to include:

- **Spice -** Open door sex scenes with knotting.
- **Violence -** blood, guts, and nasty rotting things.
- **Language -** some variation of the "F" word is used 151 times and other salty language abounds.
- **Seriously Crappy Parents -** Themes of abandonment and allusions to abuse. But note, there is nothing on page.
- **Generally unsavory behavior -** my bad guys / girls aren't good people. They do bad things and aren't sorry, but I promise they get what they deserve.

If any of the above are triggers for you, please put this novel down and back away slowly.

Still here? Awesome. Just remember, it's a fantasy, people. Don't try this stuff at home.

Senior Year, High School

FELIX GLANCED at his watch and blew out a breath, rocking back on his heels. He eyed the parking lot and forced a smile as he looked away, nodding at a couple coming up the country club's granite steps. Peggy Sherman giggled and whispered something in Seth Bradstone's ear. He choked back a laugh, ducking his head after a quick glance in Felix's direction as they hurried past.

Felix rolled his eyes. Whatever.

The music coming from inside cut off, and the DJ started making announcements. Crap. They were getting ready to serve dinner. Felix glanced at his watch again and ran a hand over his jaw, pretty sure if he ate anything he'd puke. Where the heck was Liam?

Felix's pocket buzzed, and he fumbled for his phone, his heart sinking at the text.

he there yet?

Jena. He shot back a quick "nope," wishing she was, but he got it, he did. After everything that happened last fall at the bonfire, aka the event, the Havers High prom was the last place she wanted to be seen, especially without a date.

Felix could relate. Magic prickled along the edges of his ears, and he fought the urge to disappear. The plan had been for them to come together, but then Liam had asked, and, well…Felix had never been able say no to Liam Montgomery. Him wanting to take Felix to the prom had about scrambled his brain. Talk about a dream come true.

Especially since it would mean Liam was officially coming out.

Not that there weren't rumors and one or two spectacular sightings that Felix may or may not have been involved in… but this was different. Felix smoothed a hand over his sapphire crushed velvet tux, his jaw tightening at another snickering couple.

Liam had asked him to be at his side for this, and damn it, he would be.

Which is why Felix had been standing outside the Havers-by-the-Sea country club for forty-five minutes, waiting for Liam to pull in with his crappy Jeep. Felix chewed his bottom lip. That had to be why he wasn't here yet. Stupid thing had probably broken down again.

The spring breeze ruffled his curls as he scrolled through the texts he'd sent Liam—all sixteen of them—unopened. That wasn't like him…but this was huge, and Liam didn't do well with, well, with depth. Maybe he wasn't ready to go public. Felix sighed, glad he'd never had to deal with pack politics. Not that the coven didn't have its own fucked up hangups, but aside from Maxwell Sheffield's shitty prerogative, being gay wasn't one of them.

Okay, that wasn't totally fair. It wasn't necessarily the inclination that weres objected to, it was dynastic implications. They had a thing for babies, and m-preg only happened in books.

Thank you, sweet baby Jesus, for that.

Felix puffed out his cheeks, having been subjected to more than his fair share of that topic lately. His sister hadn't even spawned whatever little hell-beast she was currently gestating, and God help all of them when she did. Felicia wasn't exactly mother material. She was barely tolerable human material, and pregnancy hormones had not improved her personality. They hadn't improved her questionable life choices either.

His phone buzzed again with another text from Jena, derailing him from that miserable train of thought.

> be there in 5

> and I hate u

His thumb hovered over the keypad, his stomach a mess. Fifty-fifty chance whether it was churning at Liam bailing on him or the inevitable shit show that Jena showing up would kick off. He hooked a flaming red curl behind the tingling edge of his ear and started texting her that he was fine. Another text popped up mid-tap.

> don't OMW

Felix smiled despite himself, envisioning his bestie's scowl. He was so going to owe her for this. Behind him, a *whoop* went up from everyone inside, followed by thunderous clapping. Liam, on the other hand, owed Felix—big time. Damn it, if he was going to bail, he could've at least had the decency to text him back.

Felix sighed, pissed, but...he really couldn't be mad. Disappointed and hurt, yeah, but Liam was in a tough situation. Felix could relate to that on some level.

And it didn't help that Liam only had two settings: squirrel and hyper-focused. He was supposed to be taking meds, but it wouldn't be the first time he'd gone off them. If he hadn't gotten stranded by that rust bucket he insisted on driving around in, he'd probably gotten distracted by something shiny and totally forgot where he was supposed to be. Felix knew he really shouldn't take it personally.

Easier said than done. He was sick to his stomach over it, but he'd be damned if he let it ruin his night.

Right, plan B. If Liam was a no-show and Jena was coming, the grand entrance Felix had envisioned probably wasn't the wisest idea. He glanced at the corner of the building where the ballroom's terrace jutted out. They could go in the side entrance and find a table. In fact, he should probably scope that out. The less opportunity they gave Crystal and her mean girl squad to home in on them, the better. Those bitches were relentless.

He shot a quick text off to Jena.

> fine meet u on the terrace

Jena gave a thumbs up, and he headed in that direction. The clubhouse was set above the golf course at the top of the highest of several rolling hills on the west side of town. The spring leaves were just starting to fill in, and everything was in bloom. In the distance, the sea sparkled beneath the last rays of the setting sun. It was idyllic, like the rest of Havers-by-the-Sea.

Pixies zipped in and out of the soft glow of the parking lot's lights, catching bugs and giggling in high, falsetto voices. Around the asphalt expanse, a pair of sprites peeked from the bushes, shying back as he walked past. A gnome paused sweeping up cigarette butts to hold the gate to the grounds open for him.

Felix gave a little wave of thanks. He buzzed his lips, his loafers crunching softly on the pristine pea stone path. Stars had just begun to break through the heavens above. On either side, tall arborvitae lined the way, then opened to a lawn and gardens that were legit straight out of a fairytale romance.

Swags of lights, a massive tinkling fountain, and an

archway of balloons threaded with sheer, sparkly scarves led to the terrace. Music played softly, and specs of quartz glimmered within the patio's wide granite flagstones, all of it just begging for a slow dance.

He stopped in the shadows, and a lump rose in his throat, suddenly very alone. Felix sighed, jamming his hands into his pockets. Man, he was stupid. Of course Liam wasn't going to show. *This is why you don't fall for boys who want to be discreet, dummy—no matter how pretty they are.*

And dear God was Liam Montgomery pretty. Muscles on top of a swimmer's build and dark, cherry cola waves with a smile that could charm a hydra at one hundred paces. The boy's looks were straight-up dangerous. He could have his pick of anyone, male or female.

But he'd chosen Felix. Said he wanted to be with him.

Well, *discreetly*. Felix ran a hand over his face. Discreet. Like everyone in Havers didn't know everything about everybody else. It was a recipe for disaster on both their parts, but Felix couldn't seem to take Liam off the menu. When they were together, the rest of it didn't matter.

Felix frowned, not sure when he'd totally fallen for him, but he had. Hard.

A giggle and then a gasp came from the terrace and was followed by a groan. Sounded like someone was taking full advantage of everyone inside being occupied. His lips tipped up, wondering if it were one of Crystal's crew. There was all that speculation about Becky Swann cheating on JC Mills…

The edges of Felix's ears tingled, and he debated for all of point three seconds before tapping into his karma and distorting himself to blend in with his surroundings. Might as well take in some entertainment before Jena got there. Lord knew they'd need any ammunition they could get when she did. He crept forward and slipped beneath the balloon arch onto the terrace.

Whoever they were, they were definitely in a

compromising position, pressed into the shadows at far corner. He recognized Jenny Rhys's swinging platinum bob first, her skirts rucked up around her waist, and—

Liam groaning, one hand slapping against the building as he spent himself inside her.

Felix gasped, his head light as he stumbled back, dropping karma.

Liam spun at the sound, quickly tucking himself into his pants. "Shit...Felix?"

Jenny giggled, straightening her skirts, and Felix gagged.

A girl. Liam had been fucking a girl.

"T-this...this is...but said you're not..." Felix ran a trembling hand over his lips, tasting bile and tears stinging his eyes as Liam zipped up. A sharp pain tore through Felix's heart. "I-I thought—"

"Yeah, I know." Liam flipped his cherry cola hair from his eyes like he hadn't just gotten caught bending someone else over. That it'd been a female was an entirely different level of fucked up Felix couldn't even begin to wrap his brain around. "But this is better. Jenny's cool."

Felix blanched, his fist in front of his lips as he gagged again. Better? How could he say that? How could he *smile* and say that?

She held out a hand to Felix. "I think it'll be hot."

"It'll all work out this way," Liam said, putting his arm around her. "The three of us."

Felix recoiled. Were they serious? That wasn't—no. No. After everything Liam had said to him, what Felix had thought they were to each other, how was that not enough now? And that Liam actually thought that Felix could be with —no. He shook his head, his stomach heaving and his knees threatening to give. He choked back the sick. "I c-can't."

"No, you can't," Jena growled from behind him, swishing up the steps in a dress that made her look like the Wicked Witch. Small hairs all over Felix's body stood at attention with the karma she was manifesting, her green eyes crackling with anger. "How dare you, Liam Montgomery!"

"What?" He looked between them totally baffled, then his face ghosted white. "Wait, I didn't—"

"Fuck you," Jena spat, hooking her arm through Felix's. "We done here?"

Felix's jaw tightened, trying to draw strength from her—at least enough to walk away. He nodded and met Liam's gaze.

"Yeah. We're done."

Twelve Years Later

FELIX RUBBED HIS FRECKLED TEMPLES, elbows digging into the blotter on his desk, silence thick in his ears. He pushed back in his plush leather chair, one of many self-serving, sinful indulgences the former mayor had pissed away tax dollars on, and stared at the suspended ceiling above.

That was bowed and had a steadily growing water stain across it.

"How?" he asked his secretary. "How is a clusterfu—I mean a *problem* of this magnitude possible?"

"It's the weres," Lorraine said matter-of-factly from her mobility scooter parked in front of his desk. Her wrinkled lips pruned. "Alway stirring up trouble. I've said it before, and I'll say it again. Decent, God-fearing folk don't truck with all that alpha nonsense. Criminals and bullies, every last one of them."

Felix's eyelids fluttered as he prayed for strength.

Lorraine shook her cane to emphasize her point, though Lord only knew why the unpleasant old woman had one, aside from using it to threaten the populace. He was more than a little convinced she'd melded with her Lark to become a terrifying geriatric cyborg.

She sniffed at his silence, her self-righteous frown making her look even more like an ill-tempered bulldog in a wig than usual.

Breathe, Felix. Trying to correct her speciest bullshit wasn't going to do anything but compound his headache. He blew out a slow breath, dispelling the power he'd inadvertently manifested. He didn't need that kind of karma tipping his scales.

He had enough problems, as evidenced by the four hundred pages of calamity Lorraine had just wheeled in, levying formal charges against Havers-by-the-Sea for the willful misappropriation of magical resources.

"Has the town's lawyer seen this yet?" Felix asked, riffling an edge of the stack.

"Our lawyer?" She pushed up the side of her glasses, sending their pearl chain swinging. "No. The Montgomery boy was on retainer—against my recommendation, I'll have you know—but he up and resigned after the mess that Westside pack of his put us in."

And it just kept getting better.

But it tracked. Felix pursed his lips with a slow nod. Who would want to come back here after getting the stuffing beaten out of them and landing in traction for eight-plus weeks?

Yeah, not it, and apparently Patrick Montgomery felt the same.

"Okay," Felix said slowly, drumming his fingers on the edge of his desk. "Do we have any local candidates for the position?"

Lorraine opened her mouth, then closed it quick, shaking her head hard enough to knock her wig awry.

Felix cocked a brow as she wiggled it back into place. He was sure that meant there was, but for whatever reason, they didn't have the Lorraine Murklin stamp of approval. Without it, he didn't have a chance of prying a name out of her. Felix raked a pale hand through his flaming curls. Maybe someone else at town hall would spill, but either way, not having a lawyer available to look at this mess was a problem.

He steepled his fingers, trying to channel authority. "If there's no one local, then we should probably be advertising the position outside of the church bulletin and the Pizza Palace community board."

"We put an ad in the paper…" She looked at him blankly. "Or do you mean like the library?"

"Sure." Felix tried very hard to remain calm. *She's like a trillion years old. Be nice.* "But we'd probably have more luck on one of those internet job sites. In fact, I'm pretty positive there's one specifically for municipal openings."

Lorraine's eyes narrowed. "The only thing you're going to find on the internet is a bunch of hoodlums asking for money and showing their feet." She scowled, probably thinking he was one of them.

Wasn't a bad idea, actually. The hours would certainly be better, and he could write off his pedicures.

"Okay," Felix drawled, putting a pin in that as a future career possibility, "but how about we post something and just see how it goes? Get me a copy of what we placed in the Havers's Herald, and I'll take care of the rest."

"Fine, but it's on your head." She muttered something about perverts, threw her scooter into reverse, and backed into a chair. She glared at him like it was his fault, then floored it, heading out of his office at a disdainful mile-per-hour crawl.

Felix pinched the bridge of his nose. Heaven help him, but it shouldn't be this difficult. Though, he suspected he should be lucky he had a secretary at all, considering the pittance the last mayor had approved for her salary. That was also a problem. They didn't have the budget to hire the kind of legal counsel they abruptly needed. Could he be more in over his head with this? Fingers crossed, maybe they could find someone to do the work pro-bono, or pay them in reclaimed granite curbing. Public defenders were a thing, right? Felix raked a hand through his hair. Whatever.

Worst case, so were foot videos.

God. Yule might almost be here, but everything that'd happened on Samhain was the gift that kept on frickin' giving. He glared at the ferret cage in the corner of his office. "I hope you're happy."

The previous mayor-turned-weasel poked his head up and chittered at Felix with zero remorse. The coven should've let Matilda turn him into a frog. That cage was far cushier than Chambers deserved, and that was even before this lawsuit had hit Felix's desk.

He fell back in his chair and closed his eyes. What had ever possessed the man to use iron in those turbine foundations instead of the approved materials…Whatever. What was done was done, and glutton for punishment that he was, Felix had stepped up to deal with the fallout from the previous administration's disruption of the leyline's flow of magic into the neighboring town of Fayet.

Unfortunately, he hadn't actually taken into consideration that it would mean having to interact with the miserable municipality. He'd put his neck in the noose because he wanted to help put Havers-by-the-Sea back together after Chambers, Malcom, and the Westside pack had done their damndest to flatten it.

Yep. Wouldn't be making that mistake again. What they should be doing was advertising for a new mayor. Approved overtime or not, whatever civic duty Felix might've felt had long since evaporated, and his qualifications were sketchy at best. Being Chamber's assistant had not prepared him for any of this.

Any inroads he'd attempted to make with Fayet on Havers's behalf had hit a wall before they'd even begun. He couldn't even see frustration in his rearview mirror he was so far past it. The animosity between the two towns was thick, and starving out their magical practitioners hadn't improved the situation. Now with this lawsuit alleging…? There was zero chance of settling out of court.

In short, they were screwed.

The alarm on his phone beeped, and Felix's headache was abruptly that much worse. Time to trade one clusterfuck for another. He silenced it and stood, grabbing his parka from the little closet. He didn't care if Jena said the white, puffy coat made him look like a man-mallow, it was warm and outside was freezing.

Felix ducked into its collar, shoulders around his ears as he slipped out town hall's side door. He swore as an icy blast of wind hit him, and he headed across the street to Haver's elementary school, rock salt and sand crunching beneath his checkered loafers. He grumbled down at the sidewalk, a frown marring his lips. If he hadn't already been in a shitty mood, the weather and having to deal with his sister Felicia's drama would've more than finished the job.

That entire situation was beyond untenable. The way his parents were constantly enabling her bullshit made him nuts, and getting sucked back into her crisis-of-the-week was trashing his mental health. As soon as the holidays were over, he needed to put his foot down. If his parents wanted to raise Felicia's kids, that was on them, but as of January first, he was out. She needed to understand there were consequences to her actions, and his parents weren't doing her any favors by picking up the slack.

Hah. Slack. More like the full monty. Felicia and responsibility weren't even tangentially acquainted. Yes, there were "reasons" but her growing the fuck up and getting sober would solve ninety percent of those.

A line of cars waited outside the elementary school, and parents milled around in tight little groups, their breaths clouding as they gossiped. Felix hunched beside a sandwich board trying to keep out of the wind. He scanned the announcements on it reminding everyone of the impending winter break and upcoming pageant. Groan. They were doing *A Christmas Carol.* Someone was getting a medal for originality in their stocking.

Felix rolled his eyes, but judging by how animated the soccer moms were, the production was a hot topic of conversation, and everyone was waiting for opening night with bated breath.

Bully for them. He'd rather gouge his eyeballs out with a—

"Hey, Felix."

He glanced up from the announcements and a molten coffee gaze caught his. His pulse jumped, and he scowled at his heart jumping, looking away. "Liam," he muttered, kicking a patch of ice.

"You here picking up Axle and Sway?" the were asked, his hands jammed into his big corduroy barn jacket. A thick, red scarf was wrapped around his throat, and his messy cherry cola waves just brushed his collar. More than one person waiting changed their stance to check him out and preen.

And damn him, but he did look that good. Better than Felix had expected, actually. The last time he'd seen the were, he was getting carted away on a stretcher. But bouncing back better than ever was just classic Liam now, wasn't it? Had the looks and luck of the gods, always getting off easy with zero repercussions. Felix's rotten mood darkened. "Yeah. Doesn't Jenny usually pick up your kids?"

Liam nodded and scratched his stubbled jaw. A group of soccer moms sighed and one looked faint. "This custody thing—"

"Nope, don't care," Felix said, nipping that in the bud. He stepped away as he spotted two of his sister's urchins pushing through the school's big double doors, though you wouldn't know they were related at first glance. Sway had definitely taken after Felicia in the looks department, but the rest of her kids favored their dads—whoever the hell they might be.

"Uncle Felix!" Sway whooped at the top of her lungs, shoving through the crowd at breakneck speed. Her messy red pigtails streamed out behind her as she threatened to take out everyone she passed with her glittery, oversized backpack.

Felix's eyelids fluttered, sure she was about to end up with a cast on her other wrist. Child had zero sense of self-preservation or any situational awareness. Axle followed at a much slower pace, the scowl on his face rivaling Felix's earlier as the nine-year-old carefully picked around each patch of ice, imaginary or otherwise.

Sway plowed into Felix, and his breath went out in a whoosh. "Can we go to the playground?" she asked, clamped to one of his legs. She tilted her head back, peering up around the bulk of his parka, only the ridiculous poof on her beanie and her bright, hazel eyes visible. "Pleeease?"

"What? No, it's like four degrees," he said, shaking her off to walk back the way he'd just come—and very pointedly away from Liam, whether he noticed or not. By all the simpering, it sounded like the that gaggle of moms had already pounced on him. Whatever. It was the principle of the thing.

"So?" Sway asked like freezing her ass to the slide wasn't a very real concern.

"So, you'll get frostbite, and I have things to do."

"Like what?" she asked, running around him in circles.

God, had he ever had that much energy? Even at six, he was pretty sure the answer was no. "Super mysterious adult-y things." Okay, so he had a date with his couch, leftover Chinese take-out, and *Snider's Creek* reruns, but mysterious adult-y things definitely sounded better.

Sway stopped at the corner to clasp her hands together

and bounce up and down. "Can we come with you? We'll be super good, Axle promises."

"No, I don't, and you won't," her brother muttered, catching up to them. He was a swarthy little dude, but hadn't escaped the Simms's family curse of freckles. "Besides, you already promised to help Gran make cookies."

Sway rolled her eyes, and Felix caught her collar right as she went to step into oncoming traffic. "If Uncle Felix is picking us up, then she's not making cookies, stupid. Something happened."

They both looked at him with the same question on their faces. *Goddamn it, Felicia. Your kids shouldn't be wondering if you're dead.* "Nothing happened. Gran and Gramps just had to take the screamer in for her rabies shots, and it ran long or something. As far as I know, you're still making cookies."

"Oh." Sway's brow creased, then smoothed. "Well, that's okay then. As long as they're not gingerbread. I hate those. Kitty Weaton told me they have mole asses in them."

Axle sneered. "God, you're so dumb. It's *molasses*, and those are the best," he said, abruptly animated. "They're like voodoo cookies, and you can bite off the heads of your enemies."

"You have many of those?" Felix asked, hauling Sway along with him as he crossed the street.

"Not for long." Axle grinned, his canines a titch too long and his freckled nose scrunched up in glee. He ran across the parking lot to Felix's car with an evil laugh.

Guaranteed, that kid's sperm donor was some shade of demonic.

Felix rubbed a temple and made a mental note to tell his mother it was time for "the talk." No matter how shitty—or predisposed for evil—Axle's parents might be, the kid couldn't just go around hexing people.

"He cries at night," Sway abruptly piped up at Felix's side.

He looked down at her too sincere face. "Who? Axle?"

She nodded. "Don't tell him I told."

"Look," Felix sighed, "you guys know your mom will be back soon, right?"

Sway frowned. "Yeah. Why else would he be crying?"

LIAM IGNORED the mom squad that'd descended upon him, plastering a grin on his face and nodding whenever there was a pause in the conversation. Shit, had he just agreed to dinner? It was hard to focus over his inner wolf's keening, but he probably had, given the way the rest of them were glaring at Miranda Clarke. Whatever. Wasn't happening. He glanced past them, his heart in his throat as Felix walked away.

Liam bit back a curse. He'd fucked up again. He'd known Felix was still pissed at him, but that'd been so long ago… Liam chewed his lip. He just—God, Felix was so damned adorable in that massive parka with his checkered loafers and wild curls. Liam knew he should've kept his distance, but he just wanted to drop to his knees and beg for forgiveness. To explain. He'd been such a fucking asshole. So stupid.

He puffed out his cheeks, kicking himself for not listening to Kelsey. His twin sister was right, he needed to give Felix space, but all her advice went out the window the second Liam had seen the warlock. Damn it, he needed to play it cool. Felix would run screaming if he had any idea of what shit show was playing between Liam's ears. He smiled at Miranda, no fucking clue what she was talking about. Some Yule party? Didn't matter. He was pretty sure all of them would be running if they knew how medicated he needed to be just to stand there.

Christ, maybe he should spill his guts.

No. He needed to keep his shit together, especially with

this damned divorce. Felix would come around. Liam had to believe that, but he couldn't rush it, no matter how badly his wolf wanted him to. He had to think, take his time, and be consistent. Show up and prove he could be there without strings attached.

No squirreling, no obsessing, and stay medicated.

Jesus, that sounded like the same laundry list the marriage counselor had thrown at him before it all went to—

"What are you doing here?"

Shit.

Liam closed his eyes for a breath before he turned, the mom squad scattering. Jenny stood just behind him, glaring. His soon-to-be-ex-wife looked haggard, far too thin and pale, with dark circles rimming her eyes. His weren't much better, but he'd found a brand of under-eye patches and some concealer that worked miracles. Unfortunately, he didn't think she'd appreciate the recommendation.

He forced himself to smile at her. *Amicable. Be amicable.* "Hey, Jenny, I just—"

"We talked about this, Liam," she hissed, glancing askance at the surrounding crowd. "You have the paperwork. There's no reason for you to be here."

He nodded, rocking back on his heels. "Right. Yeah. I know."

She shook her head hard enough to send her platinum locks swaying beneath her knitted cap and pulled her scarf tighter around her throat. "Then why did you come? Pete wants to take out a restraining order on you, and shit like this makes me think it might be a good idea. If it's about the money..."

It wasn't, but— "That doesn't exactly help the situation," Liam muttered, one eye on the listening crowd, slower than usual to hurry away, despite the cold.

A pair of slim tow-headed kids came out of the school and stopped when they saw him. That had to be the twins. Derek and Cassi. They'd still been in diapers when he'd left, and Jenny'd been pregnant with Mike, the youngest. God, they looked just like her, aside from their eyes. Those were a luminescent green, instead of a shifter's brown. Liam searched their features for any resemblance to him. It was stupid. He knew there wouldn't be, though he couldn't say he saw anything of Pete in them, either. Whatever, it didn't matter who their father was. It wasn't Liam.

You are not the father…

A fist clenched around his heart. How it was worse seeing it in black and white than it had been hearing her spit it at him still didn't make any sense, but there it was.

"I told you, the money's gone," she said, hurrying over and herding them toward a crappy minivan. "All of it."

Money. It'd never been about the fucking money. Not for him at least. What he'd sent home he could've swallowed losing, but the loans she and Pete had taken out in Liam's name, how in the fuck was he ever going to pay them back?

And if he pressed charges against her, what was going to happen to those kids?

Goddamn it. Liam's jaw tensed as the minivan door hitched as it slid to the side, and the twins climbed in. He got a brief glimpse of another little blond boy in a booster seat. She slammed the door shut twice before it latched, then glared at Liam one last time, rounding to the driver's side and joining them. He stood there, watching them drive away, not one of them looking back.

Neither had Felix.

Merry fucking Christmas. Liam blew out a breath and slowly walked down the street toward Cups. Yep. He'd fucked up all right. He grimaced, cursing himself. With the benefit of hindsight, he was able to pinpoint the exact moment he'd pissed everything away. What the fuck had he been thinking? God, if he had a time machine, he'd go back and kick his own ass for that bullshit he'd spewed at prom. Since then, nothing had gone the way it was supposed to.

And he had no one to blame but himself.

Damn it. It wasn't supposed to be like this. He'd checked all the boxes. Had gotten the wife, kids—a house with a picket fence and the stupid degree to pay for it—and everything had still fallen to shit.

He'd tried. He'd really fucking tried to keep Jenny happy, but…*"What did you expect, Liam? Even when you're here, you're not. I need someone who isn't just going through the motions, someone who's going to treasure me, and I can't keep pretending this is working."*

He couldn't either, and not divorcing her then and there had been fucking stupid, but that goddamned alpha part of him…he wasn't, and needed to stop trying to be one. Every time he let his wolf rear up, things just got worse.

Liam sighed and pulled the door to Cups open, the bell above tinging. Garlands decorated the walls and low holiday jazz played. The little tables that dotted the space were packed with people chatting over coffee and having late lunches. Greta Hornsby, the proprietress, glanced up at him as she rang a customer out, the line at the counter two people deep. He smiled at her and stepped to the back, hoping a double mocha espresso would put a better spin on the day.

"Hey, Liam," Becky Swann said, turning to him and twirling a bleach blonde lock around her finger. "Long time, no see."

"Yeah." He forced another smile and looked away, hoping she would get the hint.

"I heard your divorce isn't going so hot. You know, if you ever need someone to talk to," she said as she smoothed her hand down his chest and fiddled with his scarf, "I'm more than happy to listen."

Go away. His smile widened, bordering on rictus. "Thanks. I'll keep that in mind."

She batted his arm coyly. "Do. I'll certainly be thinking of you…I can't believe Jenny was fucking Pete Randall for all those years behind your back. It's no wonder you left. You deserve better."

Did he? Because he was pretty sure that was on him, too. Liam took a deep breath, not in the mood to discuss their open marriage, or the reasons for it. Like everything else, it'd sounded like a good idea at the time, but—

"Is it true all of those kids are really his?" she pressed, way too close to him.

His hackles rose, and he swallowed a surge of bile-tainted anger, stepping around her to the counter. "Double mocha espresso, to go." Fuck, coming in here had been a bad idea.

Greta frowned as she rang it up with something akin to pity on her face.

"Berry frap," Becky chimed in, oblivious as she added it to his tab. The rest of the shop's customers had gone silent, chewing very quietly as they waited for his answer.

They weren't getting one.

"Order up!" Kelsey called through the little window. His sister's gaze landed on him and her brows furrowed. She tilted her head toward the side entrance, and he nodded, handing Greta his card. She ran it, and he took it along with his cup, though he couldn't say coffee sounded very appetizing anymore.

"Well, like I said, if you ever want to *talk*…" Becky twirled her hair again.

"Yeah, sure. I'll call you," he said, heading for the exit.

"Wait, I didn't give you my—"

The door closed behind him, cutting her off, and Liam scooted around the side of the building before she caught up with him. Goddamn it. The last thing he needed was to hook up with Becky Swann, Miranda Clarke, or any of his other past conquests looking to relive high school.

Christ, but it had seemed so much easier then. He'd just

been having fun, male, female, it didn't matter with who—until Felix, and then—then it got complicated.

And nothing Liam had done since had improved the situation.

He leaned against Cups' pink brick wall and knocked his head against it. *Stupid, stupid, stupid—*

"You know that's not actually gonna knock any sense into you, right?" Kelsey asked, slipping outside. "Here. I screwed up an order," she said, tossing him a bag stamped with holly sprigs and shivering as she pulled her sweater closer to her throat.

"Thanks," he muttered.

"You see Jenny?" his sister asked.

"Yeah, but I didn't...she didn't give me a chance to ask about Sarah." The other kids might not be his, but their oldest's paternity test had come back inconclusive. They were running it again, but with the holidays, it could be another three weeks before they knew anything for sure. He'd hoped to spend some time with her in the interim, but unfortunately, Sarah was old enough to remember him. More specifically, him leaving.

Kelsey grunted. "She can't keep you from your kid, Liam."

"She can if Sarah doesn't want to see me." And given the shit show that'd ensued the last time he'd tried, she didn't. Christ, could he blame her? Pete had gone mental.

His sister chewed her nail. "You're still going to therapy and taking your meds, right?"

"Yeah." For all the good it was doing. If Sarah's paternity test came back as a match, his stint in the psych ward after Samhain wasn't going to help his case for joint custody, that was for sure. Regardless, he couldn't afford to fuck up again, and a restraining order would set fire to any chances he had of seeing her, period.

Especially if they found out what'd happened in Los

Huego. He'd done his best to bury it, but there'd been too many people there to guarantee his past wouldn't come knocking at some point.

Kelsey blew out her cheeks, her breath clouding as soon as it left her lips. "Look, I gotta get back inside, but why don't you come with me to Jena's tomorrow for dinner? They're having an early Yule party, and she and Chase are always asking about you. They'd love to see you, and Aggie's making lasagna again. The last time they sent me home with a week's worth of leftovers. I know there'll be enough for one more at the table."

He looked up, blinking back tears. "I dunno…"

"Liam." His sister put a hand on his arm. "You shouldn't be alone so much, and people care about you. You need to let them and get out of your head once in a while. This front you put up…it's not healthy. You're allowed to feel shit."

Like shit, yeah. He did plenty of that. He ducked his face from her and swept a hand over his eyes. "Sure, okay. What time tomorrow?"

"Six." She raised her brow like she didn't believe him.

Be consistent. Show up and prove you can be there for them.

He blew out a breath. That went for the rest of his family, too.

"Okay. I'll be there."

FELIX LEANED against the threshold to his parents' cluttered kitchen and gritted his teeth, adding noise cancelling headphones to their Christmas lists. How they could stand dealing with all the noise, noise, *noise*, NOISE!

His inner grinch winced. That child…Felix shoved his hands deeper into his pockets and glared at the screaming two-year-old in his mother's arms. The little blighter's pitch increased to a decibel just shy of glass-shattering. Whoever the kid's father was, he had to be part banshee.

Though at this point, preserving their hearing was probably a lost cause. Case in point, his mother patted the urchin's back like she didn't hear a thing. It had to be a superpower the way she was able to deal with that, oversee Sway flinging ingredients into a bowl, and keep tabs on Axle rolling out dough.

The glint in the kid's eye was definitely malevolent.

Felix pinched the bridge of his nose. "Dad gonna be home soon?" he yelled over the commotion.

His mother nodded, still bouncing the screamer. Did that kid ever take a breath? "Anytime now. He went to go pick up Cruze."

"Detention again?" To put it mildly, the eldest of Felicia's brood was "non-compliant."

His mother glanced over at him, her pinched lips answer enough.

Felix shook his head, not surprised. Cruze was all but Felicia's clone—well, how she'd been before she'd started using. His mom frowned at him like she'd caught the thought and deposited the screamer into a battered booster seat with a cookie. Felix went weak-kneed at the blessed silence that descended once the little blighter's mouth was otherwise occupied.

His mom came over to stand with him beneath the tired piece of garland strung across the doorway. She absently picked bits of food from her gray-streaked curls, then wiped her hands on her apron. She'd lost weight and didn't look like she'd been sleeping. Shocker, there. "You know, it might help if you spent some time with Cruze, maybe took her for a weekend? There's that play that's opening in—"

"You hear from Felicia at all?" he asked, not about to entertain the suggestion as he watched the other two hard at work destroying the outdated kitchen. The 1970s tract house desperately needed a makeover, everything in some variation of rust and mustard. It'd been ugly when Felix was growing up, and time hadn't improved it.

Neither had the urchin invasion. Sway squealed, spattering creamed eggs and sugar over the worn, dark pine cabinets. Not that he was in the position to critique anyone else's culinary skills, but Felix was pretty sure the beaters needed to stay submerged for them to work properly.

"No, no, Sway, honey, keep it in the bowl. That's it, great job, now add the flour." His mother turned back to him, missing the cloud that went up as the kid ignored the pre-measured cup and dumped out the bag. "You know I haven't heard from your sister," she murmured, taking the chaos in stride like every other urchin-related inconvenience. "She was supposed to pick up the kids yesterday. No one's seen her, and she's not answering her phone."

Wouldn't be the first time or the last, especially if Felicia was using again, which was pretty much a given.

His mother's brow furrowed. "I'm sure that's why Cruze acted out in class today."

Felix rolled his eyes. Yeah, having a strung-out, shitty absentee parent will do that to a kid, among other things. He eyed Axle dismembering gingerbread on the corner of the kitchen table that wasn't piled with half-finished crosswords and mail. "You try scrying for her?"

His mother nodded. "Matilda can't find her."

Damn. Scrying was Matilda Hanson's bent. If the witch couldn't find her, it meant wherever Felicia was, it wasn't on the Eastern Seaboard. "She probably hooked up with a truck driver again. I'm sure she'll be back when he gets tired of giving her money."

His mother was silent, and he sighed, running a hand over his face. He felt like a dick shutting her down about Cruze, but goddamn it, taking her for the weekend wasn't going to make anything better. How many times did they have to go through this? Not to mention it was almost Yule for fuck's sake.

The front door slammed open, racing footsteps stomped up the stairs, and another door slammed shut. The screamer detonated. Axle jammed a second cookie into her mouth, bless him.

Felix's mom forced a smile and wiped her hands on her apron again. "Sounds like your dad and Cruze are home. I'll just go see if she wants to join us making cookies."

Felix was pretty sure that was gonna be a hard no.

His dad came over and clasped Felix on the shoulder, looking far older than he had a week ago. "I'm surprised you're still here. Everything okay?"

"Peachy." He tilted his head toward Axle. The little psychopath was giggling over his dough reenactment of a

Civil War hospital, a pile of severed limbs at his side. "You going to do something about that?"

His dad rubbed his jaw. "What do you mean? He's happy, isn't he?"

"Only because he's bathing in the blood of his enemies. It's time for 'the talk.'"

Felix's dad grunted. "You know, it might be better coming from—"

"Right, gotta go." Felix turned on his heel and grabbed his jacket from the banister, low sobs and his mother's murmur coming from above. His heart dropped to his stomach, God, maybe he should take Cruze—No. It wasn't his problem, and he wasn't doing this anymore. He took a deep breath, steeling himself as he stepped outside and closed the door on the chaos behind him.

LIAM OPENED the front door of his parents' house, the knot in his stomach loosening at the silence. It was too early for his dad to be home from work, and his mom had some church thing. He breathed out a sigh of relief. The quiet ate at him, but it was better than seeing them try to hide their disappointment.

In the situation. In him.

Especially now that his dad had managed to bring the Westside weres back into the fold and create a single Havers pack beneath his leadership—making Liam the presumptive heir to the throne—or he would've been. Now that the twins' paternity test results had come back, without a son to carry on the family name, he didn't qualify.

And he didn't see that changing at any point in the future. His inner wolf whined, but he was part of the goddamned problem. God, sometimes he hated being a were.

Sorry to shit all over your legacy, Dad, but from now on, women are a no-go.

Liam slowly made his way up the hewn cedar steps, the banister wreathed in pine and twinkling lights. A massive tree dominated one corner of the great room below. He took in all the decorations, some from his childhood and more he didn't recognize, expectation weighing on him. Being back home was weird, but running into Becky had only reinforced that staying in town wasn't a good idea. He didn't need her or anyone else showing up at his door for a cup of sugar.

Living in a trailer farther down in the hollow might've been an option, but all the seasonal digs were filled with workers. The ones they kept for guests had shitty water pressure, and none of them stayed hot for more than a handful of minutes. The combo had become a weird kind of lifeline; the shower was one of the few places Liam felt at peace.

It was stupid, and he didn't care.

He trudged along the upper landing spanning the length of the great room, its big fieldstone fireplace hung with stockings, and wall of garlanded windows overlooking the forest. A part of him missed the desert with its lonely, windswept expanses and star-filled heavens, but a bigger part had missed the smell of pine and subtle salt-tinged air of Havers.

It messed with him. How could he miss a place that had always made him feel so out of place?

He pushed through the door to his room and tossed his jacket onto the bed, stripping down and heading into the bathroom. The water only took a few moments before it was scalding, and his mom had left freshly laundered towels on the vanity, his meds lined up like tin soldiers all in a row behind them.

Liam swept up two prescriptions at the far end and downed a pill from each with a scoop of water from the sink.

He locked the door behind him and stepped beneath the water, letting it sear through all the dross of the day, reddening his skin until it prickled.

Punishing himself.

Liam put one hand against the wall, letting the water soak his hair and run over his face. He ran the other over the base of his throat, wishing the node had left the nasty scar when it'd healed him. Then maybe he wouldn't wonder if everything that happened had been real, or if it was just some fucked up figment of his imagination. The lariat of sliver slicing into him, eating away his flesh like acid—

No. His pulse pounded. *Breathe. In through your nose, out through your mouth.* He dashed a hand over his face, blinking water from his eyes. That had been real. He knew it had. So had the look on Felix's face when Malcom's weres had attacked him. Felix had been so afraid for him, so scared. The memory of his concern calmed Liam's pounding heart.

It was proof Felix still cared, Liam knew he did, he just— fuck. He had to make things right between them. Had to get him back. Felix would be at Jena's tomorrow. They could talk and get everything out on the table. Liam grimaced, his guts churning, but he wasn't going to hold back about what he wanted anymore.

Because when push came to shove, yeah, he'd fucked up royally in Los Huego, but it hadn't just been the scent of pine and the sea that had brought Liam back to Havers. It'd been Felix and the way Liam felt when they were together. The way his wolf craved to be near him.

Home wasn't this stupid town, it was Felix Simms.

Liam took his time washing up and got dressed. He'd been in there for a good hour, and it smelled like his mom had gotten back in the interim. The aroma of fresh baked cookies teased around the door to his room. He scrubbed a hand through his damp hair and made his way downstairs to the kitchen before she came looking for him. There, he could leave. If she came upstairs, he'd be trapped.

His mom was bustling around the industrial-sized kitchen, her wide hips shimmying. A smile ghosted over his lips. She had to be listening to gospel Christmas music on those earbuds he and Kelsey had gotten her for her birthday. His mom had been leery of them at first, but once she'd figured out how to make a playlist, it'd been game over.

And the rest of them were blessedly spared from being subjected to her crappy Christian rock and all things Mariah.

She hipped the oven closed and turned, jumping when she spotted him, a hand to her throat. "Oh! Liam!" She pulled the buds from her ears and set them on the counter. "I didn't hear you come in! How was your day?"

He shrugged, pulling up a seat to the breakfast bar and pushed a jarred candle with balsam ringing it to the side before running a hand over the worn olive Formica. The rest of the counters were lined with baked goods in various stages of preparation, and a smear of royal icing was on his mom's plump cheek. "My day was okay, I guess, yours?"

She waved at the assembly line of cookies. "Well, if you can't tell, the bake sale's an absolute mess. What they were thinking letting Kressida Pao manage it this year…she might have an affinity for talismans, but the woman is a menace when it comes to fundraisers. How she thinks it's all going to come together in the next two days—but you don't want to hear about all that." She batted a hand at him and switched on her mixer. "Did you have an interview?"

Fuck. "No. You know how the offseason around here is."

His mom raised a brow at him. "I do, but rumor has it there's an opening at town hall."

"I don't think I'm government material," he quickly said.

"Nonsense," she scoffed, plopping down a package of manila tags in front of him and a sheet of stickers before going back to the stove. "Work on putting those together for me, would you? You certainly have the credentials after working at that big firm, and I'm sure Felix would put in a good word for you. He's such a nice young man." She shot him a knowing glance over her shoulder, and Liam felt his cheeks heat.

He took a deep breath and held it for a beat before he started peeling and sticking. He'd never discussed his preferences with his parents, but he hadn't tried to keep anything from them either. They weren't dumb, and considering his mom did his laundry, she would've smelled his mating pheromones on the tracksuit Felix had borrowed the last time he was here.

"Yeah, he is, but I don't think us working together would be a great idea." Especially with Liam's law license suspended. If he did and someone caught wind of it, he'd be disbarred. Not that she knew about that, and he sure as hell wasn't going to tell her.

"Mmm. Well, Sheila Watt said Dempsy's might be hiring after the New Year. You're not going to be able to live off your savings forever, you know. It'd be a shame to squander that nest egg of yours."

Liam grimaced, reaching for another tag. Jenny had already done that for him, but he wasn't getting into that with her either. "I'm not ready."

His mom put down her spatula to face him. "No one's ever ready, Liam. You just have to take life as it comes and hope for the best. You've got far too much to offer to keep sitting on the sidelines. It's high time you got back into the game and go for what you want."

He snorted. "Did you seriously just make a sport's analogy?"

"Oh, you know your father and football," she huffed, filling up a pastry bag. "Silliest thing I've seen, but it's important to him, so I've been trying to show more interest. It's not all bad. I do enjoy tailgating, and once I mentioned buffalo dip, I didn't even have to twist his arm to get that new crock pot I've had my eye on."

"Way to go for what you want," Liam chuckled, slapping on another sticker.

His mother shrugged. "He gets his dip, I get my crock pot, everybody's happy...except a certain son of mine, and unfortunately, no amount of my cooking is going to change that."

Liam pushed back from the counter. "Mom—"

"Stop right there," she snapped, targeting him with her spatula and glaring at him over its tip. "This needs to be said. Jenny was never right for you, and I'm furious she's robbed me of my grandbabies and dragged those sweet angels into this mess. Your father and I couldn't give a fig if they're yours or not—it kills me they won't be here for Christmas. Whatever went on between you two..." His mother shook her head. "You're better off without her and free to go after what *you* want. Correct me if I'm wrong, but I've got a sneaking suspicion that's always been a certain freckled young man."

Liam swallowed the lump in his throat. Were they really gonna have this conversation? "Yeah, but the pack—"

"Oh, screw them," his mother snapped. "There's more than one of them out there that fancies someone outside of a traditional pairing, and in this day and age, you'd think they'd be more understanding of that. Were, witch, warlock, male, female—Liam, you've tied yourself up in knots for how long? There's no point in making yourself miserable just to suit convention."

Liam stared at her, his jaw dangling. "W-what are you..."

"Honey, what I'm saying is if Felix Simms is the one who makes you happy, go get him. I can't keep watching you make yourself sick trying to be what you think everyone else wants. It's time to think about yourself."

Liam dragged a hand over his face. "What about dad?"

"What about me?" His father came in and dumped his

lunch bucket into the sink, a rush of cold air swirling into the kitchen on his heels. He kissed Liam's mother's cheek and snatched a cookie, her spatula just missing his knuckles.

Shit. Liam's anxiety surged as the big alpha leaned back against the stainless steel refrigerator, chewing.

"Phillip Montgomery, those cookies are for the bake sale, and I was just telling your son he's better off without Jenny and to go get that young man of his."

Liam's father grunted, fiddling with his eye patch. "Who? Felix?"

What? Liam's mouth went dry. How did he—

"Yes, Felix. Who else do you think we're talking about?" she asked, hands on her hips.

"It's been a long day, Tess." His dad sighed and took another bite of cookie, chewing slowly before he swallowed. "But I agree with your mother."

Liam broke out in a cold sweat. "You do?"

His dad grunted. "Felix seems like the solid sort, and the way he stepped up for the town's commendable. Thankless and more than a little dumb on his part, but commendable. You need that kind of stability in a partner, and Jenny sure as hell never had it. If he makes you happy," his dad shrugged and popped the last of the cookie into his mouth, "then it's kind of a no-brainer."

Kind of a— "What about the pack?"

His dad blew out a long breath. "Were culture is what it is. My heart led me down the traditional path and taking alpha was the natural progression. You need to listen to yours. If that's not where it's at, then you've got no business stepping up. There's plenty of other weres capable, but none of them can live your life for you."

Liam wet his lips, feeling faint.

"Don't get me wrong," his dad said, running a hand over his beard. "I think you would've made a fine alpha if you had your heart set on it, but there's no shame in stepping aside for someone else. The last thing I want is for you to shoehorn yourself into a role you'd come to resent. That's not good for anyone, least of all you…but I'm pretty sure I'm preaching to the choir there."

"Yeah," Liam hung his head, tears pricking at his eyes. "Thanks."

"We love you, Liam," his mother said. "We just want you to be happy."

He nodded as he stood. Yeah. That's what he wanted, too.

FELIX ROLLED over groaning and silenced the alarm on his phone with a dramatic sob, throwing an arm over his eyes. Ugh, he didn't wanna go to work… Five more minutes. He'd get up after five more—

Mister Meowzptlk—Myx—stirred from the tangle of bedclothes around Felix's legs, and Felix went limp, playing dead. If he was very, very still…

A furry head butted against his face, the cat's purr a low rumble as it nuzzled against him. Felix fought not to tense, knowing it for the trap it was, but if Myx thought he was asleep, maybe he would go back to—sharp teeth chomped down on one of Felix's nostrils, he howled, shoving the nineteen-pound beast off the bed. He slapped a hand to his throbbing wound, then inspected his fingers with a tentative sniff. Was he bleeding?

Myx huffed out a very human sigh and sat, tail curling around his feet. The stripy gray Maine Coon kept eye contact, nibbling delicately on one, unsheathed claw. Felix could practically hear the cat ask him, "Do you want to be?"

"Fine." Felix flipped back the covers, well aware that the furry jerk was threatening him. "Get a familiar, they said, all the best warlocks have them, they said." How convenient that *they* hadn't managed to summon a dumpster diving thug with a penchant for sadism.

Myx yawned and stomped out of the room, his footsteps far louder than a cat's had any right to be. God. And he'd been so cute when he was little. How he'd turned from a furry ball of fluff into that…Felix stumbled after him, and Myx's pace slowed to the exact speed necessary for maximum trippage.

"You know you don't make things easy, right?" Felix grumbled, stumbling over the cat. "I'm going to feed you, the least you could do is get out of my—damn it!"

Myx blinked back at him as Felix knocked into a potted fern. He scrambled to save it from tumbling to its doom and glared at the cat, his familiar suddenly acting far too innocent. Stupid plant was only up there to keep him from puking it everywh—

Oh ho. Was that the grift? Felix narrowed his eyes. "Nice try."

The cat huffed again—his insidious plot foiled for the moment—and continued to stomp into the kitchen. Felix ran a hand over his face, frowning at the scritch of stubble beneath his palm. He retrieved his majesty's kibble from the pantry and dumped it into the bowl. Myx promptly put his back to him and buried his face in it.

"Ungrateful beast," Felix grumbled, his hands on his hips. "I should let you starve. Maybe then you'd earn your keep and start policing the mouse population instead of throwing rodent raves when I'm not around."

Myx's tail thrashed twice in response, dismissing him.

"As if," Felix muttered, padding back the way he'd come and ducking into the bathroom. After his shower, shave, and third cup of coffee, Felix was almost ready for human interaction. He bid adieu to his furry overlord and drove over to town hall, with a quick stop at Cups for coffee number four and breakfast.

The line was blessedly short and the holiday music playing at a low drone tolerable. He stepped behind Miranda

Clarke and Kerry Woo, the two of them yapping away like it was happy hour instead of the ass crack of dawn.

"He really said he'd go?" Kerry squealed, clapping her mittened hands together.

"He did," Miranda gushed. "Peggy was right there, and she heard it, too."

The woman in front of them turned with a chai latte in hand. "I was, and I did. You should've seen everyone's faces. I couldn't believe it, either."

"Do you think this means he's on the market again?" Kerry asked, stepping up to the counter littered with frolicking snowmen tchotchkes. "Grande espresso, please. I didn't think his divorce was finalized."

"It isn't, but that's not like that stopped Jenny from boning Pete, or anyone else for that matter." They all snickered, and Felix felt ill. That couldn't have been a good situation—then or now.

His lingering anger over the polycule proposal aside, he didn't envy Liam having to deal with that. Pete Randall was a nail pairing shy of homophobic and somewhere along the line had fallen down the conspiracy theorist rabbit hole. Rumor had it that he'd built a bug-out shelter somewhere in the western woods and developed a serious drinking problem to go with it.

Miranda shook her head. "Why anyone would trade in a man like Liam Montgomery for Pete Randall…"

"Well, you've heard the rumors, right?" Peggy raised a poorly microbladed brow, her amber eyes flicking over Felix before returning to the group. "Apparently, Liam has a thing for men, and when Jenny found out, they agreed to have an 'open marriage,'" she finger quoted.

The other woman looked at her, stunned.

"You mean, all this time, I could've been banging Liam?" Miranda asked.

Peggy rolled her eyes. "No, stupid, he's gay."

"I can fix him," Miranda blurted.

Kerry laughed, her hand on Miranda's arm. "I'd be up for trying, too!"

Fix him? What idiots. Felix snorted, then coughed into his fist as Miranda gave him the side-eye. The gaggle collected their orders and migrated to one of the tables. Felix stepped up to the counter, pinching the bridge of his nose. It was way too early for this crap.

"Macchiato, three extra shots, and oatmeal to go, heavy on the cinnamon," he said, pulling out his wallet.

Greta rang him up, and he stepped aside for the middle-aged proprietress to take the next person in line. He flipped through a paper someone had left. Looked like they could expect a white Christmas, the livestock thefts across the county were still going strong, and the feds had issued a travel advisory way out on the West Coast.

"Order up!" Kelsey met his eye through the window into the kitchen and waved. The quirky were had an elf's cap on and candy cane ribbons plaited through her pigtails today. "Hey Felix! You going to Jena's tonight?"

"Yep, you?"

"Right after work. We have to pick a date to talk about her baby shower. I saw the cutest party favors!" She grinned, the bell on her cap jangling as she bounced up and down. "Okay, don't be mad, but I may have already gotten them."

Felix was afraid to ask. "Oh? What's the theme?"

"Yaks."

He blinked at her. "Like…Himalayan cows? The big hairy ones?"

She squeed. "Oh my God, they're adorable!" She handed his to-go bag through the window, her grin stretched ear to ear.

Greta rolled her eyes and passed it to him along with his coffee. "Enjoy."

"Mmm. Thanks." He waved at Kelsey. "Sounds cool. You

can show me pics later." Dear God, what was that girl smoking? Yaks? Though he supposed it couldn't be any worse than the opossum retirement party she'd thrown last year for a guy everyone was pretty sure was in the witness protection program. Him up and leaving in the middle of the night right after hadn't helped quell that rumor.

Felix huffed out a clouded breath as he stepped back outside, the tips of his ears and nose totally numb by the time he made it to his car to drive one block over to town hall. God, he hated this weather. Was it too much to ask for a winter home where frostbite wasn't a thing? It didn't even have to be down south. He'd go west for year-round board shorts and Tex-Mex.

Speaking of which, he was definitely due for a margarita at Snaps. Maybe he'd try to hit trivia one day this week. Jena's pregnancy and her canoodling with Chase was seriously cutting into his happy hour time. If their little blighter didn't come out cute, he'd never forgive them.

Felix deposited his to-go bag and coffee onto his desk and stuffed his parka into the closet. Chambers chittered at him from his cage, and Felix doled out a measure of the organic kibble Myx had deemed inedible, despite its hefty price tag. Once a dumpster cat, always a dumpster cat. His familiar's preferred fare was the equivalent of Micky D's, which was probably why the cat was so damned miserable. All that junk couldn't be good for his gut biome.

Not that Felix was about to try and swap it out again. The beast would murder him in his sleep. He clicked on his computer and sat, smoothing his tie as he eyed the stack of legalese from yesterday. Right, time to see if that job posting had gotten any hits.

Holy crap, he had like two hundred emails to go through.

Felix unpacked his oatmeal and started clicking.

～

LIAM JOGGED through the snow-silenced forest, everything his parents had said last night rattling around in his brain and his wolf doing backflips.

They knew about Felix, well, how he felt about Felix. What that meant. For Liam, for the pack. They hadn't come out and said it, shit, *he* hadn't come out and said it, not even to himself, but the idea of it, the label, how terrifying it'd been before—

Somehow everything seemed more possible this morning.

He grinned and picked up the pace, his breath streaming out behind him. He burst from the wooded path and into the field the tracks ran through, the tingle of the ward Jena had reenforced during Samhain tripping across his skin.

His sneakers hit asphalt, and he headed into town. Maybe he'd stop into Cups to grab a coffee and see Kelsey. She hadn't been around the compound much lately. With the holiday, Greta had her working extra hours, and his sister had been seeing some guy when she wasn't. What the hell was his name? Liam knew she'd told him, but he'd been so caught up in his own crap…Tom something. He'd been part of the EMS crew that had responded on Samhain.

Liam bit his lip. So much for first impressions, though he couldn't say he remembered talking to him. He hadn't exactly been at his best. Leave it to Kelsey to hook up with the dude that'd admitted him into psych.

Whatever. At least he knew what kind of family drama he was getting into. Liam shook his head and kept running through the neighborhood at the eastern edge of town. He purposefully didn't turn onto McDermott, though it was killing him not to see the condition of his old house. He'd driven by when he'd first gotten back into town, and the overgrown yard and blacked-out windows had just about killed him. He bet the leaves were ankle deep beneath the snow.

Not your problem. Except, it kind of was, since Jenny didn't have enough money to buy him out, and the neighborhood association kept leaving messages threatening to report him for blight. If Pete wasn't such a dick, Liam might've considered just giving the property to her in the divorce and washing his hands of it. Unfortunately, it'd been made it very clear that any kind of "charity" wasn't happening. Ironic, considering all the money they'd "borrowed" from him.

But if Liam pressed the issue, it wouldn't go well for Jenny. Though why he cared at this point...he frowned. It wasn't that he had any lingering feelings for her—not fond ones, at least—but the kids, they were a different story. Of all the men in Havers for her to hook up with, why she'd settled for a normy, alcoholic wingnut like Pete...Liam had never understood women. Not having to pretend to anymore put a massive smile on his face.

The town center was quiet, another hour before the buses started arriving at the elementary school and people just leaving for work. A light coating of snow covered everything, and the lamp posts were decorated with greenery and festive red ribbons. The shops along Main Street had gone all out for the holiday, and classic Christmas music was piping from one of them. His footsteps slowed as he passed a sandwich board letting everyone know there were only four shopping days left until Yule. His breath puffed out, cheeks pinging from the cold.

The little tables outside Cups were mounded with snow, the walkway cleared between them. Liam pulled open the door, kicking rock salt from his sneakers before he went in. Warmth hit him like a fist, and he wiped the sudden sheen of sweat from his brow. The tables were full of people enjoying their breakfasts and gossiping. He went up to the garlanded counter, and Kelsey came out from the back, a bell tinging on her cap.

Her brow rose as she flicked it from her eyes. "You're looking chipper. Anything I should know about?"

"Yeah, but not here," he said, grinning.

Kelsey smiled back. "Okay then, Mr. Mystery. I'll take it. You want your usual?" He nodded, and she started making his coffee. "You're still coming tonight, right?"

He puffed out his cheeks. "Yeah, six o'clock?"

"Six o'clock." She adjusted the drip. "I was hoping Tom could make it, but he's on call."

"Maybe next time…you invite him to Yule at Mom and Dad's?"

Her brow rose again. "I have not, but I was considering it. You think I should?"

"I don't see why not," Liam said, leaning against the counter. "Seems like you really like him."

She tried to hide a smile and failed miserably. "I do, but it's complicated."

"Of course it is. You have a normal relationship? Nah."

Kelsey rolled her eyes. "Shut up and give me your credit card."

He flipped it onto the counter. "Do I need to bring anything tonight?"

"It's BYOB. Aside from that, just you and some of this swagger you've got going on."

"I'll see what I can do," he winked at her and turned—

Directly into Pete Randall.

Liam's inner wolf growled, and he fought to keep it from his face. Pete glowered at him, his dishwater grey eyes bloodshot. "Montgomery."

"Pete," Liam said, trying to edge around him and not sprout fur.

The sallow bald man stepped with him and got in his face. "I thought I told you I didn't want you anywhere near my family. What the hell do you think you're doing showing up at their school?"

The café went silent, and Liam recoiled, cheap vodka already on Pete's breath. Liam's lip curled over an elongating canine, and the small hairs on his nape rose beneath everyone's rapt gaze, all of them waiting for the train wreck. He took a deep breath, trying to bury his rage at the pathetic piece of shit challenging him. His wolf scrabbled for release. *No. Not here and not now.*

"You did, but I went there to talk to Jenny about Sarah, not to—"

"If you want to talk to someone, you talk to me or my lawyer," Pete growled.

Liam bit back his first inclination to tell the guy to go fuck himself and put a fist through his teeth. He pulled out a chair at the nearest vacant table. "Okay. You wanna have a seat?"

Pete snorted, running the back of his hand across his mouth, stubble like iron filings rasping in its wake. "You just think you're so goddamned slick. You come back here with your fancy Jeep, waving around your money, your degree—"

Liam held up his hands. "Look, Pete—"

"No, you look!" He stabbed a grubby finger at Liam's chest. "You stay the fuck away from Jenny, you stay the fuck away from the kids, and I don't give a shit how that goddamned paternity test comes back. There's not a chance in hell I'm handing Sarah over to a fucking faggot!"

Someone gasped, and all the blood drained from Liam's face, his rage deserting him.

"The cops are on their way," Greta said into the ensuing silence, her eyes hard as she glared at Pete. "You need to leave."

"Cops." He laughed, then buzzed his lips. "And *I* need to leave, huh? Sure. *I'll* leave, but if I catch you anywhere near me or mine, I'll fucking end you." He raised his chin and knocked Liam's coffee from his hand. Two women screamed as the hot liquid spattered all over their table.

And Liam's rage was back.

"That wasn't necessary," he gritted out, his hand fisting at his side.

Pete grinned. "And what the hell are you gonna do about it, gay boy?"

"He doesn't have to do anything about it," Kelsey said, coming over and standing beside Liam, her hand clamping around his wrist. "Because I'm about ready to tear your throat out myself, you inbred piece of bigoted shit." She growled, her eyes flashing, and her canines dropped to fangs.

"Crazy bitch." Pete fell back a step. "All you Montgomerys. Weres. Goddamned supes. Every last one of you are a bunch of dirty fucking animals, heads in the sand, already staked out for the slaughter." He laughed. "Death's coming on wings, and when it do, all you freaks are gonna burn. All of you!" he yelled at the café.

Liam stared at him in shock. What the fuck?

A siren blared outside and a moment later, the door tinged open. Sheriff Nelson and his deputy, Roger, pushed through. "All right, all right, everybody, calm down. Show's over. Pete, you know the drill. You gonna come quietly, or you planning on giving me extra paperwork for Christmas?"

"You're arresting *me*?" the prick asked like he couldn't believe it. "That crazy bitch threatened me, they all heard it!" He swung around and no one would meet his eye. "Bunch of fucking pussies...You should be arresting her and that pervert brother of hers!"

"Sure." The sheriff sighed, gripping Pete's arm and hauling him toward the door. "As soon as they earn a drunk and disorderly, I'll be happy to bring them, too." He nodded at his deputy. "Roger, take statements, and get me a dark roast on your way back."

Roger tipped his hat, keeping an eye on them until Pete was in the back of the cruiser. The deputy pulled out a notepad. "Liam, Miss Kelsey. You wanna have a seat and tell me what went on here?"

Not in the fucking slightest. Liam ran a hand over his face as the adrenaline racing through his body abandoned him, his knees about to give.

"Start with someone else and give him a minute, Roger." Greta pulled out a chair for Liam. "Sit down before you fall down. Kelsey, go make him a coffee—extra sweet. That kind of a shock isn't good for anybody. And the rest of you, unless you plan on giving a statement, get on with your day," she snapped at the other patrons. "You heard the sheriff, show's over, and Cups is closed!"

Liam collapsed into the chair, his gratitude warring with his disbelief as he buried his face in his trembling hands. She was closing the café?

Greta rubbed a hand across his shoulders. "I'm sorry you had to go through that. The divorce and everything with those kids has got to be hard enough, but that man..." She sucked her teeth. "He's lucky Harold won't let me keep a shotgun under the counter anymore."

Liam snorted, but wouldn't that just solve all his problems? An image of himself asking Santa for Pete's corpse for Christmas flashed across his mind's eye, and he laughed. Greta's steel gray brows drew together in concern, and he laughed again. A corpse for Christmas, homicide for Hanukah, shit, why didn't he just round it out and string up a yokel for Yule?

Kelsey rushed over with the coffee and handed it to him. Liam went to pull out his wallet, and Greta stopped him.

"Oh no, it's on the house."

"Thank you," he said, blinking the tears from his eyes. It was a good thing the coffee had a to-go lid. The way his hands were shaking, he'd be wearing it otherwise.

She nodded back, tight-lipped. "I'm happy to do it, though I wish I didn't have to. I've got a nephew in Galleon

Falls—well. You're safe here. I personally guarantee that man will never step foot inside Cups again," she said, patting his shoulder and heading back to the kitchen.

Christ. How fucked up was it that Greta Hornsby was coming to his defense? The entire town must think he was a pathetic mess.

They weren't wrong, but it was better than them knowing how close he'd been to killing the guy. What the fuck had Pete even been talking about? It had to be some conspiracy theory bullshit from one of those podcasts always blaring from his truck. Liam chewed his lip. Goddamn it. He needed to get Sarah out of that house.

Kelsey took the seat next to Liam as he hung his head. "You need to drink that coffee."

He forced himself to take a sip and grimaced when he got a mouthful of sludgy sugar.

"You'll thank me later, and you know I'd totally do it."

"What, tear out his throat?" Liam asked, choking down another slurp and trying to play off everything that'd just happened. "Then you probably shouldn't have announced it to the entire café."

Kelsey clicked her tongue. "True, but we could make it look like an accident."

Liam's wolf howled to help, and he pushed the inclination down. "You're not killing Pete Randall. If jaundice and his smell were anything to go by, his liver's on borrowed time."

His sister nodded, chewing a nail. "You're right, he doesn't deserve a mercy killing. You okay? I mean, duh, you're not, but, you know," she said, glancing around.

"Nope. Not even a little bit." Him almost losing it aside, Pete had just outed him in gossip central. Liam was about as far from okay as possible. It wasn't that he was ashamed of who he was, he was just still wrapping his head around it and wanted to get there on his own terms without the entire fucking town discussing his business.

… "No one's ever ready, Liam. You just have to take life as it comes and hope for the best…"

Liam frowned and choked down another mouthful of coffee-flavored sugar. That was all well and good, but what was he supposed to do when it served up the worst?

FELIX TRUDGED up the Witchery's steps to the apartment above, totally defeated. His car getting impounded for unpaid parking tickets had just been the icing on the cake. He'd spent the day holed up in his office, reviewing applications and crying into his coffee. Every last one of them had either been asking for way more money than Havers could afford or been laughably unqualified. The handful that he might've considered couldn't start until late January, which he supposed was fair, given the holiday and the two weeks' notice thing, but that didn't help them now.

And dear God, they needed help now. An answer had to be filed by January second.

He scrubbed a hand through his curls and gave the door to Jena's apartment a perfunctory knock below a wreath of mistletoe and holly, pausing before he let himself in. The vibe had changed with Chase living there, and the last thing he needed was to walk in on the two of them in the middle of things again. As delightful as Chase's bare backside was, it only reminded Felix of his current dry spell. Hopefully Able would be home for the holidays. He was always up for some casual fun, and Felix really needed the distraction.

"It's safe," Aggie's acerbic voice called out as he peeked in. "I told those two if I caught them fucking on the couch again, they were buying me a new one. You know how hard it is to get lube off corduroy? It's bad enough the hallway outside their bedroom smells like the set of a porno, I don't need them fluffing in here."

All Felix could smell was garlic and sauce, but he wasn't about to disagree with the crotchety witch as he set a bottle of pre-chilled Chablis on the butcher block counter. Probably should've picked up two in his current mood, but that ship had sailed. He sourly eyed the mistletoe hanging in the kitchen doorway. "And how would you know what a set of a porno smells like?"

Aggie picked up the bottle and grunted her approval. She was in a zippered tracksuit, but her silver hair had been set in finger waves. Very ragtime chic. "Consider it a door prize for living through the seventies. You're early. What went to hell?"

"Leave him alone," Jena scolded, coming into the room. "He can help me with the charcuterie board. And by help, I mean bring plates and napkins into the other room. Though we do have enough lasagna to feed the entire Westside Fire Department, I don't want to risk him setting anything ablaze." Her brow rose at Felix's silence. "What? No quip?"

He waved a hand at her. "It's been a day, and I'm pretty sure everything is already burning at this point." It certainly would be if he lent a hand.

"Then pop that bottle, and tell me all about it." She turned to Aggie. "Didn't you want to get changed before Gorman got here?"

"I did," the older witch sniffed, eyeing the bottle. "But you better save me a glass."

"No promises," he muttered, rifling through a drawer for the corkscrew.

"Then no lasagna."

Damn it. "Fine. One glass," he relented.

"Make it two, there's garlic bread," she said, sashaying out the door.

Felix grunted. "You'd think being in remission would've improved her attitude."

"I heard that!"

"You'd be wrong." Jena laughed.

God, she looked so happy. Pregnancy was certainly agreeing with her. She had that glow everyone talked about, and her green eyes sparkled. Being with Chase had given her a confidence she hadn't had before, and the curvy girl was killing it in that little black dress. Felix's heart swelled for her, and he blinked the tears from his eyes, but whether those were for her or his own miserable existence, he wasn't sure.

"Shit," she said, her dark brows furrowing. "Something did go to hell."

He nodded, wiping a hand across his face and then grabbed the bottle. "Fayet is suing us for the willful appropriation of magic, we don't have a town lawyer on retainer anymore, my sister's in the wind again—Oh, and they impounded my car, so I've got that going for me, too."

Jena gaped at him, then put down the massive cutting board she'd hauled out from beneath the kitchen island. "I told you that was going to happen if you didn't pay those tickets, but are you serious about the rest of it?"

Felix pulled the cork with a loud *pop*. "Yep. But what we do have is a response to file by January second. Tell me you have litigation skills I don't know about."

"Unfortunately, no," she said, taking containers from the fridge. "But even if Havers did still have Patrick on retainer, he'd have to recuse himself because of his involvement with the turbines."

"Fair point, but that still doesn't do anything to help us," Felix said, grabbing a glass from the Hoosier cabinet. "We've got zero candidates to fill the position and even less funds to pay them with."

Jena chewed her lip, pausing in her artistic placement of tubed meat slices. "You have an ad running?"

"Yes, and believe me when I say, it's only highlighted what an absolute debacle this is. It's going to take a Christmas miracle to find someone on such short notice at this time of the year, willing to work for a pittance."

Jena hummed, drumming her fingers on the counter for a breath. "You should ask the coven to do a manifestation spell."

Felix blinked at her mid-pour. A manifestation— "You're brilliant. Why the hell didn't I think of that?"

"Maybe because you're also drowning in your stupid sister's drama," Jena muttered, moving on to sliced cheese. She was about as far from Team Felicia as you could get. "How long has she been gone this time?"

Felix shrugged. "More than a week and less than a month?" He swirled the wine in his glass and took a sip. "Mom had Matilda scry for her, and she couldn't find her."

"Then my money's on a trucker."

Felix grunted. "Yeah. That's what I said."

"You think she'll be back for Yule?" Jena asked, glancing up from assembling veggies.

"Is it wrong to say I hope not? Like, yes, I wish she would get her shit together and actually be there for her spawn, but dipping in and out of their lives is seriously fucking them up…right along with my parents." And him. God, he literally couldn't anymore with her drama.

Jena's lips pinched together, probably thinking about her own pending bundle of indentured servitude. She was just coming around to the idea of having a baby, though Chase was over the moon. That kid was going to want for nothing except breathing space. Felix couldn't wait to kidnap the little blighter and actually enjoy being an uncle. Surrogate parenting sucked.

"No," Jena finally said. "I think that's fair. Honestly, I don't know why your mom didn't have Matilda curse Felicia with infertility years ago."

"One, karma, and two, it's an Irish Catholic thing," Felix muttered, though he didn't disagree with the sentiment. Lord knows the sour witch had offered. "And there's no putting that genie back in the bottle. You'd think after four urchins and I don't know how many miscarriages, she'd see the value in birth control."

Jena snorted. "Don't forget the ectopic pregnancy that landed her in Klineville General for a month and cost your parents a second mortgage. Carry this out for me? I'm not supposed to be lifting."

Felix eyed the mountain of food she'd assembled. "Maybe you shouldn't have put thirty pounds of crap on it then. This is supposed to be the appetizer? How many people are coming? Maybe I should set something on fire," he said, hefting up the slab.

"Har har. Aside from you, me, Aggie, and Chase, there's Gorman and Kelsey." She glanced askance at Felix, and his stomach flipped.

"Don't say it." If Liam Montgomery was going to be here...

"Fine, I won't, but he hasn't been doing well, Felix. He got into it with Pete at Cups today, and I heard it was ugly. Not to mention how badly Samhain messed him up, and with everything else that's going on with Jenny—"

"Lalala I don't want to hear it. He looked fine when I saw him yesterday. Too good in fact," Felix grumbled, setting the charcuterie board down on the coffee table in the center of the mismatched overstuffed chairs and couches ringing the living room. Chase's renovations hadn't made it to this end of the apartment yet, and it was still a Frankensteined seventies nightmare of white paint and linoleum. But at least the tree hid the crated-up fireplace, and the swags of tinsel and fake pine were nice.

"You saw him?" Jena asked, pulling his attention back to her.

"Mmm. When I went to pick up the urchins. He was there for his kids." Felix smoothed his tie and claimed a corner of one of the big couches, pointedly avoiding the corduroy one.

"Felix," Jena said slowly, fanning napkins. "You know they're not his right? Well, the younger ones aren't. I guess the oldest might be, but they're still waiting on the results. That's one of the reasons the divorce is so ugly."

Felix just stared at her, then snapped his mouth closed for a breath. He hadn't, but— "Then why was he at the school?"

Jena shook her head. "I dunno, but you could ask him."

Felix huffed. Fat chance of that happening.

She rolled her eyes. "You know, forgiveness is actually a thing."

"So is nurturing a grudge, and in my experience, it's a hell of a lot more satisfying," Aggie said, sweeping into the room in a bedazzled, green water-silk caftan and a tiara. "What do you think? Too much bling?"

Jena's brow rose. "Umm—"

"Oh, who the hell asked you?" Aggie waved her away. "Where's my wine?"

"Still in the bottle," Felix said, taking another sip of his.

"Then I hope you've got enough upper body strength to serve yourself." She sniffed, looking him up and down. "Never mind, you'll have to get Chase to take pity on you, if he ever shows up. Where is he?"

"Probably stuck in line at Sal's trying to pick up your fancy cheese," Jena said, heading back into the kitchen. "You do know it's four days before Yule, right? Everyone and their mother are out shopping."

"Boo hoo. Sacrifices must be made, and he better not come back with the cheap stuff," she groused. "He's gonna have another thing coming if he thinks knock-off pecorino is getting anywhere near my masterpiece."

"I'm sure he knows better after the last time you

eviscerated him for not being more discerning in his dairy selection," Jena said dryly from the kitchen, china rattling.

"You'd think, but he's a man." Aggie harrumphed.

"Hey!"

"Oh, you don't count," the older witch scoffed at Felix's objection. "You had good home training."

His brow quirked. "I'll make sure to let my mom know you approve."

"You do that. Lucinda still wrangling your sister's indigents over there?" Aggie asked, lounging in a chair by the window and glancing down at the street. She crossed her legs, one foot bobbing with either anticipation or annoyance. Probably both.

"She is."

"I don't envy her that," she muttered, her gaze still on the street. "One was hard enough."

"At least I wasn't in diapers," Jena said, coming back in with a cup of tea and handing a glass of wine to Aggie before sitting beside Felix.

"True that. You weren't totally feral, either." Aggie took a sip and then pursed her lips. "Well, I made plenty, so you make sure you take a hefty portion over there. Your mom could use a break, and I haven't met a kid yet who won't eat pasta. She makes a stink about it, tell her she can return the favor in cookies. I hate baking, and her gingerbread's on point."

"Will do," Felix said, finishing his glass. Hopefully Aggie wouldn't mind getting it in decapitated pieces.

LIAM SAT behind the wheel of his Jeep, one hand on the steering wheel and the other picking his lip. He stared out the windshield at the Witchery across the darkening street, his rosy outlook from his morning run totally obliterated after what had gone down at Cups.

Kelsey had convinced him to press charges and take out a restraining order against Pete. God, just thinking about that son of a bitch made Liam want to put a hole through something. So did the look on everyone's faces that had been there. What their confrontation was going to mean for his divorce and custody proceedings ate at him.

Especially what it was going to mean for the kids.

Liam frowned, his wolf whimpering. Was it really fucking worth it? It felt selfish. Him being back in town, disrupting everybody's lives. Maybe he should just sign the papers, declare bankruptcy, and move on. Even if he spilled his guts to Felix, the chances of him forgiving him and getting a second chance were slim to none.

Christ, what if he laughed at him?

After this morning, the possibility made Liam want to puke. His nerves were fried, and his two-hour shower and double dose of anxiety meds hadn't done anything to calm him down. He blew out a breath, reaching for the ignition. He'd said he'd come, and he'd done that, but he hadn't technically said he'd go in—

Someone knocked on his passenger-side window, and he jumped.

"Hey, sorry about that. Didn't mean to scare you," Chase said, backing up with a loaded grocery bag in his arms. "You coming up?"

"Oh, um, yeah, I mean, yes." Liam fumbled with his seatbelt and opened the door—Shit. He leaned back in and grabbed the six pack he'd picked up. Not that Jena could drink it, and he wasn't supposed to on his meds, but no way was he getting through this without a beer or three.

"Cool." Chase grinned, rounding the front of the Jeep. "You know, Jena was beyond excited when Kelsey called the other day," he said, shifting the grocery bag as he waited for

Liam. "We're both really happy you decided to come, especially after Pete ran his mouth. You're a better man than me. I would've beaten the shit out of him for popping off like that. Christ, I still might."

Liam toed a chunk of ice, seeing the aftermath of what'd happened in Los Huego beneath his feet for a breath. Christ. Nope. Not going there—*Keep it together, Liam.* "Kelsey was about to, but with the divorce…"

"No, I totally get it, but it's only a matter of time before someone kicks his ass. The way I heard it, people are fucking pissed he threatened you. He's gonna have a hard time showing his face around town."

Liam's gaze jerked up to meet Chase's. "Yeah?"

His brows furrowed. "Yeah, man. That shit's not cool, and you've never been anything but nice to everyone. Him on the other hand…Pete's a serious dick, and this is pretty much the reason people have been waiting for to blacklist the prick. You know, I had a job over on McDermott, and caught him pissing on the side of my truck a couple of weeks ago? Man was stone cold sober, too."

"That's hard to believe," Liam grumbled as the crossed the unlit street. He frowned, picking his way around a patch of black ice. Shit was dangerous.

And unfortunately, so was the situation with Pete. They'd never been on great terms, but considering the guy was fucking his wife, things had been fairly amicable. Jenny had finally seemed happy, then everything went to shit after Liam had gotten that damned job offer out West. He didn't have a clue why Jenny had lost it on him when he didn't want to take it, but it'd been bad enough that he had, and Pete had jumped head first into a bottle shortly after. Prick hadn't come up for air since.

"Hopefully he abides by the restraining order. If he doesn't, you let me know."

Liam glanced over at the rumble of a threat beneath Chase's words, a lump in his throat. "I appreciate that."

Chase grunted and swept his messy caramel waves from his eyes. It was still weird to see the big man without that ratty ball cap he used to wear. "You know, you really should hang out more often."

God, he said that like he really meant it. The lump in Liam's throat grew larger. "Yeah, thanks, I've just been..." Barely keeping his shit together. He shrugged. "You know. Busy."

"No, I get it." Chase blew out a breath. "But it's better that way. Things haven't been easy for any of us the past few months. If I didn't have Jena..." He shook his head. "My family wasn't exactly the best, but it's still hard losing them."

Liam grunted. He knew all about that, but at least he had his parents and his sister. Chase didn't have anyone aside from Jena. Well, no one local. "You hear anything from Sue or Luke?"

"Luke's called a couple times, but he's pretty happy out on his boat. Think he took it up to Lost Bay for the winter. He says he'll be back in the spring, but we'll see. I haven't heard anything from Sue, not that I'd expect to." He frowned, hiking the grocery bag higher.

No, he wouldn't since the Fayet pack had grabbed her during a raid. Damn, that'd been a dumb question. She'd be in seclusion for six months, and afterwards, one of the pack members would claim her. Chase would be lucky if he ever saw her again. *Way to step in it, idiot.*

"I did hear that Patrick moved to Galleon Falls, though." Chase's frown deepened. "With all the shit he pulled, that was probably a good call on his part."

Liam snorted. "If you didn't take a piece out of him, I sure as hell would've."

"Pretty sure most, if not all, of the town would be in line."

Chase wasn't wrong. The prevailing sentiment was that

his younger brother, Patrick, was the brains to Malcom's brawn during the turbine debacle, and that the mayor had just gone along for the ride. With Malcom dead and the mayor currently doing time as a weasel, Patrick was the last man standing to take any frustrations out on.

And the town was rife with those.

Chase held the door for Liam, and he ducked inside. The Witchery was still a jumbled mess of spell stuff, but it had been decorated for the holiday and was a heck of a lot less drafty than the last time he'd been there. To the far right, the central bookcase had been removed, and what looked like the original fireplace had been restored and retrofitted for gas. Flames crackled within a scroll-worked iron insert. A bubble of leaded-glass panes surrounded it, sending warm amber light bouncing off the crystals on display.

Liam stopped in the entryway to take it all in. "You have been busy."

Chase grinned at him, pausing to admire his work. "Looks good, doesn't it? The flying squirrels were a bitch to evict, but Jena made some kind of a deal with the local pixie harem to route them. You know pixies have a thing for coconuts?"

"I did not." What the hell would they do with coconuts?

"Me either, but you should've seen them. It's a good thing they're usually wasted. If the little bastards were hellbent on world domination, we wouldn't stand a chance."

Liam cocked a brow. "Are you serious?"

"Try to take away one of their coconuts and find out."

"I'll keep that in mind." Pixies? Really? He had to be kidding.

Chase chuckled, shifting his grip on the groceries. "After they cleared the squirrels out, it was pretty much just elbow grease. Jena made me put up the glass surround. It's not historically accurate, but it didn't come out too bad."

"No, it looks great." It really did. Chase was incredibly talented. It was no wonder his business was booming.

"Thanks. What about you? Tinkering with anything lately?" he asked, starting toward the back steps again.

"Ah, no, not really," Liam said, trailing behind. "I haven't found anything that's grabbed my attention, and it's too damned cold to work outside. Just little projects, I guess. Fixed my mom's vacuum. Reading a lot of legal stuff for the divorce. I applied for a couple jobs, but you know how the offseason is."

"I do, and I'd be going nuts." Chase paused again. "You know, if you're interested, I could use a hand with some bigger projects. Nothing crazy, just grunt work and heavy lifting. It's not sexy, but if you need something to keep you occupied…"

Not sexy? Had Chase seen himself with a tool belt on? Man could be on one of those calendars. "Uh, yeah, thanks. I might take you up on that." Liam frowned, all too aware that Chase's words were echoing his mother's.

And damn it, but they weren't wrong. What Liam really should be doing was sucking it up and trying to get his law license reinstated. The idea made him ill, but as much as he hated being in a courtroom—the person he became in a courtroom—slapping an "esquire" at the end of his name again would look a hell of a lot more impressive on his bid for custody than "mechanic."

Of course, having a current job to back up either title would probably help, too. He scratched his jaw, reluctantly deciding to work on that after New Years when the prohibitionary period on his license was up—and God help him if that meant he had to head back out west.

The possibility made both him and his wolf ill.

Chase pushed through the door at the top of the steps, and Liam followed him in. The apartment smelled like cheesy, garlicky heaven. He paused, sucking in a deep breath. "Wow, that smells amazing."

"Of course it smells amazing," Aggie snapped at him from

a chair by the windows. "What do you think, this is some two-bit operation? Lasagna's not something you fuck around with, which is why you better have the right cheese!" she yelled after Chase.

He waved a wedge at her, and she grunted in approval.

"Ignore her." Jena rolled her eyes as she took Liam's arm and steered him into the kitchen. "She's just pissed because Gorman—sorry, *Manny's*—late. Does this need to go in the fridge?" the curvy little brunette asked, reaching for the six pack.

"Huh? Oh. Yeah, but I'll take one now, if that's okay," he said, handing it over and following her into the kitchen. Chase definitely hadn't had his way with the space yet. Thick plastic covered the windows behind a rickety table, and the kitchen was an avocado and baby-shit brown tiled travesty. A shockingly modern butcher's block island stood between the two like it'd been beamed in from this century.

"Absolutely." Jena smiled softly as she Jenga'd the six-pack into the fridge. "Felix will be happy he's got someone else to drink with."

"He will?" Liam asked around the lump in his throat.

"Yep. Better catch up. He's already a half of a bottle in." She tugged a beer from the six-pack. "You want a glass for this?"

"Uh, no. Bottle's fine," Liam said, trying to nonchalantly see where Felix was sitting.

She popped the beer's cap. "He's in the bathroom, making room for the rest of the Chablis," Jena said, far too perceptively. She started to hand Liam the porter, then pulled it back. "He's also had a seriously shitty day and is still fucking pissed at you. An apology would go a long way, and in the meantime, if you hurt him again, I will turn your scrotum into a coin purse."

Liam's throat bobbed, and he fought to keep from bolting back to his Jeep.

"Hey, Liam's had a shitty day, too," Chase said, coming over and kissing her temple. "And remember what I said what would happen if you threatened our guests?" She blushed and bit her lip, squirming against him, and he laughed. "Or is that why you did it?"

God, they were a cute couple. The pit of Liam's stomach churned, trying to remember what that was like.

"Fine, and maybe—but I said what I said, and I meant it," she huffed, unrepentant.

"And do you feel better now?"

"No, but I would if I got to hex someone. My karma has been accumulating way too fast lately, and I know just the jerk to spend some of it on." She shook violet sparks from her fingers, and her expression softened as she turned back to Liam. "What Pete did to you was terrible, and I'm sorry you had to go through that. If it makes you feel any better, you're not the only person he's verbally attacked with his shitty world view."

Liam stared into his beer. It didn't. "Thanks."

Jena went to say something else, and there was a knock at the door, rescuing him.

"It's open!" Aggie snapped.

Chase sighed. "I'll get it."

"That's gotta be Gorman, Kelsey would just walk right in," Jena said, shooing Liam after Chase. "Go on, find a seat and eat something."

Liam escaped into the next room, happy to have the attention off him while everyone focused on Gorman Howe arriving. The chronically unkept building inspector came into the room disheveled enough to look like he'd just survived a category four hurricane. He couldn't have been more than five-foot-five, which was tall for an imp, and all his bluster made him seem even larger.

"You know, there should be a light outside of your shop. Pretty sure that's a building code violation," he said, glaring through his askew glasses at Chase closing the door after him.

"Actually, there's a streetlight within ten feet, which puts the onus onto the city," Chase replied smoothly, "That said, I submitted plans to restore the gas lamps at either side of the front entry a couple of weeks ago, and you denied them."

"Plans?" Gorman drew the word out and scowled, his thinning auburn hair sticking up at all angles around his stubby horns. "I didn't see any plans, and if I did, I denied them for a reason. I suggest you double check your work and resubmit."

Chase somehow managed not to roll his eyes. "Will do."

Gorman didn't seem impressed by his compliance—or anything else. "Aggie. You're looking adequate."

"And you're not," she sniffed, adjusting her tiara. "Couldn't bother to put on a clean shirt? That one has ink stains all over the pocket."

He ran a hand across his short-sleeved plaid button up's overflowing pocket protector and waggled a bushy brow at her. "Why, when it's just going to end up on the floor?"

"Oh my God, I'm gonna puke," Jena muttered, hurrying toward the bathroom.

Aggie pursed her lips. "You should save your mother some work and figure out how to use a laundry bin."

Gorman slapped a bagged bottle against Chase's chest and just grinned at her. Her eyes narrowed back, as he strutted across the room, his long, arrow-tipped tail swishing, and plopped down into the chair by her side. He leaned over and raised her hand, kissing her knuckles. Aggie turned away with another sniff and a sly smile on her lips.

Liam leaned over to whisper at Chase. "They're not...?"

"Yep," he said, blowing out his cheeks. "I try not to think about it. Grab a plate and dig in. I skipped lunch for this, so it's not gonna last."

"Yeah, thanks." Liam helped himself to a plate from the

meat and cheese mountain and sat as Felix came back into the room.

He stiffened when he saw Liam. "Oh look, another reason to drink. Anyone else need more wine?"

Shit. Liam's mouthful turned to sawdust, and he killed the rest of his beer.

"No, but a couple fingers of whiskey would go a long way," Chase said, following after Felix. "Dude, be nice," he hissed.

The door flew open again as they cleared it.

"Sorry I'm late!" Kelsey huffed. "Greta got a wild hair across her ass and decided that since Cups was closed for the day, we needed to do inventory." She waved a bottle of Bownes and plopped down next to Liam, her beribboned pigtails bouncing as she unscrewed the cap. "What did I miss?"

"That the glasses are in the kitchen," Aggie said dryly. "Or are you just planning on drinking that swill straight from the tap?"

"What?" Kelsey glanced at the bottle. "This isn't swill, it's strawberry, but, yeah, I guess I can do that, if we're being all fancy." She popped back up and went into the kitchen.

Liam concentrated on chewing, wishing he'd asked her to grab him another beer. Not a chance he was going in there.

"So, Felix," Gorman blustered. "What's this I hear about Fayet suing the town?"

"Well, that didn't take long," Felix muttered, coming back in and perching on the opposite side of the couch, his back not quite to Liam. The warlock tossed a few slices of cheese onto his plate and stabbed an olive. Kelsey bounced down between the two men.

"It true?" Gorman asked, loading his plate with mortadella, Limburger, and cocktail onions. God, he probably ate kidneys, too.

Felix eyed the combo with a frown. "Unfortunately."

Gorman huffed. "Fine time for that brother of yours to up and quit." He glared at Chase like it was his fault. "From what I hear, he's left us high and dry."

"Wait, we haven't hired another town attorney?" Kelsey asked.

Felix shook his head. "Nope. We're pretty much screwed on that front."

"But—" She glanced at Liam, and he threw her a panicked look with a small shake of his head. She rolled her eyes at him and sighed.

"But…" Aggie prompted, her glower all but nailing them to the couch.

"But, um, plenty of people have gotta want that position." Kelsey squirmed, then downed a hefty swallow of her drink. "Idiot," she muttered at Liam from behind her glass.

He didn't care. Even if his license hadn't been suspended, his background was in arcane law, not civil litigation, and second, he had enough problems without taking on Havers's. He knew Fayet's council, and they'd never been on good terms. He could guarantee that this lawsuit wouldn't end well, and him being at the helm would only make the entire situation worse.

Like everything else he touched.

His gaze went to Felix, the warlock's curls just brushing the collar of his magenta satin button-up. His tie was turquoise and had penguins on it. He huffed, his cheeks pinking as he scooted farther away from Liam and crossed his long legs, tie-dye socks peeking from between his checkered loafers and olive khakis.

Despite his cold shoulder, a smile tipped up Liam's lips, in awe of how easily self-expression came to Felix. It was one of the reasons Liam had always found him so attractive. Felix was the king of confidence, and he'd never cared what anybody thought.

And now he was the frickin' mayor, for God's sake.

Granted, he seemed miserable in the role, but it wasn't like him being himself had hobbled him professionally or personally. Everyone loved Felix. Well, pretty much everyone. As for the rest of them...Liam chewed his lip, conviction settling back into his belly. If he wanted to win Felix, he was going to have to learn how to tune out the rest of them and do the same.

FELIX SQUIRMED IN HIS SEAT, all too aware of Liam's heated gaze running over him. He cursed himself, feeling his cheeks—and other parts of him—warm in response. It was the wine. It had nothing to do with the incredibly sexy were at the other end of the couch. Nope. Wasn't him at all.

Keep telling yourself that, Felix.

He took another sip, hoping to prove the point and that whatever Gorman had brought was drinkable. With Aggie guzzling glasses, that single bottle of Chablis was tapped, and if this was any indication of how the night was going to go, he was screwed.

But Chase did have that bottle of whiskey…

"Plenty of people might want the position," Felix said, reviving Kelsey's earlier statement, "but not for what we can afford. The last few months Chambers was in office, we were working under a deficit, and believe me when I say, that hasn't improved. We've had to make some serious cuts." And Felix felt like a dick every time he'd signed off on one, especially when it had cut the town's aftercare program, two weeks into the school year. The hate mail he'd gotten from irate parents had been brutal.

"Yes, but those cuts shouldn't be anything that impacts public safety. The streetlights outside should be on, regardless," Gorman muttered around his mouthful of stinky cheese.

"Are you going to have to furlough people?" Chase asked, sitting in one of the overstuffed chairs with his plate of appetizers, then pulled Jena onto his knee.

Felix felt himself pale. He hadn't even considered that. It made sense on paper, but right before the holidays?

Gorman snorted. "You do that, and they'll burn you at the stake."

The witches in the room glared at him.

"What, too soon?" he asked with another snort. "You ask me, you're better off auctioning all the frippery Chambers accumulated—starting with that suped-up golf cart of his."

As much as Felix hated to agree with Gorman, he had a point. The six-seater ATV with all-leather interior and heated steering wheel was beyond extravagant. They'd also had to lease garage space to keep the damned thing from the elements.

"If you get me a list with pics, I can post stuff for you," Jena offered. "Between the reclamation work Caldwell and Sons has been doing and the Witchery, I've been putting all kinds of things up for sale. You'd be surprised how much some stuff goes for."

"Yeah?" Felix asked, clutching to that slim thread of hope. "How much do you think we can get for granite curbing?"

Chase perked up. "Depends on the grade and how many linear feet you've got lying around. I'm actually in the market for something like that to mitigate the runoff that keeps washing out the manor's driveway. I had it graded before we dragged the Yule log up there, but after that last storm, it's already a mess."

And what a miserable hike that was going to be. Felix tapped his teeth. That wasn't exactly a short distance. The house above the node outside of town had to be a good half mile from the road. "I have absolutely no idea how much there is, aside from it taking up a third of town hall's parking lot, but you're welcome to come take a look at the pile." There was also more of it in a warehouse waiting to be delivered, pending a final payment that the town was never going to make.

Chase nodded. "I'll stop by tomorrow. I was planning on putting in a bid this week. The fact that I wouldn't have to wait for delivery is a definite selling point. That stuff takes like twelve weeks to come in, and I want to hit the ground running come spring."

"What you want and what you're gonna get are going to be two very different things," Aggie said breezily as she stood and pointed at Liam. "But what I want is lasagna. You, tall, dark and angsty, come help me plate up slices."

"What?" Jena stared at the older witch as Liam scrambled to his feet. "Tell me you didn't have a vision."

"Okay. I didn't have a vision." Aggie shrugged, making her way across the room.

"Aggie…"

"Agree to name your firstborn after me, and then we'll talk," she said, quirking her brow as she disappeared into the kitchen.

"Goddamn it," Jena seethed. "Who names a baby Agatha!?"

Felix finished his second glass of wine, snickering. "I'm going to go out on a limb and say you. It's only a matter of time before you cave. Give in now and save yourself some misery."

Jena glared at him. "How much of that wine have you had to drink?"

"Not nearly enough, and it's already gone. What did you bring?" Felix asked Gorman, eyeing the syrupy liquid in his glass.

"Blackberry Schewitz," he said, smacking his lips.

Oh God. Nope. Not drunk enough for that—yet. "I think

I'll switch to whiskey," Felix said as he stood with his empty glass and only listing slightly. He was also going to grab a slab of lasagna while he was at it. He needed carbs to bolster this buzz.

Liam was hefting a massive pan out of the oven, his stupid biceps bulging as he lifted it onto the stove. Who looked that good in a t-shirt and hoodie? It wasn't fair. The man was wearing cheap, big box store jeans and ratty sneakers for God's sake—and he was still more appetizing than what Aggie was plating up.

Which looked just shy of divine.

"Felix! Stop standing there drooling and finish shredding this cheese for me," she snapped, pointing at a wicked little contraption of jagged metal.

Drooling? He was not—okay, maybe he was. He ran a hand over his mouth. Whatever, he had a weakness for lasagna and the stupidly buff men that hefted it around, but honestly, who didn't? "As much as I would love to help you, I enjoy having skin on my knuckles more."

"I should probably do that." Liam chuckled, taking the wedge from her. "Felix isn't kitchen compatible and handing him a box grater is just asking for trouble."

"Well, figure it out. I forgot the damned fancy napkins," Aggie muttered, heading out of the kitchen.

"Now that's not fair," Felix chided Liam. "I have nothing against kitchens, aside from the whole culinary aspect. And I'll have you know, I'm quite adroit with a corkscrew."

"Good to know," he said, a sexy little smile crossing his lips.

Damn him. Felix huffed and put his empty glass on the counter, scooching behind the were. His front accidentally-on-purpose brushed across Liam's overly impressive backside, and he froze with a pained noise.

Felix swallowed one of his own, along with a tipsy smirk. Okay, so maybe his judgement was a teensy bit impaired copping a feel like that, but it served Liam right for eye-fucking him earlier. "Cut yourself?"

Liam shook his head, his cherry cola waves hiding his expression as he bent over his task.

And my, but wasn't that quickly becoming an impressive mound—*Damn it, Felix. The cheese.* Absolutely not what was in Liam's pants—or his own.

Okay, so maybe that, too. Felix cocked a brow and sauntered to the Hoosier cabinet—his smugness popped like a bubble. Great. Chase had put the whiskey on the top shelf and set it back. Was there anything less sexy than having to find a footstool? Felix cursed his genetics and blew out his cheeks. Whatever. He raised himself up onto his tiptoes, his fingertips just brushing the bottle's label—

"Let me help." The warm weight of Liam's pecs pressed against Felix's shoulder blades, their outstretched arms brushing as Liam grabbed the bottle for him.

Felix snatched it and held it to his chest, focusing on not hyperventilating. He closed his eyes, the room suddenly very, very hot and his Adam's apple bobbing. *Mayday, Mayday!* "T-thank you."

Liam grazed his hand down the outside of Felix's tricep and cupped his hip. His head dipped and warm breath teased against the shell of Felix's ear. "You're welcome. You need help with the glasses?"

Don't even think about turning your head, Felix!

Shit. Too late. His throat bobbed again. "Um. No?"

Liam ignored him, and Felix bit his lip at the bulge rubbing against the small of his back as Liam lifted his arm and leaned forward again.

Felix's pants were abruptly way too tight. *Snap out of it, stupid! Liam. This was Liam. The man who broke your heart into a thousand pieces and smiled while he did it.*

But the feel of him—the smell. A warm musk had surrounded Felix, heady and promising things he really shouldn't be thinking about. He choked back a whimper and snatched the glass from Liam's hand. "Great. Yeah, I got it, thanks," he said, spinning away.

Liam took a step back, his pupils blown. He looked away with a sheepish nod and reached down to adjust himself.

Felix went rock hard.

"Anytime…ah, you think Chase would mind if I had a glass of that?" Liam asked, motioning to the bottle Felix was still hugging.

"Nope, have at it. Pour me one while you're at it, would you? I'll get ice." He slammed what he was holding onto the counter and winced. Jesus fucking Christ. That man was going to be the end of him. Felix ripped open the freezer door and stood just shy of crawling in. The blast of cold on his heated cheeks slowly brought him back to Earth. He grabbed the ice tray and set it on the counter, not meeting Liam's eye.

"Got 'em," Aggie said, coming back into the kitchen and flipping a stack of linen napkins onto the counter," she sniffed and pinched her nose, glaring at them before throwing cheese over two of the slabs of lasagna and hefting up the servings. "Finish plating the rest of those up for me, and stop canoodling in my kitchen."

LIAM POURED Felix's drink and then himself a quick shot. He downed it, his face on fire, desperately trying to tamp down his mating pheromones. He hadn't meant to go there with Felix—at least not until he apologized and explained things—but goddamn him for flirting like that.

Jesus, the way he fit against him, that tiny whimper he'd tried to hide—

Damn it, none of that was helping to kill his erection. Liam poured himself another shot.

Unfortunately, by the look on Felix's face, he hadn't meant

it to go there, either. *Okay, Liam, focus.* He needed to keep a clear head. Divorce, think about the divorce, about Pete—and instant ice bath. Right, moving on…he could do this. Liam picked up the spatula and tried to ignore how it trembled in his hand as he started plating before Aggie came in and yelled at them again.

He cleared his throat, glancing over at Felix taking a hefty swallow from his glass. A couple more of those and the slight warlock would be on the floor. "You think you can handle adding cheese to these?"

"As long as there's no pokey implements involved, I'm willing to give it a try," Felix said, then stared blankly at the grated pile.

Liam bit back a smile. Christ, he was fucking adorable. "Wash your hands and use your fingers." He mimed sprinkling over the slab he'd just plated.

"You make it sound so easy." Felix frowned, puffing out his cheeks as he tottered to the sink, unbuttoning his shirt cuffs and rolling them up.

Liam tried not to stare at the dusting of freckles across Felix's creamy skin. *Yeah, hard fail there.* Christ, no pun intended. He turned away and closed his eyes, seriously considering giving himself a case of whiskey dick. Sounded better than hanging out with a hard on all night.

Too bad it would take the rest of that bottle and then some. A were's metabolism wasn't exactly conducive to going on a bender. Getting drunk was like an Olympic sport and required a hell of a lot more dedication than a beer and a couple of shots.

Come on, Liam. Pay attention. How many plates did they need? One, two, there were seven of them here, right? Aggie had taken out two servings already, another two were waiting for cheese, that left…three? He laughed, and Felix turned to him, his brow raised as he dried off his hands.

"Something funny?"

"Yeah. Pasta math. I was trying to figure out how many more plates we needed, and it ran through my head like one of Mrs. Abram's convoluted word problems," he said, invoking their tenth-grade algebra teacher's name. Woman had been batshit crazy.

"See?" Felix said, batting Liam's arm with the dish towel. "And you were convinced you'd never have to know what percentage of thirty pumpkins you'd need to make eighteen pies if they each averaged ten pounds, and the recipe called for twenty-six ounces per pie."

Liam chuckled. "Indeed. I stand corrected." He took another sip of his drink and then held it up. "To Ms. Abram," he toasted.

"To Ms. Abram," Felix said, returning the gesture, more than a little tipsy. "So, now what, I just…touch it?" Liam almost spat out his mouthful, and Felix went pale, then bright red. He cleared his throat. "I-I mean…"

"Yeah," Liam said, taking pity on him. God, could he get any cuter? "Grab a pinch and sprinkle." He mimed again.

Felix glanced around the kitchen like something was about to jump out and bite him. "There's no open flames around, right?"

"Nope, and I have complete faith in you."

"I'm glad somebody does," Felix murmured, his face screwing up as he grabbed a half dozen shreds and deposited them on a slab like they'd burned him.

"See." Liam grinned. "No fire."

"It was obviously a one-off," Felix sniffed, cautiously reaching for another pinch. He looked up at Liam from beneath his brows. "You do know spontaneous combustion is a thing, right?"

Oh yeah, he knew. Liam stepped to the side, leaning against the counter. "I do, but I'm pretty sure you sprinkling cheese isn't going to set off a chain reaction."

"From your lips to God's ears." Felix crossed himself and

deposited a heftier heap. The look on his face when nothing blew up was priceless. He took a sip of his drink like he couldn't believe it.

"What are you two doing in here? Giving each other a sponge bath?" Aggie grumbled, stalking back in and killing the moment.

Felix choked on his sip. "What?" he coughed, and arm over his mouth.

"Wouldn't be the first time I was subjected to seeing that up against the sink." She glowered out the door at Jena and Chase, then rolled her eyes at Felix's handiwork. "You call that adding cheese? You're not playing with nitroglycerin, dump it on there! Oh, for the love of—" She grabbed a handful and buried a slice. "There, like that. Think you can deliver it now? Here, this one too, and don't forget the napkins. I didn't dig through all that crap to have them just sit there."

"Yes, ma'am," Felix said, disappearing with two of the plates.

"And you," she groused, hipping Liam out of the way. "Leaving the garlic bread in the oven isn't going to improve it any. Didn't you two idiots hear the buzzer?"

He did now. "Um—"

"Mmm hmm." She shook her head, switching it off. "Finish putting cheese on those plates, then take them with you when you scram."

Liam did what she said and scrammed. He delivered one of the plates to Chase and retreated to the couch with his own.

"Do you think we're allowed to go back and get our drinks?" he stage-whispered, sitting where Kelsey had been. She'd stolen his seat and looked pleased as punch about it— or that could just have been because of the food. She popped a bite of lasagna into her mouth, curled up on the far end of the couch in her own little world of bliss. The sounds she was making were more than a little disturbing.

"I'll go. You two stay there," Jena said, putting her plate to the side with a funny smile on her face. It got bigger as she passed the two of them.

Felix grunted and dug into his lasagna. Liam did the same and failed to prevent the moan the first bite elicited. Okay, Kelsey was forgiven. Holy shit, this was good.

"Right?" Chase said from across the room, shoving a massive forkful into his mouth.

Liam caught Felix staring at him, and he about choked on his bite of cheesy goodness at the warlock's expression. Damn. His wolf perked up. The last time someone had looked at him like that…he started to sweat. Maybe telling Felix how he felt wasn't a lost cause.

"Yeah," Liam said, his knee ghosting closer to Felix's. He didn't move away, and Liam's heart leapt. He grinned. "This is amazing."

"Mmm," Kelsey groaned. "So fucking good."

"Of course it is," Aggie sniffed, sauntering in with a platter of garlic bread. She paused to survey everyone stuffing their faces with a supreme look of satisfaction on hers.

"It'll do," Gorman muttered, scraping his plate. "There more?"

Aggie raised her brow at him. "Yeah, and you know where to find it."

He grunted and trundled off to the kitchen as she sat. Jena came back in with Liam and Felix's glasses. They were suspiciously fuller than Liam remembered, but he wasn't going to complain. Not about the booze, not about the food, and definitely not about Felix's knee touching his, *and* he'd caught him looking at him more than once.

The warlock took a sip that he probably didn't need and

not-so-chalantly inched closer. Liam kept eating, happier than he could remember being in ages.

"So," Felix began, "this manifestation spell, you think we can get the coven here tomorrow to do it?"

"We'd have to do it at the ruins, but I don't see why not," Jena said, perching on Chase's knee again and picking her plate back up.

Liam went very still at the mention of the standing stones above the node outside of town. After Samhain, he had zero desire to go anywhere near that part of the eastern woods ever again.

"Well, that's not ideal," Felix murmured. "But you're probably right with the amount of karma we'll need to channel."

"I can send out some texts tonight and see what everyone's availability is," she said. "Matilda will bitch about the short notice, but I can't imagine that anyone won't show for it."

"Matilda would bitch if we scheduled it out three months from now and let her pick the date. The sooner we can get things moving, the better. You need anything from me?" Felix asked, taking another bite.

"Mmm hmm." She put her hand in front of her mouth as she chewed and swallowed. "Yes. You'll need to give the spell focus and shape its intent. Everyone else will be pushing it out into the aether. The more specific you can make the request, the sooner we'll get results."

"That shouldn't be a problem," Felix muttered. "I definitely know what we don't want."

"That will help," Jena said around another gooey mouthful. "I'm pretty sure Sweets should have all of the spell ingredients, and from what I've read in my mom's grimoire, it doesn't seem super complicated."

"It's not," Aggie said. "Or it won't be, as long as he stays focused. Make sure you use the bathroom beforehand. Last time I did one of those was after the town's chili cook-off. Marshall Haynes was trying to manifest goodwill between the Fultons and the Gregors, and ended up dropping a loaded port-a-potty smack dab into the well they were feuding over."

Chase laughed, and Aggie's sidhie-blue eyes flicked to him. "It stopped the feud, but you better believe he caught shit for it."

"Sounds like the well did, too," Chase snickered.

"Great," Felix murmured, taking another sip of whiskey. "Note to shelf, shit before you summon."

"Always a good rule of thumb to note the shelves," Aggie agreed, crunching into her cheesy garlic bread. She dusted off her hands as she chewed. "So is filling your plate again after you've licked the first one clean. Don't think I didn't see that," she said, narrowing her eyes at Liam.

"What?" He laughed. "I didn't lick it; I swiped it with my finger!"

"Lying's not gonna make it better. Go on, get some more."

Liam shook his head and stood. "Anyone else need seconds?"

"More like thirds." Chase scooted Jena off his lap to join him. He glanced back into the living room once they were in the kitchen. "You gonna help Felix home, or is he crashing on our couch?"

Liam froze mid-scoop. "Uhh…"

"Look, if he's slurring, he's got about fifteen more minutes conscious, half an hour tops. Trust me, it's eerily repeatable. His apartment is on the other end of Cross, that newer development at the corner of Harstand, number 58A on the fourth floor. I can give you Jena's key, so you don't have to frisk him for his."

Liam reached for Chase's plate, trying to buy time and remember to breathe. It was on his way back to the compound, but… "You really think he'd be okay with that?" he asked, scooping up another helping.

"Considering how much he bitched about his neck after the last time he spent the night here? I'm pretty sure he'd be okay with Gorman giving him a piggyback ride home. I'd ask Kelsey, but if Felix passes out, she's not gonna be able to drag his ass up all those steps. Man's heavier than he looks, and the elevator in his building's been out since Samhain. Are you okay with it?"

Liam took a slow breath and handed Chase his plate back. "Yeah, I can make sure he gets home okay."

"I appreciate it, and so does Jena." Chase clasped him on the shoulder, then stuffed another ridiculous mouthful of lasagna into his maw.

Chase was right about Felix. By the time they made it back to the living room, he was pie-eyed and fading fast. Chase grabbed the warlock's empty plate as it slid off his lap. "Hey," he said, crouching down in front of Felix. "It cool if Liam brings you home?"

"Pppttt," Felix buzzed his lips and fell back against the cushions. "Suure…why not?"

"You got the green light," Chase said to Liam. "You okay to drive?"

"Yeah." Liam frowned at his heaping plate. "You think I have time to finish this, or should I take him home now?"

They both glanced at Felix. His head was thrown back at a weird angle, and he'd started snoring softly. Liam bit back a smile.

"Take your time, man." Chase grinned. "He's not going anywhere."

FELIX GROANED and prised a gummy eye open. What frickin' time was it? His blackout curtains were drawn, and the room thick with shadow. He huffed out a breath that could've dropped a mule. Ugh, that was horrific, and a better question might be who was spooned up against him. Damn it, he hadn't thought he'd gotten *that* drunk last night, but the evidence suggested otherwise. He didn't remember getting home, and he definitely didn't remember drunk dialing anyone for a hook-up.

His blurry eyes focused on the bedside clock. Ten thirty-seven? No way. How the hell could it be that late? Myx would've been in here hours ago. Felix fumbled for his phone, and the mystery man's arm tightened around him, his breath hot on Felix's neck as he nuzzled against him.

Okay, so that was really nice. Felix wriggled back, enjoying it while he could. It'd been a hot minute since he'd had anyone to snuggle with and even hungover as hell, Felix was a cuddler.

His eyelids drooped, lulled toward sleep by the man's heady cologne…they snapped back open. Wait, what had he been doing? His phone. He'd been checking his—

Shit. It was that late. His alarm had been silenced, and he'd missed a handful of texts from Jena, three calls from the office, and double that many from his parents. He groaned, his head throbbing harder at what that could be about.

He scrolled through Jena's texts first. The coven had agreed to meet, but not until later that evening. Something about Greg Plinkin warning that the portents were wrong, and that they needed to wait until after sunset. Felix wasn't thrilled with having to hoof it out there after dark in the freezing cold, but the burly warlock would know. Portents were his family's magical bent. Felix wasn't going to complain about the reprieve.

Though he would complain about the hike out there and the cold. Loudly.

His voicemail transcriptions were a different story. Lorraine was losing her shit over having to feed Chambers, and it sounded like she'd discovered a photocopy of someone's ass on the copier again. Guess the butt cheek bandit was still at large. Felix scrubbed a hand over his face. Heaven help them if someone wasn't around to stop her from pouring bleach over the scan glass. Everything was already cloudy after the disinfectant spray and steel wool she'd used on it the last time.

A sick day. He was totally taking a sick day, and his hangover notwithstanding, it sounded like he'd need it. His mother had called seven times, but she'd only left one message.

Call home.

Damn it. He could hear the tremble in her voice without even listening to the message, but he wasn't about to ring her back with his "guest" still there. Felix closed his eyes, enjoying the man's arms around him for several breaths before he wriggled free, his head pounding. Ugh, he was still in his clothes. Guess he hadn't had as much fun as he'd thought, but that begged the question: why was the mystery man still there?

The dark shadow beside him riffled its hair, pushing up

against the pillows as Felix slipped away. Whoever he was, he was big. Beside him, a pair of malevolent green eyes cracked open, catching the scant light before they shut again.

Felix stared at the dark lump in disbelief. "Are you sleeping with my cat?" He had to be hallucinating.

"Yeah," Liam's groggy voice rumbled from the darkness. "I think he likes me."

"You!" Felix sprang away from him and fell off the bed in a tangle of sheets. "What are you doing here?!" he squeaked from the floor, then slapped a hand onto the bedside table, fumbling for the light.

It clicked on, and pain shot through Felix's temples. Goddamn it…

"Careful. You okay?" Liam peered over the side of the bed, and still fully dressed, thank God. If Felix was going to make that mistake, he damned well wanted to remember it.

In vivid, hi-definition detail.

Ugh! No! What was he thinking?! This was Liam! Felix sputtered. "Okay? No, I'm not okay. Why are you in my bed?"

"Ah…You were pretty drunk." Liam ducked his head, scratching under Myx's jaw, and the furry traitor started purring. "Chase asked me to bring you home. He said something about not wanting to listen to you bitch about your neck, and since this was on my way—"

"Bitch about my neck?" Felix stood, dashing the tangle of sheets to the floor and smoothing a hand over his rumpled dress shirt. "I'll have you know, I strained a tendon. I think I have every right to 'bitch about my neck.'" He finger quoted, the room on tilt. He put a hand out to steady himself, bile rising in his throat. Shit, he might still be a little drunk. "And that doesn't answer why you're here now." Or what he'd done to Myx. The cat looked more content than Felix had thought possible. Maybe soothing savage beasts was a were thing.

Liam shrugged, scritching the wretched animal behind the ears. "You asked me to stay, so I did."

Felix stared at him, his mouth opening and closing, his brain refusing to process that statement. He shook his head and immediately regretted the motion. "I need to take a shower," he grumbled, stumbling toward the door. "Careful, he bites."

"Nah." Liam grinned down at Myx. "He's a good boy, aren't you?"

A weird surge of jealousy flared through Felix's churning guts as he turned on his heel and stumbled over the tangle of sheets at his feet. *Nice, Felix, way to be smooth.* He pushed through his bedroom door into the hallway. And Myx? A good boy? The feline was psychotic, and it was just a matter of time before he snapped. Whatever. If Liam wanted to cuddle a furry hand grenade on his lap, Godspeed to them both.

Felix managed not to vomit until the bathroom door was closed, then he was on his knees heaving and totally losing his shit.

What the hell had he done? Had he seriously asked Liam Montgomery to stay?! What in the holy hot sauce of Jesus's blessed barbecue had he been thinking? Felix grabbed his toothbrush and jammed it into his mouth, gagging as he scrubbed. It had to be his current lack of companionship. Desperation had driven him to it, obviously.

Keep telling yourself that.

Damn it, he wasn't—couldn't—fall for Liam again. Felix tore off his clothes, the smell of the were's cologne clinging to them. He put the shirt to his nose before he thought better of it. Good Lord. If they bottled that up and sold it, he'd be buying it by the gallon to sprinkle his sheets with—

Out of the corner of his eye, Felix caught a glimpse of himself in the vanity mirror, buck naked with a semi, huffing his dress shirt. Nope. That wasn't weird at all.

"I am so screwed," he muttered, chucking it to the side of the overflowing hamper and getting under the water. He didn't have the bandwidth to unravel the squirrel's nest of emotion he had going on.

Felix scrubbed his face and blew out a breath. Priorities. He needed to call in to the office, then deal with whatever was going on at his parents'. His head throbbed, and his stomach roiled again. This fricking hangover—the urge to zap it with karma was fierce, but if he used up what he had now, he'd be spent for tonight.

He'd have to suffer through it. No matter how drunk he'd been, he deserved it for letting himself cozy up to Liam, and Chase was getting a serious talking to for putting him in this position.

Felix bit back a sob and let the hot water sluice over him. Feeling even remotely human was going to require several over-the-counter medications and more than one pot of coffee, but first, he needed to throw on some clothes—

Oh God, he'd forgotten to grab clothes.

He shut off the water and stood dripping, cursing himself for not kicking Liam out. Why hadn't he kicked him out? Jesus, it wasn't even noon, and he was already over today. Felix ripped the towel from its bar and dried off. He'd ask what the hell else could go wrong, but that was just inviting trouble. If Liam hadn't taken the hint and was still out there, Felix would just send him on his merry way.

That decided, he wrapped the towel around his waist and opened the door, the aroma of freshly brewed coffee hitting him square. His knees went weak. Okay. He'd send Liam on his way after coffee. No need to be rude, right? Felix lurched into his room and caught himself again at the made-up bed, blinking. Was Liam intentionally trying to confuse the hell out of him? Felix was fairly certain he hadn't stumbled into some strange alternate reality where he had a sexy house boy catering to him.

He pinched himself, not entirely sure he wasn't dreaming.

When he didn't spontaneously appear back in bed, Felix shook his head and pulled on a pair of pajama bottoms and a t-shirt. He blew out his cheeks, attempting to mentally prepare himself. *Thank you for everything, but I've got a bunch of work to do, and it's really time for you to leave…* Yeah. Sure. That sounded good. Felix buzzed his lips and poked his head out the door. His apartment was silent. He tiptoed to the kitchen like he was the one that shouldn't be there.

A freshly brewed pot of coffee was on the warmer, and Myx was chomping down kibble.

Liam was gone.

"Well, that was anticlimactic," Felix muttered, annoyed by the absence, though he shouldn't be, which just annoyed him more. "Though, I guess I shouldn't be surprised… You on the other hand." He eyed the cat's backside as he poured himself a cup of coffee. "Exactly what do you think you're doing cozying up to Liam Montgomery?"

Myx flicked his ears back and kept them there, still chowing down.

"Fair enough." It wasn't like Felix hadn't been doing the same, but in his defense, he hadn't known it was Liam… except there was no other man on the planet that smelled like that. God, he didn't have time for this. Felix pinched the bridge of his nose and took a deep breath before dialing in to work and putting the phone on speaker.

"Mayor's office," Lorraine's shrill voice barked after the third ring.

"Hey, Lorraine, it's me. I'm sorry I didn't call sooner, but—"

"Did you get my message!?" she squawked, the pitch slicing through his temples. "That degenerate's struck again! I called the sheriff this time, it's simply disgraceful!"

"I agree," Felix said, almost wishing he was there to see the sheriff's face when he was handed a nine by eleven of someone's hairy ass and balls by an octogenarian. "Absolutely disgusting behavior."

"When are you coming in?" she snapped.

"About that…I've been fighting a migraine all morning, and I think it's best I stay home today. I'm so sorry you have to deal with this, but it sounds like you have everything handled."

She sniffed, slightly appeased. "What about the weasel?"

"His kibble's in my closet. *Don't* open the cage. Just dump a half cup into his bowl through the bars." The last thing they needed was Chambers running amok.

"Fine. Just this once, mind you."

"Thank you, Lorraine. I really don't know what I'd do without you."

She harrumphed and hung up.

Well, that'd gone better than he'd expected. He could guarantee the next call wouldn't. Felix freshened his coffee—*not* enjoying it immensely, damn it—and the phone rang. Crap. It was his parents. He took a frustratingly delightful sip from his mug and hit the button to accept the call.

"Finally! Why aren't you answering your phone?" his mother's voice chided.

Felix's eyes fluttered, and he pinched the bridge of his nose. "I woke up with a migraine, and I did just answer my phone."

"You know what I mean," his mother tsked. "I'm sorry you're feeling poorly and hate to ask you this, but—"

Shit. "What did Felicia do now?"

There was a pregnant pause, and his stomach preemptively clenched, waiting for it.

"No, not The Renot," his mother said to someone else. "They left hair in the sink last time. Try the Grand. They might still have rooms."

Felix's eyes snapped open. Why were they looking at

hotels in Maybach three days before Yule? "What's going on?"

She sighed. "Great Aunt Helen had a fall. One of those damned cats of hers got stuck in the gutter. She pulled out a ladder instead of calling someone, slipped on some ice—she's got a broken wrist, and her hip's fractured in I don't even know how many places. I have to be there tomorrow morning to sort out the insurance paperwork before her surgery, and after, the dang rehab center's got a waiting list a mile long. The best they can do is send a home health aide to check in on her, but she can't be left alone all day."

Holy crap. His mother's spinster aunt was old enough to have graduated in the same class as Lorraine and was only marginally more mobile. Felix was also pretty positive she had a commemorative cat for every year she'd been on the planet. "A ladder?"

"I have no idea what she was thinking, but the damage is done, and we need to leave in the next hour or two to make it there by tonight," his mother said with a long sigh. "We're praying for a Christmas miracle, but it doesn't look like your father and I are going to be back in time to celebrate that or Yule."

"Okay." That sucked, but he could always go to Jena's. "So, what do you need from me?"

There was another pregnant pause.

"Oh no." Felix felt himself pale as he put two and two together. "I am not watching those urchins while—"

"Felix Christopher Simms! Those *children* are your nieces and nephew!"

His front door opened and closed, and Liam sauntered in with a to-go bag from Cups and a drink tray. Felix motioned for him to put it on the table, both irritated and somehow relieved the were had come back, even if his timing was for shit.

"How is this my problem?" Felix asked his mother. "Why can't dad stay and watch them?"

"Aren't you the one who told me I shouldn't be driving?"

God, he could practically see her raised eyebrow. And okay, yes, he had, and she shouldn't be, especially not all the way to Maybach by herself, but— "What the hell am I supposed to do with them?" He pulled at his collar, the room tunneling. Liam came over and stood behind him, rubbing Felix's arms. He fell back against him, too completely overwhelmed to protest. "I know nothing about kids, or potty training—what do they even eat?!"

"Good grief, Felix, calm down! Cruze, Axle, and Sway are more than capable of finding their own dinners and making it to the bathroom by themselves. We talked about taking them with us, but just one hotel room is so expensive, never mind two. If we could stay at Aunt Helen's, it would be one thing, but with all those cats—"

"What about the screamer?" He winced, his head throbbing just thinking about her.

"We're planning on taking the baby with us."

Felix snorted. Great, so his mom would be changing the kid's diapers along with Aunt Helen's. Like she wasn't going to be enough of a handful. "I don't see how that's going to work," he muttered, exasperated.

"We don't have any other choice."

They did, but calling the county to take custody of the urchins wasn't going to happen. He pinched the bridge of his nose. Goddamn Felicia for pushing her shitty decisions on them. His parents were supposed to be enjoying their retirement, not spending their energy and savings raising her spawn. You'd think she'd be getting state assistance and child support from one or two of their deadbeat dads, but if she was, his parents never saw a penny of it.

And neither did the urchins.

Damn it. He didn't have the bandwidth for this. It was

gonna screw him, he knew it was, but his mom was right. They didn't have any other choice. "How long do you think you'll be gone?"

"There's a spot opening up at an assisted living facility after the first of the year. As soon as we can get Aunt Helen in and settled, we'll be back. So, two weeks? Maybe three? I should've gotten her a room after the stove incident, but…"

"It's not your fault, mom. It's Felicia's for putting you in this situation."

For once his mother didn't have anything to say to that. Something rustled on the other end of the phone, and Felix's dad cleared his throat as he took the receiver. "Ah, so, we figure it's probably best if you stay with the children here."

"You think?" Felix snarked. His single bedroom aside, Myx would freak, and there was no way they were getting their grubby paws anywhere near his comic book collection. Could they even read? The last report card his parents had been bemoaning seemed to suggest otherwise. Whatever, he didn't care. "When do you need me there?"

"As soon as you can get here. The car's already packed and ready to go."

Of course it was, and his was still in impound. Fuck, fuck, fuck. "Did you leave their schedule for me?"

"It's on the fridge. It's a little convoluted for the next two days, but then they're off until January sixth for Yule. Axle and Sway you'll have to pick up around three twenty, like you did yesterday. Cruze gets out of school at two thirty, but then she meets with a tutor. We've been letting her walk home with her friends. She's usually home by four."

Usually, huh? "And if she's not?"

"She will be. They're good kids, Felix. They've just been dealt a bad hand. Your mother and I bought groceries—"

"Groceries?" His heart about stopped. "What the hell am I supposed to do with groceries?!"

"Felix, calm down." His father sighed. "Cruze can cook,

and they all know how to use the microwave. You should be stocked for the week. You know where we keep the spare cash if you need it."

"Dad, I'm not gonna—" Felix bit his tongue. "Fine, but I swear to God, if Felicia shows up, I will not be held responsible for my actions."

His father sighed and there was more rustling on the other side of the line. A door closed, and he cleared his throat again. "I don't think that's going to be an issue. Your sister called late last night. She—she doesn't plan on coming back at all."

LIAM CAUGHT Felix as he crumpled against him, his inner wolf frantic with concern. Damn, Liam wasn't totally sure what he'd just walked into, but based on what he'd just heard, it didn't sound good. It was common knowledge that Felix's sister wasn't a particularly fit parent, but Liam hadn't had any idea things were this bad.

"W-what do you mean, she's not coming back?" Felix asked, his whole body trembling.

His father sighed again. "She's living on some ranch out in Nevar. Reading between the lines, it doesn't sound particularly wholesome, but she says she's happy there. She—she also said she's giving up her parental rights."

"How high was she?" Felix snorted.

"I don't think that matters. The paperwork's already been filed."

The slight warlock went very still. "So, what happens now?"

"We either sign or they end up in the system."

Liam caught Felix as his knees gave out. His phone hit the floor, and the screen shattered. The kitchen went dead silent.

Felix put a hand on Liam's chest, steadying himself. "I-I've got to go over there..." He pinched the bridge of his nose and swore. "My car's in impound. I wouldn't normally ask but—"

"I can take you." Liam quickly offered, not about to ask any questions. The urge to protect Felix, to do whatever he could to help him, was all-consuming. "Whatever you need. If you want, I can drop you off and sort out your car, too. Jerry's a friend."

Felix nodded. "Yeah. Thanks. This…Jesus." He put a hand over his mouth, then looked at the ceiling, tears in his eyes. "Last night I told Jena I thought it would be better if Felicia didn't come back. God, if I sent that out into the universe—"

"Hey." Liam gripped Felix's shoulders and caught his gaze. "This isn't your fault. Your dad said she'd already filed the paperwork. That takes time. She had to have been thinking about this for a while." Felix ducked his head like he didn't really believe that, and Liam sighed, stepping away. He pulled a container out of the to-go bag. "Here, Greta said oatmeal's your usual. You need to eat something before you deal with all that. Five minutes isn't gonna make or break anything."

Felix nodded again and shakily took his seat. "You didn't have to do that…or come back." He popped the top of his oatmeal and stared at it for a breath. "Why did you stay?"

The smallness of his voice hurt. Liam pulled out the other chair and sat across from him. "I told you, because you asked, and I-I wanted to." Damn it. This wasn't the time to spill his guts, but…he took Felix's hand. "I'm sorry for what happened between us. How things ended, and I want to make it right, if you'll let me."

Felix watched him sweep his thumb over his knuckles. "Well," he said, forcing a smile as he pulled away. "Making me a decent pot of coffee wasn't a bad start."

"Good to know." Liam grinned, retrieving his own breakfast from the bag. He glanced at Felix from beneath his brows. "You want to talk about it? Your sister, I mean."

Felix shrugged. "There's not much to say. Felicia's the same train wreck she was in high school, but now she's got kids. They stay with my parents more often than not, and she pops in and shanghais the urchins whenever they get any inkling of stability. Cruze is a hormonal mess, Axle's a burgeoning psychopath two grades behind where he should be, Sway's got a death wish, and the screamer screams."

"And your parents?" Liam asked before taking a big bite of his breakfast sandwich.

"Have already taken out a second mortgage and don't have two nickels to rub together to support themselves, never mind the rest of them," Felix said, throwing his spoon into his half-eaten breakfast. "And living in a hotel for two weeks is going to kill whatever saving they have."

Damn. What could you even say to that? Liam nodded at the drink tray. "One of those is yours."

"Thanks." Felix found his and sat back. "I just don't get how you could leave your kids like that."

Liam winced, the question cutting too close to home. Jenny's vitriol was what had sent him packing, but—"Addiction is a powerful thing." And so were shame and regret. Leaving had been hard, but coming back had been even harder. Ignoring that little voice telling him it would be better if he left again wasn't particularly easy either.

"I thought the mother-child bond was supposed to be powerful, too," Felix muttered. "You're really okay with driving me over?"

Liam took another bite and nodded. "Yeah. I'll finish this while you get ready to go."

Felix met him in the entry once he'd put on real clothes and shaved. They grabbed their jackets, and he shoved his keys into his pocket, then touched Liam's arm as he went to open the door. "Thank you. For being here. For listening. It-It means a lot."

Liam's heart swelled, wishing he could do more. "I'm

happy to help," he murmured, wiping a bit of shaving cream from Felix's lobe.

His hand lingered.

The slight warlock's eyes closed for a breath, and a whisper of pressure from his cheek pressed against Liam's palm. His heart raced as Felix's eyes opened and their gazes met. Felix's lips parted like he was about to speak, then pressed together, tight. He nodded, ducked his head, and they got on the road.

Chapter Seven

FELIX WAVED to Liam as the were pulled out of his parents' driveway. Had all of that really happened? Felix rubbed his temple, a migraine still lurking. From the screaming coming from the house behind him, that wasn't going to get better anytime soon.

Goddamn you, Felicia.

Felix turned and trudged to the kitchen door, past the late model station wagon packed to the gills in the driveway. A smile crossed his lips despite the situation, remembering all the road trips his parents had dragged them on when they were kids. Felix sighed. His sister wasn't terrible back then, at least no more than a sister was supposed to be. She hadn't gone off the deep end until right before she'd graduated high school.

His father was convinced that was entirely due to Marcel, the guy Felicia had been dating, who was also Cruze's father. Felix couldn't disagree. The siren had certainly lured her off the straight and narrow, but it'd been Felicia's choice to stay there after he'd disappeared and left her high and dry.

Felix huffed out a breath, struggling to navigate the shovel's width of cleared space to the kitchen door. Whether Axle knew it or not, he was gonna haul his ass out here after he got home from school and do the job properly. Aunt Helen breaking a hip was bad enough, but if Felix's mom went down, they were all screwed.

The decibel level increased exponentially when he opened the door, and Felix winced as he went inside. His mother turned with a look of profound relief on her face.

The screamer wailed louder, and Felix put a hand to his ear, cringing. There was definitely a banshee somewhere in her genome.

"Oh! Thank Heavens you're here! I've been anxious to get on the road; they're supposed to get snow in the mountains." She looked out the window. "Where's your car?"

"In the shop. A friend dropped me off." Felix's brow knit. Was that what Liam was now?

"Then I hope you're planning on having them bring your bags later," his mother said.

Shit. He hadn't even thought about packing. God, this day was so not going the way he'd planned. "Um, yeah. Don't worry. I have it all worked out." His mother didn't look like she believed him. Smart lady. "So, what have you told the urchins?"

"Nothing, and I'm not going to. Neither are you." She shook out a puffy, mini-ski suit and frowned, trying to hold it up to the screamer as she thrashed. Good luck shoving her into that. It was giving him hardcore *Christmas Story* vibes. "Don't you look at me like that Felix, we will, but I can't do that to them so close to the holiday."

Considering what Sway had said about Axle crying, it might not be the most ill-received news they'd ever gotten. Felix opened his mouth to say something, then shut it again. His mom didn't need that weighing on her conscience, too.

"Fine, I won't say anything, but I'm not lying if they ask." It'd always been a personal pet peeve of his when adults spouted bullshit to their spawn, and he wasn't about to perpetuate the practice. He crossed to the mustard enameled fridge and searched for the urchins' schedule amid all the crappy crayon drawings littering the front of it. Ah. He pulled it from under an AARP magnet. Seemed straight forward enough—

No. Wait a minute.

"What's this about pageant rehearsals?"

"Oh!" His mother beamed at him and picked up the screamer. "Cruze got the role of the Spirit of Christmas Past!" She bounced the little blighter, and it wailed louder. "Yes, she did! It's going to kill us not to see her perform, she's been so excited about it. You'll do me a favor and record it on your phone so I can watch it later?"

Felix slumped, his shoulder smacking into the appliance and threatening an avalanche of bagged snacks from above. "But she's in middle school. I thought it was just for the elementary kids."

"No." His mother shook her head, trying to jam the screamer's fat little legs into the snowsuit as she thrashed, red-faced and bawling. The slag glass pendant light above the table swayed on its chain. "All the big roles are filled by middle schoolers. The rest of the cast is younger kids. Don't you remember how angry you were when they wouldn't let you audition for Rizzo in *Grease*?"

Vaguely, and he was still convinced he'd had the chops to pull that role off, but he hadn't thought his age had been the determining factor. Whatever, it wasn't important, and the school system's questionable choices in live theater productions aside, this wasn't happening.

"There's no way I can juggle work, this rehearsal schedule, and the other two."

His mother huffed a curl from her eyes and hiked the screamer's snowsuit up. Felix winced and resisted the urge to cup himself. "Now you listen here, Felix Christopher Simms. It's two measly rehearsals and then the show. That little girl has been practicing her heart out. After all her hard work, she's going to be devastated enough that we can't make it. If you take it completely away from her, I will never forgive you, and neither will she."

He rolled his head on his shoulders and sobbed at the cracked popcorn ceiling. "Why me? God, I know it's not my karma—"

"No, but it is your family," his mother snapped like that was the end of the subject. "You're just going to have to make do like the millions of other single caregivers out there trying to get by, and thank your lucky stars it's only temporary." She zipped the screamer up and shoved a hat over her curly dark hair. The urchin hiccupped and shoved her thumb in her mouth.

Felix's brows shot up. "It's self-corking?"

His mother glowered at him. "*She's* a very empathic child. All this upset isn't good for her."

"Oh, well, then taking her to the ER is a great idea."

Felix's mom gave a long-suffering sigh. "Promise me you'll take Cruze to her rehearsals, go to the pageant, and that you'll record it for me, Felix. This is important, and I'm trusting you to take good care of your nieces and nephew."

Felix rolled his eyes. "Fine. But after the New Years..." Shit. He couldn't even say that, could he? If Felicia had bailed for good, he couldn't not help his parents. Christ, they'd be in their nineties before the screamer started high school. There was no way they could do this alone. Not physically, not financially...

His mother looked like she was waiting for him to finish his thought, and he shook his head. "Yes, okay. I promise not to drown them while you're gone. I'm sure Jena will help me if I beg hard enough, and I've got to meet with her later anyway—"

His eyes widened. Shit. The manifestation spell.

"No. I won't be here for that either." His mother frowned, following his train of thought. "But twelve coven members should be enough, and you can always stand in for me. Jena can pull on the node, after all."

"What the hell am I going to do with the urchins while I'm there?" No way could he take them to the ruins, especially at night. There were way too many opportunities out there to kick off an ER visit, or Matilda would turn them into frogs—actually that might not be a bad idea…

"Get a sitter," his mom said, hefting up the screamer. "You'll only be gone for a few hours. If you order pizza, they won't even notice you're gone."

"Make sure you go heavy on the pepperoni." His dad came in and nodded to him. "Son. We appreciate you doing this. I just went around and double checked that all the doors and windows are locked. Thermostat's set to sixty-eight—and it stays there," he said, pointing a finger at Felix.

"Sure," he said like they both didn't know it was going up to seventy-five as soon as the car cleared the driveway. Felix's bigger concern was where the hell he was going to find a sitter. He turned back to his mom. "You know anybody I can ask to watch them?"

"Felix, you have so many friends. I'm sure one of them would be happy to lend a hand." Which was mom for, "I've already burned all my bridges, so good luck with that." She pulled on her jacket, wrangled the screamer onto her hip, setting the urchin off again, kissed Felix's cheek, and headed out the door.

"Don't forget to bring in the mail," his father said, trailing after her. "And garbage is on Thursdays, no recycling this week!"

The door closed behind them, and Felix rubbed his temples. Fuck.

～

LIAM BIT his knuckle as he pulled away from the Simms's house and headed to the impound lot just outside of town. He replayed those last few moments at Felix's apartment over and over in his mind. The feel of Felix's skin, slippery from the shaving cream. His cheek against his palm. The look in his eyes after. God, Liam wished he knew what Felix had been about to say.

Holding him as he slept—shit, in the kitchen this morning—had been beyond Liam's wildest expectations. But when Felix had asked last night, looking up at him from his rumpled covers all disheveled, his tie tossed to the side, and the light smattering of hair peeking from the open V of his shirt…damn, there was no way Liam was gonna say no. The sigh of contentment Felix had given, wriggling back when Liam's arms wrapped around him, Christ, he'd almost come in his pants.

His throat bobbed. Shit, he might come now if he kept thinking about it. His cock was painfully hard. He glanced in the rearview mirror, then pulled onto a trailhead. No way was he getting anything done like this. He unbuttoned his jeans, his dick kicking as he pulled it free.

Liam licked across his palm and smoothed it over his weeping tip with a low moan. He fisted himself and swirled his thumb over his slit. Fuck, he was wet. His eyes closed, imagining it was Felix's tongue exploring the fat width of his crown. He stroked himself, remembering the feel of the man's mouth wrapped around him, sucking. The slide of his lips and tongue along his shaft as he massaged the root and gently tugged on his sac.

Felix bent over, golden-red peach fuzz so soft beneath Liam's hand. His tight little pucker taking one finger, then two. The sound he'd made when Liam slid his cock between his tight cheeks—

Liam groaned, cum spurting over his knuckles. He panted, his heart pounding as he slowly milked his orgasm.

Fuck, that'd been quick, but goddamn, Felix Simms did something to him.

He always had.

The way they fit together, the scent of Felix's aftershave, and his soft little snores. Jesus, even the ridiculous sweater with cherry blossoms he'd left the house in. Liam leaned over to pull a handful of takeout napkins from his glovebox and cleaned himself up, all of it just adding fuel to the conviction that'd been smoldering inside him.

Felix was what he wanted, and damn it, Liam was gonna prove himself to him.

…*"Making me a decent pot of coffee wasn't a bad start…"*

Liam grinned, tugging his pants back up and tucking himself away. He well aware of Felix's horror of all things culinary, and Liam wasn't above using that to his advantage. He wasn't terrible at cooking and actually enjoyed housework. There was something soothing about putting everything in its place.

He put the Jeep in gear and got back onto the road. Maybe it'd been weird that he'd made Felix's bed, but he had to do something to calm his nerves after Felix bolted. Climbing into the shower with him hadn't seemed like it would've been well-received.

Not yet, at least. They'd get there, he hoped. Baby steps.

Liam pulled into the impound lot's parking area and cut the engine. A deep sense of nostalgia swept through him. He got out of his Jeep and went over to the little cinderblock building just inside the chain link fence. His gaze swept across the rows of snow-covered cars. Man, it'd been way too long since he'd been here.

His teen years had been spent helping Jerry tinker with engines and haul in clunkers to escape felling trees with his pack at the compound. He hadn't expected to fall in love with cars, but the impound lot was where that'd started. The day he'd found his Jeep moldering at the back of a foreclosure property was the day his love had blossomed into a full-on obsession. Jerry had thought he was crazy, but let him haul the rusted-out frame back to the compound, sure it'd end up rotting there.

His teeth had about fallen out the first time he saw it on the road. Liam grinned. He couldn't wait to see the old man's face when he saw it now.

An electronic sensor beeped as Liam opened the door. A trio of dogs lifted their heads, decided he wasn't worth getting up for, and went back to sleep. He crossed the long, narrow waiting area to the counter. Jerry was behind it with his feet up and his fingers laced across his prodigious gut, watching a black-and-white Western. A cigarette smoldered in the ashtray beside him.

Man, he'd gotten old. Liam stood there for a moment, staring at the man's liver-spotted scalp before he binged the bell on the counter. Jerry jumped and fiddled with his hearing aid before turning to look at who was there. His bushy brows bunched, and then a wide smile spread across his face.

"That you, Liam? Been a dog's age, boy. What can I do ya for?" he asked, slowly rising to his feet.

"I'm here to get my friend's car out of hock. You bring in something belonging to a Felix Simms?"

Jerry put on his spectacles and pulled out a thick binder. He dropped it onto the counter with a puff of grit. "Sounds familiar," he said, parsing through the handwritten entries. "Simms, Simms…Yeah. Here it is. Hauled in a sedan for parking violations." Jerry gave a low whistle and looked at Liam over the rims of his half-moon lenses. "Man owes eighteen hundred dollars with all the associated fines and penalties. No wonder he sent you to pay it. Car ain't worth near that much."

"That right?" Liam laughed. "Don't worry, he's good for it. He'd be here himself, but he's got a family emergency at the moment, and I'm trying to help him out." He pulled out his wallet and handed Jerry his card. "That and I wanted to say hi. Like you said, it's been a long time."

"You're a good egg, kid. Always have been." The old man shuffled to the machine to run it. "Tell you what, I'll give you the family discount. Makes it fifteen hundred and change. And I'm glad you did stop in son, glad you did…Say," he adjusted his glasses, squinting, "that's not the heap out there, now, is it?"

Liam grinned. "It sure is."

"Well, I'll be damned." Jerry handed the card back. "I gotta have a look at this."

They went outside, and pride filled Liam's chest as the old man exclaimed and asked about details only a car junkie would. They popped the hood and got down on hands and knees to ooh and ahh over the undercarriage and exhaust system.

Jerry shook his head, and Liam helped him back to his feet. The old man sucked his teeth for a moment. "Any chance you're looking for another project?"

"Why, you got something worth working on?"

"For anyone else, no." The old man turned away to cough into a faded bandanna. "But for you? Could be. Go take a look at the lot's north end. Got something up there under a tarp. If you like what you see, it's yours. You bring her back to life half as well as you have this one, and I will die a happy man. I'll even tow it out to the compound for ya, free of charge."

Liam's brow quirked. "What the hell have you got out there?"

"You best go see for yourself," Jerry said, a twinkle in his eye. "Merry Christmas, son. We close at five. I'll push the paperwork through and have the release waiting for your friend."

"Yeah, thanks…" He glanced at Jerry again, and the old man made a shooing motion.

Liam took off, into the impound lot. It wasn't huge, considering Havers-by-the-Sea was at the ass end of a remote peninsula, but there were more cars than you'd think. It was hard to tell what a lot of them were at first glance with the mounded snow crusted over them, but by the bumpers, most were from the last thirty years or so. Nothing he'd be interested in, but Jerry wouldn't send him out here without a good reason. The wind kicked up, and Liam's pace sped down the frozen rows of vehicles, his hands jammed into his pockets and his breath streaming out behind him.

The north end was the farthest from the shack, and a lean-to with a corrugated metal roof spanned over the lot's final row. Smack dab in the middle of it was an elongated lump covered by a rotting tarp. Liam ran a hand over his jaw and slowly approached, anticipation fluttering in his stomach. He squatted down and flipped up one corner.

His head went light as he pulled it back farther. A Bel Air. No. No way was this right. Jerry was not giving him a fucking Bel Air.

Liam didn't remember walking back to the shack, but all of a sudden, he was inside and Jerry was grinning at him from behind the counter.

"You like her?"

"That's a Bel Air."

Jerry nodded. "It is. A 1957 four-door, hardtop sedan, two-tone in India Ivory and Colonial Cream, if you want the specs."

Jesus Christ, Liam wanted it all. "And you're just going to let me take it?"

"I am."

Liam swallowed hard and put his hands on his hips, staring at the floor. He shook his head, then looked at the man. "Are you fucking crazy? You fix that up, you could get six figures, easy."

Jerry shrugged. "I could, but what the hell would I do

with the money? It'll just give my kids something else to fight about when I'm dead, and not one of them gives a shit about the car. And before you ask, I got all the paperwork. My mother was the original owner and drove that boat right up until she passed. Don't know how the hell she climbed in and out of it, I sure as hell can't with this bum hip."

"Jerry, think about this for a second—"

"I have, and my mind's made up. I'm not getting any younger, and the last thing I want is for some yahoo to fuck it up. I know you'll appreciate it. So, what do you say? Take care of her for me?"

"I—" Liam nodded, all choked up. "Yeah, I can do that, and I've got plenty of time to work on her. Let me see what I can do about getting some garage space."

"Fair enough. She's yours. I'll have all the paperwork together along with your friend's when you stop back later."

"Thank you, Jerry."

The old man waved him away and settled back down to watch his show. Liam left in a daze. First Felix starting to come around, and now this? A massive grin spread across Liam's face as he got back into his Jeep. No way had he ever expected his day to turn out the way it was, and a project like this was exactly what he needed. A Bel Air. Damn.

He couldn't wait to tell Felix.

FELIX SAT at his mother's kitchen table with his head in his hands. It'd been two hours and Liam still wasn't back. God, he'd known it would be a mistake to rely on him, but what else could he do? His heart ached with disappointment, already too invested.

And where had that gotten him? Stuck here when he needed to pick up the urchins from school in forty-five minutes. He would've called an Uber, but hello, no cell phone, and the house phone was useless without any contact information.

He sighed and stood, resigned to walking—

Liam's Jeep pulled into the driveway. The were bounded out of the driver's door with a shit-eating grin on his face and walked into the kitchen like he owned the place. Felix's heart leapt along with his anger.

"Where have you been?" he demanded, his arms crossed over his chest and his foot tapping.

"Oh, hey. Sorry. I got your car all squared away, and then I stopped to get your phone repaired." He pulled it from his pocket and held it out. "That took longer than expected."

Felix stared at it, then at Liam. "You what?"

"Um, I got it repaired? I kept the receipt in case it's under warranty."

"I…" Well, shit. Felix took it from him and ran his fingers over the new screen. It flashed on, good as new. "Thanks."

"Yeah, no problem." Liam scratched the back of his neck. "I figured you'd be dying without it. You want to pick up your car now, or get the kids first? School's out soon."

Felix just blinked at him, his pulse racing. "Why are you doing all this for me?"

Liam kicked at the floor. "Because I'm serious about making things right between us. I know it's not the time to talk about it, but I fucked up. Jenny was never…It's you Felix," he blurted, his cheeks crimson. "It's always been you. I was just too wrapped up in all the rest of it to see that."

Felix took a deep breath, his heart three sizes larger than it had been, the way it was pounding against his ribs. "And now?"

"Now things are different. I'm still scared, but…I-I want to try again. To do it right. To treat you like you deserve. I know I shouldn't get a second chance, but—"

"Okay." The word shot out of Felix's mouth before he could stop himself, and the blood drained from his face. Had he really just said that?

Liam's jaw dropped. "Okay?"

Shit, he had. Felix blew out a breath and gave a slow nod. "I'm open to being, um, friends." God, he was such a liar. What was that Larry Wall quote? *"Down that path lies madness. On the other hand, the road to hell is paved with melting snowballs."* And damn it if Felix wasn't sick and frickin' tired of being cold.

"Friends." Liam's face fell for a spilt second before he recovered. "Yeah, uh, cool. That's great. Friends." He dragged a hand over his jaw. "So, car first or kids? Car will be cutting it close."

Felix glanced at the time on his repaired screen. It would be. Too close. "Urchins, and hey, speaking of them, do you think there's any chance Kelsey could babysit for a couple of hours tonight?"

"Uh…I can ask." Liam pulled out his phone. "What time?"

"Six to eight or so, latest. I'm not sure how long the manifestation spell will take. Tell her I'm springing for pizza," Felix said, grabbing his parka and heading out the door with Liam. He glanced askance at the were. This was so freaking weird.

"Sent." Liam pocketed his phone.

Felix rounded the front of the Jeep and got in, shivering. "Thanks. What do I owe you for the car?"

"You really wanna know?" Liam put the Jeep into reverse, turning to look over his shoulder as he backed out of the driveway.

A pit opened up in Felix's stomach. "Oh God, is it that bad?"

"It's not good." Liam chewed his lip. "Fifteen hundred."

Felix blanched. "The car's not even worth half that much!"

"So I heard. Don't worry, I know you're good for it. Just hit me back when you can." What was one more drop in the ocean of debt he was swimming in? Might as well max out his cards before they pulled them.

"I have it," Felix grumbled. "I'd just envisioned spending it on daiquiris somewhere tropical, not on stupid parking tickets."

"You do know most of that was late fees, right?"

Felix glowered at him. "It was the principle of the thing, and besides, I'm the mayor. I should be able to park wherever I want." Lord knew there weren't any other benefits to the miserable position.

"Pretty sure handicapped parking and in front of fire hydrants is a federal thing."

"I'll have you know it was raining and I was wearing sueded silk."

"Oh, well, then exceptions should've been made." Liam grinned.

Felix fought the urge to return it, cursing the man's good looks. It was bad enough he was enjoying their banter. "Exactly. You can park in the town hall lot," he said as they turned onto Main Street. "Wouldn't want you to get a ticket."

Liam laughed and headed in that direction. A couple of minutes later, he pulled into the lot and idled the engine. "If it's okay with you, I'm gonna wait here."

Felix tensed, but of course Liam was going to wait there. Friends or otherwise, why would he want to be anything but *discreet*? Felix went to open the door, fuming, and Liam caught his arm.

"Hey, it's not what you think. The last time I showed up at the school, that whole thing at Cups happened. But if you're up for it..." He wet his lips. "M-maybe we can go to trivia tomorrow night at Snaps? You know...as, um, friends."

Felix's heart skipped a beat, his mouth answering before his brain caught up. "I—yeah. Sure. I'd like that." Not because Liam had asked, but because he was due for a night out.

Sure Felix, keep telling yourself—Damn it. He scrubbed a hand over his face. "As long as I can get a sitter." How was this his life now?

"You know..." Liam drummed his fingers against the steering wheel. "My parents might be up for watching them. Jenny won't let the kids see them anymore, and my mom's pretty torn up over not having them around for the holiday. I mean, I can ask, if you're okay with it? It's Friday night, so you don't have to worry about getting them up early for school the next day."

Okay, so that hadn't even been on his radar, but yes. One thousand times, yes. "Um...let me think about it," Felix said, not wanting to sound too eager to pawn the little blighters off on someone else. "But feel free to ask and see if it's a possibility." *Dear God, please let it be a possibility.*

Liam nodded, and Felix got out of the Jeep, feeling like he was in another universe again. Somehow, he managed to get across the street without being flattened and made it to the front of the school just as the urchins were clearing the double doors.

"Uncle Felix!" Sway yelled, barreling toward him. She pushed through the crowd taking down a toddler with her obnoxious backpack and lunging at him.

"Oof! Hey, you've got to be careful. You knocked that little girl down," he said, pointing at the sobbing child. Her mother glared at them.

"Survival of the fittest." Sway shrugged. "We're learning about Darwin."

Felix's brow rose. "In first grade?"

"I'm in advanced classes," she huffed, throwing a frizzy pigtail over her shoulder.

"I don't care. Advance your skinny bottom over there and apologize." She looked at him like he'd asked her to lick a public toilet. "Now, Sway."

"Oooh, someone's in trouble," Axle sang, waggling his fingers as he came up beside them.

"You can go with her for being a jerk," Felix said. God, he wasn't a big fan of discipline, but he wasn't going to live with little assholes for the foreseeable future either.

Axle gave him the same look as Sway. "Are you serious?"

Felix raised his brow and returned it with his best impression of a Joan Crawford glower. The two of them glanced at each other, then goose-stepped back to the toddler to mutter an apology.

"Thank you," Felix said when they dragged their sorry rears back to him. "And if you don't like apologizing, be more careful next time."

Sway lunged for him and wrapped herself around his leg,

sobbing. "I'm sorry, Uncle Felix, please don't be mad and go away!"

Go away? "What are you talking about? I'm not going anywhere. In fact, you're stuck with me for the next two weeks. Gran and Gramps had to go help Great Aunt Helen. They left me in charge until they're back." Actually, she was more like great squared for the urchins, but whatever.

Sway wiped her snotty little nose on his parka. Oh God, that was disgusting. Felix forced a smile and detached her from his leg. She shot him a look like he was lying.

"Then where's Poe?" Axle asked. He sounded nervous.

Poe? Oh right, the screamer. "They took her with them because I'm only rated for urchins toilet-trained and up. Come on, let's go before we freeze, and aren't you lucky? I'm staying at the house with you. Tonight's going to be a little weird because I still have to get my stuff, so my friend Kelsey is going to hang out with you for a few hours."

"Is she your girlfriend?" Sway asked. She had a death grip on Felix's hand like she expected him to bolt.

"No, stupid," Axle muttered. "Uncle Felix doesn't like girls, remember?"

"You don't?" she looked up at him, her eyes brimming again.

He scoffed. "Of course I like girls. My best friend is a girl."

"You don't like kissing them."

Felix shot a glance at Axle. "Do you?"

"Ew, no, that's disgusting."

"I don't like kissing girls either," Sway said, pulling a face.

"Then it's unanimous. No kissing girls." Felix stopped at the corner. "You guys ever ride in a Jeep?"

"Like an Army Jeep?" Axle asked, suddenly rapt.

"Um, yeah, kind of like that. I have to go pick up my car—"

"Why? Where's your car?"

Felix looked down at Sway. "At the shop. My friend

Liam's going to drive us over, and I need you two on your best behavior."

They looked at him blankly.

"Yeah. Just sit there like that," he said, herding them across the street. Heaven help him, but this was going to be the longest two weeks of his life.

LIAM GOT off his phone just as Felix and the kids came into view. Man, Sway could easily be Felix's daughter, but the boy, Axle, had were written all over him. What kind was an entirely different question. Liam rolled down the window as the kid ran up to the Jeep, his eyes wide. He didn't quite move like a wolf—

"Whoa, is this really yours?"

"Yeah." Liam grinned. "You like cars?" The kid nodded, and Liam's grin got bigger. "Then hop in, but for the record, you really probably should wait for Felix or your grandparents to say it's okay before you just climb into some dude's ride."

The kid rolled his eyes. "Duh. Especially if it's a van and they have puppies or candy. My uncle already told us you were his friend, and he's right there," he said, pointing.

"Get in the Jeep," Felix yelled across the parking lot.

"See?" Axle said, running around to the passenger side. The kid's eyes got even bigger when he opened the door. They flicked to Liam's. "Can I sit in the front?"

"No, you cannot sit in the front," Felix grumbled, coming up behind him. "You and Sway, in the back. Consider yourselves lucky I don't hogtie you to the bumper."

The two climbed in, and Felix got in after them. Liam waited until they were all buckled, then headed to the impound lot.

"You hear anything back?" Felix asked.

"Yeah, my mom's over the moon about watching them tomorrow, but she's got a bake sale thing tonight, and Kelsey can't do it either."

"Shit."

"Language," Sway yelled at Felix.

"Volume," he shot back.

She giggled, and Liam swallowed his smile at Felix fighting to do the same. "So, I was thinking," Liam said. "I could hang out with them while you do what you need to, I mean, if you want."

"You can?" Felix glanced at him askance like he was questioning Liam's sanity.

"Yeah." He looked in the rearview, and both kids had the exact same expression on their faces. "I'd really like to, actually. I miss…things." And hanging out with his kids was at the top of the list. It wouldn't be the same, but he was pretty sure it would be fun.

"Well, I'm certainly not going to talk you out of it, as long as the two of them don't mind…did I mention I'll get pizza?" he asked, overtly trying to sell it.

"With pepperoni?" Axle asked.

"Extra pepperoni."

"Can we watch *The Pretty, Pretty Princess Show*?"

Felix cocked a brow. "Does Gran let you watch *The Pretty, Pretty Princess Show*?"

Sway shrugged. "Sometimes, but she says it makes her teeth hurt and her eyes go funny."

"Then you can watch *The Pretty, Pretty Princess Show* with Liam."

"Gee, thanks." He vaguely remembered the crappy anime cartoon had a lot of squealing and flashing lights. His daughter Sarah had loved it at that age, too.

Right before he'd left.

Liam scrubbed a hand over his face and blew out a breath.

"You sure about this?" Felix asked, his brows furrowed. "You do know there's one more, right?"

"Cruze, yeah." She'd be the same age as Sarah, maybe a little younger. "Does she like pizza, too?" he asked, looking in the rearview.

"No, she likes sa-lad," Sway said, drawing out the word into disdainful syllables. "The gross kind with fish sauce and weird cheese."

"Then I'll get her a Caesar along with your pizza. I should probably order that now. Delivery takes forever to get to my parents. You'd think Pizza Palace was in Fayet instead at the corner of Main," Felix murmured, pulling out his phone. He ran his thumb over the side of the case and glanced at Liam with a little smile. "Thank you again."

"Yeah, no problem, and I'd make that at least two larges, maybe three. I'd bet good money Axle can eat one himself." Liam definitely could at that age.

"I can," the kid piped up from the back.

"Okay. Three large pizzas, heavy on the pepperoni, and a Caesar salad. Anything else?"

Liam shook his head and pulled into the impound lot. "Sounds good to me."

Jerry had moved what Liam assumed was Felix's car to the side of the shack. To say the vehicle was beleaguered would've been kind. Liam laughed.

"You really drive around in that?" After all the shit Felix had given him about his Jeep—

Felix shot him a wicked side-eye. "Zip it, Montgomery."

"Hey!" Axle said. "This isn't the shop. This is car jail."

Sway pressed her snotty nose to the window. "Why did your car get arrested?"

"It knocked over a toddler," Felix said, already halfway out the door. "So, meet you back at the house?"

"Actually, I've gotta go in for a minute. You guys like dogs?"

Felix paled. "There's dogs? Like, big dogs?"

Shit. He'd forgotten Felix wasn't a fan. "Um, yeah. Three Rotties. I think you have to sign something, but Jerry will probably let me bring that out for you, if you'd rather stay here?"

"That's probably for the best," Felix said, climbing back in.

"Don't worry, I'll stay with you, Uncle Felix." Sway leaned between the seats and patted his shoulder.

Axle bolted out of the Jeep before Felix could shut the door. "Three Rottweilers? Like real junkyard dogs?"

"I guess we'll be right back." Liam got out of the car and grabbed Axle by his collar before he disappeared into the lot. "They're inside and not nearly as impressive as you think they are."

The kid shrugged. "I don't care. I love dogs. We had one once, but my mom had to give him away when we moved, and Gran and Gramps won't let us get any pets."

"Then you're in for a treat tomorrow night," Liam said. "My dad breeds wolfhounds. If you behave yourself while you're over there, he might take you out to see the newest litter. Hey." He stopped and made Axle look at him. "You ask Jerry if it's okay to pet them first, all right?"

The kid nodded, and Liam held the door open for him. They went inside and like before, the dogs looked up, but this time they followed Axle across the room like their heads were on swivels. Huh.

"Liam." Jerry nodded as they stepped up to the desk, Axle's chin just clearing it. "Well, hey there, little man. What's the good news?"

"Can I pet your dogs?" he asked, his big brown eyes pleading.

Jerry chuckled. "Sure can, just mind Buck's ears. He's the one with the brown splotch on his nose. He don't like them messed with."

"Yes, sir. Thank you."

Liam's brow quirked as the kid scampered off. Despite Felix's warning, Axle didn't seem like a burgeoning psychopath. Maybe Felix was just being dramatic. Liam turned back to Jerry.

"I'm assuming that's not the friend you mentioned earlier," the older man chuckled.

"Ah, no, Axle is Felix's nephew. He's out in the Jeep. Does he need to sign anything?"

"Yeah, but if you want to do it for him, I won't tell. Here's the receipt and all the legal nonsense. I need initials here, here, and a signature right here." Liam scribbled his own name on the dotted line. "Thank you kindly, and this here's all the paperwork for the Bel Air."

Liam took it with a long exhale. "I still can't believe you're serious about this."

"I am, and let me tell you, I haven't felt this good about something in quite a while. You just let me know when you want me to haul her out."

"I will. My dad thinks he might have something, but I have to check the dimensions and it'll need cleaning." Along with a heavy purge. Liam was pretty positive the prefab garage his dad had mentioned had his mother's craft supplies and the remnants of a float from when Kelsey was in Scouts.

"No rush." Jerry glanced over at Axle and then did a double take. "Well, I'll be. You don't see that every day. I can't even get them to do that."

Axle crouched in front of the dogs. They'd lined up in front of him, hip to hip, rapt as the kid spoke softly to them.

"You ready, Axle?" Liam asked, tapping the paperwork against his palm.

The kid finished whatever he was saying, and the dogs huffed as he stood. "Yeah. Can we stay longer next time?" One of the Rottweilers whined, pawing at the ground.

Liam exchanged a glance with Jerry, and the old man nodded. "Sure. I have to come back and help Jerry load up a car. If it's okay with your uncle, you can hang out in here while I do."

"That would be awesome." The smile on the kid's face about lit the room.

Damn. No way had Felix been serious. Axle was sweet as pie, and whatever kind of were he was, there was no question it was of the canine persuasion. But maybe that's why he'd been acting out. Little weres needed to run around more than other kids. Otherwise, all that pent up energy came out in less-than-ideal ways. Growing up with a bunch of witches was probably akin to torture, no matter how well meaning they might be.

Liam was gonna have to talk to Felix, for the kid's sake. "Cool," he said, holding out a hand. "You ready, then?"

Axle took it without a second thought, and something in Liam's chest tightened. Before he turned into a blubbering mess, he nodded to Jerry and led the kid outside.

FELIX DROVE AWAY from the impound lot with the urchins in the back, beyond thankful his car had started. The last thing he needed it to do was to prove what a piece of crap it was in front of Liam. Though Felix expected he had it coming after all the shade he'd thrown at Liam's Jeep back in the day.

Karma, you are indeed a bitch.

Whatever. It got Felix from point A to point B—most of the time. He glanced in the rearview at the two urchins whispering. Plotting against him, no doubt. "So, you guys okay with Liam hanging out with you tonight? It's okay to say no." *Oh my God, please don't say no.*

"Yeah!" Axle said with the same feral glimmer in his eyes that he'd had decapitating gingerbread. "He said I can go back and play with those dogs again."

"Then I hope he plans on being the one to take you," Felix muttered. Dogs freaked him out. Especially big dogs, and he could thank Beverley Stinson's Dalmatian for that, thank you very little. Lord only knew why weres didn't bother him. Psychology was bizarre.

"Liam said he would, and that his dad has dogs, too."

"Mmm. He does, and they're huge slobbery things." Felix shivered as he glanced in the rearview again at the abrupt silence that had descended. Axle's face had fallen, and Sway was hugging his arm. What the hell had just happened? "Is that a problem?"

Axle shook his head and stared out the window.

"Mommy says we'll do things, too," Sway piped up. "So do Gran and Gramps, but they don't really mean it, it's just to get us to eat peas. I hate peas." She scowled, and beside her, Axle hunched lower in his seat.

"Noted." Felix drummed his fingers against the steering wheel. Telling them to get used to it because people sucked didn't seem like an appropriate response. He wanted to tell them that they were wrong about Liam, but Felix wasn't totally convinced they were. He buzzed his lips. "How about this: I promise I won't ever lie to you guys, and if an answer's going to be no, I'll tell you no then and there, okay?"

Felix took their extended silence for assent and kept driving. He needed to get back to the house and get them settled. Liam had gone home to clean up and would be back in a couple of hours, which gave Felix just enough time to deal with Cruze. Somehow, he didn't think that would go as smoothly as picking up the urchins had.

He hadn't spent a lot of time with his eldest niece, but what he had was enough to convince him that angsty, tween girls were not his forte. Felix sighed and raked a hand through his curls as he pulled into the driveway. The lights were already on. Damn it. She'd gotten there before them and had the high ground.

The urchins tumbled from the back, and Felix grabbed Axle's arm as he tried to bolt past him. "You need to finish shoveling that walk."

"I did shovel that walk," he grumbled.

"No, you traced it. Finish the job, or your dog privileges will be suspended, and you're showering after. You smell like a wet Pekinese."

Axle shot him a look that guaranteed Felix would be sleeping with one eye open for the foreseeable future and stalked to the garage. Right, that settled—on to the main event.

The kitchen was a balmy seventy-five when he opened the door. Felix pulled off his parka, setting it onto one of the low-backed captain's chairs. Sway was sitting at another, somehow already stuffing her face with store-brand cookies.

Felix pinched the bridge of his nose. Whirling Dervish. Tasmanian devil. He mentally added landshark to the list of possible sperm donors responsible for seeding Hurricane Sway. "You do know I'm ordering pizza, right?"

"We always get a snack after school."

"A snack isn't half the bag," Felix said, tugging it from her grip. "You can have more for dessert. Go wash up, hands and face. You look like you were on ground zero of a booger factory explosion."

She scowled at him and stomped off. Two for two. Fantastic. "And use soap!" he called after her, putting the bag back on top of the fridge. How she'd even gotten up there—

"Where's Gran and Gramps?"

Felix turned at Cruze's voice. She stood with her arms crossed in the doorway between the kitchen and the living room, glaring at him from beneath the rolled edge of a slouchy beanie like he was an intruding vagrant. Her dark liner winged out, accentuating her already huge hazel eyes, narrowed with suspicion. Only a light dusting of freckles smattered across her delicate little nose, and her pin-straight blonde hair was waist length. He knew she was slender, but you'd never guess it by the baggy, black skater-chic clothes she was always swathed in.

Basically, she was Skipper, if Skipper identified as a goth—or was it emo now? Felix put a hand to his temple. God, he was old. Whatever. Her brow arched.

Shit, Felix, focus or she'll eat you.

"Great Aunt Helen had a fall," he said. "They went to take care of her until they can get her into assisted living, and took the screamer with them. You're stuck with me for two weeks."

"Of course they did," Cruze snorted, her mouth screwed up, and she shook her head. "This always happens! Every time I finally—I'm not quitting, and you can't make me!" Her eyes flashed with the barest glow of karma. Oh, fun, her powers were coming in. Good to know. By the look on her face, Axle probably wasn't the only one who needed "the talk."

Felix flicked a curl from his eyes and made a mental note to ward for poltergeists with the amount of menacing angst projecting from her. "I'm assuming you're talking about the pageant, and no, that wasn't my intention, unless you keep acting like a rude little brat."

She scowled at him. "Whatever. I'm going to Sarah's."

"Uh. No. You're not going anywhere," he said, crossing his arms over his chest. "I'm supposed to check your homework, then you have a Caesar salad coming from Pizza Palace. I have to run some errands in another hour, and my friend Liam is going to hang out with the three of you while I do."

She started at the name, and Felix's eyes narrowed. "Is that a problem?"

Cruze shook her head and fiddled with her long sleeves. "Um…no, and I-I'm sorry. I just…" She looked up and blew out a breath. "If I can't go over Sarah's, can she come here? There's a biology test tomorrow, and we were going to study for it."

Her one-eighty in attitude was suspect, but Felix couldn't quite put his finger on why. God, he was so not cut out for this. "You want to study?" he asked slowly.

She nodded, looking far too innocent, eager even.

Felix clicked his tongue, assuming there was a catch, but his marching orders hadn't said anything about them not having friends over.

Oh, he was going to regret this. "Her parents have to agree that it's okay," he said, ticking off fingers. "You study here, in the kitchen. The rest of your homework needs to be done, *and* I want those dishes washed and put away before she gets here." No way was he doing it, and the urchins would probably use them for target practice if he asked them.

Cruze frowned at the over flowing sink. "Fine. I'll get my bag," she muttered, sulking away.

"And you," Felix said to Sway lurking in the living room by the Christmas tree. "Laundry."

Her lip stuck out. "I don't know how to do laundry."

Felix put his hands on his hips, mirroring her stance. "If you're advanced enough to learn about Darwin, then you can figure out darks and lights. Away with you, peasant," he said, fluttering a hand. "Gather it up and meet me by the machine."

Sway narrowed her eyes at him, the resemblance between her and her sister uncanny. "But Gran doesn't make us—"

"Gran isn't here, and I'm not about to wash the crusty skiddies out of your underpants for the next two weeks." It already smelled like a locker room in here.

She gasped. "I don't think I like you very much, Uncle Felix."

The affront on her little face was almost worth getting guilted into watching them for two weeks. "Keep it up, and the feeling might very well become mutual." He flicked his fingers. "Chop, chop."

As soon as she was out of sight, he raided the cabinet above the stove and downed a trio of off-brand aspirin, a decade past expiration. Jesus, better make it four. His headache was back in spades, and the urge to use his karma fierce. *Save it for the spell, Felix. Almost there.*

Cruze came in and dumped far more out of her bag onto the kitchen table than it should've been able to hold with a loud *thump*. He winced. Nope. That didn't help.

"How the hell did you fit all of that in there?"

"Gran spelled all our bags," she muttered.

Felix pinched the bridge of his nose. Right. That made sense. She's done the same for him and Felicia a billion years ago. Triple the capacity, a fraction of the weight, and so durable that he'd had his mom sew patches over the smiling trains when he hit fifth grade. Felix was actually surprised Axle wasn't toting it around. Stupid thing had been indestructible.

Cruze yanked out a laptop from the pile, and his brow rose. It should be in a military grade case if she was swinging it around like that. No wonder the school's technology budget was so obscene.

He pulled out a chair as Sway hauled a stinky basket of laundry past them, glowering. "What's first?"

"Elvish," Cruze said with a wicked gleam in her eye, handing him a book.

Felix took it and blinked blithely back. "Okay. What are you working on?"

Cruze gave him a funny look and opened her laptop. "Chapter six. Conjugations."

"And the assignment?" he asked, flipping through the section.

"Here." She showed him the screen.

"You're close," he said after a moment's perusal. "But you keep getting tripped up with the subordinate form. It comes before the subject and then the verb in the subjunctive mood. You've got it backwards in most of these."

She just stared at him. "You speak Elvish?"

"I do a lot of things." Especially lust after a particularly hot tutor in the subject during college. "But dishes isn't one of them. I'd suggest doing what you have to and getting on that."

Cruze glanced at him, then her screen again with a slight

shake of her head. A godawful bang came from the laundry room just off the kitchen.

"Uncle Felix!" Sway screeched.

He sighed and went to go mitigate the next disaster.

LIAM PULLED up beside Felix's car and grabbed the metric ton of cookies his mom had sent over. Man, the smile on her face when he'd gotten home and was telling her about Axle and Sway…

He clenched his jaw, not understanding how Jenny could just cut his parents off from the kids like that. She wasn't the same easy going girl he'd married. It was like she'd had a personality transplant. Liam was sure that was thanks to Pete, but damn, it was cold-blooded. It was the holidays, for Christ's sake, and they were the only grandparents the kids had in Havers. They were lucky if they saw Jenny's parents every couple of years. And Pete's…Liam wasn't even sure if his were still alive.

He shook his head, unable to change any of it, but it sucked. He'd tried calling the lab for a status update on Sarah's test, and it'd gone straight to voicemail. Liam knew he needed to be patient, but it was so damned hard thinking his kid could be living in that house. Guilt ate at him. If he'd known how bad things were with Pete, he never would've left.

All right, maybe that wasn't totally true, but he definitely wouldn't have stayed away as long as he had.

Liam went to the kitchen door, smiling at the properly cleared walkway, though the shovel had been just tossed into a snowbank. Baby steps. He knew Felix didn't think so, but he was really good with them, and it was obvious they adored their uncle. Sway had stars in her eyes whenever she looked at him, but then, Felix was easy to love.

And didn't Liam know it.

He precariously balanced the platter of cookies and let himself in. Felix was at the crappy laminate counter glaring at his phone and muttering something about stupid delivery drivers. A girl Liam assumed was Cruze was sitting at the kitchen table, and at her side—

Sarah.

She looked up as he came in, her big brown eyes going wide. "Daddy?"

"Surprise!" Cruze said, jumping up and clapping her hands.

Behind her, Felix ghosted white. "Oh, shit. This has got to be the catch. Not cool, kid." He hurried over and rescued the platter of cookies Liam was white-knuckling. "Are you, okay?"

"I—no. I-I can't—Pete...does he know you're here?" he asked Sarah.

She shook her head, staring at Liam like she was seeing a ghost. He ran a hand over his jaw. "Shit."

"Language!" Sway screamed, running into the room and barreling into Liam. "Come on! You said you'd watch *The Pretty, Pretty Princesses Show* with me, and it's starting!" She grabbed his hand, tugging.

He faltered a step. "I—"

"Hey, come here, monster," Felix said, depositing the cookies on the table and detaching her. He picked her up. "How about I watch the first part with you, and Liam will join us in a little bit? We can have some of those cookies while we wait. Sound good, Cruze? Yeah, awesome, why don't you grab them, and give Sarah and Liam a minute."

Cruze looked between them and flushed, snatching the plated mound and darting out of the room behind her uncle and little sister.

"Why are you here?" Sarah asked after a long moment.

Liam swallowed the lump in his throat. God there was no

way she wasn't his with those eyes. The roots of her cropped, bleach-blonde hair were cherry cola brown, and she had a beauty mark on her right cheek that was the twin to Kelsey's.

"In town, or here, here?" he croaked out.

"Both?" she asked, her shoulders rounding.

He puffed out his cheeks and dragged a hand over his face. "I'm babysitting for Felix tonight, but I came back because your mom—I needed to see if—I needed proof—that everything she'd said was true before I signed anything."

Sarah nodded down at her lap. "What if it isn't?"

"Then I'm fighting for joint custody. I've missed you, Sar. I-I tried to call, and don't know if your mom ever gave you guys the packages I sent—"

"She didn't, and I know you've been trying to see me, but that's not a great idea." She tucked a lock of hair behind her ear, and her sleeve slipped. A dark bruise shadowed her wrist.

That son of a bitch. Liam growled, and she glanced up, quickly hiding it. "Volleyball," she murmured, not meeting his eyes.

The hell it was. Fur sprouted over his knuckles, and he fought to keep his wolf in check.

Sarah popped up from the table and started jamming books into her bag. "Look, I-I shouldn't be here. I know Cruze was trying to do something nice, but I'll catch hell for it."

"Sarah, if he's hurting you—"

"He's not, okay. Just leave it—me—alone."

A crushing pain seared through Liam's chest. "I—is that what you want?"

She turned at the door and met his eyes, her own brimming with tears. "What I want doesn't matter."

And she was gone.

Liam slumped to the floor and pulled his knees into his chest, hanging his head. Cautious footsteps padded across the kitchen floor, and then Felix's arms were around him.

Liam buried his face against Felix's shoulder, fighting back tears.

Epic fail, like everything else he tried to do.

"Hey, hey," Felix murmured, rocking. A sob escaped Liam, and Felix hugged him tighter. "It's okay. It's going to be okay. There's not a chance that girl isn't yours, and I'm kicking myself that I didn't see it as soon as she came in. If it makes you feel any better, Cruze is beside herself. She orchestrated the whole thing because Sarah keeps talking about how much she misses you."

Liam's heart about stopped. "She does?"

"Yeah." Felix sighed. "From what Cruze just told me, the situation over there isn't great."

"She had a bruise, Felix." Liam said, sitting back and sniffling. He wiped the back of his hand across his face, too upset to worry about Felix thinking he was a headcase. "Like someone had grabbed her wrist—hard."

"Then *someone* needs to be reported," Felix said, his expression frosty. "And you go for full custody."

Liam scrubbed his face. Felix was right, but..."How the hell did this get so fucked up?"

"I don't know," Felix said, reaching out to cup Liam's cheek. The warmth from his palm—from him—choked Liam up all over again. "Hey, we'll figure it out. Okay?"

"We will?" Liam's gaze searched his.

"Yeah, we will." Felix's thumb traced the path Liam's tears had taken. "Not a chance I'm letting something like this slide. I'll report it first thing in the morning. Even without knowing about the bruise, from what Cruze said, I'd be calling anyway. You don't have to get involved."

"You—you would do that for me?" Liam stared at him, so full of gratitude.

Felix's gaze dropped to Liam's lips. "Um...yeah. I—"

The door beside them rattled at someone's knock. "Pizza delivery!"

Felix pulled back, the moment gone. Liam swept a hand over his eyes, his emotions churning. Jesus, he needed a shower or a really filthy carburetor to clean. Preferably both and not necessarily in that order.

Felix stood and pulled out his wallet. "It's about fucking time," he muttered.

"Language!" Sway screamed, plowing into the kitchen table hard enough to knock a pile of mail off the far end.

"Volume!" Felix yelled back. "Now pick that up, then get your sister to take her homework somewhere else—and go wash your hands."

"But I just did!"

"Don't think I didn't see you picking your nose in there," Felix scolded, raising an eyebrow, "or did you want a side order of boogers with your meal?"

Sway looked at him deadpan. "If we're not supposed to eat them, then why are they so delicious?"

Felix gagged. "Oh my God, I can't with you."

"I'll take her," Liam said, chuckling despite himself and getting to his feet. "Come on, Sway. I need to wash my hands, too."

Felix paid the pimply kid at the door and hauled the boxes to the table. He frowned at the pile of miscellaneous crap covering a good half of it, then ducked into a small room adjoining the kitchen. He came back with a laundry basket and swept everything off the table into it.

"Good," he said, hauling it into the living room. "You can kick Axle out of the shower while you're at it. He's been in there for forty-five minutes."

Liam could understand the inclination. A wave of searing anger went through him thinking about that bruise on Sarah. As soon as he got custody, he was going to bury that son of a bitch.

"Why were you sad?" Sway asked as they made their way to the downstairs bathroom.

"Because I'm pretty sure Sarah's my daughter, and I don't get to see her." But he was going to, and both Pete and Jenny could go fuck themselves.

Sway's brows furrowed as they walked down the ill-lit, shag-carpeted hall. Probably better that way. The middle of it was completely matted from foot traffic. Off-kilter family photos lined the walls, and Liam resisted the urge to stop and gawk at pictures of baby Felix.

"My daddy doesn't see me, but I don't think it makes him sad. He gives my mommy money so he doesn't have to."

Ouch. Liam's rage left him. He pushed open the door to the little half-bath and flicked on the obnoxiously bright fluorescents above the rust Formica vanity. "That's not the way it's supposed to be." Liam kicked a plastic step stool over to the sink, and she hopped onto it, flinging on the water. "Hey, careful with your cast."

"No, it's okay if I get it wet." she said, proceeding to do just that, and soaking the rest of the bathroom in the process. "The doctor said I could even swim with it!"

Liam throttled the rusted tap and squirted soap into her waiting hands, then lathered up beside her. "Yeah? You like swimming?"

She looked at him aghast. "Oh no. Mommy said if I go in the water a siren will come and take me away."

"Sounds serious," Liam said, feigning concern.

She nodded at him, her face uncharacteristically solemn. "She doesn't let any of us swim, ever. Not even in the pool our motel had."

Well, that was weird, but okay. He dried off her hands and then tried to slop up the overflow with an appliquéd towel. Shit. Hope that wasn't just for decoration. He hung it back on the squeaky chrome ring. "Go ahead and eat, I've gotta find Axle."

"He's already downstairs," she said, then grinned at him. "I have *really* good ears."

Liam just bet she did. "Good to know."

Sway ran into the kitchen and skidded across the faded linoleum into the seat beside her brother. Kid already had four crusts piled on his plate and was about to add another. Cruze picked at her salad, looking miserable. Felix tipped his head at her, shooting Liam a look.

Crap. "Hey," he said, putting his hand on her shoulder. "Thank you for doing that. It meant a lot, even if it didn't work out so great."

Cruze ignored him and stabbed a crouton. Well, he tried. Liam shrugged at Felix and pulled out a chair. Damn thing had to weigh thirty pounds.

"Okay then," Felix said with a too bright smile, "now that everyone's sitting here fat and happy, I've got to run. I'll be back as soon as I can. You good?" he asked Liam.

Nope. "Getting there."

"I'll take that as a win. Wish me luck." He shrugged into his parka and zipped it up.

"Good luck, Uncle Felix!" Sway screamed around her mouthful.

Liam smiled as Felix's eyelids fluttered, and he left them to their meal.

FELIX PULLED up to where the wrought iron gates of the manor had been, his car scraping against something as he parked at the side of the desolate county road. He winced at the squeal of metal and cut the engine, still attempting to process even a small fraction of what'd just gone down at the house. Whatever that'd been, it'd been intense. He'd never seen Liam so rattled or emotional, and it'd ignited an urge to protect him that Felix wasn't entirely comfortable with.

Normally he wouldn't be considering manslaughter, but if Pete stepped in front of Felix's car right now, he'd be gassing it. The only hesitation involved would be when he had to stop to put it in reverse so he could run over that miserable excuse for a human again.

Liam's divorce be damned, if Pete was even half as bad as what Cruze had said, he needed to be locked up. All the doomsday shit he spouted on a regular basis was weird enough, but the other stuff she said that was going on…

Felix ran a hand over his face, trying to center himself and purge any murderous inclinations he might have before the next pending clusterfuck. The last thing he needed was to manifest murder. He buzzed his lips and stared at the dark space shimmering faintly between stone walls; the ward Jena had set on Samhain was still active.

He frowned, dreading the frigid hike up to the tor, but it

looked like most, if not all, of the coven members were already here. Damn it, guess he couldn't sit here and wait for a buddy to show up. He was gonna have to hoof it alone. He powered on his phone's flashlight and got out of his car, icy gravel crunching beneath his loafers. Probably not the best choice in footwear, but he was already running late. Stopping for a wardrobe change hadn't struck him as wise, no matter how much it was warranted.

The ward protecting against anyone with ill-intent from entering the property tingled across his skin as he crossed through the gap in the stone wall. Shit. It had definitely been strengthened in preparation for the working. If the coven had already gotten that far, they were going to be pissed he wasn't there yet.

He hurried down the treacherous drive, trying not to break his neck. Chase may have graded it, but it hadn't been plowed, and swaths had been washed out by the last storm they'd had. A single set of tire tracks scored down the drive. By the skid marks, the driver hadn't had an easy time of it. One of the narrow ruts had been further broken up by the footsteps of everyone who had gotten there before him, and it was only marginally easier to navigate than the unbroken expanses at its sides.

Around him, the forest was silent save for icy branches tinkling in the random gusts of wind. Felix flicked up the hood of his coat, muttering as he crossed the second ward. There were a total of seven, each of them raised to contain and protect the magical node at its center. Since he'd been there on Samhain, they'd all been repaired and strengthened. Jena had been busy.

Felix scowled, annoyed he hadn't already known that. Between Chase, her pregnancy, and all the stuff Felix had going on, they hadn't been spending nearly enough time hanging out. They really needed a night out to catch up. He swapped the hand he was holding his phone with and shoved the other into his armpit. God, it was freezing, and despite the clear sky, it smelled like snow was imminent.

He didn't quite sob when he spotted Chase's truck parked ahead. Almost there. The drive came to an abrupt end, and the tor loomed up from the center of a field before him. The jagged ruins at its peak were outlined by the light of a waxing crescent moon.

A glow came from beyond.

Shit. They'd already lit the fire at the center of the standing stones. Not that Felix could blame them, but he needed to hurry.

Easier said than done. The hike up the hill was even more miserable now than it'd been in the pouring rain. He seriously hoped Chase had plans to extend the drive. This climb was absolutely ridiculous, and the fact that he was going to have to do it again in another couple of days for Yule was even less exciting. After one or two slips and a fall that had left him spread eagle staring at the stars for several breaths, he made it to the top—murderous intent definitely at the forefront of his thoughts.

The trip around the ruins to the garden in the back was marginally easier, but only because it was flat. Up here, the wind was brutal. He shivered as he traversed the garden's canted pavers and past overgrown trees. It seemed like forever before the statue of Hecate marked his passage over the bridge and into the garden's heart.

The radiant glow from the fire at the center of the standing stones grew bright enough for him to kill the light on his phone, and he pocketed it, unable to feel his fingers anymore. The last coil of the spiral path ran around a six-foot brick wall. Violet light domed above it, and God help him if it wasn't climate controlled. Keeping his focus was going to be hard enough without worrying what bits of him were about to turn black and fall off.

A break in the wall came into view ahead, and the

murmur of the coven's nattering and Sweets's booming laugh grew louder.

"What do you mean Lucinda's not going to be here?" Matilda groused. "This kind of working requires a full coven to anchor it. You're just asking for it to rebound and fry all of us."

"Oh, have some faith. Felix can stand in for his mother and still be the focus," Kressida Pao tsked. "You know very well she would've been here if her aunt hadn't broken nearly every bone in her body."

"The only faith I have is in something going wrong. And I heard it was only a hip. Serves her right mixing cats and ladders," Matilda muttered. "Next you'll be telling me she was holding a mirror while she was at it."

Matilda had a point. Felix steeled himself as he crossed into the sacred space with an apprehensive shiver. The last time he'd been here wasn't something he particularly wanted to think about. His heart sped at the prickle of magic flitting across his skin. The wind cut off, and warm air tingled against his cheeks.

Thankfully, any remnants from Samhain had been cleared away—physically and karmically. A pentagram had been re-drawn in white chalk over the wide granite flagstones, with one of the tall stone pillars at each of its vertices. At its center, a fire burned, and a cauldron was suspended over it. That steamed and bubbled; basil, rosemary, sage, and cinnamon hanging heavy in the blessedly temperate air.

Seven witches, five warlocks, and Chase stood just beyond the pillars. He looked up, and sniffed, then nudged Jena, saying something to her as Felix came in.

She looked up and left the group to hurry over. "Chase says you smell stressed."

"Huh." Felix shrugged, flicking his hood back. "Can't imagine why."

Her brows furrowed. "I can. Tell me your parents didn't really leave you alone with the urchins for two weeks."

"I could, but I'd be lying."

She glowered at him, her arms crossed under her breasts. "You owe me some serious updates, and you know I would've come to help. Why didn't you call me? Do you have your car back?" Her glower faded into concern.

He winced. "Yes, but my phone got smashed, and things have been hectic, to say the least. Any idea how long this is going to take?"

"No." She glanced back at the coven. "Who did you get to watch the urchins?"

"Ah." Felix ran a hand through his curls. "Kelsey was busy so, um, Liam, is with them."

A massive grin blossomed across Jena's face. "Then you guys are…"

"Friends," he said quickly, not wanting to get into any more detail until he figured out exactly what that meant. What had passed between them in the kitchen, at his apartment, shit, at Jena's last night…all of it was far more than friendly. Which would've been fine, if he could've trusted himself to keep it casual. Unfortunately, he'd gone down that road with Liam before, and Felix knew he couldn't stay in his own lane.

He was totally going to crash and burn.

"Friends?" Jena repeated, cocking her brow.

"Yes, we're going to trivia at Snaps tomorrow." Felix chewed his lip, abruptly anxious about their not-date.

She rubbed a hand over her belly. "Lucky. I'd kill for a margarita."

Hold up. A light bulb went on above his head. If Jena was there, it wouldn't be half as weird hanging out with Liam solo. Having her and Chase there would totally take romance off the table. "You guys should come. Mocktails are a thing, you know."

Her face brightened. "Like a double-date?"

"No." He scowled. "Like I just paid almost two grand to get my car out of hock, and you owe me a round. I won't say no to an order of nachos to go with it, either."

"Don't mind us," Aggie called across the circle. "I've got nothing better to do than stand here all night with my thumb up my ass."

Matilda snorted, and Sweets batted a hand at her shoulder. "What? Like we all weren't thinking it," the sour witch groused.

"I promise, you'll get the full story tomorrow," he said, going to join them.

Jena rolled her eyes. "With Liam and Chase there? Now who's edging who?"

"Please, you know you love it, you kinky bitch."

"Fair, but not from my bestie." She laughed, then took a deep breath. "You ready for this?"

He glanced at her askance. "Not even a little."

"If it makes you feel any better, Chase is super nervous, too. The coven asked him to help, since his bent is manifestation. He's been helping me with little spells, but he's never done a full working before."

"Oddly enough, it does." Felix's brow quirked. Way to get the poor guy's feet wet. Chase wasn't a warlock, but he was half-sidhe, and the ability to use magic an inborn talent. "Where do you want me?" he asked, dropping his parka on top of the pile of everyone else's coats by the log they'd hauled up here for Yule. Mr. Fynbender, the eldest warlock in the coven, had chosen an impressive one to say the least.

June Hill, the coven's secretary, consulted her ever-present notebook, riffling through the pages. Felix eyed her pink velvet tracksuit, wishing he'd opted to leave the house in something cozier than chinos this morning.

"Okay, Felix," she said, her smile marred by a smear of lipstick across her teeth. "You need to be at the Eastern point of the pentagram for new beginnings and setting intentions. Jena, you and Chase take the South for passion and action. Matilda, I have you in the West for endings and completion, and Aggie has the North for grounding and wisdom. Otis will stand at the fifth pillar for Spirit to assure there's no shenanigans with any entities that might try to answer our call."

Felix wiped a bead of sweat from his upper lip. Entities. Great. Had enough of those, thanks.

"Wisdom? You sure that's right?" Jena asked, raising her brow at Aggie as she and the rest of them stepped to their assigned positions.

"It's not like anyone else here knows their ass from their elbow," the older witch sniffed, tugging the collar of her robe. It looked like something Father Christmas would've worn on a postcard from the 1800s.

"Oh, yes," June said, the soccer mom oblivious to the byplay. "The grimoire I consulted was very specific, and out of all of us, you six fit the brief best. The rest of us will filter in between you and focus on raising enough karma to power the spell. Felix, you need to clear your mind and picture your ideal candidate. Otis will begin the invocation by calling corners and setting our sacred space." She motioned to the tall, white-haired warlock, and he solemnly nodded back. "The rest of you know what to do. Felix, let us know when you're ready."

Okay. He took a deep breath and ran through the list of qualities in his head, repeating them like a mantra. "Got it," he said after a long moment.

Mr. Fynbender began chanting, and the flames beneath the cauldron flared blue. Magic tripped across Felix's skin, goosebumps rising in its wake. A shimmer of opalescence wavered between them and the rest of the world, and below their feet, an answering hum rose from the node.

The cadence of Mr. Fynbender's deep baritone changed,

and one by one, the coven joined him, adding their voices to his along with their power. Their harmony twined, high and low, Matilda's sharp soprano and Rick Kleppet's flat tenor merging and adding complexity to the weave of their spell.

Felix focused on his mantra, his intent filling the holes between the notes. The air thickened. The node's power lapped at his ankles, and a thick violet mist swirled in eddies, churned by an ethereal wind.

The ghostly blue flames beneath the cauldron danced and surged. Each of the coven members at the pentagram's vertices began to glow with power. Hands outstretched and beseeching, eyes alight, sparking karma, their shadows writhed and separated from their bodies, cavorting behind the coven in a sinuous dance spiraling deosil around the circle of stones.

Mr. Fynbender's baritone increased in pitch and the magic thickened. Other voices not of this world joined the song, the node's melody far wilder. The air around Jena and Chase pulsed, the glow about them brighter than the rest. Her eyes shone with emerald fire, and behind her, Chase's had become neon sapphire.

Karma raised the small hairs all over Felix's body as he repeated his mantra, focusing on the qualities they'd need to fill the town's attorney position. A misty figure began to build in his mind's eye. His consciousness expanded, riding the wave of magic up and out. A satellite view of the continent shimmered before him, bright spots scattered across it, flaring and winking out, as his ideal candidate slowly resolved.

Distances folded, and the ethereal wind grew stronger, whipping through the sacred space. He trembled, gritting his teeth as he shaped and funneled the coven's power and that of the node, willing it to manifest what they needed.

At the far edge of the continent, a speck burned bright, fierce and determined. Felix latched onto it, and the magic surged, encapsulating his chosen candidate.

Mr. Fynbender's chant rose to a fevered pitch, his shout a crescendo over all the other voices. All at once, a massive burst of power flared, and a monumental wrenching sensation threw them back against the stone pillars. Felix's teeth clashed together, and he grunted, putting a hand to his head. The flames beneath the cauldron gutted. Above them, the bubble of power wavered, but held, significantly weaker than it had been. It cast them all in a weird purple twilight, everything silent—

"What in the actual fuck?" a woman spat.

Felix blinked as a shadow rose before him, chains clanking. Wait. Who the hell was that?

A flashlight clicked on, and the gaunt figure spun toward it, throwing its arms over its face and hissed.

They'd manifested—*physically manifested*—a vampire.

"Well, shit," Aggie said. "I didn't see that coming."

Felix choked back a manic laugh. No. None of them had. Was that supposed to happen? He'd expected an email, maybe a phone call, not the magical equivalent of DōrDash. He laughed again. Welp, guess Greg Plinkin's portents about doing this after sunset made sense.

"The fuck are you laughing at?" The vampire swore, the dangling lengths of rusted chain from her manacled wrists swinging. "Get that damn light out of my eyes!"

Um, rude, but Felix suspected he couldn't blame her. Along with the manacles, her ankles were fettered, and a wide, iron collar encircled her slender throat. He frowned at the scant rags covering her filthy body. She was so dirty Felix couldn't even harbor a guess as to the length or color of her hair, and her tribal tattoos were completely indistinguishable. She'd also very obviously been beaten recently and starved for a lot longer than that. The sharp outline of bones was grotesque beneath her battered, too pale skin.

"Oh, sorry," Chase mumbled, angling the beam away from her.

She huffed, dropping her arms. Her chrysanthemum pink eyes went wide at the dangling chains, then darted around the circle. Felix could practically hear the gears turning in her head. She quickly swallowed her surprise and struck a pose. His stomach churned. Jesus, she looked like a cabaret corpse.

"No need to apologize, handsome. How about I let you make it up to me?" Her grin was ghastly. She licked a wickedly sharp incisor, and Felix shuddered.

"The hell you will," Jena growled. Karma sparked purple at her fingertips, and her green irises crackled. Chase's arms slipped around her waist, and he murmured something. She scowled in response, dropping power.

The vampire put a hand to her pale breast, her eyes wide with manufactured awe. "Well, look at you, Lady Lightning being tamed by her thunder." She snorted and waved the performance away. "Please. No disrespect intended, but a girl's gotta eat, and I am fucking starving."

"And what, pray tell, might be the reason for that?" Sweets asked, her eyebrow raised.

"Sorry. Prayers are off the table unless they're for the big guy down below, and you don't seem the type." The vampire blew her a kiss and winked.

"*That* was what you were envisioning?" Matilda snapped at Felix. "Wrong type of bloodsucker, idiot."

He smoothed his sweater and flicked a curl from his eyes. "I'll admit that when I think of lawyers, that phrase does come to mind, but it was most certainly not what I specified."

"Are you sure?" Ms. Pao asked. The little librarian adjusted her cloudy glasses. "Magic doesn't always nuance well. What did you ask for?"

"First and foremost, a civil litigation attorney."

The vampire picked at the dirt beneath her ragged nails.

"Well, are you one?" Matilda snapped.

"I dunno." The vampire gave the sour little witch a sly side-eye. "What's it worth to you, cupcake?"

Matilda's face contorted into something far from sweet, and the vampire grinned, gnashing her teeth at her.

Aggie rolled her eyes. "Better question is, what's it worth to you? I've no problem dropping your ass right back into whatever hole we pulled you from."

Several other coven members murmured their agreement, and panic flitted across the vampire's face before quickly being replaced by contempt. "Well, aren't you just a stone cold bitch."

Aggie waved the insult away. "Thanks, it's a gift. Now cut the shit and answer the question. I'm already due to miss the first five minutes of *Matlock,* and if I don't get my Andy Griffith fix, I'm gonna be pissed. Are you a lawyer or not?"

The vampire narrowed her eyes. "I am."

"What was the second qualification, Felix?" Ms. Pao asked.

"To be desperate enough to take the job pro bono."

Matilda snorted, her white-blonde pipe curls bobbing around her frown. "If that's not desperate, I don't know what is."

"No, I don't think that you do," a rusty voice answered, "but I'm quite certain that Ophelia does."

Matilda jumped as the shadows unfolded behind her, and a tall, stooped figure stepped through them, just outside of the circle of stones. Holy shit. Mr. Brock? What was the town's archivist doing here?

Felix's throat bobbed, pretty sure it had to do with him also being the town's only resident vampire. They were insanely territorial. Crap. Had manifesting this one triggered some kind of bitey-sense?

Mr. Brock planted his brass-topped cane and rolled his shoulders beneath a thick, fur cape, straightening up. The tattoos around his eyes and dripping down his cheeks looked even more sinister than usual in the weird violet light. At full height, he had to be close to seven feet. "Don't you now, darling?"

The vampire in the circle dropped to her knees, her head bowed.

Holy shit. Felix glance between them. It was weird enough to see Mr. Brock anywhere other than the archives below the library. He rarely left his lair. Like, maybe twice that Felix had heard of, ever. And after all her bluster, the vamp's reaction to him was straight up bizarre.

"Do you know her, Thaddeus?" Ms. Pao asked.

"Only by reputation." He pursed his pale lips, as if he were unhappy about that. "Ms. Diamondé is quite the celebrity in some circles—or was. She's been rather absent from the public eye of late."

"You don't say," Aggie muttered, glancing at her watch.

"Mmm." Mr. Brock cocked his head, the pointed tip of his ear poking through his feathery, snow white hair. "My. Kremlyn's done quite a number on you, hasn't he, child?"

The other vampire didn't say anything, her head bowed.

Mr. Brock sighed. "It's a pity I didn't get here in time to return you to his tender mercies. I'll have to let court know that you'd already pledged your services. Once sworn, not even our sweet prince would dream of breaking a covenant."

Ophelia's eyes flicked up to meet Mr. Brock's dark gaze. That he was giving her some kind of an out was apparent, but Felix was dying for the details. What the hell was going on?

Her entire body whipped around to him, and she skittered forward on all fours, then popped up to stand before Felix, smoothing her rags. "It was you who called me, right, freckles? You need a lawyer?"

"Yes, and maybe? I-I mean, technically, I guess I did?" he stammered trying to take a step back and ran up against the stone pillar. His throat bobbed. Shit. She couldn't get past the containment circle, but still. Those pale pink irises were like a gas gauge, and she was about running on empty.

"Fabulous. I, Ophelia Catalina Diamondé pledge my legal services to…" The filth on her brow crinkled, and she rotated her hand, waiting for Felix to fill in the blank. He swallowed again, not certain that was the best idea.

"The town of Havers-by-the-Sea," Aggie supplied from across the circle. "Wouldn't want anything to befall your sponsor and let you off the hook prematurely."

Ophelia scowled like that'd been a distinct possibility, and Felix shuddered. "Fine," she gritted out. "I pledge my legal services to the town of Havers-by-the-Sea. By blood and fang, until my counsel is no longer needed and the earth below releases me." She raised her wrist and bit it. Blood spattered to the ground, hissing, and the magic of the node rose up in a flash of purple, leaving zero doubt that it'd just accepted her oath.

Across the circle Jena gasped, and the vamp's eyes went wide.

"Are you fucking kidding me?" Ophelia screeched at Aggie. "A node? A ghandi-damned node?! You've just gotten me stuck here in perpetuity, you stupid bitch!"

Aggie cocked a brow. "Aren't you supposed to be a lawyer? Pretty sure it's the signee's responsibility to check the fine print before they consent to the terms."

Ophelia sputtered.

Mr. Brock chuckled darkly, just shy of full on-malevolent glee. "If you all would be so kind as to drop the circle, I'll take Ms. Diamondé back with me to freshen up. I'll make sure she understands how she'll be expected to comport herself as Havers's newest resident."

Mr. Fynbender murmured a few words, and the circle was broken.

Mr. Brock extended a gnarled hand to Ophelia. "Come, child." She shot Aggie one more dark look and shuffled to him. He tucked the battered vampire against his side. "Have whatever you wish her to review sent to the archives," he said to Felix, then inclined his head to Ms. Pao, stepped back into the shadows, and disappeared.

"What the hell just happened?" Felix asked, his pulse racing.

"You got your lawyer," Aggie said, pulling her coat from the pile. "Now I get my shows. Hop to it you two," she snapped at Jena and Chase. "At this rate I'll be lucky to catch the last fifteen minutes."

Jena rolled her eyes, letting Chase help her into her ski jacket. "Like streaming isn't a thing."

"Streaming." Aggie snorted. "Half the fun of watching them's the anticipation…"

Felix tuned out their banter and grabbed his parka, hurrying to catch up with Ms. Pao as she was leaving. "Do you know what all of that was about?"

The diminutive librarian's lips pressed together. "Not entirely. Vampire culture is very different than ours," she said as they picked their way back through the garden. "From what I've been able to piece together, Thaddaeus has standing in their court, but is something of an exile. I believe that's by choice, though I'm not totally certain."

She slipped, and Felix caught her, pausing to let her regain her balance. That was one hell of a choice if it'd lasted this long. Havers's three hundred and fiftieth birthday celebration was coming up this summer, and local lore had the vampire here before the town's founding.

Felix offered Ms. Pao his arm as they went over the bridge, steadying the frail older woman. They didn't need anyone else with a broken hip. He chewed his lip, thinking about what she'd just said.

He didn't know much about vampires, save what they'd been taught in school. He was pretty sure he remembered that they were ruled by an iron-fisted, dynastic monarchy. Their tribal lands weren't considered federal jurisdiction, and their society was caste driven. The upper echelon was referred to as the court, but wasn't refined in the least, and rumored to take depravity to a whole new level.

Like, bathing in the blood of virgins, impaling your enemies, and feasting on their corpses was just another Thursday kind of depravity. Felix had always chalked that up to savvy marketing designed to keep people out of their territory after the Purge, but after seeing the condition Ophelia was in, he wasn't so sure anymore.

"What I do know," Ms. Pao said, breaking him from his thoughts as they exited the garden and started past the house, "is that Thaddaeus is very protective of the town. You're probably too young to remember, but he's kept more than one of his kind from thinning the herd in Havers. I can't imagine he'd do anything to endanger it."

Thinning the herd. Felix shivered at the vampiric term that roughly equated to wholesale slaughter. There'd been an incident a few weeks ago up north, and the footage of the aftermath was chilling. Vampires didn't need to eat often, but if they got to the point where their irises went completely white, then you got the vampiric version of a were going feral.

Except instead of running into the woods to eviscerate woodland creatures, vampires sought out cities and towns. For whatever reason, that had been on the rise of late. Felix ducked deeper into his parka, chilled at the memory of how pale the vamp's irises had been in comparison to Mr. Brock's. The town archivist's had been practically black, though who he was filling up on wasn't a mystery Felix was keen to delve into.

"If Thaddaeus allowed that girl to stay, I'm sure he had a good reason—" Ms. Pao lost her footing again, almost taking Felix down with her. No way were they making it to the bottom of the tor without breaking something.

"Aye, I'm sure he did at that," Sweets said, the big woman coming up from behind them and taking Ms. Pao's other arm.

"But whether it's in his own best interest or the town's is what I'm wanting to know."

Felix glanced over at her. She sounded like she'd heard something. "Oh?"

"Mmm." Sweets's lips pinched flat, and he didn't think it was because of the terrain. "You know as well as I that karma is never random. It's always seeking to level the scales, and that prince Thaddaeus mentioned, Kremlyn. I'd bet my eye teeth there's a connection betwixt the two, and that the fates played a hand in us snapping that vamp girl up."

"And I'm gonna bet it won't sit well," Matilda snipped from somewhere behind them. "Mark my words, but we made enemies tonight, and it's only a matter of time before they come calling."

Sweets hummed again like she agreed, and Felix pinched the bridge of his nose with his free hand. Great. Exactly what they needed.

FELIX PULLED INTO HIS PARENTS' driveway far later than he'd planned. After finally getting Ms. Pao to her car, he'd run home to pack a bag, and now it was close to eleven. He cut the engine and hurried into the house, still frozen from that trek down the tor. For Yule, he was commandeering Chambers's stupid golf cart. That heated steering wheel abruptly sounded more like a must-have than an extravagance, and no way was he hoofing it again.

Felix quietly closed the kitchen door behind him, the house silent except for the low murmur of the TV in the next room. The flickering light of the screen played in the doorway, and the lights from the Christmas tree gave everything a ruddy cast. Nope, that wasn't ominous at all.

Felix could only attribute the quiet to Liam getting fed up and selling the urchins to the circus…unless they'd eaten him and were lying in wait somewhere for Felix.

Also a very real possibility.

He tiptoed to the doorway and slowly peered around the jamb, holding his breath.

Liam lay back against the couch with his stocking feet up on the coffee table, snoring softly. Some cartoon was turned down low, thankfully not the psychedelic vomit that was *The Pretty, Pretty Princess Show*, and Sway was passed out, drooling on his thigh. Axle was curled up at Liam's other side, his face buried against the were's arm.

Felix stared, an ache in his chest, loathe to wake any of them, but he couldn't expect Liam to stay all night. Maybe if he woke him quietly enough, they could slip the two little ones into bed without any fuss. Not that Felix actually believed that, but it was worth a try.

"Liam," he whispered. "Hey, Liam, I'm back." Felix crept closer. "Liam."

Damn it. He was out. Felix leaned in and put a hand on the were's cheek, stubble prickling his palm. Felix's breath caught. He hated it on his own face, but there was something about the feel of it rasping against his skin—

Liam's breath hitched, and he nuzzled against Felix's hand, murmuring.

Felix swallowed hard. "L-Liam," he whispered again, then wet his lips. "It's time to go."

"Huh?" Liam's eyes fluttered open, and he blinked up at him. "Felix?"

"Yeah. Sorry I'm so late," he said, taking a step back. "Do you mind helping me get them into bed? Axle sleeps on the couch in the den, just through there," he said, nodding to a doorway beside the stocking-strewn brick fireplace at the far end of the room.

"Hmm? Oh, yeah, sure. I got them to put on their jammies, but they wanted to wait up for you." Liam ran a hand over his face.

Felix cocked a brow as he lifted Sway into his arms. More like they wanted to eat cookies and watch TV past their—

"Uncle Felix," Sway murmured sleepily, her little arm tightening around his neck. She buried her face against him, her voice thick. "You really came back. Axle said you wouldn't, but he's dumb."

"Your brother's not dumb, and of course I came back." Felix started upstairs. "Do you know how cold it was out there?" He brought her down the hall and pushed open the door to his old bedroom. A portable crib was on one side of it, and a narrow twin bed on the other. That had to be a delightful living arrangement. "Come on, in bed. You have school tomorrow, and I have to go to work."

"Can I have cereal for breakfast?" Sway asked, crawling under the covers.

"Sure." As far as he was concerned, she could have it every meal. He tucked her in. "Now go to sleep."

She snuggled down into the covers, the top of her head barely visible. "Goodnight, Uncle Felix."

"Goodnight, Sway." He pulled the door just shy of closed behind him and glanced at the next door down. The light was off, and it was quiet. Maybe too quiet. He should probably do a wellness check on Cruze while he was up here.

Felix buzzed his lips, about as eager to do that as he'd been to climb the tor earlier. Whatever. *Big boy pants, Felix. Time to adult.* He slowly turned the doorknob and peeked in.

"You came back?" Cruze croaked out. She was hunched into a ball in the corner where her bed was pushed against the wall, her phone clutched in her hand. By all the tissues scattered around her, she'd been crying.

"Of course I'm back. Why does everyone keep asking me that?"

He ducked as Cruze launched her phone at his head, and it smashed against the wall.

"What the hell?!"

"Because we know our mom isn't! I called her, and when she answered—why didn't you tell us!" Cruze's face screwed up, and she burst into tears.

Fuck.

Felix scrubbed a hand over his face as he stepped into the room and closed the door behind himself. He sat at the edge of the bed. "Gran made me promise not to. She wanted to wait until they got back, but I told her if you asked, I wouldn't lie to you about it."

She glared at him, her eyes red and glassy. "Then tell me why. What did we do? What kind of mom gives up her kids?!"

"A shitty one," Felix said, point-blank. "You guys didn't do anything wrong. My sister isn't very good at being a decent human being, and I'm beyond pissed at her for putting everyone in this position. You guys deserve better."

Cruze's shoulders fell like she'd just been defused. "Thanks for that," she muttered, plucking a wadded tissue from her covers to wipe her nose. "I'm so tired of everyone always making excuses for her, then lying about how she loves us."

Felix bit back the urge to refute that. Who the hell knew how Felicia felt? He'd like to think she was doing this in the urchins' best interests, but his sister was the least altruistic person he knew. Somehow, he was sure she was working an angle.

Cruze looked down at the wadded tissue in her hands, and chewed her lip. "Did Gran and Gramps take Poe to get adopted?"

Felix started. "What? No. Of course not. I told you, they went to take care of Aunt Helen. I talked to them earlier, and they made it to Maybach fine. As soon as they get her sorted, the screamer's coming back, and so are they."

"What's gonna happen to us when they do?" Cruze asked, her big hazel eyes brimming.

Jesus. Felix riffled his curls. "I don't know all the details, but I'm pretty sure you're staying here. We'll probably have a big family meeting and work it all out, okay?"

Cruze shrugged, then sniffled and wiped her nose again. "I'm sorry I threw my phone at you."

"I appreciate that," Felix said, standing. He swept it up off the floor and handed it to her, a crack crazing across the screen and pixelating half of it. "But prepared to be even sorrier, because this isn't getting fixed right way. Maybe take a second to think the next time you feel compelled to wing it at someone's head?"

She took it and huffed, falling back against her pillows. "Whatever."

"Well, then I'm glad we had this chat," he said, his hand on the doorknob.

"Uncle Felix?"

He sighed and turned back to her. "Yes?"

"When we do get it repaired, can I get a new number?"

His stomach dropped, but he got it. Blocking wasn't enough when someone broke your heart. Been there, done that, and there was always that temptation to look and see if they'd cared enough to call. Changing her number was cutting the cord completely. "Sure."

"Thanks." She rolled over, putting her back to him, and Felix let himself out, angry tears burning his eyes.

Liam was waiting for him in the kitchen. His brow furrowed when he saw him. "Hey—"

"I don't want you to say anything, I just want you to hold me for a minute," Felix blurted out. Liam opened his arms, and Felix fell into them.

Why did everything have to be so damned hard lately? He wrapped his arms around Liam's waist, breathing him in. The were's musk soothed his nerves, the slow pass of his palm across Felix's back steadying him, undoing him, putting him back together—God, he was a mess.

"They know she's giving them up," he murmured after a long moment.

"I figured something was going on." Liam sighed. "I went to the bathroom, and when I got back, Cruze was upstairs, and the other two were way too quiet. They wouldn't let me out of their sight and kept asking when you'd be home."

Felix nodded as he pushed back to look at him. "Thank you for staying—for doing this. My life is a mess right now." Jesus. Why did everything have to hit at once? Trying to wrap his head around how he felt about Liam was enough without the rest of it. The big were reached out and tucked a curl behind Felix's ear.

"I can relate." Liam smiled softly, and Felix's heart flip-flopped in his chest. Needing…something. More. The leather of Liam's belt warmed beneath Felix's palms, the edge of it pressing into the meat at the base of his thumbs. He slid his grip to Liam's hips, the bumps of his belt loops a weird torture against Felix's skin.

"I am sorry about what happened earlier with Sarah," he murmured, searching Liam's face. Close, it was so close.

"Yeah. Me, too." Liam's eyes dropped to Felix's lips, and the were wet his own, his head tilting and lowering a fraction of an inch.

Felix's pulse thudded in his ears, a cold sweat slicking his back. His breath sped in anticipation. Was Liam going to kiss him? A mishmash of emotions rose up, desperately wanting him to, yet terrified he would. His fingers tightened on Liam's slim hips—

"I'm here for whatever you need, Felix." Liam took a big breath as he stepped back. "But right now I'm pretty sure that's sleep. I'll pick you guys up tomorrow? There's no way your car's making it out to the compound. Those backroads are brutal this time of year."

Felix looked away and rubbed the nape of his neck, abruptly exhausted and hollow. "Ah, yeah. Cruze has rehearsal, and then trivia starts at seven, so, say six?"

"Perfect. I'm really looking forward to it."

A wave of guilt crashed over Felix, and he winced. "I hope you don't mind, but I asked Jena and Chase to join us. You know, so we'd have a team," he ad libbed quickly as Liam's face fell.

"Oh, yeah. Sure. Smart thinking. That sounds great," Liam said, shrugging into his coat. His keys rattled in his pocket.

"See you then."

"Yeah. See you then." And he was gone without a backwards glance.

Felix stood there staring at the door long after the Jeep's headlights had cut across the kitchen and fled down the street. "I am such a fucking idiot," he muttered, sweeping up his overnight bag.

LIAM RAKED BACK his hair as he drove back to the compound faster than was probably advisable. He should've kissed him. Yeah, it'd been less than ideal circumstances, but the moment had been there, and he'd blown it. Goddamn it. He shook his head and slowed down as he got to the tracks. If he went careening through here, he was liable to end up in a ditch, and it was too fucking cold to have to dig himself out.

He knocked his head back and sighed. Tomorrow. If the opportunity presented itself, he was taking it, and he didn't care who else was there. He knew Felix was scared after what'd happened between them all those years ago, damn it, he was too, but they couldn't keep circling around each other like this. His wolf was making him mental.

Liam pulled up to the house and tried not to slam the doors as he went in.

A shower. He needed a long, hot shower.

Unfortunately, it didn't do anything to calm his racing thoughts. He tossed and turned until the night bled into the next day. He laid in bed until he couldn't stand it anymore and got up. So much for his sleep meds. He downed his morning regimen, got dressed, and headed to the kitchen.

It was too early for anyone else to be awake, which was saying something. His dad usually had his first cup of coffee around three-thirty. Liam made a pot, then filled a travel mug and headed out to the pre-fab garage at the edge of the compound.

Thankfully, like most of the outbuildings, it had power. Based on the stovepipe snaking up the backside, it also had heat. He pried open one of the double doors at the end of it and fumbled for the light.

Jesus. It was packed with shit. Not a chance he was getting to the potbellied stove that he assumed was buried under the mouse-infested piles of crap shoved in here. Right. Well, nothing for it. He tugged on his work gloves and got the contractor's garbage bags out of his Jeep.

The sun was just peeking through the trees when his dad appeared in the doorway.

"Couldn't sleep?" he asked, eyeing the mound of trash Liam had spent the last few hours evicting. He'd made better progress than he'd thought, mostly because everything was completely coated with mouse crap.

Plus, the harder he worked, the less he had to think.

Liam looked up from stuffing what he really hoped was papier mâché into a bag. "I've got a lot on my mind."

His dad grunted and set a lunch bucket on top of a relatively clean tote. "Your mom sent out breakfast, and I figured you could use another coffee," he said, setting another travel mug beside it. "Think this is gonna work for what you need?"

Liam looked around the little garage. "I'll make it work." It was going to be a bit tighter than he'd prefer, but if he didn't give himself something to do, he'd drive himself crazy. Despite sticking to his meds, the stress of the past few days was churning up inclinations he'd rather not dwell on. Guess he was gonna have plenty to talk about at his next therapy session.

"Sounds good. I'll haul those bags out there up in the truck and stop back around lunchtime." His dad looked around, rocking back on his heels like there was still something on his mind.

Liam glanced at him askance. "I'm picking the kids up around six, if you guys are still okay with that."

"Yeah," his dad said. "Your mom is really looking forward to it. How did last night go?"

Liam closed up another bag and dragged the back of his hand across his forehead. "Okay, all things considered. Cruze called her mom, and apparently, she told her she wasn't coming back."

His dad shook his head. "Jesus."

"Yeah."

"Well, your mom's got a slew of activities planned for them. Should take their minds off it, for a little while at least."

Liam tossed the bag outside with the rest of them. "Maybe the girls, but Axle…make sure you take him out to see the dogs. It was the craziest thing at Jerry's. He had those three Rotties sitting there like he was giving them instructions, and I'll be damned if they weren't paying attention. I don't think the kid is a wolf, but he's got some kind of canine affiliation. Maybe you can figure it out. Might make things easier for him."

"If I can, I will. Has to be hard living with a bunch of witches and not knowing what your other half is yet." His father scratched his jaw. "Hopefully, I don't have to break it to him that he's a Schnauzer."

Liam laughed, flicking open another bag. "Doubtful, unless it's a giant one. He carries himself like a big breed."

His dad grunted. "Well, it will be what it'll be. How'd Felix make out up at the manor?"

Shit. "I didn't even get to ask him or tell him about the car. He was really shaken up after talking with Cruze." And as much as it'd sucked, Liam was pretty sure he'd made the right decision last night. When he kissed Felix, he didn't want the warlock writing it off as a moment of weakness, and Liam wasn't about to take advantage of him. "You feel anything out here?"

"One hell of a wave of power went through around nine. Nothing like the last time, but enough to flicker the lights. Sure we'll hear all about it as soon as Kelsey gets off shift, along with the rest of the town gossip." His dad slapped a hand against the doorframe and turned to go. "I'll let you get back to work. See you around noon."

"Yeah, see you." Liam pulled out his phone as his dad left, his thumb hovering over Felix's name. Fuck it. He shot off a quick text asking him about the spell and wishing him a good day.

Man, that was probably dumb—it buzzed as he was jamming it back into his pocket. He took it back out to glance at the screen, and a brilliant smile lit up his face.

His day was definitely improving.

FELIX SAT at his desk trying to compose an email after calling in his concerns about Pete. That had not been the conversation he'd wanted to have first thing this morning, but putting it off wasn't going to do anyone any good. A teeny, tiny part of him prayed the agency wouldn't find anything, but a bigger part knew it was going to be a shit show. Especially since he'd gotten the impression there was already an open case.

Way to ruin someone's holiday, Felix.

Although if it was Pete's, Felix wasn't going to lose much sleep over it. His gaze went to his phone for the umpteenth time after responding to Liam's text. Should he call and let him know? No. He'd tell him about it tonight. Liam didn't need that weighing on him all day, and he shouldn't find out about it alone. He should have a friend with him.

Yeah. A friend. Except a friend probably wouldn't be sending flirty texts at nine in the morning. Epic fail there, and Felix was keenly aware of the sheen of sweat that'd developed on his upper lip as he waited for Liam's reply.

spell last night go ok?

hope today is better

time will tell

and it will be around 6

God, he was an idiot. *Way to just be friends, Felix.* He sourly shoved a spoonful of oatmeal into his mouth. Obviously, his judgement was being impaired by lack of sleep. Last night hadn't been particularly restful. His parents' mattress was older than he was, and he couldn't get his brain to shut up.

His phone buzzed, and he lunged for it.

can't wait

Felix was kicking himself, but he couldn't wait, either. He smiled, watching the bubbles churn as Liam typed, then stopped, then typed again.

i hope i get another hug

Felix's breath caught, heat flushing through him—and a barrage of texts came through immediately on its heels.

i don't mean bcuz ur upset

but i would

if u wanted me to

He grinned, imagining Liam kicking himself.

see you @6

Felix put the phone back down, still smiling. Okay, maybe he was a being a dick with that last text, but he couldn't resist making Liam sweat a little. Lord knew, Felix had done enough of it when they'd been dating before—he froze, then ran a finger under his collar. Is that what they were doing?

No, it...fuck. Felix pinched the bridge of his nose. What

was it he'd told himself last night about not going down this road again? Who the hell had he been kidding? He was already strapped in and going along for the ride.

There was a knock at his door, and Lorraine rolled in, her scooter's basket full of nefarious packages. She tossed one onto his desk, and it landed with an ominous thud. "I'm on vacation next week. Merry Christmas or whatever you heathens celebrate," she grumbled, her tone definitely belying the message.

"Thanks…?" He picked it up, trying to figure out what the hell was in the brown lunch bag. She'd stapled it shut with a mangled ribbon. Felt like rocks.

"They're cookies." She sniffed, adjusting her wig. "You better not be one of those keto freaks."

Shit, was he supposed to have gotten something for her and the rest of the staff? "No, ma'am. I appreciate it…enjoy your vacation."

"I won't, but I'm taking it anyway," she grumbled, throwing her Lark into reverse. "And if you want to get me something, I'd suggest one of those hidden cameras for the copy room."

"No leads on the butt cheek bandit yet, huh?" he asked, taking a sip of coffee.

She scowled at him. "No, and that joke of a sheriff's department had the audacity to tell me they don't keep scrotum prints on file. This town's full of degenerates."

Felix just stopped himself from spitting out his mouthful. He swallowed with difficulty. "That would be quite the lineup," He daubed a napkin over his paisley tie, trying not to laugh.

She shook her cane at him. "You're just as bad as the rest of them. Mark my words, perverts like that just get bolder."

"I'm sorry, Lorraine. I don't mean to make light of the situation. I'll see what I can do about a camera. Oh—did you have those files delivered to the library archives?"

"I did, and that's another problem waiting to happen. One vampire's bad enough, two makes it a proper nest down there, and no good will come of it!" She harrumphed and floored her scooter, slowly wheeling out of his office.

He sighed, not disagreeing, but he hoped it would be better than the alternative. In the meantime, maybe Chase or Liam's dad had one of those trail cameras the town could borrow. He'd ask them tonight. Felix ran a hand over his face and went back to his email. Most of it was denying budget requests and dealing with the standard bureaucracy and red tape. But after trying several times to respond to Bertha Well's umpteenth request that the town pay for neutering and spaying the raccoons digging up her flowerpots, he gave up and fed what he had to a chatbot.

"Make me sound like less of a bitch..." he murmured.

It spat something out almost immediately. Huh. Not bad. Felix hit send, going with it. There was another knock on his door, and Chase poked his head in.

"Hey, Felix. This a bad time?"

"Nope," he said, pushing back in his chair. Christ, it was already two. "What's up?"

"I had a look at that curbing. Did you say there was more of it?"

"Yeah. Give me a sec and let me see if I can find the original order." Felix got up and riffled through one of the file cabinets lining the far wall. Behind him, Chase's stomach growled.

"Sorry," he laughed, poking a finger into Chamber's cage. The weasel hissed at him and lunged as he pulled it back. "I had to work through lunch."

What the hell had been that company's name? Argo, Arrigat... "There's a bag of cookies on the desk," he said over his shoulder. "Help yourself."

"Thanks." A moment later the bag rustled.

Ah. There it was Arinson. Felix pulled the file and turned

just in time to see Chase go green and spit his mouthful into the bag. "Uh, you okay?"

"Fuck, no." Chase gagged, spitting again as he stumbled back. "Why the hell would you feed me cat food cookies?"

Felix blinked at him. "Cat food?"

"Dude, I saw a piece of Meow Medley when I spit it out!"

Felix stared at him for a minute and then burst out laughing. "Are you serious?"

"Do I look like I'm joking?" Chase glared back. "You're lucky they weren't tuna. My auto-injector's out in the truck."

Shit. "Okay, that's not funny, but," Felix snorted, "it still kind of is."

Chase wiped a hand across his mouth and what looked suspiciously like a small smile. "Fuck you." He stabbed a finger at him. "Do not tell Jena."

"Oh, I'm so telling Jena," Felix said, going back to his desk. "She might want to ask Lorraine for the recipe."

"Fucking hell." Chase ripped one of the chairs in front of Felix's desk back and sat, scraping his tongue against his teeth. "Damn, that was vile. Now I'm sorry I agreed to come out with you guys tonight. You're lucky Jena's really missed you."

"Ditto," Felix murmured parsing through paperwork. "I told Liam to pick us up at six. We're dropping off the urchins at his parents, then heading there. I hope that works?"

"Shouldn't be a problem. Hey, you hear anything else about that vamp?"

Felix glanced up. "Nope. Why?"

Chase knocked his knuckles against the arm of the chair. "The node. It doesn't usually talk to me like it does to Jena, but when it accepted that oath..." He shook his head. "It clearly said to both of us that we'd need her, the vamp, and neither one of us thinks it was talking about this clusterfuck with Fayet."

"Well, isn't that just dandy," Felix muttered, pulling out

the sheet he was looking for, and prayed Sweets wasn't right about the universe using their spell as a vehicle to balance a bunch of vampire karma. "Here. I think this shows what's still at the warehouse."

Chase chewed his lip. "Jesus. The town took a bath on what Chambers paid."

"Color me shocked."

He huffed out a breath. "It's enough linear footage for what I'm looking to do, but I'm not paying more than market value for it. Figure on getting maybe half of that."

"At this point, I'm more than willing to cut our losses, and since we can't afford to have it installed, it's not doing anyone any good." And what Chase was proposing to shell out was still a ridiculous amount. Felix knew business was good, but damn. Jena had found herself a sugar daddy. Lucky bitch.

"It's an investment," Chase murmured like he knew what Felix was thinking. "If I can build the manor like I'm envisioning, it'll make my portfolio. What I'm doing over at the Witchery has already reeled in more business than I can comfortably handle locally. If things go to plan, by the time the manor's done, I can roll that into another location, maybe two, and can expand up the Eastern Seaboard with the buzz the press from the manor will create."

Felix quirked a brow, with Chase's magical bent, there was no maybe about it. "I wasn't aware you had plans for world domination."

Chase grinned. "Nah, but I do have plans for a big family, and someone's gonna have to pay for all those college degrees and weddings."

"Well, as long as Jena's on board, I'll be happy to facilitate that by selling you my gently used curbing."

"She's coming around. I've got her up to three." Chase grinned, standing. "I'll work up a bid and get it to you in the next couple of days." He waved over his shoulder as he left. "Thanks, Felix. See you tonight."

"That you will." Anticipation roiled in Felix's stomach as he glanced at the clock again. Another fifteen minutes until he had to pick up the urchins, then Cruze had rehearsal…shit. He was going to have to take them back to his place so he could grab another change of clothes and get ready.

Steeling himself for the inevitable ER visit the urchins meeting Myx was bound to instigate, Felix stood and crumbled one of the cat food cookies into Chamber's cage. "Merry Christmas, you filthy animal."

LIAM SWEPT the last of the mouse shit out of the garage and leaned against the broom's handle with a long sigh. After hauling garbage all day, a good dinner, and couple of beers— he was going to sleep hard tonight. His dad had come back half a dozen times to truck things out to the dump, and now, save for two totes of semi-salvageable stuff for Liam's mom to go through, the garage was empty.

He'd been pleasantly surprised by the condition of the stove and the L-shaped workbench already in there. All he needed was some pegboard, and he could start moving in his tools. Liam propped the broom against the wall and closed up the garage. Guess he was making a run to the hardware store and his storage unit tomorrow.

He grinned, more excited than he could remember being in a long time. It was like he had a purpose again, and his outlook was definitely rosier. The alarm on his phone went off, and he hurried to his Jeep. He needed to get ready before he picked up Felix and the kids.

An hour later, he stood wrapped in a towel, staring into his closet. He'd been sweating over that last text from Felix all day, trying not to read too much into it. Was he just fucking with him? He had to be, right? Liam dragged a hand over his freshly shaven jaw, praying he hadn't made a complete ass out of himself, but last night…no. Felix was into him, Liam had to believe that.

He pulled out his good, dark-wash pair of jeans and a dress shirt, then shoved the shirt back into the closet. Christ, might as well wear a sign he was trying too hard. But what…? A black t-shirt. Yeah. That could go either way, right? Casual, but kind of dressy? He pulled it on and flexed. Stupid. He shook his head at himself and grabbed a green flannel.

His phone pinged as he was mussing product through his hair. It was Felix asking him to pick them up at his apartment rather than the house. Liam texted back that he'd be there and hurried to finish getting ready and out the door.

He pulled into the parking space beside Felix's pile, shaking his head. He supposed he shouldn't talk, but it would've been a different story if the car had character. Felix's early 90s piece of crap had zero redeeming qualities. It was a rolling calamity just waiting to happen, and way too cookie-cutter to suit Felix's personality. He needed something that stood out, like the rest of—

Liam stopped short, a mental image of Felix driving around in a two-tone India Ivory and Colonial Cream Bel Air, the interior side panels and seat covers in teal and cream. Jesus, he'd be so fucking hot… Liam shook his head, getting way ahead of himself—but what if?

Maybe he wouldn't tell Felix about the car. At least not yet.

Liam grinned, jogging up the steps to the fourth floor. It was suspiciously silent as he raised his hand to knock. More so when Cruze cracked it open a moment later, then closed it again to slide back the safety chain and let him in.

"Everything okay?" he asked, slipping inside.

She eyed him up and down. "Are you two going on a date?"

Liam's cheeks flushed, and he slid his abruptly sweaty

palms over his back pockets. "What? Ah, no, we're um, just—"

She rolled her eyes. "Whatever, I don't care," she said, going into the kitchen where her schoolwork was spread out on the table.

Right. Liam ducked into the living room. Aside from the cozy leather couch in front of the widescreen TV, Felix's apartment was bizarrely utilitarian. He'd done zero decorating for the holiday, and there wasn't a speck of clutter. Most of the furniture was black laminate particle board. Instead of bookcases along the wall, he had file cabinets, probably for his comic book collection. The cabinets were also black. Superhero movie posters crowded the walls, providing the only pops of color in the room.

The other two kids were at opposite ends of the couch watching cartoons. Myx crouched on the glass coffee table in front of them, eyeing Axle and Sway like mice. The cat glanced over at Liam and huffed, apparently unimpressed with what he saw.

"Liam!" Sway jumped up and the cat hissed. Her eyes went wide, and she scrambled back to her seat.

Liam bit back a smile. "You guys almost ready?"

Axle flopped his head against the back of the couch and looked up at him. "I'm more than ready. It's boring here. Uncle Felix doesn't have anything to do, and his cat hates us. It won't listen to me, then bit me when I tried to pet him." He thrust out his arm as evidence and Sway nodded solemnly from the other end of the couch. There were definite fang marks.

Myx huffed and gave the feline equivalent of an eye roll, raising his paw to lick.

"Serves you right. I told you to leave him alone," Felix said, coming up behind Liam.

Damn. Felix was in a fitted pair of herringbone slacks and one of those ugly Christmas sweaters. It said "Merry and

Gay" in big block letters across his chest. Two reindeer struck poses beneath it with ornaments hanging from their antlers and martini glasses in their hands, er, hooves—whatever they had going on, it was adorable on him.

"Nice sweater." Liam said.

Felix flicked a curl from his eyes. "Tis the season. You urchins ready? Your sister's already packed up."

They both glanced at the cat.

Liam switched off the TV and hoisted Myx into his arms. "Go ahead, I got him."

They scrambled off the couch, past Felix who was just staring at Liam holding the cat. Myx nuzzled up under his jaw, purring, and Liam laughed as Felix's brows about shot up to his hairline.

"I can't figure out if he's doing that solely to annoy me, or if he's softening you up before he goes in for the kill," Felix muttered. "Either way, I hope you know it's only a matter of time before he lunges for your jugular. Consider this his disclaimer. My renters insurance is high enough without a personal injury claim against it."

Liam grinned, setting the cat onto the vacant couch with one last scratch behind his ears. Myx huffed and curled up with his back to them. "Noted. How did you get him to watch the kids like that? He's your familiar, right?" he asked, following Felix to the front door.

He shrugged into his parka, the kids lined up, more than ready to leave. "He is, but being on urchin duty was all him. I don't *get* Myx to do anything."

"What's a familiar?" Sway asked, grabbing Felix's hand after he was all zipped up.

"They help with spells, dummy." Axle scowled, scooting out into the hall as soon as the door was open.

Felix frowned, locking up behind everyone. "In theory. In practice, Myx hasn't shown much interest in anything outside of his kibble and terrorizing small children—though

I will admit, getting you two to behave was certainly magical."

"We're always good, Uncle Felix." Sway batted her lashes up at him.

His brow rose. "You know Santa's watching you right now, right?"

She swallowed and looked away.

"How was rehearsal today?" Liam asked Cruze as they descended the stairs.

"Painful," Felix said before she'd opened her mouth.

Cruze rounded on him indignantly. "Hey!"

"Oh, not you. I was pleasantly surprised by your performance, but the kid playing Bob Cratchit needs to learn how to enunciate. I couldn't understand half of what he was saying."

"Yeah," Cruze grumbled, slightly mollified. "He just got a new retainer, and his mom won't let him take it out for rehearsals after he lost the last one."

"Well, hopefully she does for the show. It's a musical right? There's no way he's singing with that thing in."

"Trust me, I know." She glowered. "And he needs all the help he can get. His voice keeps cracking on the high notes, and it's awful."

"Way to sell the show," Felix said, holding the door to the parking lot open. "Can't wait to sit through that, it sounds fantastic."

Liam laughed. "Aw, come on. I think it sounds great."

"Are you coming?" Cruze asked, glancing askance at Liam. "Sarah's playing Emily."

His stomach dropped. She was? No one had told him—no. Why would they? He breathed past his anger, not entirely sure how that would work, even if he'd wanted to. "Um…" He riffled in his pocket for his keys. His Jeep beeped as he unlocked it. "I mean, I hadn't—"

"We got an extra ticket," Axle said, throwing open the

passenger side door. "You can sit in Gramp's seat, next to me."

"He's not wrong, and if you don't take it, it'll just go to waste," Felix said across the front seats, helping Sway into the Jeep. "Think about it."

Liam climbed in. "Yeah. I will. Thanks."

Once everyone was buckled, he pulled out of the parking lot and drove out to the compound. About halfway out there, Felix huffed.

"Are you purposefully hitting every rut and pothole on the road?" he bitched, clutching the "oh shit" handle as Sway and Axle squealed, bouncing on the back seat. Cruze had her arms stubbornly crossed over her chest between them, but there was a definite sparkle in her eye.

Maybe. "Of course not," Liam scoffed, swerving to hit two more in quick succession. "See, I missed that one back there."

"How thoughtful of you," Felix muttered, clenching his teeth.

Liam grinned at him. "I try."

They pulled up to his parents' log cabin, and Felix got out of the Jeep with a dramatic sigh. "God, I still feel like I'm moving," he said, steadying himself with one hand against the door. The kids streamed out after him. "I'm assuming the ride back will be smoother?"

"Guess you're just gonna have to find out." Liam grinned.

Felix glowered back. "Fabulous."

"Oh, you're here!" Liam's mother cried from the doorway. "Come inside, come inside. You can leave that bag right by the door, honey," she said to Cruze as the girl scooted past her.

"Get out of the snow and inside you two! It's freezing out here," Felix yelled to Sway and Axle. They stomped back from the edge of the woods and up the porch steps, bolting into the house after Cruze. Liam couldn't blame them, he could smell the cocoa and cookies from the porch.

"Um, bye. I'll miss you, too," Felix called after them, shaking his head.

"Bye, Uncle Felix!" Sway screamed back at him.

He pinched the bridge of his nose. "Volume!"

"Thanks again for doing this." Liam gave his mom a quick peck on the cheek, and she swatted him, chuckling.

"It's no trouble. It's been far too quiet around here lately." A shadow passed over her face, and she blinked it away. "Anytime you need someone to lend a hand, you just call, Felix. We're happy to help."

"You say that now..." he muttered, then forced a smile. "But thank you."

"Well, go on. You two boys have fun." The way she smiled at them put a lump in Liam's throat. She winked at him and went back inside the house.

Liam clasped his hands together and turned to Felix. "Ready for trivia?"

"Not even a little bit after having my brain scrambled by all those bumps."

"I promise I'll let you recover on the ride out." Liam put a hand to the small of the warlock's back as they went back to the Jeep. "But, did you see the kids' faces? They loved it, even Cruze was smiling."

"As shocking as that is, I can assure you the other two don't exactly have discerning tastes," Felix muttered.

"Maybe not, but their uncle does, and I want to make sure I get this right," Liam grinned at Felix's expression as he opened the warlock's door for him. Rendered speechless, he flushed and got in.

Liam was gonna take that as a good sign.

Chapter Thirteen

FELIX STARED into the darkening twilight as the Jeep crossed the tracks and headed back into town. No question, this was a date. He was going on a date with Liam Montgomery, and they were doing it in public. *Public.* Felix glanced over at the were and covertly pinched himself. Nope. Not dreaming.

Snaps was just off Main Street on the far side of town. They passed town hall, the elementary school, and the library, before turning onto Dale. With the holiday weekend, the parking lot was even more packed than usual, but there were a few of spots left on the street. Liam pulled into one and cut the engine.

He unbuckled his seatbelt and turned to Felix. "You okay?"

"Yeah, why?" he asked, unlatching his own.

Liam shrugged. "You were really quiet on the way over. You still want to do this?"

"Do I—of course I do." Felix's brows furrowed, a pit forming in his stomach. "Do you?"

Liam wet his lips and glanced back at the restaurant. Felix braced himself, already hearing Liam backing out— "Who the hell is that?"

A woman in a short, tight dress and a motorcycle jacket was sauntering down the center of the road. Her lean silhouette was elongated by ridiculously high stiletto heels, and the glow of Christmas lights from the main drag backlit her, throwing a spike of shadow in her path.

"Since when does Havers have hookers on Main Street?" Liam murmured.

"Technically, we're on Dale, but we don't, as far as I know." And if it did, they'd be down in the waterfront district where The Blue Parrot was—aka The Dirty Bird—the town's only establishment of ill repute. Or so Felix had been told. Jena wasn't exactly welcome down there, thanks to her father, and Felix'd never had any desire to visit the strip club solo. That, and the possibility of running into his sister there wasn't a risk he was willing to take for curiosity's sake.

The woman strolled up to the driver's side window, and knocked on the glass. Liam hesitated before rolling it down.

"Well, hello, boys," she said, crossing her arms on the sill, a flask in one hand, and leaned inside. She wore heavy makeup, and her light brown hair was slicked back. "Nice ride."

"Um, thanks. Can we help you?" Liam asked.

She smiled at Felix. "Not you, champ, but freckles over there can." Her dark red lips tipped up to show wickedly pointed fangs.

Felix's stomach dropped. No fucking way. "Ophelia?" She looked like an extra from a Robert Palmer video.

"Bingo." She took a hit off her flask. "We need to talk about that lawsuit, and we need to do it now."

"You know her?" Liam asked incredulously.

"Um. Sort of." Felix's throat bobbed. "She's the town's new attorney."

Liam looked at him like he was crazy, and Felix couldn't disagree.

"Not quite," Ophelia frowned. "I still need to clear up some paperwork before I can get to work. Lucky for you, Thaddeus pulled a bunch of strings, and that should be sorted out by Monday. So, are you going to invite me in, or do I have to stand out here while we do this?"

Felix and Liam exchanged glances.

"Christ. Look, BYOB," she said, waggling the flask at them. That didn't exactly make Felix feel any better. He was positive the second "B" didn't stand for "booze." "I'm all but topped off, and even if I wasn't, neither one of you are doing it for me. I'm not into dark and angsty or pale and fabulous. Now, your big blond friend the other night—"

"Is married to his fated mate, who's also the guardian of the node," Felix snapped at her.

Ophelia rolled her dark, kohl-lined eyes. "Well, la de frickin' da."

Felix's brow arched in response. "Jena will kill you."

"Ghandi, I hope so," the vamp muttered. "Now open the fucking door and invite me in."

Felix and Liam exchanged another glance. Felix shrugged. It was better than inviting her to join them at Snaps, though she'd probably be really good at trivia.

"Fine," Liam said, stepping out of the Jeep and flipping up the seat. "Come on in."

"Why, thank you, kind sir." She batted her lashes at him and simpered before climbing in the back.

"How are you even here?" Felix asked. "The last time I saw you, you looked like death warmed over."

"Aww. Flattery will get you everywhere, and believe it or not, I'm just as shocked as you, but whatever's in the water out here, sucking on you cows is like mainlining high test. If I had to guess, that node's probably got something to do with it. It's no wonder Thaddeus has always been so stingy letting other vamps into his territory." She flippantly tipped up her flask and smacked her lips loudly. "On to brass tacks. How much of that complaint did you read?"

Felix felt his cheeks heat. "Honestly? I got through the subject line and quit. I know nothing about lawsuits and that was like three inches thick, which I'm assuming means we're in deep shit."

"Huh. You're smarter than you look," she said, taking another swig from her flask.

"Gee, thanks for the compliment."

"Don't get used to it." She popped her lips. "So, the complaint is essentially that Havers knowingly withheld magical resources and went to great lengths to divert the leyline, fully aware of what that would do to Fayet. It further contends that the town is incapable of administrating the node. This isn't just about collecting damages. They're building a case to annex Havers-by-the-Sea."

Felix's vision tunneled, and he put a hand to his chest, ill. "They want the town? Can they even do that?"

"Unfortunately, there's precedent," Liam murmured. "If that's their goal, I'm assuming Fayet's lawyer's basing his argument on *Bellveiw vs. Longmatta?*"

The vamp's eyes narrowed at Liam. "Yeah. They cited that case in the complaint."

Felix looked between the two of them. "What's *Bellveiw vs. Longmatta?*"

Liam ran a hand over his jaw. By his expression, his thoughts were somewhere else. He'd gotten the same gleam in his eye that used to mean he was going to disappear, hyper-focused on something. "It's a case that set a lot of precedent for arcane law. The initial complaint was based on a portal, not a node, but the court ruled that the town's leadership be disbanded in the best interest of its residents after it failed to prevent an unseelie incursion in 1905." He chewed his lip, oblivious to the fact that Felix was gaping at him. Where the hell was he pulling all this out of?

Liam shook his head like something about what he'd just said bothered him. "But it doesn't...I don't understand where Sperry's gonna go with it...the crux of that case was that Longmatta's elected officials held a vote the week prior rejecting the local coven's pleas to ward the area. That was cited as proof of willful negligence and ultimately won the case for them. From what I understand, everything that went down here was all behind closed doors, and no one knew Chambers swapped out the material in those turbines."

Ophelia stared at him. "Who the hell is this guy?" she asked.

Felix shook his head. "Not a clue."

Liam's head snapped up at Felix's voice, and that gleam snuffed out. His shoulders slumped, and he pressed his lips together, tight.

The vamp sucked her teeth at his silence. "Well, whoever he is, he has a law degree. Civs don't just pull cases out of their asses like that."

Felix blanched. Holy shit. That'd been what he'd been doing out West? It would certainly explain how he'd paid to fix up his Jeep and get Felix's car out of hock, but Liam? "You're a lawyer? How is that possible?" Felix squeaked. Granted, he hadn't exactly kept tabs on the were after high school, but you'd think him being a lawyer would've gotten around.

Liam dragged a heavy hand over his face. "Through a lot of student loans. I got my law degree to help my pack administer the land around the node. You know how much I hate logging, and being a mechanic didn't pay the bills."

Okay, so the Eastside pack's involvement with the node had been super hush-hush, but this was surreal. Liam? Felix pinched himself again. Damn it, still here. "Why didn't you say anything when you knew we were looking for a lawyer?" He was too shocked to even be pissed about it. Liam was the last person on earth he'd expect to go into law.

He sighed, shaking his head. "For one, I practiced arcane law, not civil, and two, I hate it. It's not something I want to do anymore."

Okay, that Felix could see, but...Liam? A lawyer? Really?

Felix put a hand to his temple, his eyelids fluttering. Later, he'd try to make sense of it later. "Okay…but forgive me for thinking that what you just rattled off sounds like it might be pertinent to our current situation."

"He's got you there, champ," the vamp said, sprawled out in the back, sipping from her flask.

"You get blood on my back seat, and I will stake you." Liam glowered at her, obviously rattled by his admission. Felix was, too. What else didn't he know about Liam Montgomery?

Ophelia licked her teeth. "Such a tease."

Liam shook his head. "Look, off the record I'd be happy to advise your main counsel, but I can't represent you. I can't…I can't go back into a courtroom."

Felix's brow furrowed, there was something else Liam wasn't saying, but he wasn't about to press him on it with Ophelia in the back. Felix's phone pinged. Shit, Jena wanted to know where they were.

"Okay, put a pin in all of that." He turned to the vamp. "What do you need from me right now?"

"A preliminary game plan. Thaddeus said Westside's old alpha and his buddy Malcom are dead, but Chambers and the attorney who filed for all of those grants are still alive, right?"

Felix nodded. "Yes, but the coven turned Chambers into a weasel. He's in the ferret cage in my office."

She snorted. "What about the attorney?"

"Chase said he thinks Patrick is in Galleon Falls," Liam frowned. "But as soon as he catches wind of the lawsuit, I'd put money on him disappearing."

"Then I suggest you keep a close eye on that weasel and figure out if it's possible for the coven to turn him back into a human," Ophelia said, leaning forward between the seats. "Best-case scenario, they can, and we get the case dismissed on the grounds that Chambers acted without the town's knowledge, putting full responsibility on him. If we have a patsy, there's a chance they'll drop the case. I'll file our response as soon as I'm cleared by the bar, but we need to be prepared for this to go to trial."

Felix huffed out his cheeks, not even a little tempted to ask what the worst-case scenario was. The thought of Havers's being swallowed by Fayet was bad enough to keep him up at night. "Okay. Anything else?"

"Yeah, after your date, stop by town hall to invite me in. I need to go through the records to see if there's anything that can help our case. Now let me out, I've got shit to do."

Liam opened the door and cold flooded the Jeep as he slid out. Felix shivered, but the vamp didn't so much as twitch. Did the undead feel cold? Her heels clicked onto the asphalt, and she fixed her skimpy skirt. Didn't seem like it.

"For future reference," she said to Liam, "you're gonna want to rescind your invitation. Otherwise, I might feel compelled to take this beautiful machine of yours out for a joyride."

His eyes narrowed at her. "Invite revoked. Stay out of my Jeep."

"Oooh, the menace," she winced, clutching her chest, then grinned. "That's the spirit. I'll see you boys around. Don't forget about the invite!"

Felix got out and joined Liam at the driver's side, watching her saunter back the way she'd come.

"I don't like her," Liam said.

She flipped them off over her shoulder and lit a cigarette.

"She certainly doesn't make it easy." Felix's phone buzzed again. "Shit, we're missing trivia." Liam locked up the Jeep, and they hurried down the street.

Felix glanced at him askance. "So…a lawyer."

Liam grunted, jamming his hands deeper into his pockets. Okay. Guess he didn't want to talk about it. Way to start their date.

Ahead, light spilled from the little cantina's frost-rimed

windows onto the sidewalk. Liam held the door open for Felix, and they stepped inside, heat hitting them like a fist.

Felix unzipped his parka, abruptly too hot as he scanned the crowded room for Jena and Chase. Ah, there they were. They'd managed to get a booth in the far corner. Felix wended through the packed space, the rafters festooned with festive lights and colorful little flags. Spanish holiday music competed with the clamor, and the trivia crowd was more than a little tipsy. Liam helped Felix with his parka before he'd asked and hung it on a hook with his own at the side of the booth. A boy could get used to that.

"Hey!" Jena smiled at them as they sat and slid over a pair of menus featuring mariachi Chihuahuas above the specials. "You guys just missed the waitress. Hurry up and figure out what you want." She glanced at Felix and tapped a pencil against the table. The first three trivia questions were already filled in on the sheet in front of her. "Nice sweater."

"Isn't it?" He smoothed a hand down its front. "It was the last one at Chatarue's black Friday sale. I had to dive through a display of mistletoe thongs to beat out someone else, but there was no way I was leaving without it."

Jena nodded. "Clearly action had to be taken."

Chase blinked at him. "Mistletoe thongs? Like with a printed pattern or an actual—"

"Sprig front and center? Yes, that," Felix said brightly. "I looked for one in your size, but no dice. Shame, we could've been twinning tonight, and it's awfully comfortable. Kind of woodsy. Seemed like something you'd like." Chase looked like he was trying to figure out if Felix was kidding or not, and Jena started laughing.

Liam shook his head and picked up a menu, in a definite mood. "Sorry we're late. You guys already order?"

"Yep. We got one of everything," Jena said, grinning at Chase. "I've been ravenous, and he worked through lunch again."

"So I heard." Felix pretended to peruse the menu, humming the Meow Medley commercial jingle under his breath. This date might be a bust, but messing with Chase was like his third favorite activity. Might as well salvage the night somehow.

"Dude." Chase narrowed his eyes, and Felix laughed.

Jena looked between them. "Do you know what that's about?" she asked Liam.

"Nope." He stuffed the menu into the holder next to the wall, and she raised her brow, her eyes flicking to Felix. *"What's his deal?"* written all over her face.

Felix shot her a look he hoped she translated as *"Later."* By her eye roll, she got the message. "So, you'll never guess who we ran into outside," he said, drawing a glyph on the tabletop to invoke a cone of silence. "Ophelia."

"What?" Jena gaped at him. "She's out? Already?"

"Mmm. Something about the node supercharging our blood." He frowned, totally grossed out. "And from what she was wearing, primed to moonlight as a hooker. Long story short, Fayet is using this lawsuit to try and take over the town and claim the node—"

"What?!" Jena hissed, halfway out of her seat, her irises crackling emerald.

"—which is why we need to keep Chambers where he is so he can take the fall instead of the town. In a perfect world, your brother would be with him," Felix finished.

"I'll drag that motherfucker in myself!"

"No, you won't." Chase pulled Jena down next to him. "If Patrick knows people are looking for him, he'll go to ground."

"Then we get Matilda to scry for him," Jena seethed.

Felix swept away the glyph as the waitress came back over with their drinks and two orders of chips and salsa for the table.

She glanced at Jena. "Everything all right over here?"

"Peachy," Felix said, batting his lashes.

"Okay then." The waitress pulled out her book of guest checks. "You ready to order?"

He blew out his cheeks. "House margarita, nachos with an extra side of guacamole, and the ceviche, please."

"Okay, and you?" she asked Liam.

"I'll have whatever's dark that's on tap and the burrito combo plate," he muttered unenthusiastically. "Can I get an order of beef empanadas with that, too?"

"You got it."

"Thanks." He pushed back in his seat, and Jena shot Felix another look.

A woman by the bar tapped a microphone, then read out the next trivia question.

"Captain Nemo," Felix said.

Jena glowered at him, but picked up her pencil. "Like the fish?"

"More vengeful, I'm sure you can relate." He chomped into a chip. "Even if Matilda found Patrick, we'd still need to haul him back, and I can't say hunting down a rogue were in the middle of winter sounds particularly doable at the moment." Or at all. There were miles of forest out there. If he shifted, Matilda scrying or not, they'd never catch him.

"Not necessarily," Liam sighed. "I know a guy we might be able to get to serve him papers. Then it's on the courts to haul him in."

"Oh," Felix said, chomping a chip. "Fun fact, Liam's an attorney."

FUCK. Liam's stomach dropped, squirming at Jena and Chase staring at him like he'd suddenly grown another head. Damn it. He knew he'd screwed himself opening his mouth like that in the Jeep, but it'd just bubbled up before he'd thought about the implications.

And he was back on that fucking country club patio all over again.

Felix chomped another chip, side-eying him, and Liam had the abrupt urge to crawl under a rock. He didn't want to lie to them, but… He scrubbed his hands over his face. Fuck. He wasn't medicated enough for this.

"For real?" Chase asked.

"Yeah, but it's not something…" Liam thanked the waitress delivering Jena and Chase's food and their drinks. He passed the margarita to Felix and took a hefty swallow of his beer. How the hell did he even begin to explain? "Being in a courtroom messes with me," Liam said as the waitress left.

"Messes with you how?" Jena repeated like she thought he was full of shit.

"I turn into a serious dick," he said, pushing back against the booth's seat. "And I'm tired of kicking myself about it after the fact." More like hating himself, but they didn't need to know that.

Jena laughed. "Sorry, but not for nothing, Liam, you're one of the nicest guys I've ever met. I don't see it. You being a dick or a lawyer."

And thank God for that. He flicked a finger across the ring of condensation his beer had left on the table. "Yeah, well, it's not something I'm particularly proud of." Though he had while he'd been in Los Huego, which was part of the problem. He'd totally given into that alpha part of himself that got off on dominating everyone and everything. "I just… I dunno. Being in a courtroom, it flips a switch, and I get hyper-focused on winning. It's why I didn't play sports in high school. I don't have to worry about that with engines." Competition, being challenged, it did something to him, and it wasn't pretty.

"I'd wondered about that," Chase murmured. "Coach Gray was always trying to get you to try out for something."

"Don't remind me." Liam's dad'd had to go in and explain in no uncertain terms to leave him the hell alone before someone got hurt. Too bad he hadn't been in Los Huego with him. Liam shook that memory away. "When I first got my degree, I was working as a law clerk. I didn't get into the trial aspect until I took a position out West." He frowned, and if he'd known how that was going to pan out, he never would've taken it. "Anyway, when Jenny filed for divorce, it made me reevaluate a bunch of things. I didn't want to be that guy anymore."

"Why did she file for divorce?" Felix asked. "Sounds like she had her cake and was eating it, too."

"Pete's not exactly lemon chiffon," Jena snarked as the next trivia question was read out.

Felix snagged another chip. "No, but he is a prepper fruitcake."

Liam blew out a breath and knocked his knuckles against the table. "Because I found out she'd taken out a bunch of sizable loans in my name. Not a clue where all that money went, but it wasn't to the house or the kids." She sure as hell wasn't driving around in a Ferrari, either. "I salvaged what I could from our joint accounts and cut her off. Now she's going for half of everything that's left."

"She stole money from you?" Jena spat. "What a bitch."

"More like Pete did," Chase muttered around a bite of burrito.

"Yeah," Liam agreed, downing a good portion of his beer. Unfortunately, Jenny had been the one who filled out all of the loan paperwork, and if he pressed embezzlement charges, where would that leave the kids? "And the answer's Merle Haggard."

"What a dick."

"Who, Merle Haggard?" Jena asked.

"No, Pete," Chase answered, taking another bite.

"Duh," Felix rolled his eyes, and they brightened as the waitress came over with their meals. "Another margarita, please."

"Do a full round," Chase said, handing her his empty plate and reaching for the stack of tacos that'd been beside it.

Liam dug into his empanadas, frowning. This was so not the date he'd envisioned when he'd asked Felix out yesterday. Next time, he was taking him out somewhere that wasn't local.

If there was a next time.

Jena squiggled something onto the tabletop. "So, Ophelia was outside?" she asked.

"She was." Felix said, dangling a shrimp on his fork. "After this, I have to invite her into town hall so she can go through the records there. You know, Sweets thinks manifesting Ophelia was more than my specs pinpointing her. When we were going back to our cars, she said something about karma seeking to level the scales. She thinks Mr. Brock and some Kremlyn guy—"

Liam dropped his fork, and they all looked at him.

"You know who he is?" Jena asked.

Fuck. Hopefully he was wrong, but Kremlyn wasn't exactly a common name. This night just kept getting better and better. "Potentially, and if it's who I'm thinking of, he's not someone you want to draw notice from." Enter reason two Liam wasn't eager to go back West ever again.

"Whoever he is, he's a prince." Felix took a sip of his margarita and cocked a brow.

A cold sweat broke out over Liam's brow. "Shit. Then, yeah. I know who he is, and the dude's hardcore. He's the court's enforcer and heads the Crimson Guard." And he'd been really fucking pissed at the outcome of that last case Liam had taken.

"Well, that doesn't sound good." Felix frowned and set his

glass on the table. "Matilda thinks he's going to come looking for Ophelia."

Liam's heart pounded. Fuck. He was fucked.

"Do you think he'll be able to track the spell?" Chase asked.

Jena frowned, flicking peppers from her plate. "We weren't exactly sneaky ripping her out of whatever hole he had her in."

Liam felt all of the blood drain from his face. "Y-you took her out of the Inchisoare?"

"If that's the same thing as a prison, I'd say that it's probable, considering what she looked like when we manifested her." She shrugged, wiping away her doodle.

Jesus, it wasn't the same thing as a prison, it was *the* prison. "I'm gonna need a shot of whiskey," Liam said to the waitress delivering the round Chase had ordered. "If you snatched her from there, then Matilda's right, Kremlyn isn't gonna let that slide. Any chance you can extend that ill intent ward around the entire town? Because we're gonna need it." No idea if it would actually keep the prince of darkness out, but Liam would feel better if there was something other than the existing treaties regulating vamp activities on federal lands between him and them.

Like an ocean. Maybe two.

He picked up one of his burritos, trying to calm his racing heart. He needed to chill out. Even if Kremlyn did manage to get a dispensation from his tribe to come out here, his focus would be on getting Ophelia back, not Liam.

Right. Just keep telling yourself that. Maybe it'll even come true.

Jena chewed her lip, doodling again. "Magic gets weird over salt water, but where the peninsula hits the mainland at our border…maybe? It would be easier if there was a circle of stones out that way—" Her and Chase exchanged a look.

"What?" Felix asked. "I know that look, spill."

She sighed, picking at her enchilada. "One of the visions I got from my mother's grimoire was of a black altar out by the western swamp. I'd planned on talking to the coven about it, but honestly, after Samhain and with everything else going on, it kind of slipped off my radar."

"Wait, what?" Liam coughed, choking on his beer.

"I really think you need to back up," Felix said at the same time. "How did I not know this?"

Jena squirmed in her seat. "Let's just say the vision I had doesn't bear repeating." Chase grunted beside her, like he knew all about it, and Felix huffed at the two of them.

"You know, you're getting as bad as Aggie with her 'need to know' disbursement of information shtick." He picked up his margarita. "You'd think you'd be more forthcoming. She ever tell you what she saw happening this spring, or are you still not naming your kid Agatha?"

"Dude, do not get her started…" Chase murmured.

"No. We're not," Jena growled, giving him a wicked side-eye before focusing back on Felix. "Look, that vision aside, there's another reason it's been on the back burner." She glanced at Chase again, and he sighed with a look on his face that made Liam think whatever she was talking about was a pack thing.

"There's something out there. Even though the swamp is a good chunk of the Western pack's territory, it was an unspoken thing to steer clear. The trail that leads out there, you can't go down it more than a half mile or so before you get totally creeped out and your wolf goes ape-shit. We used to dare each other to do it when we were kids and once was definitely enough."

Liam chewing slowed. Whatever it was had definitely freaked Chase out—enough that you could still hear it in the big were's voice. What the hell could do that?

"Okay." Felix took a sip of his drink and sat back. "But if it's a dark altar, someone's been out there practicing, and you know places like that attract the wrong kind of attention. Leaving it to just sit is a problem waiting to happen."

Jena frowned. "I know, and if there's an existing circle of stones, it's a bigger one. We can't just ignore it and set up a ward right next door. It'll resonate wrong and erode whatever we do. The circle needs to be cleansed and tied into the spell." She met Chase's eyes. "We need to go out there to see what we're dealing with."

"That we better include me," Chase growled.

Jena snorted. "No arguments here, and we should do it ASAP, as in tomorrow."

"What?" Felix looked at her aghast. "It's supposed to be like subzero, and I'm too pretty for frostbite."

She rolled her eyes at him. "Yeah, but it'll be clear. Once Yule begins, the weather's supposed to go to hell for the next week, and this doesn't sound like it should wait. Setting up a ward's going to take time as it is, and God only knows what's out there."

"Guaranteed it's worse than the flying squirrel infestation, and that took a solid week and a half to figure out," Chase said, pushing back his empty plate and reaching for the chips. "And coconuts are probably not going to be the answer."

Liam agreed, and the sooner they got the ball rolling, the better.

"Fine," Felix grumbled, pushing aside his empty plate in favor of the nachos, then brightened up. "Oh, wait. I can't. I've got the urchins."

Chase snorted. "Well, that's suddenly convenient." He ran a hand over his face. "But if it's just the two of us, I'm pretty sure I can borrow a snowmobile from one of the guys at the compound. It'll make getting in and out of there a lot easier."

"I wouldn't exactly call urchin duty convenient," Felix muttered, scooping up some guacamole with a nacho. "I've no idea what the hell I'm going to do with them for the next week."

"You could start by taking them Christmas shopping," Jena said. "When I was Cruze's age, Aggie used to give me cash, then let me spend it on whatever I wanted. I loved that."

"My parents have a pile of dollar store crap for them, but that's not a bad idea." He paused to chew. "I don't know if Axle would go for it, though."

"You could do it while I've got him at Jerry's," Liam offered.

"I could, and I'm due for a pedicure." Felix swirled the ice in his margarita. "How long do you think you'll be there?"

"I can make a day of it, then meet you back at the house for dinner. Axle probably won't mind helping set up the garage," Liam said. "Especially when faced with the alternative."

"Sold, as long as you're cooking," Felix said, then doing a double take at Jena. "What?"

"Nothing." She shook her head with a funny little smile on her face. He raised his brow at her and she laughed. "You guys just sound like you're an old married couple, and they're your kids."

Felix scowled at her. "I can assure you that I'm quite single and taking ownership of the urchins is not on my dance card. Now if you'll excuse me, I need to use the little boy's room."

Liam got up, feeling like he'd just been slapped, and Felix slipped out of the booth.

Chase reached over to smear out Jena's doodle and waved over the waitress. "Can we get the rest of this to go?" he asked the waitress delivering Liam's whiskey. She nodded and started loading up her tray.

"You guys are leaving?" Liam asked as he sat back down, his heart in his throat watching Felix walk away. Goddamn it. He'd fucked up again.

"Yeah," Jena said, snagging one of Felix's nachos and doodling again.

"Why do you keep doing that?" Liam asked, trying not to

lose his shit. He wiped his sweaty palms on his thighs, his thoughts spiraling. What the fuck was he gonna do now? How was he gonna prove to Felix he was ready for this, for them? He hadn't meant to keep secrets, but—

"Hmm? Oh. Cone of silence," she said like that explained it. "I need to corner Aggie and pry out of her whatever she knows about vampires and that altar. If this Kremlyn dude is as bad as you say he is, we need all the info that we can get, and if we have to move material out there to anchor the ward…" she trailed off, looking at Chase.

"You know I'll help with whatever you need." He pulled her close and kissed her forehead. "But do you think it will even work? I mean, Mr. Brock crossed the wards around the node."

Jena's brow furrowed. "Actually, I'm not sure he did. The way he just stepped out of the aether, that's shadow walking, and from what I've heard, it's a vampire thing that only the really old ones can do. If Kremlyn is capable of the same, I have no idea how to prevent that. I'm pretty sure it bypasses wards completely." Her gaze went past Liam and focused on something across the room.

"Can you ask the node?" Chase asked, watching the same thing.

She forced a smile and turned her attention back to the table, then glanced back again. "Um, I don't know. Maybe. Getting a straight answer out of it is harder than pinning down Aggie."

What the hell were they looking at? Liam turned around and his dinner threatened to make a reappearance, that same feeling that came over him in the courtroom pumping through his veins.

He was being challenged, and this…this he couldn't lose. He threw back his shot and stood.

Felix was by the bathroom, and some blond asshole was hitting on him.

FELIX STOOD in line waiting for his turn to use Snaps's one and only singleton bathroom. A gaggle of women had squeezed in as he was crossing the room, making him question if a clown car was on the other side of the door. He tapped his foot. At this point, if it wasn't so cold outside, he would've seriously considered watering the bushes. Frickin' winter. He resisted the urge, along with the one to lean against the sticky wall behind him and resigned himself to waiting.

The gaggle finally came out, giggling past the rest of them, and the next person went in. Felix sighed as the dulcet strains of "Feliz Navidad" kicked off. He was going to have the frickin' song stuck in his head for a week. At least the line was moving now. Only two more to—

"Felix?"

He turned at his name. A slim were beamed at him, and Felix's pulse jumped. Oh, shit. Able. He ran a hand through his shaggy blond hair and wet his lips, eyeing Felix like he hadn't eaten in weeks. Normally, he'd be happy to be on the menu, but with Liam here? Awkward, and tonight Able just wasn't doing it for him. Behind them at the bar, Peggy Sherman started whispering to Rebecca Lynn and leering in their direction. God, they were hags.

Felix made himself return Able's smile. "Hey…when did

you get back?" he asked, glancing across the dining room. Oh shit, Liam had stood up and was heading this way. Felix started to sweat.

"Just this afternoon. You're looking good." Able's teeth dimpled his lip. "You here by yourself?"

Shit, shit, shit. "Ah, no. I'm here with friends. Jena, Chase, and—"

"I've been thinking about you," Able said, stepping closer and tucking a lock of Felix's hair behind his ear. "Can I buy you a drink?"

"Actually, I'm—"

"He's here with me," Liam said, coming up behind them. Felix's heart leaped to his throat. Had Liam actually just said that? The people around them started whispering, and Peggy Sherman pulled out her phone. Had Liam seen her? Whatever was about to happen was gonna be simulcast all over town.

Able stepped back to look at him. "Damn. Where did you come from, gorgeous?"

"Eastside, and the name's Liam," he growled, pushing up his sleeves. "You mind taking your hand off my date?"

Felix almost passed out. His date. He'd called him his date!

"Oh! You two are…?" Felix somehow managed a nod, and Able took his hand from Felix's back. "Well, color me jealous. My bad. If it doesn't work out, call me. Seriously. Either one of you," he said, eye-fucking Liam as he left.

The big were ignored him, stalking to Felix. His throat bobbed, eyelids fluttering at the wave of Liam's musk enveloping him. "You do know that Peggy Sherman is right behind us and probably recording this," he said as Liam rested an arm above Felix's head, pinning him against the wall. His knees went weak. Oh, God. It wasn't fair what this man did to him.

"Good." Liam's gaze searched Felix's face, his breath

coming as fast as Felix's. "Then everyone will know you're mine."

There abruptly wasn't enough air in the room. "I-I am?"

Liam's forehead crinkled, doubt flashing across his face. His throat bobbed. "I mean, if you want?" The question tumbled out from Liam's lips, rumbly and close enough to taste the whiskey on his exhale. Their gazes locked, and the emotion in his eyes…

Felix kissed him.

Liam froze, and then kissed him back like Felix might shatter beneath his lips, softly, sweetly. Felix's hands slid up Liam's chest, and it rumbled with satisfaction, his lips becoming more insistent. Felix fisted Liam's flannel, inviting him to make the kiss deeper. Liam slid his tongue into Felix's mouth, smokey with whiskey. The barest hint of stubble rasped against his skin, and he bit back a moan, knowing the entire restaurant was watching.

And Liam was kissing him anyway. Had his tongue in his mouth, his fingers tangling in Felix's curls, and the other sliding up his back, holding him like he never wanted to let go.

Felix trembled against him, wanting that so badly, wanted so desperately to be with this man, but he didn't, he couldn't—

He choked up, and Liam broke the kiss to rest his forehead against his. "Hey, you okay?" he murmured.

Felix nodded, wiping his eyes. "Yes, I—you really mean it this time?"

"I meant it then, Felix, but now I swear to God, now I'm gonna do this right." He kissed him again—

"Get a room!" someone yelled.

"Shut up, Callaway," Jena yelled back at them.

Felix glanced over at the dining room, expecting—Yep. Everyone was watching them with expressions spanning from "duh" to "OMFG." He raised his brow at Peggy's stupid judgy face. *Try fixing this, bitch.* She scowled back, pocketing her phone.

"Um…it okay if we head out?" Liam asked, rubbing the back of his neck and nowhere near as comfortable with the attention. "Jena and Chase are calling it a night, and I can get our stuff to go."

After that kiss? Um, yes. Check please—after he peed. "Sure. I'll meet you up front." Felix scooted through the bathroom's opportunely open door, then closed it, leaning against the battered slab and waiting for the pounding of his heart to subside. He put his hand to his lips.

Had that just seriously happened?

His bladder didn't care one way or another. Felix took care of business, then flicked on the water in the sink. He washed his hands and splashed his face, the slight sting from Liam's stubble tingling around Felix's lips.

Proof he wasn't dreaming.

A stupid grin split his face ear to ear. Liam had kissed him, and he'd done it in front of the entire restaurant. God, he'd said he wanted to get this right, but, damn, if that hadn't been the grand gesture to just melt Felix's heart. He dried his hands, unable to quell his grin.

Felix opened the door and worked his way back through the whispering crowd—not smug in the absolute slightest—to where Jena, Chase, and Liam were waiting in the front.

"So, who was that guy?" Liam was asking Chase.

"Able? His mom's from the Westside pack, but when his parents got divorced, he moved to Galleon Falls with his dad until after high school. He's got a place over at the compound, but he travels for work. I think he's a medical rep or something."

"Oxygen systems," Felix clarified. "We had a casual thing." He grinned at Jena, who returned it in spades as Liam helped him into his parka. Oh, yes, a boy could definitely get used to this kind of treatment. "It was nothing serious."

Liam muttered something, and Felix's grin widened, well aware that the majority of the restaurant was still ogling them. "I think I like you jealous," he said, fiddling with Liam's jacket.

"Then I better make sure you like me more when I'm not. Otherwise, people are going to get hurt." By the look on Liam's face, he wasn't joking.

Felix had never actually swooned, but he suddenly understood the inclination.

They followed Jena and Chase outside and said their goodbyes. Liam took Felix's hand in his as they walked to the Jeep.

"I-I'm sorry I didn't tell you about my degree," he said, his palm sweaty against Felix's. "I didn't think—look, there's more stuff you should probably know before we, I mean, before you—"

Felix stopped to look at Liam, cutting him off. "Hey, there's no rush. We've got time."

He shook his head. "I'm not sure about that. Do you think it would be okay if we went back to your place and talked for a while?"

Felix's brow furrowed at the vibe Liam was giving him. Whatever he wanted to talk about, Felix had a bad feeling it wasn't an excuse to get him into bed. "Sure...right after we stop at town hall. Hopefully, that will only take a second."

"Okay, yeah. Thanks." Liam opened the passenger side door for him, and paused, chewing his lip after Felix got in. He closed the door and rounded to the other side, sitting for a moment before he started it.

Oh God, was he having second thoughts? Felix started to sweat. Liam was obviously beating himself up about something. If he changed his mind after that— "Okay, what just happened?" Felix asked, not able to stand the silence anymore.

"I-I just need to tell you some things, and I'm sorry tonight didn't go like I planned." Liam finally said.

Felix laughed. "Are you serious right now?" After that kiss? He didn't know how it could've gone any better.

Liam's cheeks flushed. "You're not mad about what happened in there?"

"Mad, no. Hard, yes." Felix fanned himself. "I'm a slut for a grand gesture, and what you did in there was huge."

Liam snorted. "It's not..." He ran a hand over his jaw, then stared at his hands, fiddling with the steering wheel. "I really like you, and I'm serious about doing this right. That's why I didn't kiss you last night. I didn't want you to think I was taking advantage of you when you were vulnerable. I asked you to trivia to prove that I'm not gonna hide how I feel anymore. All that shit I pulled in high school was wrong, Felix, and I'm so fucking sorry I hurt you."

"Hey." Felix leaned over and took the were's hands in his. "Apology accepted, and what you just did inside might cancel out standing me up at the prom. It definitely makes me inclined to let you make up the rest."

Hope lit Liam's eyes. "Yeah?"

"Yeah, now let's get going so this 'beautiful machine' warms up faster. I'm freezing."

Liam smiled and put it in gear, rounding the block to the back of town hall. "You need me to come in?"

"Nope," Felix said, rummaging around in his pockets for his keys. "I'm literally just going to open the door and holler. Be right back." He jumped out of the Jeep and jogged up the back steps to unlock the door—

"That was quick," Ophelia said. "So, did the date go really well, or did it bomb?"

Felix jumped, almost dropping his keys. "Jesus, don't do that!"

She flinched, stumbling out of the shadows. Served her right wearing those heels. They had to be six inches. "I'll think about it as soon as you stop throwing Christianity in my face. Isn't there a 'thou shalt not' about taking that dude's name in vain?" She raised her flask again, swaying.

"Are you drunk?" Was that even a thing with vampires?

She grinned. "Nope, but the cow sure was."

Cow. God, he hated that term. Why anyone would agree to sell their blood just to get slapped with a vampiric slur like that… Felix shook his head. Whatever. "Welcome to town hall," Felix grumbled, throwing the door open with a little flourish. "Come on in, and kindly lock up when you're done." He frowned as she almost turned an ankle sauntering past. Frickin' vampires…whatever.

He closed the door and got back into the Jeep. Liam was just getting off the phone.

"Everything all right?"

"Yeah," Liam said, pocketing it. "I wanted to check on the kids. My mom says they're doing fine. The girls are making ornaments and watching a movie. Axle's out with my dad in the kennel."

Felix repressed a shudder. "Well, I'm glad they haven't burned the house down yet." Thought there was still time…

"You know, I think you're wrong about Axle," Liam said, pulling out of the lot. "Weres are just built differently than witches. He needs to get out more and run around. We don't do well stuck inside."

Felix buzzed his lips, taking in all the Christmas lights as they drove. "I'm not disagreeing, but my parents aren't exactly equipped to romp around Havers with him." Neither was he. He didn't have the time or the inclination. The random hike was fine, but the kind of outdoors Liam was alluding to wasn't going to happen.

"No, I get that, but…" The were drummed his fingers against the steering wheel. "Just let me know if you want me to take him sometime."

Seriously? "You'd do that?"

Liam shrugged. "Kelsey's always getting on my case about being by myself too much. Axle's a good kid, and he says he likes cars. I'm supposed to be picking something up tomorrow. I'm not opposed to him hanging out and helping me work on it, and it's gonna take more than a day to do it."

"Well, that's certainly a step up from him decapitating gingerbread men," Felix murmured. "I hope it's in better condition than this pile was."

Liam grinned like Christmas had come early. "I'll find out tomorrow."

"Have fun with that." And speaking of tomorrow…Felix pulled out his phone and scanned the appointments Namaste Nails had open. "Beautiful," he murmured, booking three spots—no, four. Jena would want in on it, too—for late morning as they pulled into his building's parking lot. "I got us in for mani-pedis at ten."

"That'll work." Liam parked and they made their way up to Felix's apartment. Myx came out of the shadows, chittering, and Liam picked him up. Stupid cat butted the top of his head against his chin, rumbling.

"He's definitely doing that to annoy me," Felix muttered, hanging up his parka and going into the kitchen. "You want anything to drink?"

"Glass of water's fine," Liam put the cat down and shoved the to-go bag into the fridge.

"Then water it is." Felix filled up two glasses and made his way into to the living room.

LIAM SET his jacket over the back of a kitchen chair and trailed after Felix feeling like he was on his way to the gallows. Damn it, he didn't want to do this, but after seeing the way Felix had looked at him in the Jeep when he'd found out about his law degree—Liam needed to come clean, especially if Felix was serious about wanting them to be together, too.

Myx twined around his ankles, and Liam picked the cat up before he sent him sprawling. Felix sat at one end of the couch, and Liam perched on the other. Myx started making biscuits in his lap, and Felix looked at the two of them like he was about to witness an axe murder.

"So, what did you want to talk about?" Felix asked, pulling a pillow against himself as if it would protect him from the fallout.

Liam smiled despite what he was about to spill. *Right, focus, Liam.* He blew out a breath, unable to meet Felix's eyes. *The beginning. Start at the beginning or the rest won't make sense.* "I-I need to tell you why—prom." he blurted, wincing at the scowl that flitted across Felix's lips. Shit. He probably should've expected that reaction, but…*Christ. Here goes.*

"After you left, I was a mess. The only reason I'd hooked up with Jenny was because I couldn't take alpha without having a kid—a son—and she said she'd be like a surrogate. I thought the three of us…" He shook his head. "I was wrong." *About so fucking much.*

Felix gasped. "Are you serious? *That's* why you were with her?" He pinched the bridge of his nose. "Why wouldn't you talk to me about something like that?"

"I don't—I don't think it ever occurred to me," Liam said, still kicking himself about it. "Though it was crystal clear after the fact that I should've. A couple of weeks later, I found out Jenny was pregnant. I had to do the right thing, or what I thought was the right thing, but it wasn't."

Felix's brows knit. "Wait, you said you were wrong. Your pack will let you take alpha without an heir?"

Liam snorted. "No, that's never going to change, but I was wrong about it being what my parents—what everyone— wanted. The other day," he shook his head and scratched behind Myx's ears, still having trouble wrapping his mind around that conversation with his parents. "They don't care, Felix. All that legacy shit that's been eating at me...they said they don't want me shoehorning myself into a position just to suit convention if it's going to make me miserable."

Felix snorted. "Might've been nice to know that a decade or so ago."

"Yeah, I guess, but were culture..." Even if he had known, it probably wouldn't have made a difference. Not enough at least. He shrugged; there was too much there to unpack. "All I ever wanted to do was fix cars, but after Sarah was born, Jenny—she changed. She started pushing me to be more, throwing everything the Westside pack was doing in my face. That stupid competitive part of me—that's why I went into law."

"Please tell me Patrick Montgomery wasn't your *beau ideal*."

"What? No. But the fact that they had a pack lawyer and we didn't was a sore subject." Liam leaned forward to take a sip of his water, kicking himself all over again. All of it seemed so goddamned petty now, and look where trying to keep up with the Westside Montgomerys had gotten them.

He sighed, sitting back. "At first, it wasn't so bad. It gave me something to focus on. I wasn't real great with my meds back then." He ran a hand over his face and shook his head. "I dunno. I guess I thought not taking them helped, you know, hyper-focusing on shit, and it kind of did for a while. I got accepted into an accelerated program. The commute cut into that, and I decided to stay out in Klineville and come home on the weekends. I knew Jenny was messing around with a couple of different guys, but she seemed happy, so I didn't really care, and I agreed to an open marriage when she floated the idea."

Felix pursed his lips. "I heard Miranda say something about that the other day, but she seemed to think it was because Jenny found out you were quote unquote 'into men.'"

Liam rolled his eyes. "Jenny knew I went both ways from the beginning, but at that point, I knew I'd made a huge mistake. I was just going through the motions with her, and she knew it. We started going to a marriage counselor, and that led to me to individual therapy. They put me back on a bunch of meds, and I started seeing the bigger picture again. Jenny's main complaint was 'lack of intimacy.' She didn't feel treasured, and she wasn't wrong. And I felt like shit about it." He paused, running his fingers through Myx's fur. Wondering how much of what she'd said during those sessions was real, and how much of it had been just to string him along. Fucking hindsight.

"So, what happened next?" Felix prompted after Liam had been silent for several minutes.

"I graduated and started working. Things were okay for a while. I was home more, bringing in a bigger check. Made a real effort to be more attentive. Then she got pregnant with the twins. It wasn't out of the realm of possibilities that they were mine, but the youngest..." He shook his head. "At that point, I knew she was still messing around. Pete wasn't exactly circumspect, and I hadn't touched her in months."

"What did you do?"

Liam looked up at him. "Nothing. And yeah, looking back, I probably should've divorced her then. At that point, I didn't like her very much, and I've always hated Pete, but I loved the kids. Loved being a dad. The thought of losing them—I couldn't do it, Felix...and then I got a job offer. A big firm out in Los Huego had read some of the briefs I'd prepared and wanted me to work for them."

"Holy crap," Felix's eyes went wide. "You were all the way out there? That's on the other side of the country." He squeezed the pillow and tucked his stocking feet up under him, rapt.

"Yeah. That's what I said. It was too far, too much hassle, but it was a shit ton of money. I'd make more out there in a month than I would here in a year. Jenny found out about the offer and freaked out. She said…" Liam ran a hand over his jaw and closed his eyes, every word that'd come out of her mouth still living in his head. His throat bobbed. "She said a lot of shit she can't take back. We got into it, and I ended up taking the job."

"I don't get it." Felix's brows pinched together. "That meant you'd be away from the kids, which was the whole reason you hadn't left her skank-ass."

Liam nodded, watching his fingers ripple through Myx's fur. "I know, but it was supposed to be temporary to pay off the mortgage and my school loans. We had it worked out where I'd video chat with them before bed every night, fly back for holidays…except somehow that never ended up happening." And then he'd stopped taking his meds again, and everything had begun to spiral.

"Jesus, Liam, that's terrible."

He shrugged, remembering how he'd blindly accepted all of Jenny's excuses just made him feel worse. "Los Huego was okay. The firm was one of those big West Coast ones. I focused on the job…you know how I get. I wanted to prove… shit, it's stupid now, but after everything Jenny said, I wanted to prove I wasn't the fuck-up she thought I was. After about a month, the firm started grooming me toward becoming a trial lawyer."

"That's huge. You must've been really good at what you did."

He had been, but…Liam looked down at his hands. "Those last two years out there…" He shook his head. "The firm didn't represent the best people, and I didn't care."

Felix was silent at the admission, and Liam took another deep breath before he continued.

"Then I got a certified letter from the bank telling me the

house was going into foreclosure. Felix, aside from what I needed to live out there, I'd been sending every fucking penny I'd been making home. Hundreds of thousands of dollars. Come to find out, it was all gone, and she'd taken out two massive loans in my name. I was out there, away from my kids, selling my soul, and for what? I cut her off. Two weeks later, I was served with divorce papers, and she was going for full custody."

"Holy shit. What do you think she did with all that money?"

"No idea, and she freaks out whenever I mention it."

Felix snorted. "Um yeah, and rightfully so."

"Right? I don't care about the money. I mean, I do, but I care about the kids more, and the threat of losing Sarah set me off. I lost it. Made some bad decisions. Got rip-shit drunk, ran my mouth, started a fight in some bar. The pack out there, I had a temporary stay to be in their territory. When they showed up to handle the situation, I-I almost killed their beta. One of their members knew what was going on back in Havers. He convinced them to let me walk, but I had to do it then and there. I couldn't even grab a change of clothes from the apartment I'd rented."

Felix went pale. "You must've really messed him up."

Liam ran a hand over his mouth. "It wasn't...it wasn't good, and it gets worse. I was scheduled to be in court the next day. I was co-counsel on a case for the vampire court. They ended up losing, and that prince, Kremlyn? His brother's in jail because of me."

Felix just stared at him, and Liam regretted every bite of dinner churning around in his stomach, afraid it was going to come out with the rest of what he had to say. Before he totally chickened out, he swallowed raggedly and spat out the rest of his story.

"I can't represent Havers because they slapped me with gross neglect for abandoning the case, and my license has been suspended." Liam hung his head and chewed his lip. "I haven't told anyone else that. My parents and Kelsey know about the fight, but not about the rest of it. They don't know about the money, either."

"I can't even," Felix said, a hand over his mouth and his eyes wide. "How could she—what are you going to do?"

Liam sat back against the couch cushions with his glass of water. "I dunno. I've been waiting to get the results of Sarah's test before I figure it out. I just...I don't understand how it got so fucked up, Felix. Jenny...she wasn't a bad person. I still don't think she is, but I don't understand what happened to her."

"Sounds like Pete happened, and this is just as much on her for staying with him and co-signing his bullshit." Felix picked at a corner of the pillow. "I know you're worried about what will happen to the kids, but believe me when I say, sometimes they're better off without. Lord knows the urchins don't need to be living in a brothel somewhere out in Nevar right now."

Liam spat out a mouthful of water. "Is *that* where your sister ended up?"

Felix grunted with a little shrug. "Reading between the lines, it's firmly within the realm of possibilities. The last motel she had them in wasn't far off."

"Are you kidding me?"

"Nope," he said, popping the P. "As awful as it is to say, they really are better off without her." He glanced up at Liam through his curls. "And I have a feeling it's going to be a similar situation over on McDermott. When I called CPS earlier today, I got the distinct impression I wasn't the first person to have dropped a dime on Pete."

"Great." Liam clenched his jaw, then ran a hand over it, taking a deep breath—simultaneously feeling like shit and somehow better that Felix knew about all the baggage he was hauling around. Well, almost all of it. "There's one last thing I need to tell you."

"If it has to do with you lobotomizing my cat, I'm already aware," Felix said, frowning at Myx flopped across Liam's lap, while he absently rubbed the feline's belly. "If I tried to do that, I'd lose a hand."

Liam grinned at him. "I told you: he likes me."

Felix rolled his eyes. "That's apparent. Okay, so what's this last thing?"

"You know that after Samhain, I ended up in the psych ward for a couple of weeks. I'm better, but my mental health isn't great," he said, focusing on the cat instead of Felix. "I'm sticking to my med schedule and meeting with my therapist like I'm supposed to. This project I'm picking up tomorrow—I'm hoping that's going to help, too, but if I—if I disappear, you know, go dark on you…it's not because I don't want to be with you. I just get stuck in my head, and sometimes it's hard to come back out."

The couch cushions shifted, and Felix moved beside him. "Hey. Samhain screwed all of us up. I still have nightmares about what they did to you along with everything else that happened. Not for nothing, but you were lucky you missed the lion's share of what went on in that circle. If you need time, just let me know. I get it."

"Yeah?" Liam looked up at him, fighting back tears.

"Yes." Felix kissed him softly. "We're doing this right this time, right?"

Liam nodded, sniffling and took his hand in his. "God, I hope so. You really think we sounded like an old married couple at Snaps?"

"I resent being called an old anything, but yes, and for you, I'll do my best not to take offense." Felix's lips quirked. "That said, we should probably go get 'our' kids."

Liam laughed as he moved Myx off his lap and stood with

Felix, still holding his hand, and really liking the sound of that.

FELIX SAT in the passenger seat of Liam's Jeep as they drove back to the house with another platter of baked goods on his lap. The urchins were passed out in the back, and the distinct scent of dog tickled Felix's nostrils. He sniffed, weighing the merits of making Axle take a shower when he got back home versus letting him stink up his sheets.

Felix sighed. Whatever. They probably needed to be washed anyway.

Everything that Liam had said tumbled around in Felix's brain. He was still unable to process what a shit show the were had been dealing with. How the man could show up every day with a smile on his face and pitch in to help Felix with the magnitude of his own problems weighing on him was mind-boggling.

It was also absolutely infuriating that Jenny and Pete had treated Liam as badly as they had. The small hairs on Felix's arms rose with his temper, and he made a concerted effort to release the karma that was gathering around him. Those two had plenty of negative energy coming their way. He didn't need to accrue any of his own on their account, though he wouldn't say no to being the vehicle that dealt it out.

Any latent guilt Felix may have felt at making that call to child protection services had definitely left the building.

"What do you think about me picking up Axle around

eight?" Liam asked softly, glancing in the rearview mirror. "Is that too early? I want to hit the hardware store and my storage unit before I head over to Jerry's."

"Sounds fine to me, but you're sure it's not too much taking him?"

"No. I told you I want to. I really like kids and did you see the smile on his face when we picked him up? Hanging out at the compound is good for him, and my dad said he was a marvel with the pups. Worst case, if I get overwhelmed, Axle can help out with them. My parents loved having the kids there. I can't remember the last time my mom was so happy… it really messed with her when Jenny stopped letting them go over there."

Felix wasn't entirely sure what to make of that, but he wasn't going to argue. Liam wasn't exaggerating about his parents' enthusiasm; his mom had practically begged to watch them again. "Well, then I suspect you'll have to ask me on another date just to make everyone happy."

Liam grinned, taking Felix's hand. He'd been doing that a lot since they'd talked, like he needed to reassure himself that Felix wasn't going anywhere. The quiet show of vulnerability made Felix's heart melt.

"I've already got a place in mind," Liam said, "but it'll require an overnight trip. Not that my parents would be opposed to taking them again, but have you heard anything from yours?"

Felix sighed. Yes, and it hadn't been very encouraging. "Aunt Helen's surgery went as well as could be expected, but the woman's like ninety-three years old, and they ended up admitting her to the ICU. Something about her blood pressure bottoming out, and her being delirious. She didn't recognize my mom and got really agitated. The nurses ended up asking her to leave."

"Ouch." Liam winced. "That's tough."

Felix grunted. It was, and his mother wasn't dealing with

it well. She'd grown up in Maybach, and after her dad had been killed in the Purge, Helen had helped raise her. "They're keeping her there until they can get her stabilized. In the meantime, my mom's been stress-cleaning Aunt Helen's house. You know she has thirty-six cats?" And those had just been the ones his mom had seen.

"You're kidding. *Thirty-six?*" Liam asked, pulling into the driveway.

"Yep, and every last one of them needs to be re-homed. I guess she's talking to a rescue out there about it." And delirious or not, Aunt Helen was going to be devastated when she found out. His mom was terrified the shock of it would kill the old woman, but there wasn't any other option. Most residences didn't allow one pet, never mind thirty-six of them, and claiming they were all her familiars wasn't going to fly.

"That's...wow. How's your dad holding up? He's got the littlest right?"

"All day, every day. My mom didn't say much about that, but I'm anticipating he'll come back completely deaf and have developed a tic," Felix said, getting out of the Jeep.

He flipped up the seat and pulled Sway's comatose little body into his arms. She was completely out. Cruze woke up as her sister's weight left her shoulder. "Hey, grab that plate for me," he whispered as she groggily slipped from the Jeep. She snagged the mound of baked goods on autopilot and stumbled to the back door, unlocking it.

Liam hefted up Axle, and they all followed Cruze inside. Felix brought Sway upstairs. He tugged off her sneakers and jacket before tucking her in. *Mental note, send them to Liam's parents with their pajamas next time.* Not that Felix hadn't slept in his clothes recently, but his hadn't been covered in glitter glue.

She snuggled down into her blankets, and he stood there for a moment, watching the slow rise and fall of her tiny shoulders. An odd feeling had begun in his gut, and the low rumble of Liam's voice from the room below compounded it. Axle must've woken up. Felix ran a hand over his stomach, trying to dispel the weird sense of longing.

He backed out of the room and knocked softly on Cruze's door before cracking it open. All he could see of her was a mound of blankets.

"Good night," he called in.

She muttered something back, rolling over, and he closed her door.

Shit, should he have made them brush their teeth or something? Felix shook his head. Whatever. They still had the ones that were going to fall out, right? At least the little ones did. Cruze was probably about ready for braces. His footsteps slowed as he went downstairs. Yet another expense his parents weren't going to be able to afford, but would find a way to pay for anyway. *Damn it, Felicia.*

Felix got to the first floor and meandered toward the sound of Liam's voice. Axle had been sleeping on the ratty couch in the converted den. Originally, it had been a screened-in porch they'd retrofitted—poorly. The cramped space was at least ten degrees colder than the rest of the house. When Felix's dad had still been working as an accountant, the little room had been organized within an inch of its life. Now it was a catch-all for whatever didn't fit somewhere else, and most of it was crammed full of unidentified junk. The poor kid barely had room to change his clothes, and those were heaped into milk crates balanced on the couch's arm against the faux-wood paneled wall.

Felix stopped just outside the doorway. Liam sat at the edge of the blanket-mounded couch, tucking Axle in. Felix frowned at the chill in the air. How the heck was this going to work on a permanent basis?

"...tomorrow. Think you can be ready that early?" Liam was saying. The top of Axle's head bobbed, and Liam grinned, ruffling the boy's hair. "Cool. I'll see you then. Now get some sleep."

Liam stood and came out into the hall, leaving the door cracked behind him.

"You're really good with him," Felix said as they walked back to the kitchen. "Thank you again for offering to take him tomorrow."

"Yeah, like I said, it's no problem." Liam stopped by the kitchen table and jammed his hands into his pockets. He chewed his lip, then looked at Felix through a fall of wavy hair. "Have you ever thought about it? You taking them instead of your parents?"

Felix went to say no, and the word died on his tongue. He reached out, fixing Liam's collar. "I'd be lying if I said it hadn't crossed my mind, but I don't see how it would work. The logistics alone are daunting." No way would all of them fit in his apartment, and that wasn't even taking the screamer into account. His neighbors would murder him.

Liam nodded, then looked down, their toes almost touching. "Yeah, it's a lot."

Silence thickened between them.

"So, I'll see you tomorrow at eight?" Felix asked.

Liam raised his head, and kissed him.

Softy, then insistent. Lips, tongue, and teeth, his mouth fed on Felix's. He gasped, tangling his fingers in Liam's hair, fisting his shirt. A sudden desperate need rolled over him, all the emotion from the past few days—God, he just needed to be touched. To be held. For someone else to make all the decisions.

A chair clattered against the table as Liam walked him backwards, pressing him against the kitchen counter. His hips ground against Felix's, and his cock went rigid. Oh God...he needed this man like his next breath.

"I'd rather see all of you now," Liam rumbled, his lips trailing over Felix's jaw, working to his throat. "Let me take care of you, please? You work so hard, I want to make you feel good."

Liam's hand slid to the bulge in Felix's slacks, tracing the outline of his rigid cock before lightly pinching his tip. Felix whimpered, sure the were could feel how wet he was through the thin fabric.

"Mmm. Please, baby?" Liam murmured, nuzzling Felix's ear.

"Not here," he panted, pushing Liam back and taking his hand to lead him into the small space that acted as a laundry room and overflow pantry adjoining the kitchen. They closed the door. Liam's mouth found his again. He pushed Felix against the wall, the sundries on the shelves beside him rattling at the impact. His hands were on Liam's belt, then slipped inside his briefs.

He slid his fingers around Liam's throbbing cock, and Liam groaned into Felix's mouth. Jesus, had he always been this big? Liam's breath sped as Felix stroked him, root to tip, his palm slick with pre-cum, his own cock aching.

"You going to come for me already?" Felix teased as Liam's dick kicked in his grip.

"No. Not until you do." And then he was on his knees. He unbuttoned Felix's pants and groaned as they fell to his ankles. "You weren't joking," he murmured, lightly nuzzling against Felix's thong. "Do you need me to kiss you under the mistletoe, baby?" He flattened his tongue, running it over the wet spot, then suckling.

Felix's mind blanked, and Liam chuckled. He slid his hands up Felix's thighs, beneath the fabric and slowly pulled it down to bury his face against Felix's groin, inhaling against the mound of strawberry curls, then kissing and licking around the base of his cock.

Felix's eyes rolled back in his head. Sweet Jesus, how many times had he jerked off to a fantasy like this? His pulse raced as Liam slowly worked his lips along Felix's rigid shaft to its weeping tip, lapping pre-cum from its slit with a low groan.

"You taste so damn good. Be a good boy and come in my mouth."

"Yes, Daddy," Felix gasped, fisting Liam's hair as the were swallowed him. Wet, velvet heat enveloped his cock, and Felix's eyelids fluttered, his knees going weak, the sensation shorting out all rational thought. He fell back against the wall, canned goods crashing to the floor. Liam bobbed against him, meeting his eyes as he took him deeper. He moaned around Felix's dick as it kicked to the top of his mouth with another burst of pre-cum.

Liam wrapped his hand around the base, his tongue flattening, then swirling around the tip, sucking—

Felix's vision began to tunnel, his aching balls tightening and drawing up. "You keep doing that, and I'm going to come," he panted raggedly.

Liam pulled off him with another low chuckle, sweeping his tongue up the underside. Felix's toes curled, and he fought for breath. "Not yet, I want to make sure it's more than a mouthful," he rumbled.

That wasn't going to be an issue.

Liam laved down Felix's dick, lapping at his sac and gently drew his balls into his mouth, saliva dripping. He hummed and pulled back, sweeping a finger through the wetness and running it down Felix's taint to his pucker. His knees buckled, widening his stance to give Liam what they both wanted. Felix gasped at the slow swirl and burn of Liam's finger penetrating him, pressing inward and curving to caress his gland. His mouth teased the tip of Felix's dick, tracing his slit, his crown, then swallowed him, bobbing—

Felix's hands slapped against the wall, his back arching. Stars exploded across his vision, ecstasy blanking out every other sensation save for the intensity of his orgasm. It pulsed through him, long ropes of cum spurting, filling Liam's mouth. The were moaned, sucking down every drop, then lapping at him, slowly removing his finger. He dipped his head and licked over the stretched ring of muscle, the pressure from his tongue electrifying the sensitive nerve endings and shooting waves of pleasure through Felix. He spasmed again, slipping down the wall. Liam grinned and glanced at a bottle of olive oil on the pantry shelf.

"My turn. You ready for me, baby?"

LIAM LICKED the salty tang of Felix's cum from his lips. The warlock had collapsed against the wall, his pants pooled around his ankles and his cheeks flushed. His cock lay against his thigh and twitched at the question. Jesus, he was fucking sexy. Liam leaned over and kissed him.

Felix groaned, sweeping his tongue through Liam's mouth. "You want to fuck me?" he murmured all coy, his palm stroking over Liam's dripping tip.

"So damn bad," Liam groaned, his hips moving of their own accord. "And I'm gonna breed you when I do. I want to see my cum dripping out of your pretty little hole." He reached up and grabbed the bottle of olive oil. "Bend over, now."

Felix shivered, and his cock twitched again, coming to attention. "Yes, Daddy." He positioned himself onto his knees and dropped to his forearms.

Liam's breath caught at the two perfect globes and Felix's pucker winking between them. He smoothed a hand over the warlock's ass. "Goddamn, you're perfect," Liam murmured, opening the bottle of olive oil and drizzling a small stream down Felix's crack.

He flinched. "Cold!"

"It'll get warmer," Liam murmured, running a finger over the ring of tissue, reddened from his earlier intrusion. Jesus, that was hot. His dick throbbed, dripping pre-cum. The need to claim Felix, to fill him with his seed and make him his was doing fucked up things to Liam and his inner wolf. Saliva filled his mouth, the urge to bite him intense. *No. Not yet.* Oil pooled, and he slipped one finger inside Felix's pucker, then two, his breath speeding as it sucked him in, so damn tight around him. Felix moaned, rocking them deeper.

"Stroke your cock while I get you ready to take my mine." He cupped Felix's balls with his free hand, gently caressing them as his fingers pumped inside the warlock's ass, the heat of Liam's anticipation making his head go light. Felix moaned, pressing farther back. "Good boy," Liam murmured. "Loosen up for me."

Felix whimpered again, the sound going straight to Liam's dick. It bobbed, weeping, its head an angry purple. Liam drizzled more oil onto Felix's pucker, then slicked himself between Felix's cheeks with a low moan. Christ, he wasn't gonna last.

He spread Felix's knees farther apart with his and set his fat crown against Felix's hole. His breath sped, watching Felix's flesh part to take his, clamping down around him—so fucking tight—

"Oh God," Felix panted, pressing back against him. "Yes, just like that…more…"

Liam slid deeper, trying to slow his stuttered breath. He spread Felix's cheeks farther apart, and the warlock whimpered. "Shh…you can take it, almost there," he murmured as his pubes ground against the cleft between Felix's cheeks. "Goddamn, you feel amazing." It was more than amazing. It was where he belonged. Liam slowly began to slide his dick in and out of Felix's asshole, subtle ridges rubbing against Liam's engorged length, griping him tight—

Felix groaned, rising up to slap a hand against the washer. "Jesus, Liam, stop teasing and fuck me."

"Yeah? You want it harder?" he asked, thrusting.

"Yes. Oh God, yes, more—"

Liam drove into him, flesh slapping, his sac bouncing against Felix's. He pulled the warlock against him, fumbling up under his shirt, and groaning at the crinkle of Felix's chest hair beneath his palm. His fingers found the pearled tip of the warlock's nipple and pinched it.

Felix cried out.

"Mmm. You like that?" Liam rumbled against his neck. He sure as fuck did. His fangs extended, lightly scoring the warlock's flesh. Holy hell, the temptation. The urge to bite him, to claim him—

"Oh, sweet God, yes," Felix gasped, offering up his throat.

Liam's pace faltered, shocked. "Y-you *want* me to bite you?" Was he kidding?

Silence descended between them.

"T-that means I'm yours, right? And you can't take it back?" Felix glanced over his shoulder, insecurity etched across his face.

"It does. And I won't ever. I swear it, Felix. I want this. Us. I more than really like you, I-I love you, I always have." Liam kissed him, tenderly, desperately, trying to put all the things he couldn't articulate into it. Jesus, he'd fight for this man, take care of him until his dying breath. Felix was all that he wanted, all he'd ever wanted, he'd just been too stupid, too scared, but— "You want that? Even after everything I told you?"

"Liam, I want that *because* of everything you told me. I-I've always loved you, even when I hated you, and we've wasted enough time."

Warmth bubbled up, filling Liam's chest and rising to choke him. He blinked away tears. His hand strayed down to stroke Felix's rigid cock, moaning at the smooth slide of skin over its iron length. "Then let's start making up for what we lost. I need you to come for me when I claim you."

"Not an issue," Felix groaned, his hips rocking, pumping his dick into Liam's fist.

His inner wolf howled, the little room thick with pheromones.

Liam began to move again, the slow slide of his cock a building tempo, their tongues tangling. Felix's dick wept, crying for release. He whimpered and gasped, turning away, palms flat against the washer. Liam stroked him harder, his grip rough.

"Oh God, please…"

"Come for me, baby." Liam nuzzled at his neck, breath ragged, trying to hold back his own orgasm. Searching for the right angle until Felix cried out, Liam's dick sweeping across the warlock's gland with every thrust. Felix's cock grew harder, pulsing in Liam's fist as he pumped it. His own cock throbbed, painfully hard, Felix's tight walls pulling at him, taking him deep.

"Liam, I'm gonna—" Felix's asshole clenched, and hot cum spurted over Liam's knuckles. He sank his fangs into the warlock's shoulder with a sob as his own pleasure took him, his balls drawing up and heat zinging from the base of his spine to the top of his head, the room washed in white with an influx of euphoria—

Liam's eyes went wide as the base of his cock expanded, and his orgasm intensified, rolling through him like an echo. Beneath him, Felix came again, searing bursts of cum spattering to the floor. They fell against the washer with a loud clang, panting.

"What in the actual fuck?"

Liam swallowed raggedly, pushing up off the warlock, and stared down at where their bodies were connected, speechless for a moment. "Holy shit. I think I knotted you."

"What do you mean 'you think?' It feels like you just shoved an apple up my ass!"

"I mean, it's never happened before." Liam laughed,

running a hand over his face. "I guess my wolf approves of you being my mate. Give it a sec, it's supposed to go down after a couple minutes."

"What?! A couple—"

There was a knock on the door, and they froze. "Uncle Felix?" Sway's voice trembled.

Felix and Liam stared at each other, wide-eyed. "Um… yes?"

"Are you okay?" The doorknob rattled, and Liam flailed back to hold it shut. "I thought I heard fighting."

"No, nope, no fighting," Felix squirmed, but the knot wasn't going anywhere yet. Liam bit back a moan. That wasn't gonna make it go down any faster. "Just, um, cleaning some pipes."

The fuck?! Liam slapped a hand over his mouth, his shoulder shaking, and Felix gave him a dirty look. Yeah, that didn't help, considering he was still on hands and knees with Liam's dick knotted in his ass.

"Oh. Is Liam in there with you? Can I help?"

Abject horror flashed across Felix's face. "No! Um, I mean, um, yes, he is, but it's really filthy in here, and we're almost done. You should go back to bed. We have a big day ahead of us."

"Can I have cereal for breakfast?" she asked, her slippered foot toeing at the crack beneath the door.

"All the cereal you want. Now bed, hurry, shoo, Santa's watching."

The last sent her scampering, and Liam fought not to burst out laughing. "God, I hope not. He'd probably have a coronary if he saw this."

"Forget him," Felix snorted. "I almost had a coronary just now, and I can't see anything."

"It's a really nice visual," Liam murmured, running his hand over Felix's fuzzy cheeks as the knot slowly started to abate.

Felix opened his mouth like he was going to say something and then closed it again. Liam cocked a brow, and the warlock huffed. "You've really never knotted someone before?"

"Nope." Liam shook his head as he slipped free. He grabbed something out of the hamper to clean up. "I haven't left my bite on anyone either. Trust me, it was cited more than once as proof positive of my 'lack of intimacy,' but knotting isn't something weres can control. It's all my wolf, and he just claimed you as his mate as much as me biting you did. You're mine now, Felix, for better or for worse."

Felix dropped the cloth he'd been cleaning up with and put a hand to the two tiny puncture wounds. They'd already scabbed over. "So, you're telling me that in were culture, we just got married fucking on my parents' laundry room floor?"

Liam grinned at him and tossed the bundle of sticky fabric into the washer. "That's exactly what I'm saying."

Felix huffed. "Well then, you better come upstairs and clean up with me. I'm not enough of a deviant to have sex in my parents' bed, but there's no way I'm spending my wedding night alone."

"Are you asking me to stay over and cuddle?" Liam grinned, standing to pull on his pants.

"No, I'm telling you," Felix said, doing the same.

"Then that's what I'll do." Liam pulled him close and kissed him. "I love you, Felix Simms. From here on out, whatever you want, if I can give it to you, it's yours."

"Lucky for you it's a short list. Shower, cuddle, and make me some of that coffee tomorrow morning." He huffed softly and looked up at him, his expression so vulnerable Liam's chest ached. "You're really serious about this?"

"Yeah. You're mine, Felix. There's no undoing what just happened."

The warlock smiled coyly. "Good. Because I love you, too,

Liam Montgomery, and if you ever break my heart again, I'll have Matilda turn you into a frog and feed you to Chambers."

"Before or after Jena makes my scrotum into a coin purse?"

"She threatened you?" Felix grinned at Liam's nod. "Nice. She would definitely get first dibs."

"I'll keep that in mind." Liam kissed his forehead. "And if I ever do anything to hurt you, I'll offer it up myself, but right now, that shower sounds awfully good." He cupped Felix's rear and pressed his hardening length against the warlock's belly. "And I promise I'll make it feel even better."

Felix grinned as he took Liam's hand and led him upstairs.

Chapter Sixteen

FELIX SAT at the breakfast table nursing a cup of coffee. It was the ass crack of dawn, but Liam had wanted to talk to his father before he headed out for the day. Something about informing the alpha of the pack about taking a mate. Were culture made Felix's head ache, but the rest of last night made it spin. It'd been like some weird fairy tale come true.

Liam was his husband.

How was that possible? If he wasn't so deliciously sore, he'd think he dreamt it. And good lord, was he sore. A smirk slid over Felix's lips. He might not be enough of a deviant to have sex in his parents' bed, but apparently that hang-up didn't translate to their shower. Whoops.

He made a mental note to scrub it down before they came home, which by the voice message waiting for him this morning, would be sooner than he'd thought. His mother had called late last night to tell him that Aunt Helen had passed. They were staying one more day to finalize arrangements for her and the cats, then would be back tomorrow in time for the Yule ceremony. Settling Aunt Helen's estate would wait until after the holidays.

Felix ran his thumb over the handle of his coffee mug, staring into the living room at the long brick mantle. Dollar store stockings for the urchins hung beside the older, church craft fair ones for Felix and his sister.

Fucking Felicia.

He sighed, taking another sip of coffee, his thoughts going back to last night, to all of the pillow talk he and Liam had shared. Where they would live. How they were going to tell their families. Liam's hopes and dreams if he got custody of Sarah. Felix chewed his lip. The plan right now was for Liam to move into Felix's apartment, but if he got custody, they'd need something bigger.

How much bigger had been on both of their minds.

Wrapping his head around being someone's stepfather was surreal enough, but the rest of it...Felix scrubbed his hands over his face. God, somewhere along the line he'd definitely fallen into an alternate reality where everything was moving at the speed of light. If someone had told him four days ago that he'd be mated to Liam and have a ready-made family waiting in the wings, he would've laughed in their face.

He didn't know when his mindset done a one-eighty about the urchins not being his responsibility, but that was where he was at. Felix's gaze slid to the kitchen, taking in all the wear and clutter. The bills on the fridge, too many of them stamped overdue. Granted, the situation here wasn't tenable, but would it be if he stepped in? He wasn't hurting for cash now, but he would be with four additional mouths to feed. And, despite Liam's assurances of support, after everything he'd gone through, Felix was hesitant to take him up on that.

He sighed, falling back against the chair. His parents wouldn't be home until tomorrow, and even then, he still had time to think, but it weighed on him.

Footsteps thumped down the stairs, and Sway plodded into the kitchen with Cruze behind her. Felix's brow rose at the tween's early appearance. He'd figured he'd need to pry her out of bed with a crowbar.

"Good morning," he said as Sway scaled the counter like some bizarre red-headed lemur and rummaged for her cereal in a cabinet. "You're up early. Make sure you brush your teeth after breakfast—you both skipped it last night."

She shot him a venomous look as she hopped down and poured a heaping bowl of tiny marshmallows with maybe three flakes of what he'd actually consider grains.

"More like we didn't sleep," Cruze muttered, shoving slices of bread into the toaster.

"Yeah." Sway pouted at him from beneath furrowed brows, her hands on her hips. "You clean pipes really loud, Uncle Felix."

Felix almost choked on his coffee. Shit. Probably shouldn't have made that quip when she'd interrupted them last night. He swallowed with difficulty. "Oh?"

"Oh." Cruze glared at him. "Is Liam still here or did he leave?"

Felix debated playing dumb for all of three seconds. "He went home a while ago, but will be back to take Axle out with him."

She slammed the lever on the toaster down, and Felix's brow rose.

"Is that a problem?"

"Yeah," Cruze said, spinning on him. "Sarah's already pissed at me because he's been here so much and that I got to spend time with her grandparents. She's gonna freak out when she finds out you two are f—dating," she quickly amended, going beet red.

"Uncle Felix is *dating* Liam?" Sway squealed, splashing as much milk onto the table as her cereal.

"You are?" Axle asked, shuffling into the kitchen and grabbing a bowl. "Cool. Does that mean we get to spend more time with him? Liam's awesome, and I wanna go play with those dogs again."

Felix pinched the bridge of his nose. This wasn't exactly how he planned on broaching the subject, but— "Yes. Liam and I are together, but I'm not sure about the rest. Aunt Helen passed last night, and Gran and Gramps will be home tomorrow."

Cruze's toast popped up in the ensuing silence.

"Then things will go back to how they were," she said after a long moment.

"I don't want them to!" Axle yelled, dashing his bowl onto the floor and storming out of the room. Sway burst into tears and scrambled into Felix's lap.

He stared at the mess as she sobbed against his neck. What the fuck just happened? His eyes flicked to Cruze, and she scowled at him, her hands fisting at her sides.

"You're just like *her*. You pretend to be all nice and then leave."

Then she was gone, stomping up the steps before he could even open his mouth.

"Please don't leave, Uncle Felix," Sway sobbed, clutching at him.

"What? No." He smoothed her hair, an awful, sick feeling in the pit of his stomach. God, was Cruze right? When he'd first gotten here, leaving was exactly what he'd planned on doing. Suffering through this, then getting back to his life as soon as their car pulled into the driveway. He put his nose to Sway's frizzy curls, trying to remember why. He had a job he hated, a cat that thought he was a pet, and spent most of his time waiting for either Jena to call or Able to wander back into town.

It suddenly seemed so empty.

His arms tightened around Sway. "No. I'm not going anywhere. Come on, we need to go talk to your brother and sister." Felix scooted her off his lap and stood. He took her by the hand, going into the living room. "Cruze! Axle! Get in here. I need to speak with you both. I-it's important."

Axle stomped in and flopped onto the ratty Berber couch, his arms crossed over his chest. His eyes were red from crying. Sway went over and sat beside him, hugging his arm.

Through the front window, Felix caught a glimpse of Liam's Jeep pulling into the driveway. Good. He should probably be here for this, too.

"Cruze!" Felix yelled again. "Seriously! We need to talk, and I only want to say this once."

Another minute passed before she huffed to the top of the steps and sat. "What?"

Felix's eyelids fluttered. Jesus Christ, he couldn't believe he was going to do this. "Look, I'm not saying you were wrong about my intentions when I first got here, but your mom filing papers changes things. Gran and Gramps aren't exactly young, and I'm sure you know money around here is tight. I'm not—I can't make any promises, but I'm planning on being around more, okay?"

"With Liam?" Axle asked, his eyes on the were as he stepped into the room behind Felix.

"They know we're together," Felix said, sensing his hesitation.

"Oh. Um, then yeah. I told your uncle I was hoping you could help me with a bunch of stuff out at the compound, and I am going to come to the pageant tomorrow, if that's still okay with you?" he asked Cruze.

"Whatever," she muttered, disappearing back into her room.

Liam looked at Felix. "Do I wanna know?"

He rolled his eyes. "She's pissed because Sarah's mad at her for spending time with you and your parents."

"Oh. Yeah, I guess I can see that," he said, stoic for a moment before a smile bloomed over his face. "But that means she does want to see me."

Felix's heart swelled at the hope on Liam's face. "It certainly sounds like it...how did it go at the compound?"

His smile bloomed into a full-out grin. "Really well. My mom wants everyone to come over tonight for Yule's Eve dinner to celebrate—I mean, if you guys don't have any other plans? We can ask Jena and Chase, too."

"We don't, and you know very well that I'm up for anyone cooking that isn't me."

"Great. Ask Jena and let me know, so I can get back to my mom." Liam squeezed Felix's shoulder. "You ready Axle?"

"So ready." He bounded up and ran into the kitchen to grab his jacket.

Felix scowled after him. "Have a great day, Uncle Felix, thanks for letting me go, Uncle Felix."

"Bye, Uncle Felix!"

"Whoa, hold up," Liam said, giving Axle a look. "I'm pretty sure you need to clean up the mess in the kitchen first. That's your bowl smashed all over the floor, isn't it?"

Axle rubbed the back of his neck. "Oh yeah, that."

"Dustpan is in the laundry room," Felix called after him, pointedly not meeting Liam's eyes. Just remembering that sordid chain of events that'd taken place in there last night was enough to get him all hot and bothered.

Liam chuckled and gave Felix a quick peck. "I'll make sure he does a good job. We'll be back here to pick you guys up, say five?"

"Make it six. Cruze has her last rehearsal at four."

"Perfect." Liam waved and headed into the kitchen to oversee Axle's cleanup.

Felix pinched the bridge of his nose, then his eyes snapped to Sway. "Why are you so quiet?" It was off-putting to say the least.

"I'm thinking," she said, picking at her cast.

He leaned against the kitchen's doorway, broken shards clattering behind him as Axle swept. "You do that?"

She looked at Felix like he was an idiot. It didn't bode well for her teen years. "I think *a lot*, Uncle Felix."

"Oh really? What about?"

Sway shrugged. "Cats, mostly, but nice ones, not like yours."

"That's fair." It also reminded him that he needed to feed Myx. He should probably do that sooner than not. His majesty wasn't going to be pleased his victuals were late. Neither was Chambers, but there were bars between them, and the weasel could deal with it. "And what do you think about when you're not thinking about cats?"

"How much I hate Kitty Weaton," she said deadpan.

Well, okay then. His brow quirked. "Isn't she the one who told you gingerbread had mole asses in them?"

Sway nodded. "She also said that you can't be my pretend daddy when we're playing house at recess because you don't like girls, and I told her that you said you just don't like kissing them, and she called me a liar, but if you like kissing Liam, then she was right, and you can't be my pretend daddy even if I want you to be," she said without taking a breath, then teared up.

Felix abruptly didn't like Kitty Weaton either.

He sat on the couch next to Sway, and she threw herself around his neck. He grunted, shifting her knee away from his crotch and sighed, rubbing her back. "Hey, shh. It's okay. Kitty sounds like an opinionated little hag. I don't know what her deal is, but forget her. You can pretend whatever you want."

She sniffled. "But what if I want it to be real?"

A fist clenched around Felix's heart as his thoughts raced. The look on Liam's face when Felix had jokingly called the urchins "our kids." The oppressive silence of his apartment when he'd gone back to pack the other night. The meltdowns he'd just witnessed in the kitchen.

Had he thought about taking them? Yes. Had he discussed it with Liam? Yes.

But.

"We have a lot to talk about when Gran and Gramps get

back, okay?" he finally choked out, smoothing her frizzy curls. Girl needed a serious moisture treatment.

Sway pulled back to look at him, her hazel eyes narrowing. "You promised."

His brow furrowed. "I—"

"You promised that if the answer was no, you'd say so," she said, planting her hands on her hips and glowering at him.

He had. Felix sighed, scrubbing a hand over his face. How the hell did he explain this to a six-year-old? "You're right, and I did. It's just—it's more complicated than yes or no. Even if I wanted to—"

"Do you?"

"I don't know," he said truthfully.

Sway searched his face. "Okay." She shrugged, climbing off his lap. "Can I go finish my cereal?"

"Y-yes?" Felix blew out his cheeks and just sat there as she scamped into the kitchen. Hurricane Sway indeed. "Brush your teeth when you finish and get changed. We're going out," he called after her, his gaze rising to the top of the stairs.

He really didn't want to go up there.

Goddamn it. Felix pushed off the couch and clomped to the second floor with leaden steps, the hallway leading to Cruze's door elongating like something out of a horror movie. *Ugh. Stop being dramatic.*

Right. Big boy pants. He pinched the bridge of his nose and knocked. "Cruze?"

Nothing. Then— "What?"

Felix cracked the door. She stood at the window with her back to him. "So, I forgot Jena had something to do today and accidentally booked an extra mani-pedi appointment. I thought we could do some shopping after. Do you think Sarah would like to go with us?"

Cruze shrugged.

"Do you want to use my phone to text her and ask?"

She spun and Felix instinctively ducked. "You know she's like my only friend, right?" Cruze spat. "Gran and Gramps, you. Nobody understands what it's like to be abandoned and stuck in house you hate."

Felix sucked in a breath. "You hate it here?"

She raised her arms and slapped them down, at a loss. "No, that's not—I hate knowing that I'm a burden, always waiting to get passed on to the next person. You said it yourself downstairs, Gran and Gramps are old and money's tight. I don't have to wait until your stupid 'family meeting' to figure out what that means," she said with tears in her eyes.

"Cruze," Felix sighed. "Look, whatever you're thinking…" he pressed his fingers to his temples. "We're going to figure this out, together, and I swear to God, you guys aren't going anywhere. Can we just put all of this on hold and go out for mani-pedis and some thrifting? I've got fifty bucks with your name on it to spend however you want."

Her brow cocked. "Fifty bucks?"

Felix's breath went out in a whoosh, and he pulled out his phone. "Yeah. Fifty bucks. So, you want to text Sarah or not?"

"Can I get black polish?"

"You can get whatever color you want."

She chewed her lip, hesitating. "Is it okay if it's just us?"

"As long as Sway's included in that, but I'll let you pick where we have lunch."

"Fine." Cruze rolled her eyes. "And I want to go to the noodle house."

"Fabulous. I'll meet you downstairs in ten." He closed the door behind him as he left and leaned against it for a breath. God, he was so not cut out for this.

But he really wanted to try.

∽

LIAM GRINNED and put an arm over Axle's shoulders, looking at the progress they'd made throughout the morning. The kid was a hard worker. There was no way Liam would've gotten this far by himself. Pegboard lined the walls with a bunch of his tools hanging from hooks and more had been stored below the L-shaped workbench. The little stove was crackling, and the wood box full beside it.

And, after last night and this morning, so was Liam's heart.

He hugged Axle to his side. "Looks good, think we've earned some lunch?" The boy nodded, his grin as wide as Liam's. "What do you say we go up to the house and see what my mom's got to eat?"

Axle nodded again, and they piled into the Jeep.

"Are we going back to the junkyard after this?" he asked as they bumped along the forest track. "You said we were, right?"

"Yeah. Jerry's got a car for me to work on, and I need to help him load it up to tow over here. You still okay with that?" Axle looked at him like he'd lost his mind, and Liam laughed, pulling out his phone as it buzzed. He glanced at the screen and smiled, showing Axle. Looked like Felix and the girls were having fun at the nail salon.

"Why is it such a big deal you and Uncle Felix are dating?"

"Ah..." he glanced at the kid. "Well, because it's more serious than that. Were culture isn't like witches, it's more—"

"Like animals," Axle supplied.

"Yeah, I guess, though some people would be offended by that."

"I don't understand why," Axle said, rolling his eyes. "Animals are better than most people I know."

He had a point, though God help the kid if Liam's Aunt Selma heard him say that. "You're not wrong, there's less thinking with some stuff, more relying on instinct. Last night, your Uncle Felix and I worked out a lot of things between us, and one of those things was that we're mates."

Axle's eyes went wide. "You *bit* him?"

"Um…yes?" Exactly how much did this kid know about the way things worked?

He chewed his lip. "Then that makes you my stepuncle."

"Ah, yeah. It does," Liam glanced over at him, not sure how that was gonna fly.

"That's awesome," Axle grinned after a long moment. "If you claimed Uncle Felix, you'll be with him forever and can't leave. I wish I could do that."

Okay, so he had a solid grasp on that part. Liam pulled up to the front of his parents' house and idled the engine. "Your uncle's not leaving you, and how do you know about claiming a mate?" he asked, not sure he wanted to know the answer.

Axle shrugged. "My dad did it to some girl, and my mom yelled at him on the phone about it a lot, then we moved."

Ouch. "You ever meet him?" Axle shook his head again, and Liam killed the ignition.

"No, she made sure none of our dads came around."

Wait—what? Liam went to ask him why, but the kid was already out of the Jeep and running up the front steps. Liam sat there a moment longer. What the hell was that about? Between what Sway was telling him about not being allowed to swim and this, Felicia was turning into even more of a headcase. Whatever. He got out of the Jeep. Not his circus, and he had three rings of his own to handle.

Liam's mom opened the front door before Axle could knock and wrapped him up in a big hug, then shooed him to the kitchen. She turned to beam at Liam. "You hear back from your friends?"

"No, not yet, but they had something to do this morning." And Liam sure as hell didn't envy them tromping through a swamp right about now, it was frigid.

"Well, just let me know. Kelsey's supposed to be bringing that young man of hers for us to finally meet. We're all so happy for you, Liam. I just knew everything was going to work out."

He snorted, stepping into the house with her. "It's hardly everything, I still have to get through the divorce and all the crap that comes with that."

She shut the door behind him with a harrumph and rubbed her arms. "True, but having the right someone by your side can make all the difference. Now hurry on and wash up. I made you two some sandwiches. Go eat something before I have you both peeling vegetables for me; I'm making a roast tonight."

Liam's mouth watered. His mom's roast was hands down his favorite meal. He joined Axle washing up at the sink.

"Axle, honey, you want juice or milk?"

"Milk, please, Meme."

Liam's brow rose as he dried off and the kid went to the table. "Meme?"

His mother huffed. "Well, I can't have him Mrs. Montgomery-ing me. Besides, he's family now," she said with a wide smile, ruffling the boy's unruly dark locks.

Axle grinned around a mouthful, his sandwich already half gone.

Well, shit. Liam scratched his jaw and claimed his lunch before the kid snagged it. They finished up and headed back out the Jeep. Liam drove away from the compound in a daze. Never in his wildest dreams had he imagined last night happening with Felix or how thrilled his parents would be to hear they were together. His dad had actually shaken his hand with tears in his eyes.

And the kids were just the cherry on top.

Yes, Felix was terrified by the idea, but damn, if there was some way they could figure out how to make it work…Liam ran a hand over his jaw, frowning. Getting back even a fraction of what Jenny and Pete had stolen from him would go a long way towards a downpayment on a house, and if he could get his license reinstated?

Lunch churned in Liam's stomach, but he'd actually enjoyed working as a law clerk. Not as much as working on cars, but if he could find something he could do remotely and tinker with things on the side—

"Are you okay?"

Liam glanced over at Axle. "Huh? Oh, yeah. Sorry, I just… get lost in my head sometimes. Thinking big thoughts, you know?"

"You're not mad I called your mom Meme, are you?"

"What? No. I'm glad. She really misses her other grandkids. Their mom won't let them see her anymore, and she was pretty devastated about it. I'm glad hanging out with you guys makes her so happy."

"I'd be mad if someone did that to me," Axle growled, his little hands fisting. "And I'd be even more mad if someone I knew hurt Meme's feelings like that. Really, really mad, and I'd make them sorry for it."

Liam glanced over at the menace in the kid's voice, and almost swerved off the road at the pricks of red light flaring around Axle's irises. He steadied the wheel and blew out a shaky breath. Holy shit. Felix hadn't been being dramatic, and the kid's first shift was gonna happen any day now. Liam was also abruptly positive he knew exactly what kind of were Axle was.

There wasn't a doubt in his mind that the kid's father was a hellhound.

Chapter Seventeen

FELIX PICKED through the racks of secondhand clothes at ReRun. Sway was on the other side of the store rifling through the estate junk, and Cruze was somewhere by the shoes. He smiled, pulling out a chartreuse, satin poet's shirt. *Hello, beautiful.* This had definitely come out of Old Lady Ames's theater wardrobe. Her loss. He added it to the pile with his other finds.

"Hey," Cruze said, coming up beside him. Predictably, everything in her stack was over-sized and black, just like her nails.

The mani-pedis had gone over surprisingly well with both girls, aside from discovering Sway had toenails that would put a troll's to shame and was ridiculously ticklish. Having to watch Cruze struggle in the beginning wasn't ideal either, but she'd come around. He'd had no idea her fingers and toes were webbed or that she had patches of very fine, iridescent scales running up the sides of her legs like racing stripes. It made sense, considering her father was a siren, but she was incredibly self-conscious about it. Personally, he thought it was cool, though the webbing was a definite impediment to wearing flip flops.

"Hey, you find everything you wanted?"

"Yeah. I think so." Her brow rose at the poet's shirt. "You're really getting that?"

"Absolutely." Felix held it up against himself. "Tell me it's not divine."

"It's something," she said under her breath.

"Rude." He snorted at her almost giggle. "You and Jena have the exact same lack of vision. Next time you can come with her—"

"Uncle Felix!" Sway tore around the aisle with something clutched against her chest. "I found what I want!"

She thrust a taxidermy squirrel posed beside a beer can at him.

He and Cruze recoiled.

"Ew! Gross, Sway, that probably has bugs!"

"It does not, and Uncle Felix said I can get whatever I want, and I want Pablo!" she yelled at her sister, hugging the furry little corpse.

Pablo. Good grief, this child...Felix's eyelids fluttered, and he pinched the bridge of his nose. "You do realize that 'Pablo' used to be a real squirrel, right? Like alive?"

Sway rolled her eyes. "Duh. Why do you think I want to take him home?"

Cruze sputtered. "We are not bringing that thing back to Gran and Gramp's—"

"Not our home, stupid, *his* home." Sway glowered at her. "He doesn't like it here and wants to go back to the woods."

"And he told you this?" Felix asked, intrigued despite himself.

"Yes," she said decisively, raising her pointed little chin.

Felix cocked a brow back at her. "And you're going to leave him there?"

"Yes."

He puffed out his cheeks. "Okay, go put him on the counter."

Sway squealed and disappeared in that direction.

"You're really going to let her buy a dead squirrel?" Cruze looked at him like he'd officially lost his mind.

"I did say you guys could get whatever you wanted, and if she wants to spend her money on that…" Felix shrugged. "It's her Christmas present."

Cruze shook her head. "You are so weird."

"I'll take that as a compliment," Felix said, flicking a curl from his eyes. "You get everything you wanted? You need to be at rehearsal in forty-five minutes."

"Um, actually…there's this pair of boots…"

"Ohh, show me." Felix hadn't made it over to the shoes yet. Cruze headed in that direction, and he followed her.

She looked back over her shoulder and chewed her lip when they got to the section. "Those," she said, pointing to a pair of glimmery dark green shit-kickers with black and white laces. They looked like they'd been made out of wyvern hide.

"Nice find," Felix said, picking one of them up and really hoping it'd been ethically sourced. Whoa. They were certainly sturdy. The one in his hands had to weigh two pounds. They also happened to be his size. Too bad those black velvet loafers with gold tassels weren't. "Why would you think I wouldn't let you get them?"

She shrugged. "They're kind of expensive."

He glanced at the tag. Thirty-five bucks was a steal as far as he was concerned. "Tell you what, I'll either pay the difference for you to get these along with the rest of your stuff, or get your phone repaired. Your choice."

"The boots," she said without hesitation.

Felix put a hand to his heart and gasped. "There's hope for you yet, and I get to borrow them."

"Fine." She forced a glower, failing to hide what looked suspiciously like a smile.

"Right, let's settle up," he said, working his way to the front of the store.

They dumped their finds on the counter, and Melvin Wert bellied up to the register. "This all together?" he asked, brushing crumbs off his painfully bland gray button down.

Talk about lack of vision, but Felix supposed the man's red suspenders were a titch festive.

"Yes," he said, pulling out his wallet. "And the squirrel."

"He's really special," Sway piped up, her nose barely clearing the counter.

Melvin grunted and stabbed a blunt finger at the antique register's keys. He glanced at Felix as he rang up the poet's shirt. "You know, I got more of this stuff in the back."

Cruze groaned, and Felix shushed her. "Do you?"

"Yeah. There's a whole trunkload from Old Lady Ames's attic. I wasn't gonna put it out until next Samhain, but if you're in the market, you're welcome to parse through it now."

Felix checked the time on his phone. He'd been planning on stopping by the apartment to feed Myx before Cruze's rehearsal, but it wasn't like the cat was going to starve. He tucked his wallet back into his pocket. "That would be amazing."

Forty minutes later, Felix pulled into the parking lot behind town hall, a few hundred dollars poorer, with the entire trunk shoved into the back of his car.

And a very happy tween in the front seat beside him.

Who knew Old Lady Ames was a closet goth in her youth? Felix certainly hadn't, but as soon as they'd opened the steamer trunk of sparkly black corsets and long shredded skirts, Cruze had been entranced, and Felix had his eye on a bunch of it as well. They'd made a deal that she could have the lot of it, as long as he could borrow whatever he wanted. Sway had fixated on a pointy witch's hat and refused to take it off. Whatever, representation, right?

They hurried to the auditorium and took two seats while Cruze headed backstage. Felix sighed. God help him if he had to suffer through that kid mangling his lines again. At least this was the last one before the show tomorrow. He pulled out his phone, scrolling. Jena's last text had been suspiciously blunt, especially after giving her the CliffsNotes from last night. Something was definitely up. He chewed his lip, sure it had to do with her and Chase going to check out that altar.

"Thank you for my hat and Pablo, Uncle Felix." Sway piped from the seat beside him. "He's really happy he's going home, and so is the kinip-kinap."

"Kinip-kinap?" The word sounded vaguely Elvish, but if it was, the translation eluded him. He raised a brow, and she rolled her eyes.

"You know, Uncle Felix, they live in the wind and sing. They said they'd come and take care of Pablo. I told you, he's *really* special."

Alrighty then. "You know where you want to leave him?"

She nodded beneath the wide brim, sending the tip of the hat bobbing. "He needs a big tree. Maybe we can find one at Meme's house?"

Felix looked at her blankly. He knew she was speaking English, but something was definitely getting lost in the delivery. "Meme...?"

"Liam's mom. She said Mrs. Montgomery was too much of a mouthful. Pablo will like it there. There's lots of animals, and the trees are happy."

"Oh? How can you tell?"

"They said so the other night. Can't you hear them?"

His brow quirked. "Nope, can't say that I do."

"That's okay," Sway sighed. "No one else can either, but I have really good ears. Do you have any snacks?"

Felix pulled a tin of breath mints out of his jacket. "Knock yourself out."

She sat back with them, and Felix ran a hand over his jaw, ignoring the moms filtering in and the kids gathering on stage as he pondered Sway. What kind of supe understood the wind, trees, and taxidermy animals? He shook his head. She was six. It could just be a vivid imagination.

Keep telling yourself that, Felix.

Whatever. At least that was less concerning than whatever Axle had going on. Felix blew out his cheeks and glanced around the auditorium just in time to see Jenny hustle in with Sarah.

Neither of them looked happy. Sarah tugged her arm from Jenny's grasp, and fled backstage as her mother took a seat away from the rest of the mom squad. She didn't quite collapse into it. Felix frowned at her unhealthy pallor. The woman obviously wasn't well.

Serves her right, he thought uncharitably.

The inevitable whispers from the mom squad started up at the interaction, and Felix didn't feel bad for Jenny in the slightest. Quite the opposite, actually. Whatever was going on with her, it reeked of divine retribution—karma seeking to settle the scales. He made an effort to breathe, dispelling it from gathering around him. The urge to hex the duplicitous bitch was intense.

"Uncle Felix?" Sway put a hand on his arm.

He glanced down at her. "Hmm?"

"Is that blonde lady a bad person?" Sway asked, looking at Jenny, or at least he thought Sway was looking at Jenny. It was hard to tell what was going on beneath the brim of that hat, but Jenny was the only blonde woman over there. Sway's hat tipped toward him. "Your face got mean when she walked in."

It did? "Oh, um…kind of? She's made some bad choices that are hurting Liam."

"Then I don't like her either," Sway huffed, crossing her arms over her chest.

Fair enough. The mom squad abruptly started laughing, and Jenny stiffened. Felix tried not to look too interested, though it was apparent something had just gone down. Ooh, damn him for picking seats way over here—

Sway giggled. "Those other ladies don't like her very much either."

His brow rose again. "You can hear them?"

She nodded. "Yeah. I told you. I have *really* good ears."

Okay, so there was probably something morally or ethically wrong with using your six-year-old niece to eavesdrop, but— "What did they say?"

"That lady in the red hat said she should've kept riding the gravy train with biscuit wheels instead of hopping off to bend over for the mule behind it, and then the lady with the scarf said a mule would be an upgrade to what she was riding now, 'cause there's no way Pete's hung like one."

Felix coughed into his fist. "And you think that's funny?"

"Yeah, a train made out of gravy with biscuits for wheels and a hanging mule? That's real silly."

"It is, indeed." And thank God she'd taken all of that literally.

Felix cocked his head at the shrill ring of a phone. Jenny fumbled in her purse and then held hers up to her ear. She glanced at the stage and chewed her boney thumb. Whatever the person on the other end was saying, it didn't look like good news the way her face blanched and went slack. She grabbed her purse and hurried out.

"There's people at her house," Sway said without prompting.

Felix wet his lips, not quite salivating for more info. "Do you know who?"

"No, but the man that called sounded scary and called her bad names."

Shocker there. Pete was less than eloquent. The rest of the rehearsal was much less entertaining, and when Cruze came out from the back with Sarah, Jenny still hadn't returned.

"Hey, Uncle Felix, I hope it's okay, but I told Sarah we could give her a ride home. Her mom texted that there was some kind of emergency and to stay here, but they're closing the auditorium."

Felix pursed his lips, dying to know what that call had

been about. The police sirens that'd kicked up in the distance a few minutes ago didn't bode well for whatever it was. "Sure, but we need to make a couple of stops first, and we have to do it fast to get back in time to meet—ah, your brother," he amended, just stopping himself from mentioning Liam at Cruze's expression.

"Cool." She blew out a relieved breath as they all left the building. "Hey, can we wait in the car while you feed Chambers? I want to show Sarah what I got."

"Sure—"

"I want to see the weasel!" Sway yelled.

"—Sway and I'll pop inside real quick," he continued, clamping onto her hand before she sprinted through the intersection.

They all crossed the street, and Felix unlocked the car. It was a tight fit with one of the seats folded down to accommodate the trunk of clothes, but the two girls managed to squeeze in, oohing and ahhing before Felix closed the door behind them. He hurried to the back of town hall with Sway in tow.

"Can I feed him?" Sway asked as they went in and headed to Felix's office.

"Absolutely not, but you can get his kibble out of the closet for me. Right over there," he said, pointing at the door beside the wall of filing cabinets. A red folio was on his desk with a sticky note. "Filing on Monday" was written on it in big block letters.

Felix thumbed through it. Looked like the town's response to the lawsuit, but legalese was not a language he understood, though Liam would. Felix glanced up at Chamber's irate chittering.

"Whoa! Hey!" Felix dropped the folio and rushed over to the ferret cage where Sway was glowering at the former mayor. "Did he bite you?"

"No." She pouted. "But he's even meaner than your cat."

"Don't let Myx know, he might take that as a challenge." Felix quickly filled up the weasel's bowl. "Okay, put that back, and let's go," he said, handing her the kibble and grabbing the folio from where it'd fallen. He took one last glance around his office and shooed her out into the hall.

Felix locked the door behind them, and they got back into his car. He wiped a hand across the fogged up window and started the engine. "One more stop. You guys okay back there?" he asked, throwing an arm over the seat to back up. Stupid curbing was a hazard.

"Yep," Cruze said with a wide smile on her face.

"Good." He pulled out of town hall's lot and onto the street. "I'm going to be at the apartment a little longer than my office, are you going to stay with them?" he asked Sway.

She shook her head. "No. All they talk about is boys."

"Sway!" Cruze sputtered, and Sarah giggled into her mittens.

"What, you do!"

"Oh really?" Felix's brow cocked at the girls in the rearview. Cruze was several shades past pink. "Any boy in particular I should know about?"

"Dustin Remy," Sway replied gleefully.

Cruze fell against the seat with her hands over her face, and Felix swallowed a smile. Well, looked like he was going to be doing some light internet stalking after dinner. He pulled into his spot and cut the engine. "Pull out your phone, Sarah." He rattled off his number. "I'll be back in five minutes. Text me if you need me before that."

He and Sway headed into the complex, and Felix frowned at the "Out of Service" sign still on the elevator before hoofing it up the four flights of steps. He unlocked the door to his apartment and groaned. The fern was on the floor, and dirt had been tracked up and down the hallway.

"Goddamn it, Myx," he muttered, hurrying Sway in. "Go hang out in the living room while I clean this up." Felix pulled off his parka on the way to the kitchen, the furry perpetrator perched on the kitchen table. He looked far too satisfied with himself.

"Ew! There's cat puke on the couch!" Sway shrieked from the living room.

Because of course there was. "Was that really necessary?" Myx yawned.

Felix glared at him and grabbed the broom and dustpan. "Since you've already eaten, you can wait for second breakfast."

Myx's ears flicked back, and he huffed. Whatever. Stupid cat. Felix cleaned up the mess in the hall, then the puke in the other room. It was between the cushions, because why wouldn't it be?

"You know, I really hate you sometimes," he muttered, dumping kibble into the cat's bowl.

Myx huffed again, stomping down the hall and ignoring his tribute.

Felix threw up his hands. "Whatever. I don't have time for your attitude." He shrugged into his parka and absently pulled out his phone as it pinged in quick succession. "Come on, Sway, we're going to be—"

DRAGON!!

pissed off!

stay inside!!!!

Felix's jaw dropped at Jena's texts. A what? There was no way. A fucking dragon? There were like twelve on the planet, what the hell was one doing in Havers? He furiously texted her back.

R U OK?!

His chest heaved, waiting for Jena to respond, and a text from Sarah pinged.

> we need u!!!

Fuck, they were still in the car. Felix shoved his phone in his pocket and hustled Sway out the door. Myx shot out into the hallway between their feet. "Damn it, Myx!" Whatever, he didn't have time to chase him. Felix quickly locked up and hurried Sway to the stairwell, the cat keeping pace with them.

"I think he's coming with us, Uncle Felix."

"What do you mean you think, can't your really good ears hear him, too?"

"No, he doesn't talk to me, but he mutters a lot."

Well, that was on brand. Felix frowned as they jogged down the steps. "Great. Just what we need, two ill-tempered beasts on the loose."

The cat's ear flicked back, racing down the stairs ahead of them. Felix opened the door to the parking lot and froze. In the car, Sarah and Cruze's white faces were pressed to the glass, staring at the monstrous serpentine shape circling high above the town. Holy shit. There really was a dragon.

"Is that Santa?" Sway asked, squinting at the darkening sky.

Felix's throat bobbed. "Um. Yes. Better get in the car before he sets fire to all your presents." She squealed and dashed to the car.

Felix followed her lead, and Myx jumped into the car as soon as the door was opened. He bounded across the front seat to Sway buckling in. She gasped as he plopped down on her, and she went still, holding her breath with her eyes screwed shut.

"Holy crap, that's a cat?" Sarah asked, tearing her gaze from the circling dragon. Myx yowled at her, hissing, and she cringed back.

Cruze's eyes went wide. "W-why is he here?"

"You'd have to ask him," Felix grumbled, hurrying to start the car. Jena still hadn't texted, and the dragon's circles were getting lower. Fuck. Executive decision time. Felix shot Liam a quick text and threw the car into reverse.

"Text your mom and let her know I'm taking you to the Witchery with us," he said to Sarah.

With all the wards the building had on it, it was the safest place in town, and it was also a lot closer than his parents' house. "Everyone buckled?"

The two girls in the back nodded, clutching at each other, and there was no way Sway was going anywhere with Myx on her lap. She tentatively tried to put her hand on his back, and he nipped at her fingers, growling.

A much louder growl came from above, rattling the car windows, and Felix floored it.

LIAM GOT BACK to the house before Felix and the girls, and hustled Axle into the shower. Kid was ripe after all the work they'd done. Liam sat at the kitchen table, sniffing a pit as he sat. So was he, but it would have to wait. Getting the car over to the garage had taken longer than he'd expected.

One of the axles had been totally busted in what Jerry referred to as "the pothole incident," and the frame on that side needed more than a little help. It wasn't anything that couldn't be fixed, but it had made loading and unloading the car more difficult.

But it was back at the compound now, and Liam had made himself walk away without even opening the hood. He was stupidly proud about that. His fingers were itching to get started, and he was dying to know what was under there, but —no.

No squirreling. No obsessing.

He was gonna show up and prove to Felix that he could rely on him. And as soon as they got back to the compound for dinner, Liam needed to take his meds to guarantee it. He probably should've stopped off before coming here, but he hadn't wanted to be late. He blew out a breath and grabbed yesterday's paper to kill time, antsy about getting off schedule.

The front page of The Haver's Herald was taken up by a massive article on the lawsuit threatening the town. Somehow, they'd gotten a copy of it, and of course the details were sensationalized. Liam chewed his lip. He did not envy Felix having to field phone calls come Monday morning. The way this read, Fayet was massing at their border and Havers's town government was already being disbanded.

Liam shook his head, flipping to the next page. More missing cattle, library bake sale…ah. National News. His brow's furrowed. They'd extended the travel advisory out on the West Coast. Holy shit. At first glance, he figured it'd been because of a quake or wildfires or something, but this was talking about civil unrest in and around the vampiric tribal lands.

He dropped the paper and sat back, feeling ill. There had been rumors of something going on during that last case. Bits and snippets he'd overheard, alluding to things being tense, but he hadn't thought it was anything other than the typical court infighting.

Obviously, it was way bigger, and he had a bad feeling Kremlyn's brother being in jail hadn't helped ease tensions. Liam scrubbed a hand over his face and fumbled for his phone as a text pinged through.

DRAGON!!

taking kids to witchery, safest there

i have sarah, meet if u can

b safe. 🩶 u

What the fuck?! Liam shot out of his seat and went to the window just as town hall's emergency siren blared on for everyone to shelter in place. Holy shit. Where the hell had it come from? He stared agog as a massive black beast swooped above the town and let out a roar that shook the windows, then dive-bombed at something far too close for comfort. Shit, that was right about where his house on McDermott was. Liam's stomach clenched, but Felix said he had Sarah, so at least she was safe.

Liam had a bad feeling no one else in the neighborhood was.

The dragon came up flapping with a police car and wheeled away to drop it somewhere on the other side of town, then returned for round two. Liam knuckled an eye. How the hell was this real? Dragons kept to themselves in the middle of nowhere, like mountain peaks, remote islands, deserts, not Havers.

Thought that would explain all the missing livestock.

"What was that?" Axle yelled, running into the kitchen wrapped in a towel.

"A dragon," Liam said, his throat bobbing as gunshots rang through the twilight. "We gotta get to the Witchery. Your uncle and sisters are there, and it's not safe to stay here." They stared out the window as the dragon swooped again and came up with another car. "We probably shouldn't drive."

Axle shook his head, his mouth hanging open. "N-no."

Fuck. "If I shift, do you think you can stay on my back while I run over there?" The kid nodded, and Liam started undressing, eyeing Sway's *Pretty, Pretty Princess* backpack. The Fluorescent rainbow glitter wasn't exactly subtle, but it was big enough to hold all his stuff. He dumped out her books and more crayons than he would've thought possible. "Okay, go get dressed, quick."

Axle disappeared and a moment later he was back. Liam finished shoving his clothes into Sway's bag and zipped it up, cinching it tight onto Axle and clipping it across the kid's chest. He handed him the house keys. "Lock up while I shift."

Liam stepped out into the freezing cold and took a deep breath, his wolf taking over. Fur sprouted over his body while his bones cracked and reformed, thickening and growing longer. Fangs dropped as his face elongated, and his ears migrated to the top of his head and sounds sharpened.

He shook himself, sneezing at the abrupt influx of brimstone and the dry musk of reptile flooding his nostrils. He looked back at Axle and dropped to his belly. The kid grinned and climbed on. "That was so frickin' cool! I can't wait until I can shift."

The dragon glided over them, and he flattened himself to Liam's back. Hopefully, they lived that long. Axle's hands tightened in Liam's fur, and he slowly got to his feet, waiting for the right moment to sprint from the deepening shadows…

The dragon roared again, and there was a godawful crunch and squeal of metal.

It rose with a fucking firetruck in its talons.

Liam took off, Axle's weight plastered to him, his feet and knees digging in on either side of Liam's spine. Twin points of pain flared at his shoulders where the kid had a death grip on his fur. Liam picked up speed, running toward town. He took full advantage of people's yards. They needed to give whatever had the dragon's attention and all the gunfire a wide berth.

Curiosity won out on the hill above McDermott, and Liam glanced down a cross street. Flashing red and blue lights cordoned off an entire section around Liam's old house, and an ambulance was parked in front of it, along with an unfamiliar SUV.

Shit, what the hell had happened? It looked like the entire Havers Sheriffs Department was out in force, hunkered down behind trees and bushes, clutching their side arms and watching the sky. Two of the remaining cruisers were equipped with LED spotlights. A deputy with a death wish was manning one of them, following the monster's path through the sky.

Fuck that. Liam turned away and kept going. As long as Sarah was safe, he didn't care about the house, and now he needed to make sure Axle was safe, too.

A burst of wind raked over them as the dragon flew above, and Liam ran faster, swearing at the lack of cover. Night rapidly falling helped, but he wouldn't put it past the fucking reptile to be able to see in the dark. Shots fired again somewhere behind him, and a man's scream cut off sharply.

Liam's pulse sped as they reached the town proper, and he slipped into a cleared alleyway. Rock salt around the dumpster dug into the pads of his paws. Only three and a half blocks to go, but there was even less coverage than in the surrounding neighborhood. He glanced back the way they'd come. Aside from the emergency siren at town hall still wailing, everything was far too quiet. Liam slunk into the shadows.

Light slashed across the rooftops above them and a burst of air blasted down the alley. The facade of the building beside them crumbled as the dragon landed, clutching a lax form in its talons. The sour smell of cheap vodka and ruptured viscera hit Liam's nose. Holy fuck, was that Pete?

Well, what was left of him.

The dragon raised its sinuous throat, each razor-sharp scale outlined in horrific clarity by that fucking spotlight. Liam had thought they were black, but up close they shone with a midnight iridescence that rode over a deep shade of bruised plum.

It was the color of death on wings.

What the fuck? All that vitriol Pete had spilled back at Cups—had he known about the beast?

The dragon let out another roar, the stench of brimstone thickening. Liam's eyes watered, his lips drawing back in a soundless snarl. Above, the monster's barbed tail thrashed like a cat's, gravel and chunks of masonry peppering them. Its head lowered, scanning the streets and looking for something. Its tail thrashed again. More masonry fell and Axle bit back a cry. Liam pressed against the dumpster, trying to shield the kid from the debris.

The dragon's head whipped around, its slit, luminescent green pupils widening, then narrowing as it focused on them.

Fuck, it could definitely see in the dark.

Liam growled, his hackles rising, and the dragon's maw gaped in a parody of a grin. Its head pulled back, and a malevolent chuckle rumbled through its belly. The dragon flicked Pete's corpse from its long black talons, and his mutilated body landed in the center of the street with a sickening thud.

Holy fuck. Liam's eyes flicked from the pool of crimson spreading around the mangled lump of flesh just in time to see the dragon spit a cloud of noxious green vapor at them. Liam bolted, the cloud cutting into his lungs and tunneling his vision. His legs gave out beneath him, and Axle's weight rolled from his back as he collapsed.

Sharp talons rutted against the concrete, scooping them up in an iron grip. The beast launched itself into the air, the pavement crumbling beneath it, and Liam's head lolled, everything going black.

Chapter Eighteen

FELIX STOOD at the Witchery's third story windows, really, really trying not to freak out. *Okay, Felix. Just the facts.*

Fact one: the dragon had very obviously cornered something.

Fact two: it had left, carrying whatever that was away.

Fact three: one of those things had borne a striking resemblance to a certain small, doggy-scented child wearing what looked like Sway's obnoxious backpack, and the other was wolf-shaped.

Did he *know* that'd been Liam and Axle? No. But was he pretty positive that it had been?

Abso-fucking-lutley.

And Felix was freaking out again.

*Don't panic, don't panic…*He rubbed his arms, his racing breath fogging the glass, and his head growing light. He slapped a hand against the window frame, feeling like his heart had been ripped from his chest. His knees buckled, and he staggered backward.

Oh yeah. He was panicking.

"You know, losing your shit's not gonna help anyone, right?" Aggie's acerbic voice echoed through the empty room behind him.

Felix turned to see her standing at the top of the stairway and laughed as she drew a glyph in the air. It flared purple, and an unnatural sense of calm came over him. God, she'd hit him with a tranquility spell. He should be annoyed by that and still freaking out, but everything was abruptly remote. For now, at least. That spell's life span wasn't particularly long.

"Yes, I am aware, and thank you so much for noticing, but neither is sitting downstairs, pretending to drink tea," he grumbled.

"Actually, I was gonna offer you a quaalude." She shook a bottle and raised her brow.

And now she had his attention.

"I'm not saying no, but didn't they pull those off the market like forty years ago?" he asked, not that it was a deal breaker.

"Let's just say I know a guy." She tipped two pills into her palm. "You gonna come downstairs and take 'em with some tea, or crunch into them up here like a heathen?"

"God no, who does that?" Felix asked, running a trembling hand over his face. Yeah, that spell wasn't going to last.

Steady Felix, you can do this.

Aggie shrugged. "Personally, I like to let them dissolve under my tongue, but to each their own. They'll be in the kitchen waiting for you. I warmed up the lasagna you were supposed to take. Come down and eat something."

Felix sighed, not hungry in the slightest, but also able to think again. Aggie's spell had alleviated his full-on panic to a gnawing anxiety. He supposed she was right. They needed a plan, not for him to crumple into a sobbing heap. He glanced out the window one last time at the point on the horizon where the dragon had disappeared.

At least Jena and Chase were okay. She'd texted that they hadn't even made it a quarter mile into the swamp before the dragon had burst into the sky, making a beeline for town. They'd gone to ground at the Westsiders' compound. God only knew if the beast leaving meant it was safe for them to come back, but when they did, Jena would have a plan. She always did, right? Right. He pulled out his phone, sending her a text with trembling fingers and giving her a rundown of the situation.

Felix closed his eyes. *I swear by everything that's holy, we'll get you back alive and well,* he thought as hard as he could at the universe, setting his intention. He blew out another breath, attempting to center himself as he padded through the superstructure of scaffolding holding up the Witchery's sagging ceiling. Water dripped into several strategically placed barrels. Thank God the dragon hadn't decided to roost on the roof. Despite all the wards protecting the building, it would've collapsed.

He shuffled down the steps and shouldered the crappy composite door at the bottom closed, scrabbling for his phone as it pinged.

> OMFG!!!

> on our way.

Jena. His stomach roiled and he sent out a quick prayer that they'd make it back safe. Felix re-pocketed his phone and trudged down the hall to the other side of the apartment, focusing on not hyperventilating.

Myx had claimed one of the loveseats, and by default the rest of the living room. Sarah, Sway, and Cruze sat at the kitchen table, silent, while Aggie bustled around behind the stove. The kids looked at him expectantly, and he jammed his trembling hands into his pockets.

"So, good news and bad news," he began, not about to lie to them. "I think the dragon left, so there's that."

"Where did it come from?" Sway asked.

"Swamp," Aggie said, plating the reheated pasta. "Put these on the table, and those are for you." She nodded at a cup of tea with two pills on the saucer. Felix eyed her, wondering how much of this she'd seen in one of her stupid visions. He downed one pill, then pocketed the other, positive this day wasn't going to improve.

"Enjoy." She smirked as he washed it down with a mouthful of tea. "That'll give you an entirely new outlook."

Which begged the question why she was so miserable.

"What's the bad news?" Cruze asked, her voice full of apprehension.

Felix attempted to steady his own as he doled out the plates Aggie shoved at him. "Um…I'm like, ninety, ninety-five percent sure it took Liam and Axle with it."

The kids stared at him, aghast.

"The dragon has my dad?" Sarah asked, her face ashen.

Sway started crying, and Cruze's eyes went wide. "H-how are we going to get them back?"

Shit. *Don't freak out. If you freak out, they'll freak out and everything will just be that much worse.* He took a deep breath. God, he hated adulting.

"It does, and I'm not sure yet," Felix said, answering the two girls and putting his hand on Sway's shoulder. "But Jena's on her way, and she'll have a plan." *Please, please, please, dear God in heaven, let her have a plan.*

"Probably won't be a good one," Aggie said, blowing on a forkful of pasta.

Felix glowered at her. "You're not helpful."

"I prefer accuracy to blowing sunshine up people's asses."

Oh, he knew. "Still, I don't understand how you can be so nonchalant about it," he muttered, his anxiety seeping back in. He was all too aware of the girls marking his every move. He blew out another breath. He could be strong for them. For Liam and Axle. He *would* get them back, damn it.

"When you've lived as long as I have, it takes more than an overgrown lizard to ruffle your feathers. Besides, dragons are easy. Guaranteed, someone screwed with its horde. Put whatever they took back—problem solved," she said, handing him a plate.

Felix rolled his eyes. "Oh, well, if it's just that simple…you didn't happen to 'see' any of this happening, by chance, did you?"

She raised a smug brow at him, answering that question. "Now, that would be telling, and I don't expect you to have any firstborn children to name after me."

"And thank you, sweet baby Jesus, for that, but you could just answer the question and take Cruze," he said, trying to make light of the situation.

"Hey!" the tween protested, glaring at Sway's sniffling giggle.

"Careful, you're next on the list," Felix said, putting a plate in front of her. He supposed he shouldn't be freaked out if Aggie wasn't, but— "I don't understand why everything has to be a state secret with you," he said to her. "It's cruel and inhumane to keep things to yourself while the rest of us are working on full-blown panic attacks—"

Footsteps stomped up the steps.

"You're gonna want to get that," Aggie said, plating up more lasagna. "Chase has got his hands full."

Felix rubbed his temples as he went to the door, resisting the urge to wring her neck. Stupid visions. He opened it just as Chase reached the landing, carrying Jena. Felix sucked in a breath.

"Oh my God, are you okay?"

"I'm fine," Jena scowled around a document tube. "I rolled my stupid ankle again when that frickin' dragon burst up out of the swamp right in front of us. How are you guys?" she asked, her brows drawing together.

"Shitty."

"You know we're getting them back," she said, without a hint of doubt in her voice.

Felix nodded, struggling not to break down. "I do."

"Good, 'cause we will, and the dragon was like a half mile away when it came up from wherever it was," Chase said, stepping into the apartment. "Is that lasagna I smell?"

"It is," Felix said, wiping his eyes as he closed the door after them. "Apparently, Aggie knew all about the impending dragon invasion and prepped extra the other day specifically for sheltering in place."

The big were frowned, shaking his head. "Of course she did."

"I knew you were up to something!" Jena yelled at the kitchen as Chase set her down on one of the loveseats and left the room, mumbling about being starving.

"Your point?" Aggie asked. She sashayed into the room with a portion and held it just out of Jena's reach.

She rolled her eyes. "Whatever, just give me the fucking plate."

"And that's what I thought." Aggie smirked.

"Wait, you didn't even get near the dark altar?" Felix asked, his eyes on the darkening sky over Jena's shoulder. *Please be okay, please be okay.* "I don't get it. I thought you guys headed out way before noon."

"Two birds, one stone," Chase called from the other room. "We wanted to check out the border."

"This morning, we stopped at the library and pulled a bunch of records. There's a copy of the last survey map the town commissioned in there," she said, nodding at the document tube. "There was supposed to be an old stone wall that ran a good portion of our border with Fayet—what is Myx doing here?" she asked as Felix took a seat on the couch opposite her, giving his familiar a wide berth.

Felix shrugged. "No idea. We were at the apartment when all hell broke loose, and he decided to come along for the ride."

"A good familiar usually knows what their practitioner needs before they do," Aggie said, depositing a small bowl of pasta on the floor for the cat. Myx trotted over and started stuffing his face.

Felix scoffed. "Trust me, he's not, and that can't be good for him."

"Psh." Aggie waved a hand. "Lasagna's good for everybody, and if you want any, I'd suggest you hop to it. Chase is already having seconds."

"Sorry, I'm starving," he said around a bite as he came into the room with another slab of lasagna, and settled beside Jena. She shook her head at the rate it was disappearing, and Felix had to agree, it was freakish how quickly he could pack food away.

"Anyway," Jena said, "when we asked Mr. Brock about the map, he said the wall was there because Havers didn't like Fayet back then, either. Then, like a hundred and fifty years ago, there was a minor earthquake. An entire portion of the peninsula broke off up there, and the land that was left sank, turning some poor farmer's pasture into a swamp."

"And you used the latest survey the town had done?" Felix asked. "I love that for us."

Chase snorted. "You should see the town's schematics. Cross street doesn't even exist on them. That's why Gorman won't give me a permit to put in those lights. He's got no idea what's under these streets. No one does."

"Luckily for us," Jena said, ignoring them, "the water's fresh, not brackish, so it shouldn't interfere with putting up a ward. We snowmobiled along the remains of the original wall this morning, and it's in the same condition as the ones I used around the node. It should work to tether the ward between the big granite outcroppings on the northern shore and the cliffs in the south."

Well, a bit of good news then, but it wasn't like they could do anything with a big, pissed off lizard camping out next to it.

"Then where were you when you saw the dragon?" Felix asked.

"Trying to cut across pack territory," Chase said. "The woods out there are a shit show, and you wouldn't believe the detours I had to make. We'd just hit the trail, headed out there to it, when the dragon exploded into the sky. Thought for sure it was after us. Jena and I abandoned ship and dove into the rough."

"That's when I rolled my stupid ankle," she muttered.

"As soon as we were sure we weren't its target, I grabbed her and floored the snowmobile back to the compound. We sheltered in the root cellar with everyone else at the compound until we got your text. It really took Liam and Axle?"

Felix nodded, still oddly detached. Aggie's quaalude must be kicking in. Myx jumped up beside him and started licking his rear. How delightful, dinner and a show.

"There's something else you should probably know," Jena said. "We were listening to the police scanner on the drive back—

"You have a police scanner?" Felix asked, frowning as the cat lapped at its pucker.

"After Samhain? You better fucking believe I do," Chase muttered around a mouthful.

"Anyway, like I was saying," Jena said, jumping back in, "there was some kind of standoff going on between the sheriff's department and Pete when the dragon showed up. It sounds like Liam's house is a pile of rubble, and it took off with Pete after destroying half of the town's emergency vehicles. They found what was left of him a couple of blocks away."

"H-he's dead?"

They all looked at Sarah standing in the doorway to the kitchen with Cruze and Sway behind her. Shit.

"Oh my God! I am so sorry," Jena said, her hand flying to her mouth.

"What about my mom?" the girl asked, less upset than Felix would have banked on.

"Uh, I don't know," Jena stammered. "No one does. They put out an APB on her and the kids…Felix, they think Sarah is with them."

"No, Jenny left at the beginning of pageant rehearsal to deal with some emergency and never came back. We were going to drop Sarah off on our way home, but dragon."

"You think she left because she knew about the standoff?" Chase asked, sitting back with his empty plate on his knee.

"I don't think so," Felix said, his eyes going back to Myx. The cat shot him an evil glare and kept licking. "I heard sirens as we were leaving, but she'd been gone for over an hour at that point."

"What I'd like to know is why the cops were there to begin with," Jena said.

Felix chewed his lip, a sneaking suspicion taking root. "I called CPS yesterday. If they showed up to take the kids—"

"Then Pete definitely would have lost his shit over that," Jena muttered, then winced, glancing at Sarah. "Sorry."

"Don't be. You're right, and he was a jerk. I'm glad he's dead," she muttered, settling into one of the big, overstuffed chairs with Cruze. Sway climbed into Felix's lap, eyeing Myx as he curled up with his back to them on the other cushion.

Felix barely registered the little girl's weight, blinking at Sarah along with the rest of the room. Okay then.

"Do you have any idea where your mom might have taken the other kids?" Jena asked.

Sarah chewed her lip, and Cruze murmured something in her ear and tilted her head in Felix's direction with a pointed look at her friend. Sarah shook her head, staring at her lap, and Cruze said something else to her. Sarah's gaze swept over the adults in the room, and she took a deep breath.

"Yeah, I know where they are, and my dad and Axle are probably there, too."

~

LIAM ROLLED OVER, the ground shifting and chiming beneath him. Fuck. He fell onto his back and put a hand to his head as he tried to open his eyes. Wherever he was, the light was weird, and it reeked of brimstone with an odd metallic tang riding beneath it.

Slowly, a rough stone ceiling came into focus, light flickering across it and casting long, wavering shadows. He slowly sat up, and ran a hand over his eyes, not believing what he was seeing.

He was in a cave, sitting on a pile of gold coins.

Others spilled across the floor, torchlight playing over the uneven glittering mounds and sparking random flashes of color from gems scattered throughout the cavernous space.

It contrasted sharply with the stark white protrusion of bones.

His stomach clenched and sweat broke out across his brow. The dragon. This had to be its horde.

Axle. Liam's pulse spiked as he spun around, coins skittering beneath him—oh, thank God. The boy was just behind him, still unconscious, his chest rising and falling, and the backpack beside him. Liam grabbed it and ripped it open, searching for his phone.

No service.

He sighed, but at least he had his clothes. Until he got a handle on the situation, shifting probably wasn't the best idea, and he really didn't have any desire to hang around there naked. He got dressed and pocketed his cell. Maybe he could pick up a bar or two of signal somewhere else.

Liam turned, taking in the rest of the cave, coins shifting beneath his sneakers. It wasn't huge, maybe the size of his parents' great room, but he didn't see any way in or out. He glanced at the ceiling. The light from the torch sputtering against the far wall made it tough to tell if there was a hole up there. He pulled out his phone and shined the flashlight at it.

It was higher than he'd thought, easily three times his height, and completely solid. Liam sniffed, searching for a thread of fresh air, a subtle current...nothing but dank brimstone. Okay, there weren't any holes or tunnels, maybe a hidden door? He made his way over to the torch, slipping on coins and tripping over a femur.

He picked it up and took it with him, feeling better about having some kind of a weapon, no matter how crude.

The wall was roughly hewn, claw marks clearly visible where they'd gouged out chunks of stone. He ran a hand over it. No seams, no cracks. The torch was just a bunch of rushes bound together and stuck through an iron ring in the wall. It was also past the halfway mark, and he had a bad feeling they'd be stuck in here longer than that would take to burn down.

Liam ran a hand over his face and made his way back to Axle. The boy didn't stir. Liam sat beside him, abruptly dying for some water. He turned the femur over in his hands, toothmarks scoring its ivory length.

Positive thirst wasn't going to be what killed them.

FELIX'S HEART leapt into his throat at Sarah's admission. "You do? You know where they are?"

She gave a slow nod, and Cruze poked her. "All right!" she hissed back at her. "Look, I'll tell you, but you need to promise I get to live with my dad. I don't—I don't want to see any of them ever again."

Felix pinched the bridge of his nose, things abruptly making sense. Cruze hadn't been talking about herself the other day, she'd been talking about Sarah. "You're the one with the house you hate living in."

She looked away, tearing up. "It wasn't that bad until after my dad left, but she's—my mom—she's not my mom anymore, and the twins, Mike—"

"They whisper like snakes," Sway's piping voice interrupted, looking up at Felix. "I hate them even more than Kitty Weaton. They're not very nice. Cassie laughed when Derek pushed me off the swings at recess. Does that make them hags, too, Uncle Felix?"

"She sounds like one, but it makes him a little prick," Felix muttered before he thought better of it. "Sarah, I can't promise that, but I know it's what your dad wants more than anything. And if we can get him back, I know he's going to move heaven and earth to make it happen, and I'll help him do it."

She chewed her lip again, uncertainty written all over her face.

"Uncle Felix doesn't lie," Sway said. "He promised that if the answer was gonna be no, he'd say so, instead of making us eat peas."

"Shut up, Sway, you're not helping," Cruze huffed at Sarah's furrowed brow, and put a hand on her arm. "But she is right about Uncle Felix. He doesn't lie, and he keeps his promises." She met his gaze, and suddenly they weren't just talking about Sarah and Liam anymore.

"They're in the cave," Sarah said, her voice a thready whisper.

"The cave? Can you tell us how to find that?" Chase asked, leaning forward in his seat.

She glanced at him. "Um...yeah, maybe? I've only been there once. Pete called it the bug-out shelter, but it's not—" She shivered, and Cruze put an arm around her friend. "I know it's off the main road going to Fayet. There's a trail through the woods you go down, and it's by a bunch of big rocks."

The adults exchanged glances. "Can you see the swamp from the rocks?" Jena asked.

Sarah nodded. "Yeah, and it's super creepy. The shelter's in a cave on the cliffside above a circle of stones. You have to get really close before you can tell it's even there, and then it only looks like this little crack, but it opens up once you squeeze through."

"Then what's inside?"

Sarah looked at Felix. "*He* is."

LIAM LAY BACK against the coins, staring at the ceiling, his hand on Axle's back, taking some comfort in the steady rise and fall of breath beneath his palm. There wasn't much to be had elsewhere. After a painfully thorough search of the cave walls, Liam had come to the conclusion that however they'd gotten in here had to be some kind of sorcery.

Meanwhile, the torch had gutted lower, and his mouth had gotten drier, an acrid tang at the back of his throat.

"Comfortable?"

Liam bolted upright at the rough, hissing drawl. A tall, lean man in a long black robe stood at the center of the room. He was incredibly pale, his skin and hair an unnatural alabaster, with luminescent green eyes, vertically slit above bitingly sharp cheekbones.

Oh, yeah. This was bad. No way was that a man.

"This is one of the nicer chambers in the lair," he continued, looking around before meeting Liam's eyes. A strange pressure accompanied his gaze.

"Why are we here?" Liam growled, putting a hand to his head.

The creature smiled, his teeth a series of sharp points, serrated like a shark's. "Why to bargain, of course. I'm afraid you coming back has upset the status quo, and that won't do at all...but come, I'd be a poor host if I didn't offer you succor." He held out a long-fingered hand, his nails black and curved.

"You're the dragon."

"I am."

"I'm not going anywhere without Axle."

"You say that like you have agency. I assure you, you do not."

"If that were true, you wouldn't feel the need to bargain."

The dragon laughed. "Touché, Counselor. Fine. Bring the boy, if you must."

Liam stood, hefting up Axle and paused. Wherever they were going, it had to be an improvement over this, right? Liam's thoughts flew through everything he'd ever heard about dragons. None of it made him feel any better about taking the creature's hand.

"I'm waiting," the dragon said, more than a hint of malice in his tone.

Liam exhaled roughly and stepped closer. The room wavered and spun before he'd taken a second step, then reality solidified around him, and he stumbled.

It wasn't an improvement.

They were in another cave, this larger than the first and far hotter. A sickly glow came from a deep crevasse bisecting the space, and beside it, a long stone table with a feast laid out. Jenny sat at one end, her face slack, with the twins and her youngest at her sides.

"Please, sit," the dragon said, his tone brooking no argument. "Eat."

Liam took a seat on one of the stone benches, shifting Axle to his lap. His gaze ran over the spread, that pressure in his head sharper than it had been. Every dish on the snowy tablecloth looked like something out of a magazine, the places set formally with gold-rimmed dinnerware and crystal goblets.

The dragon sat at the end opposite Jenny and began to fill his plate. Liam's gaze flicked to her and the kids. They'd begun doing the same, the children with far more relish than her. He tried to catch her eye, but she avoided his gaze, her lips pressed firmly together. Liam reached for a chicken leg, and the barest waft of carrion hit his nose as he put it onto his plate. Sweat beaded his forehead.

Illusion. Dragons were supposed to be adept at illusion, to the point that it became tangible to the unwary. Was that why he'd smelled rotting meat? It looked amazing, but, at this point, he was definitely fucking wary.

And now, not hungry in the slightest.

Liam kept his face blank and reached for the potatoes,

fighting to ignore the sense of skittering legs running up the spoon to his arm as he spooned them onto his plate.

"So, what's this bargain you'd like to discuss?" Liam asked, his stomach clenching at Jenny lifting her fork to her lips. Her eyes flicked up and she smiled at him as she chewed.

"The last consort my bride chose was less than ideal. He failed to abide by the terms of our agreement and brought too much attention to my brood." The dragon's gaze slid to the children at Jenny's sides, gorging themselves on the feast.

They'd forgone the silver utensils beside the fine china. Dark bits flecked their chins and spattered the fronts of their shirts, ruddy liquid running to their elbows in long greasy streams.

Jesus. The longer Liam looked, the more filth he saw, and he had a bad feeling that the truth of what was on this table would send him straight back to the psych ward.

"So, you killed him," he said, tearing his gaze away, his stomach churning as he pushed whatever the potatoes really were around his plate.

Jenny's brow crumpled then smoothed, that pressure on Liam's mind increasing.

"I removed an impediment. You, however, have proven yourself to be an adept provider. I've taken action to allow you to step back into that role." The dragon raised his glass and smiled, nodding toward Jenny and the kids. "You'll return with them to town a hero, having saved them from the clutches of an evil wyrm."

Liam wiped sweat from his brow. It was so hard to think. His thoughts spiraled and jumped like one of his episodes. He blew out a shaky breath and focused on Axle's slack weight against him. Liam needed to keep his shit together for the kid. "Yeah, and what would you get out of it?"

"The continuation of my line and more gold to feather my

nest. My dearest Jennifer can continue to take care of the minutia of our arrangement, can't you love?"

"Yes, Salsibar, whatever you need of me," she murmured at her plate.

"That's all I have to do?" Liam asked, struggling to focus on the conversation and not obsess on what the hell was really on the table or squirrel on all the variables. "Get a job?"

The dragon laughed. "Oh no, Counselor, you're also going to get me access to the node."

Liam started, shock clearing the swarm of random thoughts threatening to overwhelm him. What? "The node? Why—how the hell do you expect me to do that?"

"No more than you already are." He took a sip of whatever was in his goblet, and Liam swallowed, parched. "Jennifer tells me you're quite friendly with its guardian. As to the why, that's simply a matter of aesthetics. I like shiny things, and the node is very, very shiny. I was drawn to these shores by its power, but another had, shall we say, prior claim. However, playing the long game has always served me well. Now that he's been removed from the equation, the sharks have begun to circle, and the only thing standing between me and all that delicious power, is an unproven witch and several bothersome wards."

"Killing her won't get you past them." Something large skittered behind the fruit bowl, and Liam fixated on the motion, his wolf scrabbling for release so he could chase it. *NO.*

"I'm aware, and if she wasn't the only one who can remove them, she'd already be in the ground." The dragon frowned, not missing Liam's reaction. His slitted pupils widened, then contracted. The pressure in the room tightened like a fist around Liam's skull. He gasped, pinching across his temples. *Fuck, what was that?*

"Interesting," the dragon murmured, the pressure receding. "But no matter. The gears are already in motion, and I have no intention of killing her. She'll be much more useful as my thrall." He smiled at Jenny. "Won't she, my love?"

"Yes, Salsibar."

Liam panted, blinking as the pain behind his eyes subsided. Was that what'd happened to Jenny? The dragon had brainwashed her and was planning on doing the same to Jena? Then why bother to bargain with him and Pete? Why not just hit them with the same whammy? Variables clamored through Liam's mind, and the dragon grimaced.

"I tire of this form, and there are preparations to make," he said, standing abruptly. "Explain his role to him and then attend me in my chamber." The cavern wavered and spun, and he was back in the room of coins, his heart trying to beat out of his chest. He clutched Axle to him. Fuck. They were fucked.

"You shouldn't have come back," Jenny said in a hollow monotone from the center of the room.

Liam looked up at her wan face, a thin, stained shift hanging to her filthy, bare feet. Holy shit. She was pregnant again. "I guess now I know where all the money went," he said, flicking a coin.

She put a hand to the rise of her abdomen, neither confirming nor denying the statement. "You have to do as he says. Otherwise, people will get hurt." Her gaze went to Axle.

Liam growled, holding the boy closer. "Why isn't he waking up?"

"Salsibar doesn't want him to, and he won't, unless you comply."

Liam laughed. "Comply. Why doesn't he just fuck with my mind like he did yours?"

"My mind is my own, and the way your brain works, atypical thought patterns—he can't work with broken tools. He couldn't compel Pete when he was drunk, either," she said cruelly. "Which is why you have to accept his bargain."

"It's not a fucking bargain. I'd be agreeing to be his slave, and there's not a goddamn chance I'm living under the same roof as you and his spawn." After what Liam had seen out there, those weren't kids, they were little monsters in the making.

"It's your only chance to save Felix when he comes for you. If you agree to Salsibar's terms, I may be able to persuade him to let the warlock go. If you don't, he will die."

"What? Felix—" Gorge rose in Liam's throat. That's what the dragon had meant about wheels in motion. Felix had gone to the Witchery. Jena would've been there, and as soon as they found out the dragon had taken him and Axle, they'd be on their way.

"Think about it, Liam. You don't have much time to save him," Jenny said smugly, raising her brow. She turned on her heel and walked out of the chamber, through the solid wall.

Liam stared at the space where she'd disappeared for a breath before running over and crashing into stone. He slid down its face with tears in his eyes.

She was right. He never should've come back.

FELIX WET HIS LIPS, at loathe to ask the question, but—"Who is *he*?"

"Salsibar," Sarah croaked out miserably. "The dragon."

"You knew it was out there?" Jena asked, exchanging glances with the rest of the adults in the room. "I think you need to tell us what else you know about him."

Sarah sniffed and ran the back of her hand beneath her nose. "I didn't know about him until after my dad left, but I think my mom had been seeing him for a lot longer. She used to come home sometimes…" She paused, chewing her lip and worrying at the ends of her sleeves. "I don't know how to explain it. It was like she was in this happy dream and nothing bothered her. That happened a lot more after Dad left."

"Dragons can rapture their victims," Aggie murmured from her chair. "If this has been going on for that long, then I'd hazard a guess that Jenny's been completely enthralled by him."

Felix sighed. "Liam said that she'd turned into a different person." God, he almost felt bad he'd been hating on her so hard.

"Yeah, because she got lobotomized by a lizard. Then what?" Aggie asked Sarah.

"Mom found out about some job offer, and she and my

dad got into a really big fight. S-she said some really awful things about him and how he is." Her eyes flicked to Felix. "I don't blame him for leaving. I would've, too. And then Pete moved in. He was a jerk, but he really loved my mom." Sarah looked around the room, then ducked her head again.

"She didn't come home one night, and he went out looking for her. When they came back…things were different, and he started drinking a lot. They would fight, mostly about money. I didn't understand why, because I saw some of the checks Dad would send home, and they were really big, like *Total Housewife* big."

"They shouldn't have been fighting about money." Felix frowned. "Liam said he'd sent hundreds of thousands of dollars back, and that Jenny had recently taken out two massive loans in his name without anything to show for it."

"Dollar to a donut, she was funneling it to the dragon," Aggie said.

Sarah nodded. "Yeah. That makes sense. The first time I met him, I had a swim meet in Klineville, and she made me wait in the car outside of this big, green brick building—"

"That had to have been O'Shay's Exchange," Chase said, scratching his jaw.

Jena's eyes bugged out. "Your mom took you there? That part of town's shady as hell."

"It's the only building out there that fits the description." Chase shrugged. "And dealing with leprechauns is the only way you'd be able to move that much gold without flagging the feds."

"I-I don't remember what it was called," Sarah stammered, "but it was really scary. I hid in the back seat under a blanket until she came back with two men carrying a big case, and the whole van dipped when they put it in the back. She seemed really nervous driving home."

Jena snorted. "With that much gold? I would be, too."

"I-I don't think that was why. We pulled off at that

trailhead I was talking about. By then, it was dark. She made a call and almost as soon as she hung up, this tall, pale man was standing in the beams from headlights. He's—the twins and Mike look just like him. He's their dad."

"Well, that's an issue," Aggie murmured. "If you're right about that call to CPS, it's no wonder he went apeshit. Dragon spawn wouldn't survive for long away from his horde, and their diet's not something anyone would be keen on providing."

"Do I want to know?" Jena asked.

"Probably not, but I can tell you exactly where all that missing livestock ended up."

"Talk about livestock later," Felix said, focused on Sarah's story. "Then what happened?"

"My mom got out, yelling about how she couldn't do it anymore, and h-he hit her," Sarah rasped. "Then he looked at me and said something to her with an awful smile on his face. The next thing I knew, it was morning, and I was in my room."

"Then when did you go to the cave?" Jena asked.

"The next time I had a swim meet. We just had bags that time, and she made me carry one. It was really heavy, and I dropped it when I was squeezing through the crack." Her throat bobbed. "He got really mad and told her if she brought me again, he'd kill me."

"Charming." Jena huffed out her cheeks and fell against the cushions. "So, this asshole has been pulling Jenny and Pete's strings for years right under everybody's noses, and I'm gonna bet that's why your pack can't stand to be around the swamp. That fucking altar has got to go. There's no other reason he would've landed in Havers."

"Maybe," Aggie said, raising her brow. "Maybe not. An untended node would've been an awfully ripe cherry, just waiting to be plucked."

Jena threw up her hands. "Great, so it's my fault."

"You said it, not me."

She glowered at the older witch. "Then where does that leave us?"

"Sounds like we need to rout the dragon, rescue Liam and Axle, then cleanse the altar and put up that ward. If the others stopped it from getting to the node, another should keep it out of Havers," Chase said.

"Oh, well, if that's *all* we have to do," Felix quipped, rolling his eyes.

"Yeah, no joke," Jena muttered. "I'm sure it's gonna be a piece of cake."

"Speaking of which, I've got some in the fridge," Aggie said, standing. "How about you kiddos come help me eat it. And by help, I mean get your asses in the kitchen and let the adults talk."

The three of them shuffled out after her, and Felix blew out his cheeks, trying to wrap his mind around this grand plan of Chase's. The logistics of everything else aside, the ridiculous amount of karma they'd have to raise to power the ward was daunting. Granted, Jena's mom had done that herself around the Eastern pack's territory, but she'd had the node right there—he was jolted out of his thoughts by Jena and Chase's fervent whispers.

"Oh God, you have a plan, don't you? Please, tell me it doesn't involve sneaking out the coal chute," Felix moaned.

Jena sighed. "No, no coal chute, but you're probably going to be as excited about it. I've been going through my mom's grimoire, and when she put up the wards around the pack's lands, she had to create a reserve nexus of the node's power down in the hollow to fuel her spell. It being there was the only reason I was able to reestablish them when the Westside pack attacked. With the scope of we're talking about, I would need to do the same to create a border ward."

Felix looked between them. "Which means what?"

Chase ran a hand over his face. "It means that she's

planning on eating all that sin around the black altar and pushing the karma to me so I can manifest a channel from it to the node and establish another nexus."

Felix felt himself pale. "You're fucking kidding, right?"

Jena shook her head. "No, even if we performed the rite to cleanse the altar, that kind of karma leaves a stain, but if the node extended out that far, we'd have warning of anything going on out there and fingers crossed it eats away any lingering residue."

"That's a big fricking if," Felix said. "And I doubt the dragon is just going to let us waltz right in."

Jena nodded. "No, but I don't see another way to do it, and if the dragon's adding to the negative karma out there, it might pack enough of a punch to banish him while we're at it. That vision I had of the altar was of Malcom crossing the veil through the fire at the center of the standing stones. If it's already been compromised, maybe we can open it again and send the dragon through."

"I'm going to assume that today's killing and maiming of people while inflicting widespread property damage alone will guarantee that, but I'm more concerned about you," Felix said, frowning at her rounded abdomen. "How the hell are you going to safely channel all of that?"

She chewed her lip. "If we can get the node to reach that far, I don't think I'll have to do it alone. It's…it's like a spider. All the wards are part of its web, and everywhere I walk, I carry a thread strengthening its connection throughout Havers."

Felix cocked a brow. "Wouldn't that make you the spider?"

"Shut up, you know what I mean. My point is that the node naturally wants to expand. If we provide the channel, it will rush to fill it, especially if I'm feeding karma into it at the other end."

"Your shitty mixed metaphors aside, I get what you're

saying, but that still leaves the dragon," Felix said. "How are we supposed to get him out of his cave?"

Jena and Chase exchanged another look. "If Aggie's right about the node drawing him here in the first place, I'm pretty sure he'll come to us when we start raising power," she said with a measured breath. "And if the wards around the tor kept him from the node, one around the dark altar when I call corners and set the circle should keep us safe."

"Well, isn't that just tidy." Felix clapped his hands together, and Myx popped his head up, hissing at him. "Deal with it," he muttered at the cat, then turned back to Jena and Chase. "I'm going to go out on a limb and say we're doing this sooner than not?" God, it was already almost eight. They were supposed to be eating dinner with Liam's parents, not—

Shit. Liam's parents had no idea he'd been taken.

"Moon's almost full, and there's not a cloud in the sky," Chase said, looking out the window. "The sooner we get out there, the better. If the dragon took Liam and Axle, there's a reason for it, and I'm pretty sure we don't want to give him enough time to find out what that is."

He had a point. Felix frowned down at his loafers. "Cruze, I'm borrowing your boots!" he called into the kitchen.

"Don't mess them up!"

"Are you leaving now, Uncle Felix?" Sway asked, running back in.

"Yeah. We're going to get Liam and Axle." He looked up at Aggie standing in the doorway. "You have them?"

"Go do what you need to. I'm gonna light a fire under the coven's asses and see what we can do from here to help. There's no way the rest of those geriatrics'll be able to hoof it out there."

Jena's brow rose. "'Those' geriatrics? You might want to add yourself to the list."

"And you might want to wear something warmer," Aggie smiled, batting her lashes. "Cold front's coming through."

"And you have to take Pablo," Sway said, her little face uncharacteristically serious.

"Pablo?" Jena looked at Felix for help.

"It's her squirrel—"

"Her dead squirrel," Cruze shouted from the kitchen.

"He's special!" Sway yelled back.

Jena looked horrified. "She has a special dead squirrel?"

"Long story," Felix sighed. "Sway, we're not going to have time—"

"He wants to go there. Please, Uncle Felix?" she wheedled. "You just have to leave him under a nice tree, and the Kinipkinap will come get him." Her eyes got big and she went still, then cocked her head like she was hearing something they couldn't. "As long as it's in the woods. They said not the swamp. If you bring him home, they'll help you, I know they will. That's how it works, so everything balances, and you promised, Uncle Felix!"

Felix just stared at her, his mouth hanging open.

"Is this some weird witch thing I don't know about?" Chase asked.

Felix scrubbed a hand over his face. "No, it's a weird Sway thing," he muttered. "Okay, fine." Leaving Pablo out there was probably a better alternative than gifting Liam's parents with questionable lawn art, and it would get it out of Felix's car. Goddamn it, he was going to have to call Liam's parents. Maybe he'd just text Kelsey. He didn't even know how to begin to explain this.

Sway clapped her hands and scampered back to the kitchen. Aggie followed, giving the little girl a side-eye that Felix didn't have time to unpack.

"I'm going to put on something warmer," Jena said, glowering at the kitchen. "I'll meet you guys at the truck."

Felix zipped up his parka, muttering as Chase did the same, then opened the door. Myx jumped off the couch, his tail swishing as he passed between them and went down the steps. Chase's brow rose.

"Just—don't ask," Felix said, holding up a hand and following the cat outside. Sway's weirdness was enough to deal with. He couldn't handle his cat's right now.

Felix pulled the boots and Pablo out of the car and trudged over to Chase's work truck. Myx was already in the back seat when Felix climbed inside. The big were raised an eyebrow again as Felix set the taxidermy squirrel on the seat between him and the cat and started swapping shoes. They were surprisingly comfortable, considering how much they weighed. The passenger side door opened a moment later, and Jena did a double take as she got in.

"That's Pablo?"

"It is, and he'll be riding bitch to his final destination."

She snorted. "I can't believe you let your six-year-old niece buy a taxidermy squirrel posing beside a beer can with her Christmas money," she said, buckling up.

Chase snickered as he pulled out of the parking spot.

"Okay, so it sounds bad when you say it like that." Felix huffed, his finger hovering over his phone's screen as he tried to figure out what the hell to text Kelsey.

Jena rolled her eyes. "You think?"

"Look, I never claimed to be a fit role model, but it's not like it's loaded or anything."

> dragon has liam @swamp
>
> going to get him with j & c
>
> sorry about dinner

There. That worked, right?

> WHAT?!

Felix tucked his phone away. Maybe not. He was just gonna pretend he didn't get that.

"You sure?" Chase asked. "Maybe if you pull its tail a cigarette will pop out somewhere."

"Har har. Just drive, Montgomery," Felix grumbled. "Or I'll feed you another cat food cookie."

"Wait, what?" Jena laughed

Chase put a hand over his face. "Dude!"

"Cat food? Is that what the Meow Medley theme song at Snaps was about?" she asked.

"Mmm." Felix smirked. "Apparently, they're part of Lorraine's secret recipe. You're more than welcome to the rest in case Chase gets the three a.m. zoomies and needs a little treatsie to calm him down."

"The fuck she will. That was vile." Chase shook his head. "Damn, I can't believe you just told her that."

"I can't believe he held out this long! That's gold right there," Jena said, still laughing.

"Well, it's not like you've been in the mood to text lately. I couldn't even get a GIF out of you after I told you about Liam and me," Felix said, affecting a pout.

She turned in her seat to look at him. "I know, I suck, but I am so fucking happy for you."

"Thanks—are you crying?" God, this was an alternate universe.

"What? No," she snapped, turning back around as she sniffled. "Ugh, okay maybe. These stupid pregnancy hormones are ridiculous."

"They are," Chase said. "I caught her crying over a block of cheese this morning."

Jena flushed bright red. "Shut up. It was really good, okay? Now, let me focus. I need to start summoning the node."

"Well, then obviously tears were warranted." Felix bit his lip. "You both do realize the sheer stupidity of this, right?"

"Yup." Chase nodded as he turned a corner. "But that just means the dragon'll never see it coming." He glanced over at Jena. She'd begun chanting softly under her breath beside him, violet sparks of karma manifesting around her fingers. "Look, if she thinks we can do this, we can. The node…it's more powerful than people think, and she's been spending a lot of time with it and going through her mom's grimoire."

"But it's *a dragon*."

"Yeah." Chase chewed his lip. "Still, I'm betting her father was worse, and she managed to banish him. Her mother couldn't even do that," he said, glancing at Felix in the rearview.

That was also true, but Felix was pretty certain there was more to that than met the eye. Jena's father wasn't exactly on the up and up. But maybe Chase was right. Felix sighed. The element of surprise had to count for something, didn't it?

Chapter Twenty-One

FELIX BLEW out a shaky breath as they pulled onto the trailhead, and Chase cut the engine. Whatever Jena was doing in the front seat had sent Felix's nerves jangling and his skin tingled with power. She got out of the truck, still chanting softly, and they followed suit. He grabbed Pablo, scowling. Hopefully there would be a likely tree sooner than not. The squirrel wasn't super heavy, but he didn't particularly want to carry it all over the place.

Myx jumped down landed in a puff of snow, flicking his feet.

"Hey, you wanted to come," Felix muttered. "Trust me, I don't want to be here either."

"It's not as bad as it could be," Chase said, rolling his shoulders closer to his ears and pulling on a pair of heavy gloves. "We'll have the tracks from the snowmobile to follow for part of this at least."

Well, thank heaven for small favors.

They started down the broken path, the wind flitting through the tops of the trees and rattling their ice-covered boughs. Their boots crunched across the treaded path, too loud, raising the small hairs on Felix's nape. The forest was otherwise silent, and the moon a luminous globe above them. Shadows cut starkly across the snowy landscape, slashing ominously over the stark unbroken drifts below.

Felix's breath puffed out in an erratic cloud, scanning the woods for Pablo's new home. "How far is it?"

"About a half mile in," Chase said, falling into step beside him. "We've probably got another ten minutes at this pace."

"Fabulous," Felix muttered, rolling his shoulders closer to his ears and shivering. It was frigid out here.

He stopped dead, and Chase looked back at him.

"You okay?"

"Shh. I thought I heard something," he said, a sensation of song building around him, then fading. Was he hearing things? Chase glanced at Jena, still chanting and getting farther ahead of them. "Go ahead, I'll catch up," Felix said, wondering at the same time what the hell he was doing.

Chase shrugged and hurried to catch up with Jena.

Felix waited for another breath and shook his head, about to follow them—

No. *I'll be damned.* There it was again. He turned, and to his left, Myx was perched on a spar of bare stone, and, maybe a hundred yards off the path behind him, a massive oak tree stood in a small clearing.

That'll do.

Felix blew out another breath as he clambered toward it, over a drift of snow, and sank up to his ankles. Myx bounded ahead of him. Stupid cat. Must be frickin' nice. Felix struggled after him, sweating profusely yet somehow still freezing by the time he reached the base of the tree. It was enormous. Three of him couldn't span it fingertip to fingertip.

Especially if he stayed out here much longer. He wouldn't have any fingers at all. God. The things he frickin' did for people. He flicked a sweaty curl from his eyes, the wind teasing past the collar of his parka.

"Well, Pablo, this is it, buddy." He put the squirrel down and took a few steps back, feeling like there was something unfinished about Sway's weird request. Myx sauntered from around the back of the tree and sat at Felix's feet. The air went dead calm, and the little clearing gained a heavy sense of expectancy.

Felix glanced at the shadows beneath the trees, the small hairs on the back of his neck rising. Was there really a kinip-kinap? Something was out there, but he'd be damned if he knew what.

What he did know, was, unfinished or not, he wasn't sticking around to wait for it to make an appearance.

He went to turn, and the wind kicked up again, funneling around them in a microburst. It sent him to his knees, and he just caught himself before he went face-first into a drift, the air thick with karma and the oddest sensation of song.

And then it—and the squirrel—were gone.

What the fuck was that? Felix panted, staring at the remaining beer can, frozen.

Myx butted against his face, trilling, then turned, with his tail in the air, and his puckered asshole way too close to Felix's nose. He scrambled back and stood, dusting snow off his trousers, scowling, and backed away from the tree, hurrying to catch up with Myx.

"Really, you had to flash me your rear after that?" he muttered, glancing back at the clearing once they'd reached the path. Like it wasn't bad enough that Sway had somehow gotten him to summon a bunch of air entities to take Pablo to that great nut factory in the sky. Talk about adding insult to injury.

Myx huffed, heading towards the swamp. They hit the point where Chase and Jena had jumped off the snowmobile, the snow rucked up and the frozen ground poking through. A mounting sense of dread stole over Felix not long after. God, if this is what Chase had been talking about, it was no wonder he'd turned back as a kid and the pack left this part of their territory alone.

Sweat trickled down Felix's temples. He focused on Myx's tail waving like a furry flag just ahead of him, following Jena and Chase's footprints. If something was out there, Felix was fairly positive it would've gotten them first, or the cat would be tearing past him to save his own skin. Unless, of course, Myx had a death wish, but then whatever it was would probably eat him first.

Felix's dread increased to the point where he was seriously questioning if he was about to shit himself when the woods opened up. Jena and Chase crouched behind a bunch of boulders just before the path cut down into a hollow. A circle of stones stood to the side of a vast swamp, and the gibbous moon hung directly overhead. Behind them, a cliff face rose, craggy with shadows. Crap. How were they supposed to find the little crack Sarah had been talking about?

"Nice of you to join us," Jena murmured as he crouched beside him. "Were you successful in sending your squirrel off to Valhalla?"

"Pretty sure Viking funerals require flaming arrows and a boat, but something took him." Felix shivered and shook his head at her furrowed brows. "Later. What's the game plan?"

"Apparently, Felix's cat thinks we should just stroll on in," Chase said, nodding at the furry pain in the ass picking his way to the circle.

Myx hopped up onto the stone slab and lifted a leg, chewing ice from between his toes.

"I don't have any better ideas," Jena muttered. "Chase and I will go down and call corners to raise a circle. The dragon shouldn't be able to get past it." She looked at Felix. "You need to stay out here and use your power to distort yourself when it makes an appearance, then find Liam and Axle."

"You think getting him out of his cave's going to be that easy?"

She rolled her eyes. "Trust me, the dragon's not going to be able to ignore the power we're talking about raising in his front yard. At the very least, he's poking his head out to see what's going on."

"Then what?" Felix asked, not completely sold.

Chase shrugged. "And then I'll do something to piss him off."

"Like what? Moon him?"

"There's an idea," Jena snorted.

"Yeah, but not a very good one," Felix muttered. Unfortunately, they didn't have any others.

LIAM FLICKED another coin with his thumb and watched it flip through the air and into Sway's backpack. Double Eagles, Saint-Gaudens, Liberty Heads, and Sovereigns. There were others. Jesus, so many others. Older, newer. Most weighed an ounce, some more, some less.

Each of them worth around four grand a pop, and God only knew how much the gems were worth. Diamonds, rubies, emeralds, cut, and uncut. Those didn't fly as well, a fortune of them scattered around the open bag along with the coins that'd missed the mark. Still, he'd been here long enough to fill the stupid thing to overflowing, and that hadn't even made a dent in the pile of treasure he was sitting on.

Liam dashed a hand through it, sending coins skittering. He didn't give a shit about any of it.

"Enjoying yourself?" Jenny asked, appearing back in the center of the room.

"I don't get it," he said, resting his forearms on his knees. "If you were miserable enough to fuck a dragon, Pete, and whoever else you spread your legs for, why bother staying with me or going through all the marriage counseling? All that shit you said—I would've taken Sarah, and you could've been free and clear to live your life however you wanted."

She stared at him, stone-faced, and he shook his head, turning away with a laugh—

"You know how we met? It was a dare. 'See how far you can go down the path, Jenny.' 'No one's ever made it to the swamp, Jenny.' Except, I did, and he was waiting for me." She smiled. "No one thought I could do it. No one ever thought I was good enough for anything. But he did. Salsibar listened. Cared for me. Showed me so many things. How the world worked and how to make it work for me."

"He fucking groomed you."

She shook her head. "No. He chose me. He treasured me. Put *me* above all others." Her face fell. "My own husband couldn't even do that, but you will be a means to an end. I didn't want you to get hurt, Liam. I didn't want anyone to get hurt."

"Too late."

"Mmm." She nodded, but didn't seem overly upset about it. "They're out there now, did you know? Jena, Chase, and Felix. Salsibar is, too. He's going to kill them and glamor her. Then he'll drag their corpses to his great stone table, and all of us will feast."

Jesus Christ, was that what— "You've fucking lost it."

"Oh, Liam," she shook her head. "If you weren't so wrapped up in yourself, you'd have known that I never had *it* to begin with."

FELIX CROUCHED JUST outside the ring of standing stones, with an awful sense of déjà vu. The karma that'd been raised on the dark altar was thick and cloying, the blackness of it settling on his tongue and at the back of his throat. He put his hand on Myx's shoulders, and the cat flicked an ear, tail twitching, his focus rapt on Jena.

She'd called the corners and set the sacred space, blue flames erupting around the broken shards of an iron cauldron at the circle's center. The wind had picked up, tossing her long, dark locks, her eyes glowing a brilliant emerald. Chase stood behind her, karma prickling through the air as he called on it to manifest his will. A glow brightened around them, his irises sparking sapphire, and the flames around the cauldron leaped wildly.

Dark threads of vapor rose from the stones as she chanted. It teased around them, traveling up her body. She inhaled, her lips parting to eat sin, and the glow around them grew brighter, the air thickening with magic.

Beneath Felix's palm, Myx's fur rose, and a low growl rumbled through his chest. Felix's gaze went to where the cat was looking. A triangular-shaped head separated from the shadows by the cliffside, followed by a sinuous neck.

Holy fuck. The dragon was coming.

Its eyes narrowed at Jena and Chase, stalking closer. The

absolute silence in which it moved was terrifying. A beast that enormous was supposed to lumber, not slip through the outcroppings of rock like smoke.

Felix's ears tingled, distorting himself and Myx before he'd thought about it, a strange resonance humming between him and his familiar. Well, that was new, but he didn't exactly have the liberty to figure it out right now. Felix stood, edging around the circle to keep the dragon in view. It slipped around the stones, as if testing the sacred space for weaknesses, then came to a stop by the swamp. It raised a talon and scraped it down one of the standing stones, sparks flying with a horrific grating squeal. Chase's eyes flicked to the monster, his knuckles whitening on Jena's shoulders, then he raised a hand and flipped it off.

The dragon snarled, its head snaking closer, and its pupils narrowing, totally transfixed.

Jena's brow furrowed at the sound, but she continued to chant, her tone more urgent. The flames tinged a sluggish purple, like the node was struggling to answer her call, and the dragon's tail thrashed. The flames faded back to blue as ice and muck peppered around the space, and her chant grew louder. Chase's voice joined hers. The dragon raised its head and roared, a venomous green cloud spilling from its jaws—

Myx's claws sunk into Felix's leg, and he bit back a yelp, glaring at the cat. Myx huffed, and started climbing to the cliff face, then looked back and huffed again. Felix scrambled to his feet. Oh, shit, right, he needed to go.

… "A good familiar usually knows what their practitioner needs before they do…"

Aggie better be right about the stupid cat…not that he'd tell her if she was. Felix swallowed the lump in his throat and followed Myx.

The cat bounded up a narrow path, and Felix fought to keep up with him, even though he was pretty sure Myx was leading him right into a solid wall. No. There was a crack in the stone. Myx disappeared inside it, and Felix squeezed through after him. Stone closed around him, the narrow passage continuing for long enough to make him question his life choices, and then it was gone.

A cavern opened up.

To one side, the earth had split, the air thick with sulfur, and a long black slab of stone rested at its side. Thick tallow candles burned along its length, light dappling over the rotting carcasses of several eviscerated cattle. Rats and insects feasted on the remains. Felix's stomach clenched, and he turned away, retching.

A furious roar came from outside, and Myx butted against him, leading him further in.

Felix stumbled after him, wiping his mouth. God, this was so not what he wanted to be doing right now. Honestly, who did these things happen to? He bit back a sob and hurried after his familiar. The light of flickering flames played over the stone at the back of the cavern. Was there another chamber back there? Voices echoed from within as he neared. Felix stopped beside a ragged passageway in the stone, listening.

"I need your answer," a woman snapped.

Wait, was that Jenny? Myx looked at Felix and stepped through the opening. He lunged after the cat. Goddamn it—

Holy shit.

Jenny and Liam stood with Sway's backpack in the center of another cave piled with gold, and Axle lay prone behind them. Oh God. Was he hurt? Felix swallowed roughly, his pulse pounding in his ears. Myx huffed at him over his shoulder. Outside, the dragon roared again and the stones around them trembled.

Right, right. One way to find out. Felix gingerly stepped around a mound. Distortion didn't render him completely invisible, and if he knocked into one of the piles, she'd know something was up. Jesus, how many billions of dollars were in this room? Guess all that stuff he'd heard about a dragon's horde was true.

"An answer, Liam," she barked, her hands fisting at her sides.

"No," he growled back.

Felix picked up a jeweled ale mug. He didn't want to hurt her, but if he could knock her out—

Coins chimed and his eyes snapped to Myx. He'd jumped onto to Axle's lax body and was crouched on the boy's chest. The cat sniffed Axle's forehead, then licked it, karma sparking between the two.

What the hell was he up to?

"Not even to save, Felix?" she asked coyly, oblivious to whatever the cat was doing. "He will die, and Salsibar won't be merciful."

Axle twitched, and her head snapped to him. "How—"

Felix hauled back and swung the mug, cracking her across the back of the skull.

LIAM OPENED his mouth to tell Jenny to fuck off, and she crumpled into a heap. He fell back a step. What the fuck—

Felix popped into view dropping a heavy jeweled mug like it'd burnt him.

"Shit. Do you think I hit her too hard? Oh my God! She's pregnant?" He put his hands to his mouth horrified. "I am so going to hell."

Liam threw himself at the warlock and hugged him tight, burying his face in Felix's neck. Any stoicism he'd cobbled together left him in a rush of tears. "I don't know how you got in here, but I am so fucking happy to see you," he wept.

"Ditto. I was so worried about you two," Felix said, sniffling as he hugged him back. Another roar sent the stones trembling and coins slipped down the piles around them.

"But it's not over, and we need to get out of here. The dragon's outside with Jena and Chase. I don't know if they're going to be able to do what they planned on. We need to go."

Shit. They really were out there with that monster?

"Liam? Uncle Felix?" They turned at Axle's voice. The boy stood shakily, his eyes enormous. Myx butted him, and he stumbled off the pile of coins. "Why is your cat here?"

"He missed Liam, obviously," Felix said as the cat wound around the were's legs. "What are we going to do with her?"

They all looked down at Jenny, and an enraged roar shook the cavern.

"Shit. Leave her. We'll figure it out later." Felix bolted from the room the same way Jenny had earlier, and Liam came up against solid stone, swearing. Fuck!

"Felix!"

The warlock reappeared. "What? Come on, we gotta go!"

"Yeah, I know, but we can't. You just disappeared through solid stone!"

"What? No, I didn't, it's wide open. There's not even a door."

Shit. That had to be the dragon's illusion.

"Well, that's not what I see." Liam glanced back at Axle, and the boy shook his head, dragging over Sway's backpack. How the hell was he moving that? It had to weigh over two hundred pounds with all those coins stuffed inside of it.

"I don't understand!" Felix wailed, popping back into view. "I'm not—did the dragon mess with your minds?"

"No, Axle's been out cold since we got here, and Jenny said it couldn't because there's a shit show between my ears," Liam spat, eyeing her lax form. Felix should've hit her harder. "It's gotta be an illusion, but I've got no idea how to break it or why it isn't affecting you."

"Okay, not for nothing, but Jenny's a bitch, and I have no idea how to make you not see what isn't there. I can't sense anything at all." Felix raked a hand through his curls, and

Myx jumped up, licking at his pants pocket. He batted the cat away, and it went for him again. "What the hell? Hey, stop it. There's nothing—" Felix's face went slack for a breath, then he dug into his pocket. "God, I hate her," he muttered.

"Who?"

"Aggie." Felix pulled out a little white pill and snapped it in half with his nail. "Eat it," he said holding out the two halves to them.

Liam's brow bunched. "What is it?"

"A quaalude. It'll give you an entirely new outlook." Felix pinched the bridge of his nose. "Oh my God. Just eat it, there isn't time to explain."

Liam and Axle popped them into their mouths. "Now what?"

"I don't know? Chew? You're either going to be stoned out of your gourds, or the damned illusion you're seeing—"

"Will disappear," Liam finished as the wall melted and an opening stood in its place. He grabbed Axle's arm and threw the backpack over his shoulder. Maybe he could get some of his money back, unless that was an illusion, too. "Come on, it's gone. She said that was a quaalude?"

Felix grunted as they entered into a wide cavern. "Holy shit," Liam said, his gaze falling on the rotting corpses littering the table. He put a hand at his mouth. That's where he'd been—

A hiss came from the shadows, and they all spun towards it.

One of the twins grinned at them from the shadows, its teeth as pointed as the dragon's. Jesus. Liam blinked, running a hand over his face. Was this what they really looked like? Its features were sharp and reptilian, and its spine was misshapen. The little monster raised a talon-tipped finger, pointing up.

Before Liam could look, the other twin fell on Felix, and a third creature rushed them. Liam went down hard, the breath knocked out of him, then he screamed as the dragon spawn's serrated teeth sliced into his shoulder.

"No! You leave him alone!" Axle screamed, rushing forward in a burst of black vapor and whoosh of crimson flame.

Liam recoiled, his hands over his face. What the fuck?! One of the little monsters shrieked, its body crushed between the massive slavering jaws of a hellhound. Liam scrambled back, his eyebrows frizzling and the skin on his face tight. Jesus fuck, the heat—he clambered to his hands and knees, pulling Felix away from the fray.

The creature in Axle's jaws dangled limply, and he flung it against the cave wall with a sickening crack. Axle growled at the other two, standing between them and Liam and Felix. The ground beneath Axle's dinner plate-sized paws smoked, the stone burning, and long ropes of saliva dripped from his jaws, clouds of acrid smoke rising from where it spattered.

He lunged at the other two. One fell beneath his flaming paw, its pale skin blistering and splitting as it writhed, then burst into flames. Its head exploded, searing gray matter and gore shooting across the cave.

The last of them ran into the stone chamber with the horde, Axle on its heels. A horrific scream rent the air and then cut off sharply. An inferno erupted from the opening, and the stench of burning stone and metal seared Liam's nostrils.

"Tell me I'm not seeing that," Felix squeaked against him, fisting Liam's shirt, his eyes enormous. "A hellhound. A fucking hellhound! I knew he was some shade of demonic."

"Yeah. Good thing he likes us," Liam croaked, licking his cracked lips.

Felix laughed manically. "Fucking Felicia. Sirens, hellhounds, I swear Poe's part banshee, and whatever the hell Sway is—you'd think my sister could've settled down with a nice warlock. Hell, I'd even take a sidhe at this point."

Liam slowly got to his feet and helped Felix up. "She definitely has a type."

Felix glowered at him. "A type is blond or brunette, not the upper end of malicious—"

Axle staggered out of the inferno and collapsed. The flames behind him snuffed out.

"Shit," Liam said, helping Felix to his feet. "I'll get him."

"Is he hurt?"

Liam pulled off his flannel and wrapped the boy up in it, wincing at the wound on his shoulder. It was hard to tell with the black tee, but he had a bad feeling it wasn't bleeding red. God help him, but he was positive that little shit's bite was poisonous, and Liam didn't think his tetanus shot was gonna cut it. They needed to move before he couldn't.

"No, but your first shift takes a lot out of you," he said, picking Axle up and trying to keep calm for Felix's sake.

The chamber beyond was thick with smoke and the stone glowed red. Nothing remained of the dragon's horde but heaps of carbon. Liam blew out a slow breath and carried the boy back to Felix. "You're gonna want to bring Sway's bag. Everything else is gone."

Felix slipped it over his shoulder with a grunt. "Remind me to thank my mom for spelling it then." Another roar shook the cavern and their heads whipped around to the entrance. Myx was waiting for them. Felix's throat bobbed. "You ready?"

Liam shook his head. "Nope. Let's go."

FELIX AND LIAM squeezed out of the cave and into a shattered landscape, bathed in violet light. It was obvious that the dragon had raged outside of the circle of stones. Huge furrows rent the blackened earth, and the air was striated with thick smoke. Stumps of trees smoldered and burned, and massive stones had been torn up and thrown at the circle. They weighed on the ward Jena had created around them. She slumped against Chase, and even at a distance, her face was haggard and pinched.

They were in trouble, and the dragon knew it.

A malevolent chuckle rumbled through its chest as it paced around the stones, playing with them and waiting for her ward to fail.

"Shit," Liam muttered.

Yeah. Felix's throat bobbed. That about covered it. Why hadn't the node responded? Aggie was supposed to be getting the coven to help, and that'd been hours ago.

It didn't matter. He had to do something. "You need to get Axle out of here," he said to Liam, handing over Sway's bag. "Myx will go with you. If he could wake Axle up, he can hold the distortion around you long enough to get back to the path."

Liam's brows furrowed, shouldering it with a wince. "Felix, we're not—"

"Yes, you are. I need to distract that dragon long enough for Jena and Chase to do what they need to do, and I can't do that if I'm worried about you two, so go," he fought to keep the tremble from his voice. "I've got this."

Liam searched his gaze and then pulled him close, kissing him fiercely. "I love you."

"I love you, too," Felix said, struggling to keep his emotions in check. "Now go, before I totally chicken out."

Liam kissed him again, and then he was gone, following Myx along the cliffside and out of the hollow. Felix took a deep breath as they slipped from view. Right. He had this. He just needed to piss off the dragon, right?

"Hey, asshole!" he shouted, dropping his distortion spell.

The dragon's head snapped to him, and it hissed, its neck weaving like a snake.

Felix swallowed his fear. "You might want to see if your homeowner's covers charred corpses and vaporized gold, because all of it's gone."

The dragon eyes narrowed at him. "Liesss," it hissed.

Felix cocked a hip. "Mmm, no, I'm pretty sure, one, two, three nasty little lizard spawn and one psycho bitch are inside doing their best rendition of brisket," he said, ticking off his fingers. "And I hate to break it to you, but I'm a *terrible* cook."

The dragon cocked its head like it was listening, and then the beast's jaws parted. It hissed again, its wings snapped open as it reared up, screaming into the sky. Felix distorted himself again and ran like hell, a stream of liquid fire blasting the cliffside where he'd just been standing. The dragon crashed back to the ground, the earth shaking and boulders tumbling from Jena's ward.

"That all you got?" Felix screamed, changing direction.

The dragon charged, and Felix dove into a deep furrow. He landed in slushy, half-frozen mud, his heart in his throat. The earth trembled again and stones peppered down around him. Long, black talons curved over the edge of the gash, flexing, and Felix looked up.

The dragon stood above him, his scales close enough to touch. Heat radiated from the beast and sweat broke out on Felix's brow, the stench of brimstone thick enough to choke him.

And his karma was rapidly coming to an end.

The dragon's talons flexed again, clods of frozen earth falling around Felix and swamp water seeping higher around him. Above him, the monster's chest rumbled, and it let out another roar—

Karma prickled against Felix's skin, and the light from the circle grew brighter. He bit back a sob. The node. It'd finally answered them.

The dragon shrieked again and lumbered away. Felix held his breath until the last flick of the monster's tail passed him. He gingerly shifted his position, climbing over scree to pop his head out of the furrow.

The circle of stones glowed a brilliant violet, cleansed of sin, and in the distance a shimmering curtain had begun to rise. Felix bit his lip so hard it bled. But Jena…she was on the ground cradled in Chase's arms. He glared through the circle at the dragon, his features half-man, half-wolf.

Oh, fuck. Felix stare at them aghast. *Oh my God. She couldn't be—No. No!*

He scrabbled out of the furrow and raced across the broken landscape, summoning karma. Fuck the balance, fuck his scales— "You bastard!" he screamed, etching a glyph into the air and clashing his wrists together over his head, throwing everything he had at the dragon.

The wind kicked up around him as the beast whipped toward him, taking a step back as the wind became a gale, then a hurricane, Felix's curls writhing around his head, pushing more karma into his spell. He screamed at the universe: *I don't care what happens to me, save them!*

A horn sounded in the distance and a thunder of hooves raced toward them.

The dragon reared back, as a ghostly host of riders thundered into the hollow. Felix fell to his knees, panting. Otherworldly spears flew over his head, sinking deep into the monster's hide. It bellowed in shock and pain, its wings snapping open as it scrambled to get away.

The dragon launched itself into the air, and a volley of arrows met it, shredding its wings. The great beast listed, fighting to gain height, then crashed into the swamp, a tidal wave of muck exploding outward and drenching the shore. Felix spat it from his mouth, not understanding. What the hell was going on?

The dragon thrashed, flames and green vapor spilling from its jaws, the earth rumbling and the beast's irate screams splitting the air. The leader of the host dismounted, a curved horn at his hip, and a crown of hawthorn across his brow. He grimly marched toward the dragon, weighing a long silver spear in his hand. He lightly tossed it, once, twice, and then reared back, and threw it.

It sped true through the night, starlight flickering in its wake, and pieced the dragon's breast as if sinking into softened butter. The great beast shuddered, then went still. The luster fell from its scales, then dulled completely and clouded over. Its massive carcass turned to stone.

Felix's throat bobbed. Holy shit.

The host, the world—all was silent. The man turned and strode back to his horse, remounting. He turned to Felix, his eyes greener than the greenest of springs, and nodded solemnly, a squirrel peeking out of his collar.

"You gotta be fucking kidding me," Felix murmured.

The man grinned and kicked his horse forward, the rest of the host streaming after him and disappearing into the night.

Felix blinked, his gaze going from where they'd disappeared to the dragon's petrified corpse, and then back to the circle, slowly becoming aware of the baying of wolves in the distance. He staggered to his feet, tripping over frozen muck and stones.

The ward was still up, and he put a hand against it. Chase was cradling Jena, but he'd lost the wolfish cast to his features. That had to be a good sign, right? Felix's fingertips tingled and the ward slowly dissolved. He stepped through, into the circle and fell to his knees beside them.

His throat bobbed. "Is she…?"

"She's okay," Chase said with tears in his eyes. "But it was close. The dragon was doing something that blocked us from reaching the node. If you hadn't come out and distracted it…" He shook his head. "Never again. That was too close. You get Liam and Axle out?"

Felix nodded, the distant baying closer. "Yeah, and it sounds like the rest of the pack is on its way. I texted Kelsey when we were back in the truck and probably should've explained more than I did."

"Dude, that's not the only thing you need to explain. What the fuck was that out there?"

Felix scrubbed his face with his hands and frowned at how filthy they were. "I've absolutely no idea, but I have a horrible suspicion that Sway does, and that her kinip-kinap just saved all our asses."

Chase just looked at him.

A red wolf burst into the circle and morphed into Kelsey fast enough to turn Felix's stomach. "Oh my God, are you guys okay? Shit, I mean, duh, no, you're not, but damn it! I always miss the good stuff!"

Felix snorted. "I can assure you, it wasn't that great."

"Whatever, you're just saying that." She jumped up and down and rubbed her arms. "Whoo, it's cold! Tom's coming with the EMS crew, but I just wanted to tell you Axle, Liam, and your cat are fine. My dad took them straight to the Witchery when we saw how bad off he was. That bite Liam got was really nasty, but don't worry, Aggie says his arm won't fall off."

Felix's heart about stopped. "What? He got bit?"

"Um, yeah," she said like he was an idiot. "Good thing Aggie had the coven make up a batch of dragon antivenom after you guys left. I guess that kind of thing's pretty serious."

Felix's eyelids fluttered as flashlight beams dipped down into the hollow along with men's voices.

"Ah! There's Tom. I'm gonna run, but I'll see you guys back at the shop." Kelsey sprinted over to a huge tattooed guy in an EMS uniform and kissed his stubbled cheek. Felix's eyebrow rose, and he and Chase exchanged a look. That was Tom? Kelsey grinned over her shoulder at them, then shifted and bolted out of the hollow. Whoo. Guess so.

"Hey," Tom said, directing the rest of the crew to lay out a stretcher for Jena. "You guys mind if I check you for injuries?"

Chase sniffed, and a low growl started in his throat.

Tom sighed. "You really want to do this now or can we get your girl out of here first?"

Felix put a hand on Chase's arm. "Can we please go home?"

Chase's gaze slid from Tom's to Jena, and he frowned. "Yeah, sorry about that, it's—"

"Don't worry about it," Tom said, obviously irritated despite his words. "We'll take good care of her, I promise, and you can ride in the back with her to Klineville General."

Chase nodded and let them load her up. They stood as the crew started away and followed them out of the hollow.

"What the hell was that about?" Felix asked when they were out of ear range.

Chase snorted and shook his head. "Kelsey's dating a cat."

LIAM LAID BACK against one of the couches with his feet up at the Witchery, his bandaged shoulder a dull throb. It wasn't quite as bad as the one in his head after being subjected to watching black and white *Matlock* reruns with Aggie, but he'd take it. He smiled as Sarah hugged his good arm tighter, snuggling beside him with Cruze. Axle was snoring obnoxiously loud at his other side, but the kid sure as hell had earned the right.

On the screen, Matlock objected to something, and Liam rolled his eyes.

"You know that none of that really happens, right?" Liam asked, unable to stand it anymore. "Cases don't move from filing to trial in under a week, and you can't have last minute evidence like that because of discovery rules."

Aggie glowered at him. "Did someone tell you Santa wasn't real when you were little, and now you've gotta spread that joy?"

"Santa's not real?!" Sway screamed from one of the overstuffed chairs.

Cruze and Sarah groaned, snuggling closer together like puppies.

"Of course he's real," Aggie scoffed. "And let me tell you, he's a lousy tipper."

Liam snorted, his eyes going to Sway as she bolted upright. Felix must be close. A couple of minutes later, Chase's truck pulled up outside the shop, and tired footsteps dragged up the stairs.

Sway was in Felix's arms before he'd even gotten the door open all the way, and shockingly silent. He picked her up and closed the door behind himself, his gaze running over the rest of the kids and then meeting Liam's eyes.

A broad grin stretched across his face at what he saw there. "Hey."

"Hey," Felix said, smiling back.

"God," Aggie grumbled. "Get a room."

Two months later

"OH, my God, get in the car." Felix pinched the bridge of his nose, so incredibly done with all of this. Visiting a paint center should not be this complicated.

All he wanted was a warm neutral, damn it. Preferably one that wasn't too pinky. Not that he had any issues with the color, but the couch Liam had picked out for his office would look horrendous against it. Felix should just let the were suffer with it, since he was the one that would have to stare at it all day working remote for that big firm up North. God, the man had zero eye for design. If he wasn't so wonderful otherwise…

Liam grinned at Felix like he knew what he was thinking and strapped Poe into her carseat. Thankfully, Liam's ability to sooth savage beasts like Myx had extended to Felix's youngest niece, and the screamer had become strangely tolerable. Almost cute, even—well, except during baths and when she was supposed to go down for a nap, but it was a vast improvement over the twenty-four-seven cacophony she'd subjected Felix's parents to. They'd more than earned their extended "vacation" in Maybach clearing out Aunt Helen's house.

And they were definitely enjoying it. To the point where

Felix wouldn't be surprised if they decided to move there and sell the house in Havers. Aunt Helen's was in much better repair, and there would be room for everyone when Felix and Liam brought the kids up to visit.

That and they kept finding cats.

The move would necessitate Felix taking his mom's place in the coven, but after Yule, the gaggle of old farts had definitely been looking at him with more respect. He wasn't about to tell them that calling the Wild Hunt—aka the kinip-kinap—had nothing to do with him, and everything to do with a certain frizzy, red-headed girl in the Bel Air's back seat.

Aggie, of course, knew all about it, not that she'd tell anyone.

Sway fumbled a ridiculous stack consisting of every paint chip in the store and sprayed them all over the back seat. Poe clapped her hands, laughing.

Felix's eyelids fluttered at the mess, and he slipped into the front, buckling up.

"You ready to go relieve my mom from urchin duty, or did you want to make another stop?" Liam asked, starting the engine. A wide smile crossed his face as it "purred" for him. The man really was obsessed with cars, and after Chase had mentioned its restoration during an interview about his work, Liam was fielding calls from all over the country. It was just a hobby for now, but Felix knew that wasn't going to last.

"I think we have an adequate amount of paint samples to choose from," Felix muttered as they pulled onto the road. "Besides, every minute we let your mother stay at the house, another baked good appears on my counter, and I'll be forced to eat it."

Liam laughed. "Still mad about having to let your pants out?"

"They're trousers, and yes." Between Liam and his mother's cooking, Felix had become decidedly fluffy. Not that

Liam seemed to mind, but Felix couldn't say he wasn't jealous of the were's metabolism. At least he and Jena had something new to commiserate about. She might only be six months pregnant, but she was huuuge.

Not that he'd ever tell her that.

Thankfully, everything that'd happened at Yule hadn't had any lasting effects. She'd been admitted at Klineville General for dehydration and exhaustion, but was out two days later. Chase, on the other hand, had become a helicopter husband and was at her side before she could even attempt to lift a finger. It was cute, but Felix could totally see why she wanted to punch him.

They drove through Havers, and he rolled his eyes at one of the "Wanted" posters Lorraine had insisted they put up. The butt cheek bandit was still at large, though how she thought the photocopied evidence with the "bits" redacted was going to help catch him... Whatever. Now the culprit got to moon the entire town instead of just whoever opened the copier.

Felix shook his head, smiling despite that as they passed town hall. Part of the dragon's gold had gone to balancing the town's budget, and the streetlights were on again. So was the aftercare program for the school, and Felix had an entirely new appreciation for it.

Unfortunately, Ophelia had been correct about Fayet's lawsuit going to trial, and opening arguments were scheduled to start in a few weeks. Still, he had hope. It was almost spring, and Main Street was beginning to showcase all things for Imbolc and Valentine's. New beginnings were on the horizon.

A smile flitted over his lips, looking forward to the getaway he and Liam had planned for the holiday. He didn't regret taking over guardianship of his nieces and nephew, but they definitely put a cramp in things. Especially the one in the back seat with "really good ears."

Liam turned onto Bruntwell, and the landscape opened up. The house they'd bought with another portion of the dragon's gold stood at the top of a rise, overlooking the harbor. Back in the day it'd been home to a ship's captain, and Chase had wholeheartedly approved of the rambling Victorian complete with a widow's walk. From there, you could just see the top of the tor where Jena and Chase's manor would eventually stand.

The Victorian was more house than Felix had thought he'd ever need, but with him, Liam, five urchins, and Myx, it didn't feel too big.

It felt like home.

THE END

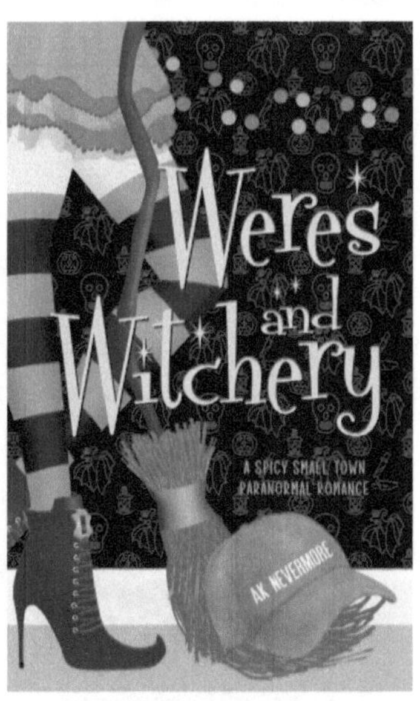

Karma's a Witch.

WHEN WITCH JENA SEYMORE returns home to Havers-by-the-Sea to care for her dying aunt, old town politics and prejudices are rekindled. Between the local Westside Pack's vendetta against her family and the coven pressuring Jena to complete the rite to become guardian of the node of magic outside of town, she has enough problems without adding Chase Montgomery to the mix. Especially after he broke her heart and started the devastating rumor that sent Jena running from town in the first place.

But Chase has plenty of problems of his own, and how to make amends with Jena and win her heart is at the top of the list. Unbeknownst to his pack, Jena is his fated mate, and after her leaving the first time almost killed him, he's not letting her get away again—no matter what the backlash might be.

And meanwhile, outside of town, the node is turning wild, jeopardizing the town's existence, as tensions inside of it threaten to tear it apart. Deep-seated small town secrets hold the key to its future—but only if they're discovered before Samhain, when the blue moon rises.

Magic happens and sparks fly in the small town of Havers-By-the-Sea when a sassy witch with curves for days crosses paths with an irresistible alpha shifter. WERES AND WITCHERY, the first standalone spicy paranormal romance novel in the Star-Crossed Chronicles series by AK Nevermore.

Karma Sucks.

OPHELIA DIAMONDÉ never asked to be summoned to Havers-by-the-Sea, but when the node makes her an offer she can't refuse, she officially becomes stuck representing the crappy little town. Having to clean up their messy legal issues isn't what she wants to be doing, but anything's better than being returned to the vampire court's clutches—or at least she thought so before she met the opposing counsel.

Gideon Sperry isn't known for his patience or his giving nature, but he is one hell of a lawyer. Unfortunately, all that goes out the window when Ophelia shows up, and the lawsuit between Havers and Fayet becomes personal.

But the facts aren't adding up. When it becomes clear that karma's had a hand in bringing them together, they need to find a way to build a case against who's really at fault for the turbine debacle. If they can't, it's not just the town itself that's in danger, but every resident's very lifeblood.

Magic happens and sparks fly in the small town of Havers-by-the-Sea when a sharp-tongued vampire crosses paths with a broody gargoyle. VAMPS AND VENDETTAS, a spicy slow burn paranormal romance novel in the Star-Crossed Chronicles series by AK Nevermore.

So, weird. I wasn't going to write this book. I'd planned on *Weres and Witchery* being a standalone, but after it was released there was an overwhelming demand for Felix and Liam's story. I hope it lived up to your expectations!

Especially since there's more coming.

Me being me, now that the door to Havers-by-the-Sea has been firmly opened, my brain is on overdrive, and I'm already noodling on the third installment, which I'm pretty sure is going to be Ophelia's story. Keep an eye out for that one.

So, thank you to all of my readers for your overwhelming support, and for my team dealing with my insanity and busting ass to get everything on the backend rolling to get this out. Lori Walker, you are a magical editor, and I've no idea how you do what you do. I mean, I know alcohol was involved, and cheers to that. Thank your cat, Joan Didion, for me while you're at it. I'm pretty sure she was giving you the stink eye to keep you motivated.

A huge thanks to JJ Graham, alpha reader extraordinaire, who keeps me on my toes and makes sure all of my facts are fact-ing. I really wanted to do Felix and Liam's relationship justice, and your input was instrumental in that.

And as always, Mom, thanks for slapping upside the head when I need it (and oftentimes when I don't.) Tossing around plot lines and trying to figure out where I'm going is always easier when you have an aggravator in the front seat.

No that wasn't a typo.
Now on to the next installment…

THE DAE DIARIES - URBAN FANTASY WITH SPICE

One Night in Bliss — Flame & Shadow — Air & Darkness — Playing with Fire

THE PRICE OF TALENT - SPICY DYSTOPIAN ROMANCE

*Breeder — Breaker — Destroyer — Binder — Conspirator — Split Overlord — Exile — Dyad **

THE MAW OF MAYHEM - PRN MC EROTIC ROMANCE

*Bites of Mayhem — The Maw of Mayhem — Grimdarke Darker — Kit-Kat — Katherine — Deuce **

STAR-CROSSED CHRONICLES

Weres and Witchery — Wards and Warlocks — Vampires and Vendettas

ANTHOLOGIES & STANDALONES

Secrets We Keep — Sense, Sensibility, & Shifters — Fairytale

**Forthcoming*

ABOUT THE AUTHOR

AK Nevermore is a bestselling author of paranormal, dystopian science fiction, and urban fantasy romance. She enjoys operating heavy machinery, freebases coffee, and gives up sarcasm for Lent every year.

A Jane-of-all-trades, she's a certified chef, restores antiques, and dabbles in beekeeping when she's not reading voraciously or running down the dream in her beat-up camo Chucks.

Unable to ignore the voices in her head, and unwilling to become medicated, she writes full time. Her books explore dark worlds, perversely irreverent and profound, and always entertaining.

Want more Nevermore?
Sign up for her newsletter and never miss a release!

aknevermore.com

www.ingramcontent.com/pod-product-compliance
Lightning Source LLC
Chambersburg PA
CBHW030147310726
48970CB00005B/1618